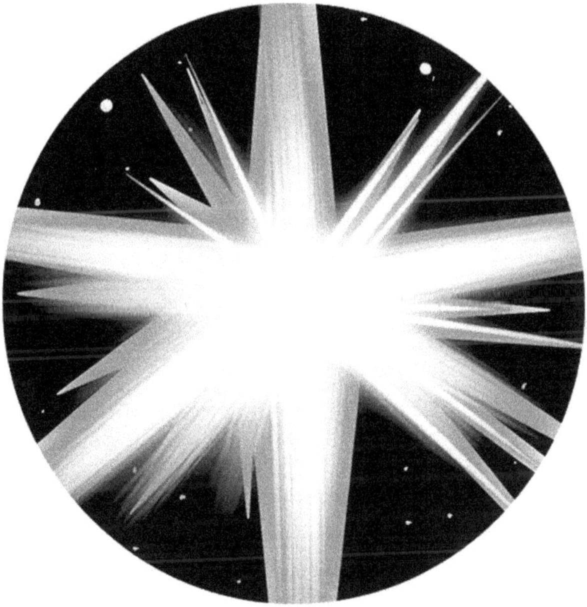

By Ann Christy

The Silo 49 Series
Silo 49: Going Dark
Silo 49: Deep Dark
Silo 49: Dark Till Dawn
Silo 49: Flying Season for the Mis-Recorded

The Between Life and Death Series
The In-Betweener
Forever Between
Between No More
The Book of Sam
Savannah Slays
Christmas Between Life and Death
Dead Woman's Journal (Prequel)

Strikers Series
Strikers
Strikers: Eastlands
Strikers: Outlands
First Strike (Prequel)

Into The Galaxy Duology
Portals
Portals: Saving Earth
Portals: The Hub of Life (VIP List Exclusive)

Dark Collections
The Ways We End
And Then Begin Again
Bringing All The Bad

Novels
Girard, The Guardian

THE NEVER-ENDING END OF THE WORLD

Ann Christy

Campfire Publishing
Knoxville | Lisbon

First Published by Campfire Publishing 2023

Copyright © 2023 by Ann Christy

All rights reserved. No part of this publication may be reproduced, stored or transmitted in any form or by any means, electronic, mechanical, photocopying, recording, scanning, or otherwise without written permission from the publisher, with the exception of brief quotations included in critical reviews and certain other noncommercial uses as permitted by copyright law.

This novel is entirely a work of fiction. The names, characters and incidents portrayed in it are the work of the author's imagination. Any resemblance to actual persons, living or dead, events or localities is entirely coincidental.

For Dad

Adorably impatient, inspiring, and lovable. My favorite days are the ones I spend with you, especially when there's food involved.

Prologue

Year 39 of the Loop

Coco: Age 51

The books seem so much more present when laid out this way. The piles are uneven, and the books grow more tattered as they move backward in time. Each tottering stack represents five years of Coco's life, or rather, five years as she has counted them. She may not be correct in her counting. There were times when even recording a mark to count the passing of a day couldn't be managed.

She is missing the earliest books; those precious early journals filled with childish drawings and uneven letters remain tucked away in her childhood bedroom. They'll stay hidden forever if the world stays as it is. Those are remnants of a lost world, a world where mothers helped their children learn to form letters and called it a journal. Those books will slowly crumble to dust as what remains of her family move around the rooms, forever the way they were on that day, forever entangled in the small allotment of time that is theirs alone.

She sighs, then sorts the stacks to order the books by age. The earliest on top, the latest on the bottom. If she somehow managed to layer all the books into one stack, it would almost reach the ceiling. Perhaps not quite, but it certainly wouldn't be shy by much.

Jorge clears his throat as he enters the room. He doesn't want to startle her. They've all learned the importance of subtle noise. The emphasis is on the word *subtle*. Sudden clamor is always bad, a lesson they have also learned more often than they would have liked. In this place, at this time, it's vital they don't break the rules they have lived by for so long.

She looks over her shoulder at him and whispers, "What's going on out there now?"

He looks grim, and his words offer no reassurance. "They're moving closer. I think they'll try to breach the building soon."

"We can't hold them off forever. You know that, right?" It's not so much a question as a confirmation of what they both know to be true. Both sides of this conflict understand the rules of their world, but desperation can make even the worst decision seem logical.

Jorge nods. They both know that time is no longer on their side. He approaches and eyes the books.

"Wow," he murmurs. "It looks like so many when you have them in piles. I don't think I've ever seen them all in one spot before. Not like this."

Coco smiles at his tone, the wrinkles around her eyes deepening when she does. As always, she smiles with her lips closed. Though they have both become competent dentists over the years, there's only so much either of them can do. She lost one of her bottom teeth a few years back and this kind of self-consciousness has become second nature.

When she doesn't offer any explanation, Jorge lowers himself to sit next to her with a grunt of effort. They've swept the industrial carpet many times, but decades of dust cannot be easily removed. He brushes it from his hands and drapes his arm over her shoulders, squeezes, then releases.

"What are you doing with all the books?" he asks.

She gnaws at her lip for a moment, unsure. Jorge is her partner in all things and has been for so long that she knows how he'll respond to almost anything she could say. She also knows how to counter-respond to anything he might say. When there are so few people in the world, there are even fewer secrets or surprises between them.

His lip quirks up in amusement when she looks at him. He already knows. Of course he does. With a little shake of her head, she says, "I just want to make sure they find these books. I want them to know they should read them. That they aren't trash. If the world comes back, they should at least know what happened."

Jorge's glance shifts toward the snug alcove where Joey sleeps. Coco looks too. Her son. His arm has flopped out from beneath his covers, which has been his habit since he was small. They have agreed it's the result of spending so much time sleeping on floors with a bedroll instead of in a proper bed. He never had to fear monsters lurking in dark spaces beneath him, where dust bunnies and stray socks congregate.

Jorge's eyes shine as his gaze returns to her. "You want them to know him."

Coco nods. Really, that's what it all boils down to. All of them existed, including her son. She does not want her son erased from time.

"Where should we put them?" he asks. He knows it will have to be close by. This place will be their last place.

"I'm not sure. It has to be somewhere obvious, someplace where they'll be recognized when they're found. A place with context. You know what I mean? I was thinking downstairs."

Jorge sucks in a deep breath and eyes the stacks. "I understand, but definitely not the offices below. Too many important loops cross that area. We'd have to make too many trips. We can't risk breaking those loops now."

"I might just leave them here. It's not a bad spot and the right people will see them, eventually." She pauses and pulls out a small box. It had once been bright with colorful butterflies and improbable flowers, but the decades have faded those vivid shades to muted pastels. She flips up the lid to reveal sealed packages of index cards. Even behind the plastic, the paper is yellowing with age. Stuffed into the empty spaces are colored pencils. Pens are a thing of the past, but the right kind of pencils are still perfectly serviceable, even after decades. Finding them is the problem.

She's lost pages and pages of writing after picking up a pencil, only to realize later it was part of someone's loop. All of these pencils are safe, untied to any loop. The marks these pencils make will last. They won't disappear. She picks up a blue pencil and opens a pack of index cards.

"I'm going to read them," she says. "I've never done that. I've searched for specific entries when we were tracking loops or mapping supplies, but I've never actually read them. Once I write something, I don't look back. Now, I think it's time. I thought I'd mark the important entries and make notes with the cards. You know, for science, for history. Well, for the history of non-history, anyway."

His eyes flick toward the ragged books on the far left of her stacks but shift back quickly. Worry fills them and he rests an age-spotted hand on her knee. When they'd met, they'd both been young. She can still remember his young hands. Was that a moment ago or decades?

"Coco, maybe you shouldn't read the early ones. Do you think that might be best? Not to read the early ones?"

Coco hadn't known Jorge at the beginning. She had been alone then. She was alone for many excruciating years. Confusion, fear, hunger, and pain were her only company for so long that she'd almost not recognized another loopless person when their paths crossed.

That didn't mean Jorge didn't know about those early years. He did. In whispers at first, and later using the adult voice Coco hadn't even known she'd developed, they shared all they'd experienced. Those conversations marked the start of their joint path as the last true Seekers, though neither of them had known that at the time. Back then, they had naively thought there would always be those who searched for a way to end this strange, timeless, endless apocalypse.

Patting the hand he still has on her knee, she smiles sadly and says, "Even the early ones. Especially the early ones. Maybe I'm silly, but I want whoever might be left to know us. All of us. It may be all that's left of *our* world when the old one returns. Just our words. I want to give them that, even if I can't give them anything else."

Jorge pulls her close, her head tucked against his shoulder. He rocks them both back and forth, gently and quietly. Far away, they hear a door closing as someone's loop begins once again.

Part One

Coco

Coco's Journal: Age 17

Year 5 of the Loop

I've been whispering for so long I can't remember what my voice sounds like. It's an alien thing living in my throat somewhere I can't reach. If I speak too loudly, a looper might break their loop. That's when the bad things happen. Bad for me. Worse for them. I don't want any more bad things.

One

Year 5 of the Loop

This stretch of street is the safest one for Coco. She's had it mapped in her mind for years. It was the first one she memorized once she understood she needed to. On her arms are seventeen watches, each one meticulously cared for and synchronized for a different loop. Each loop is a hurdle she must clear without flaw.

One watch ticks over. She takes two side steps then turns to present a narrower profile. This particular spot is a tight one. It's not the only clear path she has, but it is the quickest, and food lies at the end. She'll need the wide spots in the loops when she returns loaded down with as much food as she can carry. The return path is much, much slower. It will take over two days to walk this short distance and return.

A woman stutters into existence on the sidewalk mere inches from Coco, so close that her perfume creates a soft, floral cloud. It's not overbearing, but light and sweet. It smells like sunshine and clean clothes and fresh flowers in a vase across a room. Coco breathes it in. The scent is a bright spot in her day, in this entire trip. It's one of very few such bright things.

The woman is smiling, holding a phone in her hand. There are white earbuds in her ears. They stand out against her skin, which is beautiful and gleaming with health. She walks on. She will walk three blocks, then turn left and enter a building.

The woman does this every twenty-nine minutes and has for the last five years.

Coco glances up for her next cue, not needing a watch for this one. It happens every six minutes. The cab rounds the corner, honks, then jerks to a stop next to the curb. The man who emerges will cross the sidewalk and enter the building closest to Coco. He's in a hurry.

There's a risk of collision, so she waits for him to rush inside, checks her next watch, then hurries to the corner. The cab will come again, but foot traffic is light. The looping began on a Sunday morning, and even in New York City, even on the quasi-island of Manhattan, early Sunday morning is quiet.

Well, relatively quiet anyway.

This city is never truly silent. The sounds of cars, horns, people talking or laughing, and a thousand other things surround Coco. The looped people are doing what they've been doing for years. It is only her that must remain quiet. She must leave their bubbles of sound and life undisturbed. Looking ahead, she spies her goal for today.

The church is so close she can see the people in front of it already. Like everything else in Manhattan, the building butts up against the street. The sidewalk is barely enough to contain those passing through the doors. It's also chock full of loops, far too many for even Coco to account for.

Getting inside is tricky, but buried there is a life-saving gift. A veritable treasure trove of canned and boxed food, ripe for the taking. Almost all of it is unlooped, which also means it's edible. Only one small section is tied up in a loop and therefore, inedible. A woman wearing a blue shirt passes through the room, going from one door to another at the beginning of her loop. Blue shirt's eyes must pass over the closest shelves during her walk. None of it is dusty.

That's a trick it took Coco ages to learn. Enough time had to pass for dust to settle, but she still shakes her head when she thinks about how long it took for her to notice that particular detail. Unlooped things age. They decay. They go stale. They collect dust. Looped things remain as they were, renewing with each loop of the person tied to the object. If it's dusty, it's free to take.

It took her far less time to figure out taking looped food was a terrible idea. She'd eaten a plate of hot bacon and eggs in a nearby diner the first time she ventured beyond her building for food. The looper controlling the plate got up from the table, holding up his hand to greet someone. She'd snagged the plate and wolfed it down silently, thinking she'd found a loophole in the loops.

It wasn't a loophole. When that man's loop reset a few minutes later, the food in her belly disappeared as if it had never been there. She'd felt it, a twisting and terrible pain, followed by hunger.

No, unlooped food is the way to go. And this church has loads of it.

It takes nine of her watches, and nearly eight hours, to twist through the looping people and into the cool, green space hidden in the center of the block. Once inside, surrounded by buildings reaching into the sky, Coco can at last take a breath not tight with stress. This is a peaceful place, despite windows and balconies by the dozen overlooking her.

There are, no doubt, many loops that will bring people to windows or balconies. Some of them may look directly at her. None of them will see her. To them, she does not exist. All they see is what they expect to see, what they saw in real time before the looping began. As long as she doesn't touch them or distract them with noise, she is effectively invisible.

Getting into the rear of the church takes three of her watches and a lot of careful maneuvering. There's a large congregation and little space to maneuver around them. She makes it inside, rushing past the moment a man opens the door and holds out his arm, motioning for someone who is no longer there to precede him. Whoever might have been a part of his loop is either dead or trapped in a different moment of time, but during every loop he smiles at the air where they once were, his expression warm and loving.

Like she's done with hundreds, or possibly thousands of others, she looks for some evidence in the man's eyes that he understands his situation. Is there any hint of horror? Desperation? As always, there is nothing. No matter how many times each looper repeats their small fragment of time, for them it appears no different than it did the first time.

Unlike the loopers, Coco has no time for dawdling, so she slips into one of the few spots in the lobby that isn't crisscrossed by loopers. She checks her next watch and prepares for the last few hurdles. This church had a robust feeding program for those without homes. None of this is evident in the loops she winds her way through now. There is one loop involved, though only tangentially, and that loop is how she found this glorious stash of shelf stable food.

Coco times everyone, everywhere. It's vital to survival. She spends most of her time creating charts of loopers and their loops. Her graphs and charts are hung everywhere, most covered in plastic film to keep out rain and snow. From 80th and Madison all the way to 82nd and 3rd, there are charts posted on walls, on windows, on lobby desks, and even inside apartments. There are charts on parked cars, along with flags to help those unlooped vehicles stand out.

A parked car that isn't inside a moving loop is a valuable safe haven. Several of her paths call for a break on top of a car while particularly complex loops reach their peaks. As long as she's quiet, no one pays her the slightest attention. She stashes supplies on those without loops when she has more than she can carry. It's not great for the paint jobs.

Long loops—time fragments that take many hours or more—are interesting to Coco, mostly because they're so rare. Or maybe they aren't, but only lacking in her neighborhood. Regardless, they're rare for her. In the case of this food pantry, she'd found a homeless man with an astonishing thirty-two-hour loop. Her motion activated cameras caught him and the time stamps made her doubt her equipment.

She'd checked her setup, then sat quietly in the apartment where her survey was headquartered at the time. Sure enough, his loop time was thirty-two hours and four minutes. Coco had cautiously mapped and followed him, thinking there had to be some clue to be found. Such a uniquely long loop had to mean something. It took two weeks to map a safe route, but it was worth it.

In the end, his loop offered no clues or answers, but it *had* led to a food pantry when she really needed it. Sixteen hours into his loop, he went into this church, which was running on all sorts of other loops. Once she got inside, she found a dining room, and behind that an industrial kitchen, and behind that, a massive pantry.

In a stroke of major luck, only one female looper interacts with the food. Most of the huge pantry, with its tall shelves packed tight, is unlooped. She'd known the moment she walked in. After nearly five years, the room was almost gray under a thick layer of dust.

An even greater shock greeted her that day. A huge, tattered spiderweb stretched between the racks. It was out of place and wonderful. It was evidence of a living thing not trapped in a loop. A spider who was like her, who had lived and died and strung a web that remained long enough to become tattered by the passage of time.

That dead spider's curled legs and stillness gave Coco hope when she had almost lost her last shred of it. If there were two of them without loops, then there could be many more. If an unlooped spider and human existed, there could be unlooped members of all species. The dead spider represented the potential for life. Real life.

There had been other indicators of life over the years, but nothing as certain and unmistakable as the spider. In the very beginning, she found the occasional body. At the time, Coco assumed they were either loopers that didn't disappear in death for some reason, or possibly people who died because their loop didn't start properly. Every looper she disturbed disappeared, but she was never certain.

There were also the rare, nibbled packages of crackers, or tiny spills of flour near bags that sprang mysterious holes. Other signs. Maybe there are unlooped rats somewhere. If *anything* managed to stay unlooped, wouldn't it be a New York City rat? Coco left bait and rigged cages hoping she might find one, but nothing came of the effort.

Since she found the pantry a few months ago, the food stocks have dwindled, but her hope has not. If anything, she feels more of it with every survey. Are there more spiders, more rats… maybe even more people somewhere?

She no longer focuses solely on the loopers and their times, but on the details around them. Positions of curtains, trash levels in bins, debris locations. Anything could be a clue, so she looks at everything.

Inside the pantry once again, Coco does a quick count. Nothing is missing since her last visit, which is both good and bad. Good because it means more food for her. Bad because it means no unlooped person has found it despite the huge sign she posted nearby.

The big industrial cans of vegetables and soups are remarkably heavy. She can carry only so many. They're also usually less valuable from a calorie standpoint, but she knows she needs vegetables, even if they are five years old and canned in too much salt.

She checks the church's menu planning book, which rests on a metal cart inside the pantry. She's using the back of each page as her own sort of logbook. This time, she should take mixed vegetables. Last time was peas. The time before had been carrots, and before that, green beans.

Swinging off her backpack and unzipping it, she pulls out the second backpack inside, as well as several dirty canvas totes. Her load needs to be balanced so she can carry more without slowing down, and nothing can be allowed to interfere with her movements through the loops.

Coco yawns and glances at her last watch, the one that tells the actual time. It's getting late, and she's exhausted after hours of intense concentration and furtive movement. In the corner of the pantry, just in front of her dwindling supply of powdered milk, rests her overnight gear. She has such kits stashed all over her mapped territory.

She never knows when she might need to hunker down and stay put for a night or two. It happens. The cycles where loops meet and converge and leave gaps aren't always convenient. Sometimes, an extra minute inside one of her supply depots can mean missing her window. Patience is absolutely necessary for survival, so Coco is always prepared to wait out the loops, no matter how long that takes.

She lives by the two most important rules of this world: Never disturb a looper and watch where you step. Patience in all things might qualify as a close third in the rules governing this new world. She's disturbed loopers in the past. She's broken their loops. Coco has the scars to prove how costly that is. The long, jagged lines of nails raked along her arms, the gouges and divots left by an enraged, grabbing hand... more. For the disturbed looper, the outcome is far worse than a scar. They die, then disappear forever.

There are more rules, of course. The looped world is complicated. The rules on noise are important, but so subject to interpretation that it's more like a calculation than a steadfast rule. Gravity versus apparent weight. One is determined by an equation, while the other is judged by a single number.

Coco learned about noise the hard way. Touch and noise disturb loopers. Touch is simple and straightforward, but noise is based on whatever sounds they were being exposed to during their loop. Loopers dancing in a now powerless nightclub might not hear her shouting, but someone reading a book in a coffee shop may react to a single misplaced footstep. It's safer to be quiet all the time. For her and for them.

It's still a mystery why the loopers can be disturbed at all. And why do they react with such violence and rage when they are disturbed? Coco isn't sure those are questions she'll ever be able to answer. She'd like to know but can't imagine any path to finding those answers. And as strange as it is, the whys of the loopers aren't important to her survival. Obeying the rules is what matters.

Once her sleeping bag and pillow are neatly laid out, her stomach rumbles. There's no way to cook food at the moment. Too risky. Instead, she pulls out a rather tattered bundle of flatbread. The napkin had once been exceptionally fine, but now it's dirty and smudged, the color more gray and less pale blue. Her mother would have called it unsanitary. She unfolds the cloth and breaks off pieces of the bland bread, which is more like a poorly formed tortilla. Boiled rainwater quenches her thirst.

As she tucks herself into the sleeping bag, relaxing into the darkness of the pantry, a woman opens the door to the staff bathroom, passes her by no more than fifteen feet, then exits into the church kitchen. Coco barely registers the disturbance as she drifts off to sleep. The exact same scenario will play out four more times before she wakes again.

Coco's Journal: Age 17

Year 5 of the Loop

The library is great, but it's a huge pain in the butt too. It wasn't open when the looping started, which is good. They were re-shelving books when it started, which is bad. Many books inside the library are part of a re-shelving loop, which keeps them in pristine condition. Reading them can get annoying, though. It's hard to stay engaged in a story when the book disappears from my hand every hour or two. I have to get it off the shelf again, and by then, the mood is broken. Luckily for me, the comic book section is unlooped. My mother would be appalled at how much time I spend reading those.

Two

Year 5 of the Loop

Once Coco gets the heavy canvas bags settled onto the hood of an unlooped car, a silver Mercedes, she finally feels like she can breathe again. The loops she has to navigate on the way back take her on a different route but leave her more room to maneuver. It's also a much slower route, one that requires many of these breaks.

As if she needs an additional drain on her energy, Coco must also check for problems on her way back to her current base of operations. There have been a few significant changes in recent weeks and those tend to break loops, creating more mayhem. She likes to try to fix things if she can. On her last trip, she found cans of paint exploded on a street. An unlooped portion of a scaffold lost some boards up high and dropped the cans.

Now, she uses that spot as a crosswalk because all the loops there are gone. Exploding paint cans hitting the street would have been loud. Loud is bad. For loopers, the result of noise is always the same. They're enraged, then dead, then gone. Forever gone.

Fixing problems isn't the only reason a longer return route is worth the bother. Trading longer travel time for being able to carry more food and gear is a fair exchange. Less chaos to navigate, more room for baggage, and more time to rest between each free moment of travel. The basic math of making fewer trips because she can carry more food is terrifically clear. She appreciates clarity wherever she can find it. Her world is already too complex. Simplicity is welcome.

According to her newly set watches—the schedules synchronized with her logbook for this stretch of her territory—she has nine minutes to wait. The Mercedes is the center of her sanctuary. She can lean on it, or climb on it, or stand in front of it. The only rule is that she can't move more than thirteen inches from the tip of the front bumper. If she does, she will be crushed when a red convertible appears at the start of its driver's loop in three minutes and forty-seven seconds.

Today, with heavy, overfilled packs on her back and front and bags taking up all the hood space, Coco opts for a lean. It will take some weight off her sore feet and give her a little relief.

Slipping her logbook out of her pocket, she opens to the pages for this area. It's always wise to confirm her loop maps, even if she's done it a hundred times. Mistakes are deadly and those fallen paint cans changed a lot of patterns. She can afford no mistakes. She has no end-of-the-world health insurance, and all the doctors are eternally playing the same round of golf.

With a dirty fingernail, she taps an entry, checks a watch, then glances across the street. Coco mouths the words as she counts down in her head. *Three, two, one. Dog.*

As she thinks it, a woman stutters into existence in exactly the spot Coco is looking. This particular looper is remarkable only in that she and another living thing share the entirety of a loop. Her dog appears with her, toenails tapping at the end of the leash, steps jaunty and eager for a Sunday morning walk along lively Manhattan streets.

They are both relaxed. They look happy and, even better, utterly content in that happiness. Coco watches as they move down the street. While she doesn't know how it was accomplished, or perhaps designed, it remains a source of wonder that these two beings share a loop.

Equally baffling is why none of the loops intersect. As the pair take their walk, other loops stutter out of existence in front of them, or into existence just behind them, or traverse the area mere inches and microseconds after the pair.

Why don't they bump into each other? Why don't they appear in the same place at the same time? Why don't their paths ever, ever intersect? An even weirder question is why everyone is on different loops at all? If the looping began at the same moment, why isn't everyone doing what they were doing at that moment? Why do some repeat a few minutes from Sunday morning and some an hour of Saturday night?

She knows that's how it works. She just doesn't know *why*. In the building where she spent her entire childhood, she knew many people and mapped their loops. By tracking her neighbors and friends, she survived those first confusing and fearful weeks. By knowing the people she was studying, she could tease out the quirks in their loops. It prepared her for the world beyond the building. The strangeness of loops was evident even during those first days.

Coco's first survey project involved her neighbors, the Martins. They lived on her floor and always took a walk on Sunday morning. Only if the weather was exceptionally bad would the Martins skip their morning walk. Coco knew this because they had a dog when she was very young. Even after the dog died, the Sunday walks remained.

Once the world went crazy and she ran out of food in her apartment, she thought of them first. Expecting both to be gone on their Sunday walk, Coco went to scavenge their kitchen for food and water. Given the time the looping began, and the fine weather on that day, the couple should have been on their walk. They weren't. Or rather, only one of them was gone.

Their apartment wasn't empty. Mrs. Martin was—and still is—reading in bed, her head wrapped in a colorful scarf to protect her hair during the night. Coco found Mr. Martin later. He's still taking that morning walk, smiling and chatting with his hand out as if he's still holding hers. He never stops his walk. His loop is just over nine minutes long. He has been walking for years.

That's just one example of the way loops are divided. Everyone is like that. Almost everyone, anyway.

When Coco really thinks about it, and what it would take to accomplish something as complex as the looper paths, her head swims. She can't remember attending church before the world ended, but trying to comprehend this intricate dance between loops on a global scale is almost enough to make her believe in God.

Out of all the loops she's seen, Coco thinks the woman with the dog must have done something spectacularly good in her life. Her loop —an eternal happy walk with a happy dog—is the closest thing she's seen to heaven. If Coco were ever to be bound in a loop, she would want one just like that.

Her attention never wavers too far from her watches. As her current timer ticks down, she straightens, grabs her bags, and faces the sidewalk, readying herself to move quickly. Right on time, a child appears with a hand up, as if in the grip of an adult next to him. He complains and makes a pouty face.

She steps behind him. Matching his steps, she counts down. At zero, she steps to the side, joining the next looper, who is arguing with someone on the phone about money. The dance continues for twenty minutes but gains her only one block of progress. This short stretch of street is particularly hectic.

As the final looper for this block raises his arm for a cab, she breaks free, takes three steps, then ends on the stoop of an ornate building that might actually be a home instead of a cluster of apartments. She has two minutes and thirteen seconds to breathe.

Leaning her head against the cool stone, she closes her eyes for a moment to catch her breath. The packs are heavy, and her back is aching. The straps make her shoulders feel like the bones are slowly bending beneath her skin.

A sharp and unexpected sound makes Coco's eyes pop wide. A roundish bit of blue glass bounces on the sidewalk, little chips flying away from the impact. She shrinks into herself, holding her breath as she listens for a yell, a scream, or the sound of angry feet. There's nothing. No loop was broken by the sound.

Where did the glass come from? This isn't part of any mapped loop, and she's been making this trip every three weeks for months. The sidewalk in front of this door should be clear. The conflicting loops requiring her break here begin about twenty feet away. There are several static loops, the people in them forever stuttering, never entirely in or out of existence. The complexity comes from all the loops that appear around and between them. Her timing must be exquisitely precise there. A glance at her watch reveals she has one minute and twenty-three seconds. The glass must have come from above.

Peeking out from the alcove and twisting to look upward, Coco isn't sure what she might see. An unlooped bird or rat?

Neither. It's better. An old face framed by wild gray hair stares back at her, her hand moving in a tremulous, but extremely excited, wave. Though worn by time, the woman's eyes reflect the disbelief and overwhelming emotion of seeing another living person. Coco recognizes it because she feels it too.

Coco's mouth drops open and she comes so close to shouting that she slaps a hand over it. The old woman above her must understand the danger, because her hand stops waving, and she presses a finger to her lips. She mimes that she will come down and motions for Coco to wait.

A looper is coming her way, a man with his arm still crooked as if someone has their arm tucked under his. He's dressed for a night out, entirely handsome in his Manhattan-level stylish clothes. His loop must be from the night before it started, an eternal snippet of a Saturday evening date, perhaps. Coco jerks her head back as he passes. She glances at her timer. She has less than a minute to decide what to do.

She's never had to stop here to wait for loops to synchronize after missing a window, but she keeps a mental log of every safe spot. Coco thinks this might be one of the longer ones, maybe even a full day. The loops in this area are complex. Timing is everything.

It doesn't matter, and she knows it. She's just seen another unlooped person. A *living* unlooped person. Even if this loop pattern took a week to return to this point, she wouldn't leave. Even if that face hadn't belonged to an old woman unlikely to be a physical threat, she wouldn't leave. It's possible she wouldn't leave even if it were someone with 'serial killer' tattooed on their forehead. Coco drops her arm, pointedly ignoring the watches, and gazes at the closed door.

It takes several long, awful minutes before the sound of an inner door opening reaches her through the heavy door. It's so long that she begins to wonder if she hallucinated the entire event. It takes another eternity for the noise to shift to the outer door. Her stomach does jumping jacks inside her.

But the door eventually opens. It opens and there is an actual person. A person who is looking into her eyes and seeing her, *really* seeing her.

It's too much. Coco bursts into silent tears.

Coco's Journal: Age 17

Year 5 of the Loop

I'm still pinching myself, wondering if I'm dreaming. I've done that before, dreamed of people and talking to them. Sometimes, I do it even when I'm awake. I'll see a looper just like every other day, but it will seem like they're looking at me. They might be talking on the phone or to somebody that isn't there, but it will sound like they say my name. I know it's not real. This time, I think it was real, but how can I be sure?

Three

Year 5 of the Loop

Coco stands just inside the door, her heavy packs entirely forgotten. She stares at the person facing her while she cries. The woman gazes back, her eyes also streaming. She's old, quite short, and her body looks frail, like it might shatter into pieces at the slightest touch. Oddly, her stomach is quite round and big, almost like she's pregnant.

It seems like they might never break eye contact, but then the woman's eyes squint in pain and she looks away, reaching to steady herself against an ornate table just inside the door.

"Are you real?" Coco whispers, still wondering if she might be hallucinating. She's read enough in the library to know such visions are entirely possible when someone is left alone for too long. She's always wondered if the fact that she's surrounded by loopers every day might exempt her from potential hallucinations.

The old woman takes a couple of hitching breaths, her free hand pressed to her side, then looks up and smiles. "Oh, honey sweet, I am definitely real. I've been wondering if you might not be me seeing things. I'm glad to know I'm not the only one doubting my eyes."

"Oh my gosh, I love your voice!" Coco whispers too loudly, then slaps her hand over her mouth. It comes out before she can stop herself.

The woman's southern accent is strange and lovely, her words soft and round, like words themselves are luxuries to be savored. Coco has never heard an accent like that in real life, but she has in movies and on television. Its graveled texture is from age, which Coco remembers from her grandmother's voice. It makes the words sound even better somehow. It's beautiful.

The woman chuckles and says, "I'd love your voice if it sounded like nails on a chalkboard. You're real." She pauses, her expression shifting into something like fear as she glances toward a closed door made of metal and glass. There's a faint sound beyond the door. She presses her finger to her lips and whispers, "Follow me."

Coco nods, ready to follow this frail old woman with her lovely accent into actual fire if necessary. Cartwheeling, even. She is real and alive and here. More practically, she will know the loops in her territory. Coco doesn't. The only safe way to go is the way the woman tells her.

The inner door to the building is beautiful and ornate, with swirling patterns of dark metal and etched glass. The contrast between the woman's jaundiced hand against it is stark. Her sallow skin and frailty tell Coco much. She is sick, probably very sick.

Coco waits in silence even though every nerve is firing, each one urging her to grab onto this old person, keep her close, and never let her go. Finally, there's a soft shuffling noise, then the click of a door closing somewhere deeper in the building.

"Alright, she's passed now. We'll go directly up the stairs. After that, it's clear for a bit," the woman says, then looks at Coco for confirmation.

"Got it," she whispers, and moves closer to the woman, ready to match her steps or take instruction.

Despite how heavy it looks, the door swings smoothly and soundlessly. The woman steps through, points at the staircase, and motions for Coco to close the door. She does, then hurries across the open space toward the stairs. She needn't have hurried. The old woman climbs at a ponderous pace, breathing hard at the effort of it. Coco can barely stand it. Her body is in hurry mode.

The slow progress gives her a chance to look around without being rudely obvious about it. She's certain this entire building is one house, and therefore, the home of rich people. Her parents' home was considered a place of relative wealth by most standards, though the reality was quite different. Coco's building belonged to her mother's family for a long time, bought generations ago when Manhattan was a different place.

When the building was sold and renovated to go co-op, a large apartment became theirs and the windfall ensured permanent residency. Such spacious accommodations in this city, especially so near the park, were normally for the wealthy. Coco's parents, aside from their ownership of an apartment, had never been genuinely wealthy. Money was managed.

This place is definitely not one of managed finances. The floors are made of some gleaming pale stone. Marble? Rich people always talked about marble in the movies. The ceiling is high and sculpted in fantastically detailed reliefs in creamy white. Even the banister under her fingers feels too fine for Coco to touch with her dirty hands. This is a palace compared to any home she's ever entered.

Coco's wandering gaze returns to the woman. She's panting, and the last few steps seem almost too difficult for her. Hurrying to her side, Coco slides her arm under the woman's and whispers, "Let me help you. Point the way."

The woman seems relieved, and despite her slight frame, the weight she puts on Coco is substantial. Her hand trembles as she points toward an open doorway. Soft, bright light spills out and Coco can't see anything beyond it.

The woman's steps falter, and she loses one of her slippers as they enter. The gleaming stone gives way to a soft carpet. The space resolves into a bright and airy bedroom with open windows overlooking the street where Coco stood only moments before.

The panting breaths are alarming, so Coco eases the woman down onto a large bed. Now that she's not overcome by the bright daylight, Coco can see how dingy the sheets are. Drifts of dust are piled in the corners. The sheer curtains are yellowing from dirt carried in through the open windows. Stacks of canned and packaged food almost fill a room just beyond the bedroom that was probably once a dressing room. The whole area reeks of being occupied for too long without a thorough cleaning.

As the woman settles back onto the pillows with a sigh, she gives Coco a wan smile and tries to catch her breath. After a long moment, she says, "I'll be alright. I just need a minute or two."

Not knowing what else to say, Coco whispers, "My name is Coco."

The woman's smile widens, and her eyes move over Coco's face and hair. She says, "That's just the right name for you. Yes, that's perfectly right. My name is Ruth."

For some reason, this information absolutely tickles Coco. A real person with a real name. Covering her mouth with her hand to keep the noise down, she giggles.

Ruth raises an eyebrow and asks, "And what, exactly, about my name is so funny?"

It's a good question, but the answer is complicated, so Coco shrugs and whispers, "I believe you're real now. I would never have hallucinated someone named Ruth."

"Why ever not? Ruth is a perfectly serviceable name."

"The only Ruth I knew used to pick on me in school. I don't know why, but she used to wipe boogers on me. Other kids thought it was hilarious."

"Boogers? No, surely not."

Coco nods, looking around for any evidence of nearby loops. There are no clean spots, no suspiciously unworn tracks in the carpet, no areas free of dust. This room seems safe, but safe is relative. Noise can travel beyond the confines of a room. It's safer to whisper.

"Can I put my backpacks down?" she asks, still whispering. Now that she's not overcome with adrenaline, the weight of her packs has returned.

Ruth seems distressed to have forgotten about that. She waves her trembling hand and says, "Oh, dear. I am sorry. This room is safe, so make yourself at home. Please, do move a chair closer to the bed."

Coco does, and sighs as she sinks into a plush chair she takes from a vanity. It's upholstered in beautifully embroidered silk and feels divine. It's also the only piece of furniture in the room she could have possibly picked up. Everything is oversized, overstuffed, and overly decorative.

Ruth reaches over and takes Coco's hand. Her skin feels soft and cool. She squeezes once, then says, "Well, now that we've both determined the other is quite real, tell me more about yourself. Are you alone? Have you been here the entire time? For all these years?"

At each of the questions, Coco nods, causing Ruth's expression to fall into sympathetic lines. "You poor, sweet girl! Alone for so long. How old are you? You couldn't have been more than a child when all this… whatever this is… started."

A tiny part of Coco almost bristles at the tone. She's managed well on her own. She's proud of her ability to survive. She made mistakes, yes, but she's not helpless. At the same time, it's so good to hear an acknowledgement of how difficult life has been that she wants to climb into bed next to Ruth, hide her face and cry.

She does neither. With a small shrug, she whispers, "I'm seventeen. I was twelve when it started. And yes, I've been alone the whole time. You're the first unlooped person I've seen."

"Unlooped," Ruth mumbles, as if testing the word. "Looped or unlooped. Why, that's exactly what it is, isn't it? I've never really decided on a term for this thing. I suppose I think of it as cycles. They cycle through their patterns."

"That works too," Coco says.

"Honey, I can barely hear you. Why are you whispering? It's safe here. You can speak up. For now, anyway."

For a long moment, Coco doesn't respond. She just looks at Ruth. How can she have survived for so long and still be able to speak out loud like that? Coco can count the number of times she's raised her voice on her fingers. Aside from the first time… that terrible, horrible first time… she has always reserved such outbursts for locations where there are no loops to hear.

Other than those rare occasions, she whispers. Even when she talks to herself—which is shockingly often—she whispers.

"I'm not sure I can," she says.

Ruth examines Coco's face for a moment, then squeezes her hand again. "I understand. I really do. However, if I can't hear you, this will be a rather one-sided conversation." She pauses, then smiles slyly and says, "Which, I confess, will not be substantially different from every conversation I've had for an exceptionally long time. I've become something of an expert at one-sided conversations."

"Me too. I even argue with myself," Coco says, this time a little louder, but still not approaching the volume Ruth is using. She realizes she also doesn't yet know how this woman knew about her. "How did you know I would be on the street today? Or that I was even around?"

"Oh, that's an easy question to answer. You started leaving bags on cars. That must have been, what, six weeks ago now? When something is different, it stands out. Once I realized someone had been nearby, I decided to sit at that window right there until I saw you. Well, during the day I sat there. And here you are."

"I wish I'd known you were here earlier. We were so close to each other all this time, and I didn't even know."

Before Ruth can answer, her face twists in pain and she gropes for a small brown bottle next to her on the bed. Her hand trembles as she opens it, then squeezes a few drops of liquid into her mouth.

Coco wants to ask what the liquid is, wants to ask what's wrong with Ruth, wants to find out if she's going to be alone again. Instead, she waits patiently. Ruth's pain-tightened expression slowly shifts to something less tight. When she opens her eyes and looks at Coco, the pain is still there, but it's not as sharp.

Ruth opens her palm to show the bottle and says, "Morphine. I went and found as much as I could when I realized I would need it. I'm sorry to say I caused quite a few cycles to break in the doing of it."

"Oh," Coco says. She's read at least a dozen medical books and searched for solutions in many others over the years. All she knows of morphine is that it's addictive and meant for severe pain. Either option is bad. How can she ask what's wrong without sounding like a terrible person?

Ruth must see the question in Coco's expression, because she says, "I have cancer. No, that's not the whole truth. I'm *dying* of cancer." Her tone is quite matter-of-fact despite the dire nature of her words.

"How do you know?" Coco asks, confused. It's a good question. During her infrequent bouts of illness since the looping began, she's often felt fear because there's no one to confirm she isn't dying of something horrible. Only surviving is left as an indicator that an illness isn't fatal.

Perhaps understanding the source of Coco's confusion, Ruth says, "I've had this before. I was in remission when this mess started. I think I was in remission for a good many years after, too." She gingerly pats her swollen belly and adds, "I wasn't truly certain until this began. Liver cancer. It does this when it gets near the end."

A soft ding sounds out, and Ruth holds up a finger for Coco to be quiet. She grabs a digital timer from the bedside table and pushes a few buttons. As she puts the timer down, there's a noise beyond the room. Coco cocks her head to listen. It sounds like it's coming from downstairs.

Heels click against the stone steps. Coco looks at Ruth in alarm, wondering if someone on a loop is coming. Again, Ruth holds up her hand for patience.

The clicks stop, then a young woman's voice reaches them from the stairs. The voice is raised, but the tone is teasing, almost amused. "Grandma, you are the slowest person ever! You're going to make me late." There's a pause, then more talk from the same person in a lower tone. The short spans of silence between make it clear there's a conversation going on with someone who is no longer there. Then, the voice comes again, almost laughing. "Mom is bringing you coffee, but you can't have it until you get out of bed! She'll be up in ten minutes."

The steps fade as the heels march down the stairs. They sound jaunty, happy. A door opens and closes. Silence returns.

Coco looks away from the door and is surprised to see tears in Ruth's eyes. After five years? Why didn't she move to another building, like Coco did? She glances at the digital timer on the table. Seventeen hours and fifty-eight minutes. It must be an eighteen-hour loop. There are very few loops that long. Most run from a few minutes to an hour.

"Are you okay?" Coco asks.

Ruth nods, blotting away tears. "That's my granddaughter, Sophie. Her mother is my daughter, Hannah. We had an appointment that day. It was going to be quite the affair. Her entire bridal party flew in for it."

"Bridal party? You mean for a wedding?" Coco asks.

Her experience of such things is minimal and generally limited to leafing through wedding magazines at the library while her younger brother sat through his Paws for Reading sessions. Chase loved watching people read to the dogs. He'd been excited when told that he would someday get to read to them as well. Coco pushes thoughts of Chase away. She can't bear them. Those are wounds that will never heal, and the scabs remain tender. To push him into the shadows of the past, she focuses on Ruth and nods to show she's listening.

"Well, no, not the actual wedding. That was still months away. She was to try on her gown that day. Sophie was so excited. It was designed just for her, but she wanted to be surprised, so she didn't micromanage the process. It would have been the first time she saw her wedding dress."

"I'm sorry. That's… well… that's pretty bad timing," Coco says, somewhat at a loss.

With a dry, half-chuckle, Ruth says, "Well, at least you're honest. And yes, it is quite unfortunate she never got to try on that gown. I suppose it could be worse under the circumstances. I mean, she's happy. For years, I would sit at the top of the stairs so I could watch her face and see how happy she was. Even after what happened, I took comfort in that."

Something in the way she says the words 'what happened' tells Coco there's more to the story. The emphasis has a tale wrapped inside it. She wants to ask. She also isn't sure she should. Coco has a story that could be wrapped in words just like those, one she tries very hard to avoid thinking about.

As she always does when remembering that first day, Coco touches her forehead, her fingertips tracing the ragged scar there. The raised flesh twists from her forehead to her temple in a curving line, a terrible reminder she can never tuck away in a box. One she sees every day in the mirror when she brushes her hair or her teeth. Lowering her hand before Ruth sees and asks about the scar, Coco decides she probably shouldn't ask what happened to Ruth on the day the looping began.

Despite her resolve and almost without thought, Coco asks, "What happened?" She quickly counters herself and adds, "No, I'm sorry. I shouldn't have asked."

Ruth examines the little bottle in her palm for a long moment. She doesn't look up as she answers. "Soon enough, I won't be here to tell this story to anyone. All that will be left is my granddaughter downstairs and the housekeeper in the kitchen. No one will ever know the story if I never share it. Stories should be shared. I've always believed there's a good reason why we have them in our minds. We have stories so people live on. I think that's what heaven really is. It's the story told about us when we're gone."

She looks up, meeting Coco's eyes. Her face is pale, and the lines of pain are still evident, but she also looks more at peace somehow.

"If you want to tell me," Coco says.

"I think I do."

Coco's Journal: Age 17

Year 5 of the Loop

I think I've decided there *is* something worse than being the only one not in a loop. It's finding out there is someone else and then losing them.

Four

Year 5 of the Loop

"I've never been an early riser," Ruth begins. "I'm not lazy. I'm just not a morning person. My husband used to tease me that if we didn't have children, he may have never seen me with my eyes open before ten o'clock."

She pauses and smiles, as if looking into a more pleasant past. The smile fades.

"I had liver cancer before, as I told you, but after I went into remission, my body clock never seemed to recover. It became difficult to get up in the morning and I couldn't fall asleep until very late. When this mess began, my day started just as you heard, but with a couple of additions.

"When my granddaughter arrived, my daughter was with her. My housekeeper, Tammy, was in the kitchen, though I didn't think about that at the time. She'd agreed to work so the bridal party could meet here for refreshments. I remember smiling when I heard Sophie's voice, then deciding I could let myself drift until my daughter brought the coffee. I'd just give myself those extra few minutes in bed. Do you understand what I mean? Those wonderful little stolen minutes before you simply must get out of bed?"

With a sigh, Coco nods. "Oh, I remember."

"I suppose I knew there was a problem as soon as I woke up again. The light was different." She gestures toward the windows, then goes on. "Morning light is quite different from afternoon light, here with all the buildings in the way. Anyway, I could tell it was afternoon, but no one had come up. I was a bit confused, wondering if I'd dreamed them arriving. I looked at my phone, saw it was Sunday, and realized it couldn't have been a dream.

"I called out, but no one answered. When I tried to call my daughter, there was no signal. No cell signal in Manhattan? Not possible. That's when I got frightened, so I went downstairs."

Ruth stops talking, her face drawn into lines of pain and regret. Coco presses a fingernail into the tender skin of her wrist. It's what she does to erase thoughts of her family. She wonders if her expression is like Ruth's. After a long, silent moment, Ruth pulls in a sharp breath, like she's forcing herself to push everything else aside and simply tell the story.

"I went directly through to the service area. That's the door you saw when we came up. We have rooms through the arch meant for living areas, but my family is a kitchen sort of family, if you know what I mean. At first, I didn't understand what I was seeing. Not really."

"What did you see?" Coco asks, remembering how it had been for her.

"My daughter. She was at the island with a tray. It was so strange. I thought I was having a stroke. She was just… I don't know the right word for it… fluttering? Flickering? There, and not there. Of course, I've seen it more now, but at the time, I didn't understand. I must have stood there for a while, because she would stop flickering, put the tray on the counter, then reach for the little coffee press I particularly like, hit the kettle switch, and begin making coffee. Then she would flicker, and it would happen all over again."

"She's on a tiny loop? One that only lasts for a few seconds? Or maybe a minute?"

"Yes, that's right. You know, I do think loop is the right name for it. Not cycle. It *is* more of a loop, isn't it? Like the same short scene of a movie forever repeating."

Coco senses Ruth is diverting from the story, shifting into the safer harbors of nomenclature to avoid what comes next. But she has to hear it. Coco needs to hear her tale. Perhaps it will help her deal with her own. She also thinks that Ruth, even if she's afraid, desperately needs to tell it.

"What happened?" she asks, but she tries to ask kindly.

Ruth looks down and twists her fingers around the small bottle. "I touched her arm. I'm not sure what I was thinking, or if I was thinking at all. I just took hold of her arm, as if I could stop her from flickering or maybe she could take me with her. I don't know."

Coco knows the rest. It's the same with all of them. Loopers always do the same thing when disturbed. She says nothing, trying not to indicate she knows what will come next.

"I don't know if you've seen it yet, Coco, but I've seen it many times since that day. I know it wasn't just my daughter that acted like that. In a way, it's a comfort to know that. Until I saw it happen again, I had this terrible notion that she was angry with me.

"She screamed in a way I'd never heard anyone scream before. It was truly frightening. Fear right down to the marrow of my bones. Her hands curled into claws, and she did this." Ruth turns her arms so Coco can see the inner surfaces. They are latticed with purple scars. Dozens of scars.

"It would have been worse, but I held my arms up to protect my face. That's when I realized she couldn't move from where she stood. Her body could shift, but from the hips down, it was like she was planted. I've never seen that particular thing since that day, so I'm not sure what it means." She looks at Coco in question.

"Oh, yeah, I've seen it. When you break a loop, they can only go where their loop goes. You got lucky. Well, I mean… well, not lucky… uh…"

Ruth reaches out to pat Coco's knee and says, "It's alright. I understand what you mean." She withdraws her hand. "If you've seen that, then you know what happened next."

Coco glances downward, wondering what it would be like to be a mother and see her daughter go crazy, die, and disappear. She wonders if it's more painful than what she experienced.

Perhaps Ruth understands these thoughts, because she says, "In the end, she simply disappeared, and I had no idea what to do. The whole episode was so strange that I thought I'd died and gone someplace awful, or that this was more evidence of a stroke. Before she disappeared, I touched her neck and there was no heartbeat, but then she was gone, so I couldn't be sure."

"Didn't you wonder what happened or if anybody would come? It took me forever to figure out anything at all."

"Oh, honey, of course I did. I didn't think what happened was just another Sunday. I tried to call for help. The power was out. Then I saw all the people outside when I opened my front door. I tried to get help from a man on the sidewalk. That resulted in the same disastrous outcome as my daughter.

"Finally, I remembered Tammy was here, or should have been. By that time, I'd already been the cause of two possible deaths, so I was quiet and careful. Tammy was in the laundry room. I didn't disturb her. I just watched. She didn't flicker, but even when I stood right next to the folding table, she didn't see me. She hums and folds the tablecloths. And like the people outside, she didn't seem to know I was there as long as I was quiet. She finished the laundry, took up the basket, went back to the kitchen and did her work."

"How long is her loop?" Coco asks.

"Just under two hours. I didn't know it, but I'd caught up with her when she was well over halfway through her loop. She flickered too, eventually. I didn't want to disturb her. She's still down there. Anyway, by the time I realized this was everywhere, I also realized I wasn't having a stroke and that my daughter's body had, in fact, disappeared. I still don't know if that means she's truly dead. Do you know why they do that? Scream and attack us?"

Coco shakes her head. "No, but I know they all do it. It's not personal, I don't think. I used to wonder if maybe having all this reality shoved back into their heads might be too much, but I'm not sure how we could ever find out exactly why they react like that."

"I can't either."

"I'm so sorry that happened," Coco says, because it's true, but also because she isn't sure what else to say.

"That's sweet of you. It's in the past now. I can't undo it and I can't change what's happened to everyone else." Ruth's eyes shift upward toward Coco's forehead and the terrible, twisted scar there. Putting one hand over the scars on her arm, she says, "I think you must have a story much like mine, Coco. I hope not, but I think you do."

As her hand rises to cover the scar and her face grows hot, Coco feels the same strange panic she felt at the beginning. It rises so quickly inside her she can't even find words. "I… I can't…"

Raising a hand to stop her stuttered words, Ruth says, "It's okay, Coco. You don't have to say anything. It's alright. I didn't mean to upset you."

Her breaths come fast, but the gentle tone of Ruth's voice works. Looking away, Coco squeezes her eyes shut and focuses on regaining her calm. It's been too many years. There's been no one to ask her about the beginning. No one to confide in when she was still confused and frightened and wanted to be comforted by talking about what happened that Sunday morning with her family in their apartment. This took her by surprise.

When her heartbeat recedes to a dull pounding, Coco opens her eyes and says, "I'm sorry. I just…"

"It's alright, Coco. Truly. You can talk about it… or not… whenever you want to. Just know that I'm here if you do."

In the old woman's pain-racked eyes, Coco sees something more than sympathy. Ruth really does understand. She lived her own horror and can probably imagine what Coco must have gone through. Even without telling Ruth the details, Coco feels an easing in the tightness in her belly. Something like relief.

"Thank you," Coco says.

Ruth smiles and looks away, but Coco senses she's not done. She twists the little brown bottle in her hands, her brow creased as if debating if she should say whatever it is she wants to say. Coco can guess what it is.

Reaching out, Coco touches her hand and takes the bottle, tucking it next to Ruth's leg where she can get to it later. Taking the now empty hand into hers, she says, "It's okay. Just say it. I'm right here. I'm not going anywhere."

Ruth's eyes shine with tears when she looks up. One tear drops to darken the worn nightgown when she nods. Swallowing, she says, "I want to ask something of you. I'm not sure I should. I'm not sure it's right. It might be selfish or borne of fear or… I don't know… wrong. You're so very young."

"If you're asking if I'll stay, then yes. I will."

Despite her frailty, Ruth squeezes Coco's hand with a sudden and surprising strength. Choking out a sob that seems more relieved than sad, she says, "I don't want them to find me like this. After. If it ends.

Will you… can you? It's so much to ask. I know. Too much. If I had any courage at all, I'd take myself to the park and lie down, but it's really too late for that. I haven't got much time. I can barely make the stairs once a day to empty the pails."

The helplessness in Ruth's eyes is too much. Coco knows she missed a lot growing up in a looping world, but this reaches all the way down to the deepest part of her. This is primal, and she understands it because she's human. It's also crushing. After all this time alone and soon, who knows how soon, she'll be alone again.

But Ruth won't have to be alone. Coco can do that much.

"You're not asking too much, Ruth. I won't leave you. I'm not sure I could even if I wanted to. And I'll take care of everything. I understand. We're in this together now. I'm here."

Coco's Journal: Age 25

Year 13 of the Loop

I like to remember Ruth as she was for the two weeks we were together, not the way she was when I walked out the door for the last time. Really, that's her story, the living part. A person's death, or even the way they die, isn't their true story. It's everything that came before.

That's what I've kept of her for the last eight years alone. It's the part I'll share with the new people I've found, Tamara and Jorge. For me, Ruth was a sign of hope. Hope that there were more of us out there. Hope that I would find them. Hope that I wouldn't be alone forever. That's a lot of hope to give someone.

It's the best gift I've ever received. I'm pretty sure it's how I survived all the lonely years between then and now.

Five

Year 13 of the Loop

Coco enjoys the sunshine while lying on the roof of the auto parts store. Spring has well and truly sprung, but today is a reminder that winter isn't entirely gone. The roof soaks up the sun and feeds it right back to her. And bonus, there are no loopers on auto store rooftops, at least as a general rule. That means she can relax.

The winter here in Salem, New Jersey, couldn't hold a candle to the fierce and biting cold of Manhattan without a power grid, but it wasn't precisely balmy either. It feels like Coco has been cold for half a year.

She lowers her chin to peer at the black and white cat resting on her chest. With his paws curled in and his eyes half-closed, he looks supremely content. Stroking a finger under his white chin, she says, "But I have you to keep me warm, don't I?"

Tuxedo's eyes open and his nose twitches, but within seconds his eyes drift closed again, and his purr ratchets up to a rumble on her chest.

"You are so lazy and unhelpful," she says, smiling.

It's true. Tux is spectacularly unhelpful with most things that need doing. He is also spectacularly good at the one thing he really needs to do, which is to simply exist. Living company. And this little bundle of fur is probably the reason she's not stark, raving mad by now. Thirteen years is far too long for a human being to be alone.

"We should actually get up and map the loopers soon. That's why we're up here. I need to get into that vet clinic and find more kibble for you. So, you know, you do have a vested interest in this, Tux."

The cat either tires of her chest moving as she speaks, or decides fresh kibble is, in fact, a good idea, because he yawns hugely and stands, arching his back in that way only cats can. Leaping off her chest, he strolls away, his ears radar-dishing around as he scopes out the rooftop.

Sitting up, Coco unpacks her gear for a mapping session. Notebooks, colored pencils, a big roll of art paper to make diagrams, and binoculars. After so long doing this on the road, she's pared her tools down to the essentials. She's also been pared down to the essentials. A spare-framed woman with her hair tied back and nothing except a cat to slow her down.

Not until she left Manhattan did she realize how much stuff she had accumulated and how easy all that gear made certain aspects of her life. Not everything, but some things. Food was never easy. Food became a problem.

It took eight years for Coco to summon the courage needed to venture away from Manhattan, but logistics finally demanded she go. The winters were hard and got harder every year. She interrupted too many loops in her search for unlooped food. Canned food froze and exploded in winter. Boxed food went gooey from summer humidity.

There was a period when she was so hungry, she ate looped food just to feel her stomach full. The pain of it disappearing when the loop reset was terrible, but she'd done it several times out of sheer desperation. It was a horrible thing to experience. Coco would dash between loopers to reach a hot plate of food tied up in a loop, then gobble it down. It felt so good as her belly filled, and every time, she hoped against hope that this time, she could keep what she ate.

But she never could. The loop would reset and there she would be, looking at that same hot plate of food as it reappeared on the table where it had been before. Her belly would twist and cramp as everything in it disappeared like it had never been there.

Finally, she did the last thing she wanted to do. It was that, more than anything else, that made her leave. Rather than face starvation, Coco broke loops so the food tied up in those loops would be free.

Breaking a loop to take things is a wasteful endeavor. It doesn't always work. Half the time, the food disappears with the looper, along with other objects tied in the loop. Usually, only small things disappear, but strangely, large things can go as well. Even cars.

The other half of the time, food is released from the loop and stays behind. It becomes unlooped, though Coco has no idea why or how that happens. She only knows that it works, but only half the time.

Even more strange is the fact that the food is exactly as it was the moment it was tied into the loop. If it was fresh and hot, it will be fresh and hot. If it was a chilled soda in a glass of ice, it will be that too. Milk, eggs, meat. Constant hunger made the temptation too much to resist.

Worst of all is how happy she was to have the meals. It was hard to live with the fact she broke a loop to take someone's dinner. If Coco is right in her belief that the loopers truly die when their loops are broken, that means she killed more than one person during those years. She did it to avoid death by starvation, but she did it.

In the end, there was no way to reconcile what she was doing to the loopers, so she left Manhattan. She's been on the road for five years now, and only regrets leaving when she is particularly cold or hot or lost.

As she meandered away from Manhattan, she marveled at how easy it was to get around loops when the land wasn't crawling with people. At first, all she wanted was to go south, hoping for less severe winters and better conditions for growing food. Beyond that, it was all wandering and guesswork.

At the first farm she encountered, one absolutely filled with unkempt and unlooped vegetables and weeds, she sat down and cried. She pulled undersized and odd-looking tomatoes toward her until she had a pile around her like a fort. That night, Coco camped under the stars with only a sleeping bag and ate tomatoes until she threw up so violently that red tomato slime dribbled out of her nose.

Even with that inauspicious start, Coco knew it was the beginning of a more hopeful period. She'd read many books on gardening and farming, anticipating the need to do some of that herself. With little thought, she realized the farm had probably used hybrid or GMO seeds, which resulted in poor regrowth of the seeds left by uncollected vegetables. Seed companies did that on purpose.

Despite human design, what Coco found was nature forging a path. The few seeds that grew created more seeds that would grow. She inherited an uneven patch of small, red tomatoes so delicious that eating them felt sinful.

And, she found Tux.

Not far from Morganville, New Jersey, Coco decided to stop for a year and see how many of the hundreds of seed packets she'd obtained would sprout. The goal was to collect more seeds, fresh ones, which she might then plant with confidence much further south. With the spring springing, she began the backbreaking work of clearing a good-sized plot of unlooped land once covered by some crop that had not regrown.

Unlooped gas wasn't hard to find once she was away from Manhattan, but none of it seemed to work by the time she really needed it. Engines sputtered and wouldn't catch, so motorized garden tools were out. Hand tools were all she had, but she also had nothing but time.

When she sighted Tux, her first thought was that she was getting sloppy and not recording the loops around her as thoroughly as she should. She retrieved her current logbook, made a note of his location, then waited to see where the cat's loop might take her. Instead, the tiny, underfed cat sat down, licked its paw a few times, then stared at her. He was such a small thing. And adorable. A classic tuxedo patterned cat, with white paws, chest, and chin on a background of fur so black it glinted blue.

Noise was still the enemy, but Coco wasn't new at this and the field she'd selected was entirely free of human loops within range of her noises. She couldn't even see any people. In this small area, the world was blissfully free of reminders.

She looked around, waiting to be surprised by some other loop she'd missed, then waved her arms in sudden movement. Loopers couldn't see anything that wasn't in their loop. They could be broken from their loops by touch or noise, but not sight.

To her surprise, the little black cat crouched, tensed, and poofed its tail. That was the beginning of a new chapter in Coco's life, one in which there was another heartbeat in the night, a pair of ears to hear her, and a brain between them that could respond to her existence.

Coco is brought back to the present by Tux's head butting against her cheek. She shakes her head to clear away thoughts of the past. Too much sun does that to her. Gathering her gear, she ambles to the edge of the roof. The couch cushions she brought up here two weeks ago are getting a little battered, but they're comfortable. She plops onto one and pats the empty cushion next to her. "Come on, Tuxie. Sit with me."

The cat ignores her, ears pricked forward as he stares at something over the edge of the roof.

"Tuxie?"

One ear flicks toward her for a flash, then it's back to facing whatever it is he's staring at. This isn't usual behavior for him. He's rarely interested in the loopers. If anything, he's afraid of them. So why is he interested now?

Her heart thuds an extra hard beat in her chest. It's unpleasant, like heartburn with a shot of adrenaline behind it. Crouching behind the low lip of the roof, Coco peers out into the bright spring day.

The same stores line the opposite side of the street, cars moving along the four lanes of blacktop between. A few people are visible in a parking lot. A car caught in a static loop a little way down the road flickers in and out of existence, shooting bright flares of sunlight into her eyes every time it goes momentarily solid.

And there. Beyond the flickering car, on the grass near a fast-food place, are two people who do not belong in this picture.

Coco knows the two people aren't loopers the moment she sees them. They look around with the same furtiveness she recognizes in herself. She almost shouts but claps a hand over her mouth before she does something foolish. She doesn't know who these people are, and she isn't stupid enough to believe every unlooped person managed to stay sane after over thirteen years of this mess.

Ducking back from the lip of the roof, Coco crawls toward Tux until she can grab him and pull him away from the edge.

"There are people. *Unlooped* people," she whispers, stroking Tux's head. "It's alright. It's going to be alright."

Tux bumps his head into her palm, but otherwise has no comment.

Coco has no idea what she should do. Here she is, five years into her long journey, and she has finally seen another living unlooped person. Two of them, in fact. It's almost too much to process. She has a strange, but strong, urge to simply fade away, to avoid the people and let them pass. She has Tux to think about. What if they want her cat?

She shakes her head, realizing how silly that notion is. Why would they want Tux? They have each other. He purrs under her hand in a buzzsaw rumble. He has the loudest and strongest purr.

"What should we do?" she asks him. His eyes are half-closed in pleasure. "Never mind. You'd have us walk right into the middle of something."

She settles for watching the people. It's not as if she has anywhere urgent to be. She came to the roof to map loopers. It's a firm rule: Never go anywhere that isn't mapped. Too many loopers have disappeared because she broke their loops. An incautious door slam, a yelp when she hurt herself, and once, an accidental fire that burned down an entire house when she didn't realize a fireplace was decorative instead of meant to be used.

Her methods are not foolproof by any means. Animals and insects have loops too. Every step she takes probably breaks countless loops. She disturbs ants or mites or whatever small insect might be in her path, but she can't help those. The unseen must take care of itself. She has time to watch before she acts.

She makes a little nest out of the cat's favorite blanket on the cushion, then eases Tux down onto it, patting his head. His fur is warm from the sun, despite the chilly air.

"You stay there," she says, holding up a finger. He licks his chops in reply.

Staying low, she hurries to the edge of the roof, then plops down onto her stomach. The two people are plainly visible, but she brings up her field glasses to get a closer look anyway. They're both older than her, but not old. Or maybe they are. It's hard to judge. The woman has a streak of bright white in her dark hair, sort of like a superhero Coco has seen in comic books. It's eye-catching.

The pair are across the street, which is peppered with cars inhabited by loopers. They've stationed themselves on a perpetually freshly mowed lawn between a fast-food joint and a drugstore. To either side, loopers move in and out of the businesses, but the lawn remains clear.

It's exactly the kind of spot she would choose as a way station. Because so many eyes see the lawn, it stays looped and mowed, but because it's a place never meant to be traversed, it's clear of interfering loops that might walk through.

As she watches, the two people spread a large piece of paper on the ground. It's not a map like the ones she has. It's obviously hand drawn or traced, more like a diagram.

The man stabs a finger at a spot on the paper, then turns and jabs at the air, pointing generally northwest. The woman waves her hands in negation, points at something else on the paper, then gestures westward. They're clearly arguing silently, using extravagant hand gestures in place of shouts.

After a moment, the man stands and bows. Even without words, Coco can read the sarcasm in the movement.

He folds the paper and hands it over his shoulder. She takes it and tucks it into his pack, then bends to tighten the laces on her boots. He slips a water bottle from the side pocket of his pack and drinks, then, when she stands again, he hands it to her and bends to tend to his laces. It's all very routine looking, like a dance done so often the dancers don't have to think about their movements.

Because the pair were gesturing away from her spot, Coco thinks they'll also be heading away from her, which might be good and might be bad. If they leave, she might never find them again. Or, if she does, it will be only after running headlong through an untold number of loops she hasn't mapped. Then again, what if they aren't nice people? What then?

She still hasn't decided when they both turn and look directly across the street. Not to the northwest or the west, but north, where she lies in full view on top of a flat roof with a pair of field glasses. Coco freezes. Motion draws the eye, so she doesn't move.

Coco gets the feeling the pair hasn't exactly mapped and timed all the loops, because they pause for a long time, examining the cars zipping along the road between them. She keeps still, but the initial panic is wearing off. The two are so engrossed in the road activity that they haven't so much as glanced at anything beyond.

There's no way to map or time all the loops here without at least a few days of intense tracking. Crossing an entirely empty street can be deadly. If a loop resets and a car suddenly materializes where she's standing, Coco will be even deader than if she'd been hit by a car. Normally, she would give a road like this a full day, finding the sweet spots in the loops she can count on to be clear.

These people won't wait that long. They point at a few things, make a few motions, and watch a little, but she can tell they're about to move. They seem focused on the static loop in the road.

Static loops are weird, but surprisingly common. They're as looped as any other, but in such a brief loop that the object never really exists or ceases to exist. It simply flickers, forever stuttering in a loop so short it can't be measured. Static loops are great waypoints because they don't move. There's always some space around static loops too, but that space is limited. They're always surrounded by many other loops, like the static loop is a roadblock of some kind. Coco has no idea why that should be, but it is.

Right about the time she starts to relax, believing these people are probably so used to seeing loopers that her presence won't stand out, Tux appears and strides right up to the edge of the roof. Coco reaches for him, but he hops out of the way, then looks out at the world.

"*Meooow*," Tux wails.

It's the loudest noise he's made since he swiped at a looped mouse, which then rounded on him in a fury and bit his foot. Coco's mouth drops open as she gapes at him. When she looks across the street, thinking surely the people couldn't have heard the noise, she meets two pairs of eyes. They are staring directly up at her and the cat, who is now washing his face as if he's done nothing wrong.

Coco's Journal: Age 25

Year 13 of the Loop

I've decided that people are a bit like head lice. If you find one, you can be sure there are a lot more nearby.

Six

Year 13 of the Loop

"Thirteen years? You've been alone for thirteen years?" the woman, Tamara, asks Coco. She looks horrified at the idea, but also intensely interested in what the experience would be like, as if Coco were a particularly nasty car accident the woman can't stop watching.

It's been an hour since they met, but the weirdness of other people isn't easing. Coco can't get used to meeting their eyes, of them recognizing that she exists. It seems alien to converse with something other than a cat after so long. Not since Ruth… now eight years gone… has Coco seen acknowledgement in another human's eyes. She'd accepted she never would again. It's too much, too fast.

Weird or not, Coco can't stop looking at the two people. It feels like a dream. The white streak in the woman's dark hair is just as cool up close as Coco thought it would be, but other things are also now visible. Tamara looks worn, like someone who hasn't truly rested in so long she's forgotten how. Uneven freckles from sun damage dot her cheekbones and faint lines fan her eyes from too long squinting in the sun. Her skin isn't the smooth, pampered one of a looper, but the hard-used hide of a human from an earlier, less gentle time. It's all the imperfections that finally allow Coco to believe she's real.

The man, Jorge, touches Tamara's side discreetly and gives her a look when she turns to face him. She either doesn't understand or decides to ignore the hint, because she looks at Coco again and repeats, "Thirteen years?"

"Tam, don't be like that," Jorge says, like he's soothing a potentially dangerous wild animal.

"Like what?" she snaps.

Coco cringes.

Jorge eyes Tamara for a moment, then says, "Try to remember what it was like when you first met me. Just try."

For a moment, Tamara's expression doesn't change, then it does. She sucks in a deep breath and returns her attention to Coco. "I'm sorry. I know this is weird for you. We don't have to talk more. Not yet. There's time for history when you're ready."

With that, Tamara grabs her big pack and starts removing things like toiletries and packets that might hold food. Coco looks away, not quite sure what to do with herself. She wants to talk. She wants to grab both of them and see if they're real. She wants to hug them and dance around and cry and possibly glue herself to their sides.

For whatever reason, she can't. She can barely open her mouth to whisper.

All three of them, plus the cat, sit in the living room of the small house Coco claimed as her temporary headquarters in Salem. It's close to the auto parts store and has an almost entirely unlooped path between it and a field where she planted some quick growing vegetables like radishes, carrots, and beets.

Coco planned to be here just long enough to harvest, and she has lots of seeds for cool weather crops. It takes a long time to travel, and preparation is key. Her traveling season is meant to begin soon, and her destination for the year, Delaware. The year after, Virginia. That plan probably won't work out as scheduled. She wonders if she should plant more since there are now three people who will need to eat.

She always leaves some crops in the ground wherever she goes. It's her way of leaving hope behind in case another survivor happens along. If she doesn't leave any in the ground here, perhaps she can stretch the harvest to fill three bellies.

Tamara retrieves a few bar-shaped objects. The wrappers are wrinkled and so worn that some of the color has come off, leaving plain white behind. Old food picked up somewhere. She hands one to Jorge and offers another to Coco.

"Thank you," Coco whispers. It's some sort of granola bar. It's also probably as hard as a rock. She puts aside the bar, swallows hard, then forces her voice above a whisper when she says, "There's leftover stew outside. It's in the pot by the firepit, and probably still warm. It's just the winter veggies, but it's good. Cabbage, carrots. That kind of stuff."

Jorge lowers the bar he was about to bite into and gapes at her. "You mean, fresh? As in fresh vegetables?"

They look at her so eagerly that Coco has to avert her eyes. It's too much. She strokes Tux's head and keeps her eyes fixed on his placid face as she answers. "Fresh enough. I grew them during the winter. They keep pretty well as long as the weather is cold."

The two scramble up and are out of the door in seconds. Jorge comes back a few seconds later and smiles as he heads for the kitchen. "We forgot bowls," he says.

When they return, the room is silent except for slurping noises. That's not so bad, and Coco watches them from the corner of her eye. They seem alright. She tries to remember what it was like before the looping, what it was like to have people doing their own thing without some set path or pattern. It's hard to remember that. Not what it looked like, because her actual memory is fine. It's more that she can't recall what it felt like.

All the movement feels chaotic now, but she doesn't remember it feeling like that before. Maybe she'll get used to it. Or maybe she won't.

Maybe she won't get the chance. Who's to say these two people will want to stay with her? They must have plans, a goal… something. What if those plans can't include her, or even worse, are something Coco doesn't want to do?

Jorge leaves to refill their bowls from the big pot, but only after he asks if that's okay, which Coco appreciates. She made a huge pot and left it outside in the cold air. It was intended to last her a few days, but it doesn't matter if it goes before then. She knows there's enough bagged, boxed, and canned food in this town to last a year. Towns like this aren't like Manhattan. There are usually loads of unlooped items in sleepy, mid-sized communities. Some of it will be edible, if not particularly tasty.

Tamara lets out a huge, reverberant belch once she's finished her second bowl, which elicits a groan from Jorge. Even Coco lets out a quiet, surprised laugh.

Turning to her, Jorge waggles his eyebrows. "I should have mentioned that Tam over there is gassy. Cabbage makes it much worse. You have no idea what we're in for later. She is the acknowledged champion of burps and farts."

Coco smiles and for the first time since she laid eyes on them, it feels natural.

From the other end of the room, Tamara says, "There she is. I can see you now, Coco."

* * *

It surprises Coco how quickly she gets used to other people. Tux appears to appreciate more hands to stroke him and more warm laps to snuggle into. Perhaps his comfort is what helps her to loosen up. Or maybe it's just their easy familiarity that does it.

When she wakes on her second day with them, she feels ready to ask them questions. She feels ready for them to ask her questions. They'd held back, being polite and quiet. The only conversations had been brief and dealt with the daily business that needed tending; the newly planted seeds, the cooking, and the mapping of loopers.

Their breakfast consists of thirteen-year-old oatmeal that is still surprisingly delicious with a bit of brown sugar. It's so quiet that Jorge actually looks surprised when Coco asks, "Have you two been together since the beginning? Or most of the time? Or did you know each other before? And why do you have matching tattoos on your hands?"

Tamara motions for Jorge to answer. "I met Tam about a year and a half after the Break," Jorge says. "I was out looking for survivors to bring to our community and I found her. As for the tattoos, they show that we're members of a community. That way, if we meet someone while we're traveling, we'll know if they're new, like you. We can show tattoos without making noise."

The spoon stops halfway to Coco's mouth, her lips still parted. "Community? You mean, there are more people? Where?"

A wide smile splits his face. "Ohio. And yes, there are more. Back when I met Tam, we had what, maybe eight? Now there are twenty-three people in town. Or at least there were when we left for our trip."

"Twenty-four," Tamara corrects. "Remember, Lydia had her baby right before we left."

"Oh, yeah!" he says. "I can't forget the baby. Twenty-four. There might be more now. Who knows? We've been gone about a year. I hope there are more by now."

There's no way these two people can understand the impact of their words, but the sheer number of shocking facts packed into those few sentences is almost enough to send Coco back to bed with the covers over her head. It's almost enough to make her doubt her sanity again.

Twenty-four people? A baby born? A community?

"Are you okay?" Jorge asks gently, lowering his voice. He places one hand flat on the table between them, as if to offer her comfort without presuming to touch her.

Coco can feel the sting of tears in her eyes. She doesn't want to cry, so she sniffs and leans her head back for a moment. When that moment is over, she meets his gaze and shakes her head. "How? I don't understand. How can there be so many? I've only found one in all this time. Just one unlooped person! And you've found so many. Why would you leave them?"

"Oh boy, here we go," Tamara says, with a roll of her eyes that isn't unfriendly. "You have just opened a huge can of worms. This boy is what you might call a science nerd. He's never going to shut up now."

Confused, Coco looks at Jorge, who is grinning. "So unfair. Ignore her, she knows nothing." He elbows Tamara, his grin growing wider at whatever inside joke they're sharing that Coco isn't a part of. Shifting to a bizarre accent, he says, "You know nothing, Tamara Reese."

They both chuckle while Coco looks on, completely confused. Jorge clears his throat and says, "Uh, that was from an old television show. It's one of the few we've got all the episodes for. Someone had it downloaded to a computer we found, so we've watched it at least twenty times. Sorry."

Rather than repeat her many questions, Coco opens her hands, encompassing everything she just asked. "And?" she prompts.

Jorge holds up a finger for patience, then gets up to retrieve his pack. After a bit of rummaging, he returns with a computer and a few battery bricks. He opens the screen, then crosses his fingers while the machine boots up. As the light flickers on his face, he urges, "Come on, baby. You can do it."

He claps his hands together when the computer apparently boots up successfully. He starts working the keyboard, and without looking up, he says, "Okay, this is easier if we don't go in order. The easy answers are complicated, and the complicated answers are impossible in plain words, but we can get there with a little patience. Are you game?"

Coco nods.

With an exaggerated sigh, Tamara flops back in her chair. "Oh my god. If I have to hear this again, I will definitely stab myself in the eye."

Jorge pulls a face. "Oh, right, because being one-eyed would make you so much more useful. Why don't you go map some routes or something? No, how about you find a good route into that general store. They'll have loads of packaged food."

Tamara gets up and flicks Jorge on his ear as she leaves the table. He yelps and jerks in his chair, which just makes her laugh as she hurries across the room, beyond reach of any retaliation. "Don't bore her to death," she says as she closes the door behind her. The house feels empty when she leaves.

These two people are so easy together that Coco can't quite figure out the relationship. They act like family, like her older brother had been before he turned into a teenager and decided she was a pest. They also act a bit like her parents did, back when she was young and they were happy, before they got divorced.

She doesn't think they're related. Both have dark hair, but it's a different kind of dark. Jorge's skin is a few shades deeper, his nose sharper, and his eyes a brown so dark they seem almost black. Tamara's skin is tanned, but quite pale when she pulls up her sleeves. Her eyes are blue.

Before she loses her nerve, she asks, "Are you two together? Like a married kind of together?"

Jorge was in the middle of sipping some water and almost chokes at her question. "No! Just… no. That would be weird. I suppose you'd say she's my best friend. Besides, she's already married."

"She is? To someone in Ohio?"

Jorge stops typing, then looks at her, his eyes no longer laughing. "No. Her husband is a breaker. A looper, I mean." At her expression, he says, "Yeah, I know. Most of the people in our community who were married or in relationships have moved on. They're getting together, breaking up, and everything else in between. Not Tam. She just can't seem to do that. It's her story to tell if she wants to. But to answer your question, no. We are definitely not together."

"Okay," Coco says, a bit embarrassed. "I didn't mean to be nosy."

Jorge glances at his screen, then at her again. Coco knows her face is blazing red. She can feel it. He must see it too.

He chuckles and looks down at his screen, resuming whatever he was doing. "Don't worry about it. It's natural to wonder. No, Tam and I are good traveling partners and we're out here for a reason. Some of us can't forget the Break. Some of us want to fix it more than we want to move on. That includes me, so here I am."

It's the first time Coco has heard they have a goal other than traveling. And their goal is to fix what's happened? Over the years, Coco has dreamed of finding some magic key that will fix the looping. Of course, she has. But a dream is a different thing than reality. How could they ever possibly fix all of this? Her belly clenches with nerves and a dash of hope.

"Is that possible? Can we fix the world? How?" she asks, leaning forward. Coco doesn't even notice that she spoke in a normal tone of voice.

Coco's Journal: Age 25

Year 13 of the Loop

I finally remember what it's like to be a part of something. It's strange, but good. The way Jorge and Tamara have folded me in almost makes it seem like we've always been a trio. I'm in the middle of their warmth and laughter and it's so very wonderful. I'd forgotten what that's like.

I also know that if I'm ever alone again, I won't be able to pretend it's normal. I only know how terrible those years were because of how good it is right now. There's no way I could survive being on my own again.

Seven

Year 13 of the Loop

Jorge rubs his hands together, then grabs a slip of paper from a pad meant for grocery lists. He cups his hand so Coco won't see what he writes, jots some quick strokes, and folds the paper into a small square. Only then does he turn the computer around so Coco can see the screen.

"So, here's the first part. This is our list of standard questions for new people. On the paper, I wrote what I think your answers will be. With me so far?"

Coco glances at the screen, sees a few of the questions, and frowns.

Jorge holds up his hands. "I know, I know. These may seem nosy, but trust me when I say it's for a good reason. It's how I can show you what we've figured out about the Break so far. I won't ask you to elaborate. Your story is yours. You can share or not, whenever you want. Okay?"

She nods, then glances at the screen again. They aren't really personal questions. It's probably fine to answer them.

"You think you know my answers?" she asks.

He makes an indecisive noise, like he's hedging his bets, then slides the pad of paper toward her. He rolls over the pencil he used as well. "Not exactly or precisely. It's more like I know an either-or option. Your answers will help me with my data, and maybe confirm it a bit more if I'm correct. Just write your answers on the pad. If none of the options are close or you don't know the answer, leave it blank. Got it?"

Coco takes the pencil and reads the first question.

When the Break happened, you were in what kind of location?
A: A large, densely populated metropolitan area.
B: A city or large town, surrounded by less developed areas.
C: A small town or rural setting, with many farms or undeveloped lands nearby.

Coco writes an A, then moves to the next question. That one asks how many people lived within one mile of her location. The next, how many micro-breaks were within that distance.

Coco frowns and asks, "What's a micro-break?"

"Ah, well, you've seen the breaks—the loops—that are so short that the person doesn't move? Maybe they just seem to flicker? Like the car on the road where we met?"

Her heart sinks, her mind conjuring the image of a small, chubby foot kicked out from under the covers of a bed. Squeezing her eyes shut for a moment, she pushes the memory back, erasing the image. Without thought, her hand rises to the scar on her forehead.

"Are you okay?" Jorge asks, his tone compassionate, as if he really understands this pain. Maybe he does. His eyes move toward the scar she's rubbing on her forehead. He tugs up one sleeve and holds out his arm, revealing silvery lines scoring it. So many scars. "Almost everyone has their marks. These questions aren't meant to pry into that. That's your story to tell, just like Tam has hers."

Lowering her hand, Coco nods. "Okay."

"You want to stop for a while?" he asks.

"No, I'm fine," she says, then pushes away all thoughts of her family. "I know what you mean now. I call them static loops. Static because they look sort of like static. Like when the cable went out and my mom tried to switch the TV input to the digital antenna thingie. You know how it makes that horrible noise and is, well, static?"

He leans back in the chair, crossing his arms behind his head. "Man, I'm really digging your nomenclature. It *is* just like static. Holy moly, that's good. You know, I'm actually a little bit jealous I didn't think of it. If I start using it now, I'll be copying."

Coco smiles despite herself. "You can use it. It's okay. You have my official permission."

Jorge nods toward the paper, urging her back to her task. Coco finishes the rest of the questions quickly. For the most part, they aren't difficult. Some are unanswerable, so she makes a guess. When she finishes the last question, a multiple-choice one asking how many breakers, whether human or animal or insect, were within 100 feet of her initial position, she slides her answer sheet toward him.

"Now what?" she asks.

Jorge pushes her answer sheet back toward her and then the folded-up paper with his answers. "Go ahead and check them for yourself," he says with a knowing smile.

She unfolds the sheet, then looks at his projected answer for the first question. He's written A or C on his sheet. Her answer was A. She glances up at him, her eyes narrowed. "That's not a guess. It's a two out of three bet, which is pretty easy to get right."

He waves his hands to indicate she should continue. "I'll explain, but you need to see this for yourself. It won't make sense otherwise."

With a sigh, Coco looks at the rest of the answers. In every case, he has selected two answers. In every case except two, her answer is one of the two he selected. The two incorrect ones also happen to be the ones she doesn't know. The ones she guessed. One correct is an easy two out of three chance. Fifteen such correct answers are something else entirely.

When she's done, she lowers the pencil to the table, still staring at the two sheets, wondering if she hadn't somehow given away what her answers might be. Was this some sort of trick? Was he some sort of mind reader?

Without coming to any conclusion about any of those possibilities, she looks up and asks, "How did you do that? Is it a trick?"

Jorge glances at the papers. "May I?"

She nods and pushes them over, watching his expressions as he compares answers. He looks at the screen when his fingers run over the questions he got wrong. He shrugs, as if the two he missed weren't important.

"So? How did you do that?" she prods.

Jorge stacks the two papers, then places the pencil neatly on top. "Okay, this is complicated, but bear with me. You answered that you came from a city. Can I ask where? You don't have to tell me if you don't want to."

Coco doesn't answer at once. Instead, she tries to figure out why she shouldn't tell him. Is there some value to knowing that? Other than potentially leading to follow on questions that might bring pain, she can't see any risks.

"I'm from Manhattan," she says.

Jorge's eyebrows draw together. "As in, New York? Or is it one of the others? Manhattan, Kansas, maybe?"

"No. I'm from Manhattan, New York."

His eyes widen, and he gives a long, low whistle. Then he looks at her with something like wonder. "How in the world did you survive that? We were in D.C. last year, and it took us forever to get through, even on a Sunday morning. Before that, the largest city I'd been in was Pittsburgh. No one goes near big cities."

His questions probably seem innocuous to his ears. She can tell he's asking out of genuine curiosity. He can't possibly know how loaded the question is. But how is she supposed to answer?

"*Ugh*, I'm sorry," he says. "Never mind. Don't answer my totally inconsiderate question. Let me answer your question instead, because Manhattan is a prime example. Your answer for how many people who aren't breakers within one mile of you was one I got wrong. You said earlier that you only found one. Was that person there? In Manhattan?"

Coco nods. "Yes, but I didn't find her until about five years after it started. There were probably others that I never met. Some bodies in the beginning, but I figured they were loops that didn't disappear for some reason."

"Okay, I think I understand how that came to be, but I'll talk about it later. The other one I got wrong was how often you'd seen breaker paths reshuffle. You answered zero. I would have thought that number would actually be much higher in a city."

That was one of the questions that confused Coco, because she's never seen that happen. There were periods when her loop maps and timers no longer seemed to work, but she attributed it to flaws in her timing. She never actually considered the possibility that they were changing. Not even once.

"I'm actually not sure I understand that question," she says. "When you say reshuffle, do you mean they change? As in, the paths that the loopers take changes?"

"Yes, I mean exactly that. You obviously know what happens when a breaker is disturbed from their slip… their loop. They go crazy, sometimes chase you or attack you, then fall down dead and disappear to who knows where. You probably already know they never, ever bump into another loop. Not ever. And they can scream, but no one hears them. If you scream, everyone hears it. Right?"

She nods. All of this is old news.

"Well, all of that is true with everyone I've spoken with, no matter where they come from. What it took time to figure out was that when a loop disappears, the other loops will fill in the space. The timing changes can be so small that they don't matter much, but they can be big too. I noticed it with a car. That's big enough to notice."

Again, she considers, trying to dig through her memories for details of a time when her loop maps seemed wrong. There are too many memories. Nothing comes. She was always careful not to break loops. Desperation drove her to do it in the past, but never for any reason less than that.

"Sorry," she says. "I just don't remember any. I really try not to disturb them. I still don't understand what this has to do with why the looping started in the first place. Or why I'm not one of them."

Jorge does something with the computer, then turns the screen to face her again. It's an image of buildings and people, looking slightly down and outward, as if the picture were taken from a rooftop. It looks like a decently sized downtown area.

Until she'd left Manhattan, Coco had never even seen a moderately sized town before. She's seen plenty since. There's a name she doesn't recognize in a label box in the right-hand corner.

Jorge points to the various clusters of people and says, "This is one of the towns we mapped in its entirety. Or at least as entirely as we could. There's no way to count every ant or spider, but you know what I mean, right?"

"You tracked the loops."

"Exactly. We can't do that anymore because so many loops have been broken from unlooped stuff falling down or decaying or whatever. This was about two years after the Break. We mapped this town in every possible way. The length of the loop, the time it takes, when it starts, when it ends, where it starts and ends… all of it. As much as possible. You with me?"

"Yeah, sure."

He hits a key, and a new image replaces the old one. "This is what the loops look like when we take all the distractions out and make them dots and lines. Pretty chaotic, right?"

It is exactly that. White space has replaced buildings and streets. Lines and dots cross over and around each other until some parts look like big black blobs.

He hits the key again, and a chart appears, then he keeps clicking. More charts. All of them look like nonsensical blobs or jagged, overlapping lines. He speaks and keeps on clicking. "We tried charting and mapping them in all sorts of ways, using every combination of factors. Nothing stood out. Nothing made sense."

He pauses, his finger hovering over an arrow key, but not pressing it. "Keep in mind that it took us more than five years and a whole lot of mapping to get to the next graph."

She nods, wondering what in the world could be on the next slide that's so momentous.

He jabs the key, and a new graph comes up. At first, it looks as chaotic as the others, and Coco is disappointed. Rather than say so, she looks harder. Jorge is watching her, as if he's waiting for her to see what he knows is there.

It's when she leans back, about to give up, that something stands out. Only when she doesn't focus on the graph does it appear. She holds up a finger for patience, then closes her eyes for a moment. When she opens them, she doesn't focus on the graph, but rather, its edges.

"There are clumps. I see them now. Here and here and here. It's hard to see them, but there are definitely clumps in a sort of line."

He grins widely. "Yep. Well, dense clusters of dots, really, but clumps work too. That's when we realized we needed to map things differently. There's a program people use in science and engineering for complex visualizations like this. I'm a pure math guy, but we figured it out. Let me bring up the video. It'll take just a sec."

He gets up from the table and sits next to her, sliding the computer so that it rests between them. He brings up a new window and a still image of a black screen with a few bits of computer code fills the frame.

"What this video shows is the maps with multiple vectors. It's three dimensional... well, four if you count time, but that's sort of the broken bit. Just watch."

The video starts and at first, it's more of the same chaos. There is more code, more cursor movements, and then the charts expand into a three-dimensional representation. Jorge sucks in a slightly harder breath, so Coco knows the important bit is coming. She focuses.

And there it is. The chaotic curves and lines spread apart and resolve into a shape any human from the modern age would recognize.

"It's waves!" she exclaims.

"Exactamundo," Jorge says, beaming. "Watch."

There are more charts and more graphs. With some explanations peppered in, it makes perfect sense, even to someone like Coco, who had gleaned her education past seventh grade entirely from books she selected herself.

When it ends, Jorge meets her eyes, as if waiting to explain anything she doesn't understand. And yes, while Coco would like to learn all the details, the big questions are the ones she can't shake at the moment.

"Then why aren't we in loops? And how did you know I either came from a city or the country? What does it all have to do with each other?"

His smile broadens as he says, "Density. It's all about density. Everyone who comes to Solace—that's what they call our community—is questioned in detail about everything. And everywhere anyone goes, they take notes on certain things. About ninety percent of all the unlooped people and animals come from places with an exceedingly high density of life. I'm including all the dead bodies in this too, because we record that. We have two unlooped people from Pittsburgh, including me, and both of us had a higher percentage of micro-breaks—what you call static loops—near us. That seems to be an indicator. The more static loops, the more likely we are to find a living thing unlooped. We don't know why, specifically, but basically, I think it's a matter of space between loops. We just, I don't know, didn't fit or something. There are a couple of theories about observer bias or biological factors that might have some merit. We can never prove it, though."

"Okay, so that accounts for cities. Manhattan is certainly filled with people, but the country? Wouldn't it be the opposite? And why didn't I find more people if my city was dense enough to keep me unlooped?" she asks.

"All life, remember? Do you have any idea how many animals and bugs there are in the country? That matters. And no, we didn't count bugs, obviously. It took us a while to figure out that they influenced things no differently than humans when it comes to loops. As for you, well, you found one person alive, but you answered that you'd seen between ten and fifteen dead bodies, regardless of species. I'm betting there were more you didn't find. Probably more alive, too."

A memory surfaces. Packages of unlooped food that sprung leaks. Little nibbled holes in boxes and bags. "I think there were some unlooped rats, but I never saw them."

Jorge nods eagerly. "Oh yeah, rats. Seen plenty of evidence of them. Animals don't seem to survive well except for rats. Most animals don't know to avoid food tied up in a loop, so they starve. Rats are smarter, or just meaner. Either way, rats are common enough. Well, if anything unaffected can be called common."

Coco glances around for Tux at those words. She'd never found his mother or littermates, but he was thin and sickly when she found him. He'd been eating a bowl of looped food set out on a back porch. More than likely, Tux ate that same food over and over again, never getting nutrition, his belly full and then empty again.

"Yeah," she murmurs. "I know how that goes."

At that moment, the front door opens and Tamara breezes in, bringing with her a swirl of cool, fresh air and her own peculiar form of friendly, high energy. With a glance at the computer, she looks at Coco, then mimes her head exploding with her expressive hands.

Coco laughs and nods. "Yeah, basically that."

"I hope you're done, because I am. I've got a nice path into the store and about half of it is covered in dust, so there's plenty of food. Grab bags. Many bags. Also," she says, then stops to turn in a celebratory circle, poking her index fingers into the air like she's just done something worth celebrating, "I've found a breaker pair! That would be a looped pair to you, Coco. They're so cute I want to pinch their cheeks. You have to see them."

After so much information, Coco could use a respite. Despite not learning how it all started, she's at her saturation point. It will take time to settle into this new knowledge. It will take time to process the million regrets she'll have for the things she didn't do and would have done if she'd known all of this at the beginning. She stands, stretches, then moves toward her neat pile of stacked totes.

"Sure thing. I'll be ready to go in a minute. I could use a walk."

Coco's Journal: Age 25

Year 13 of the Loop

If there was one thing I wish I'd learned earlier, it would be toilets. Toilets. If you can catch a toilet that's tied up in a loop, and get in before the looper, then you have an eternally fresh toilet. Yeah, I didn't figure that one out for a long time. And where does the water come from? I have no idea. I do know one thing, for sure. If this ever ends, there are going to be a lot of people really mad about the state of their bathrooms.

Eight

Year 13 of the Loop

Jorge and Coco walk along the spray-painted path, both of them swinging their empty bags as they wait for Tamara to catch up. Coco feels good. Amazingly good. Just knowing there is a pattern to the looping is comforting, even if it's far beyond her ability to comprehend. This isn't just some inexplicable cataclysm that left her alone and frightened. It has a pattern. It's a complex dance between all living things, including her.

Tamara jogs out of the looped section of the field near their temporary home, pushing through unlooped, overgrown weeds that reach her chest. She's still doing up her pants, the two ends of her belt flopping as she runs.

The looped bit of the field is their unofficial bathroom. Since it's looped, it returns to its original state when the loop restarts. Everything they leave behind, including wrappers, bits of garbage, and their own biological trash, disappears. It's very handy for keeping things tidy.

When Tamara catches up, she lets out a big breath, then flashes Coco a wicked grin. Jorge chuckles, like he knows what's coming.

"Did you know," Tamara asks, "that if you eat food on a long enough loop that you have time to shit it out, not all of your shit disappears when the loop starts again? How does that work? Have you ever wondered how in the hell that works?"

The tone of her voice sets Coco to laughing. She waves a hand and refuses to look at Tamara, laughing hard while trying not to do it too loudly. There are no human loops anywhere near the house or the path, which is why Coco chose it as her headquarters, so it's probably safe. But probably isn't the same as being certain, and Coco uses a hand to muffle her laughter.

For her part, Tamara ramps it up by bending over as they walk, trying to meet Coco's gaze while repeating the words, "Do ya? Do ya? Do you know the mysteries of looping shit?"

Jorge nudges Coco's leg with his bundle of bags and says, "Don't answer her. For the love of all that's edible, do not feed that beast. She will go on and on. She has an entire catalog of really gross stuff like that."

When Coco laughs so hard that she snorts, that gets them going even harder. The pair tease her with exaggerated snorts of their own.

They've arrived at the edge of the street and take a moment to calm down so as not to disturb the loopers across the street. Coco's cheeks actually hurt. It's a strange sensation. She only remembers it now that she's felt it again. It's been that long since she's laughed that hard. Thirteen years.

Directly across from them is the Salem General Store. According to the signage, most items are a dollar or less. In Coco's experience, these stores are often chock full of looped items, but they often have an astonishing array of useful or edible things.

Tamara pulls a small notebook from her back pocket, then nods toward a spot just to the left of the big doors. "The looped pair I told you about is right inside the doors. Other than that, the back room is one huge loop, so I didn't bother with it. Inside, there are only a few loopers, and you can see them fine. Clear path for us if we're quiet."

They move across at Tamara's cue. Roads are always dangerous, so Coco does her best to avoid them, but this one is surprisingly easy. Sunday morning is good for traffic.

They move in a curving path along a line of dots that Tamara spray painted to indicate safe passage. A few dots have disappeared as loops reset, but most remain. Smart. Spray painting safe paths had never occurred to her before.

Their path meanders, taking them around the parking lot, then back and forth till they approach the doors. There aren't that many loops compared with Manhattan, but there are some. There are a few parked cars, each one still shiny and with full tires. One of them flickers and disappears as they pass.

Tamara stops them and gestures toward the side of the building. "The back door is completely out because the stock room is looped to hell and back, but also, there are a couple of loops behind the store that I didn't bother to map. It looks like drugs to me, but I didn't check."

Jorge looks around. "That leaves just one way in or out. How tight are the loops at the door?"

With a firm shake of her head, Tamara says, "Not bad. The store wasn't open. There's some Saturday night traffic inside, but not by the doors. I think the pair I want you to see is the reason the door isn't busy. They take up a lot of room. It's a short loop. I'll get the door when it's time and you'll see."

There's a mirrored coating on the glass, so Coco can't see the interior with any clarity. Some of the coating is bubbled, but she thinks it was probably already like that when the looping began. Most of the glass is far too clean to be unlooped. Coco isn't in a rush. She's spent too much of her life waiting for loops to be impatient anymore.

No more than two minutes later, a young woman carrying a toddler on her hip flickers into life near the door. She has long, pale blonde hair. It's absolutely straight and sways behind her. Her face is a bit too broad to be classified as conventionally beautiful, but she has a certain something. Maybe it's her obvious happiness that makes her beautiful.

The woman isn't walking so much as dance-walking. The exaggerated motion makes the whining toddler in her arms rock back and forth as she hums softly. She's wearing a uniform shirt with a name tag that reads *Candace*. When Candace reaches for the door, she swings her head around and smiles up at someone who's no longer behind her.

Tamara holds up her fist and whispers, "Hold, and walk close to me when I go. Get ready."

Before the door swings closed, Tamara hurries forward, yanks it wide, then presses her back to the other door, sliding along it until she's stopped by a large display bin filled with colorful inflated balls. It's a tight squeeze, but Coco presses her side against Jorge, eyes on Tamara for her next instruction.

With her finger over her lips in an entirely unnecessary reminder to keep quiet, Tamara holds up her fist again. Coco risks a glance at the pair. The woman is swaying back and forth and soothing her child. She looks up at someone as she hugs the child to her chest and rests her cheek on the soft, white-blond curls.

She mouths, "It's okay. He'll be okay," toward whoever is missing from their tableau. Coco smiles at them and feels a sting in her throat. They are beautiful. Even with one member of the trio missing, Coco can see the love in the young woman's eyes.

A man walks past them and turns left down the far aisle. He's wearing a nice shirt and the same kind of name tag as Candace. There's a woman with a basket examining an obviously looped rack of gum and mints near the registers. Another man leans against a cart filled with energy drinks. He looks tired. The line must have been slow at some point on Saturday evening.

When the man nudges his cart forward, Tamara waves for them to move. They follow quickly, close on her heels as they cross the open area and slide into the relative safety of an aisle. A quick glance around shows Coco what's looped and what's not. The floor is mostly looped, as are the items near the head of the aisle. Even there, it's not complete. The bags of chips nearest the front are clean and vibrant. Behind that first row, more bags bear colors dimmed by the years and gray with dust.

Jorge raises his hands in a mime of victory and heads for a candy display. They're hard candies, which usually last better than most kinds of sweets. He reaches for the packages in the rear, each one shedding a curtain of shimmering dust as he stuffs them into an open bag as quietly as he can.

Most items aren't going to be even remotely edible after thirteen years. These two people must have a running catalog of such things just like Coco, because they skip over the ones she would have skipped. A few things need to be tested. They're worth taking and sorting later. Soon, the looped floor is littered with bits of foil and plastic.

At the end of the aisle, they set down the filled bags with care in a wedge of dusty floor. Tamara holds up her fist again, then looks around, cataloging the status of the loops. It must be fine, because she twirls a finger, then points them toward the next aisle.

Another woman appears there, near the other end, going through a rack of small t-shirts meant for babies or toddlers. She holds up one after another, each sporting some slogan like, *I'm With Stupid* or *World's Cutest Baby*. Most she puts back, but a few are draped over her arm.

Tamara pulls both of them close and whispers, "Stay on this end. She's going to grab shampoo too."

Coco looks in the direction of Tamara's nod. The shampoo is about halfway down the aisle, the bottles all bright and free of dust. That's too bad. Cheap shampoo seems to survive best, and Coco has been out for a while. Her hair stinks.

They fill more sacks with potentially useful items. Soap and other toiletries. Batteries, which will probably be drained, but are worth checking. Notepads and pencils. Coloring books and colored pencils. A surprise batch of cheap underwear, which might have rotten elastic, but are always worth taking just in case. T-shirts. Socks. Hair bands.

By the time they traverse the safe parts of the store, all their bags are overflowing. They raid a display of unlooped reusable grocery bags and fill those as well. Most of what they take probably won't be edible or usable, but it's easier to discard what doesn't work later than it is to check everything within hearing range of loopers.

Through it all, Coco has kept half an eye on the pair at the front of the store. A rare paired loop. Like the woman and her dog so long ago in Manhattan, these two are captured in a moment of closeness. The loop can't be more than ten minutes long, but so much information can be gleaned from the right ten minutes.

The woman is about to start her shift, which must include pre-opening duties here at the store. The child doesn't want his mother to leave him. The now-invisible person who makes up the trio is clearly dropping off the mother. The noises of the other looped shoppers aren't enough to drown out what the woman says to her child. Coco listens as she works, her ears pricked to not miss a single word.

Candace bounces and soothes her child, speaking softly about him going to his grandma's. She tickles his neck and tells him how much fun it will be to help grandma cook and reminds him they will be making cookies. It's all loving and beautiful and tender, a private moment between a small family before her workday begins.

When they finish, Tamara leads them to the front, leaving Coco with the first bags while she and Jorge collect the others. There are too many for them to carry in one trip, but using a cart is out of the question. Squeaking wheels would mean death for any looper who hears them.

Coco watches the loop as it comes to an end. The woman shifts position and looks up at the invisible third party, then lifts the now-happy child from her chest and into unseen arms. Just before she lets go of the child, the loop ends. It's a strange conclusion, with the child almost caught in mid-air.

Next to her ear, Tamara whispers, "I'll never get used to seeing things like that."

Coco hadn't heard their approach, and she starts a little, but doesn't make noise. She nods, because really, who could get used to seeing such things?

"Ready to go?" Tamara whispers.

Coco stares at the empty space where Candace and her child just were. "Can I leave a note?"

The others seem confused by the request, but nod. The confusion clears as she jots her message on a sheet from her notepad and pulls out the roll of tape she keeps in her pocket. Quietly, she wipes dust from an unlooped section of the interior window, then tapes her note there.

Jorge smiles and touches her shoulder when he reads it, giving her a nod she takes as approval.

To Candace and family. You were trapped in a moment filled with love. I watched it. It was beautiful. Remember that love when things get difficult.

Love, Coco. Year 13 of the Loop.

Coco's Journal: Age 25

Year 13 of the Loop

I used to leave photos with my notes. That was when I could still print things. I found this little photo printer and would set up my power wherever I stayed using unlooped car batteries. I wanted the people to see what I saw if this ever ended. Once all the ink was gone and dried up, I tried using one of those cameras that ejects the picture for you right away. Those are too loud to use in most situations, so I eventually had to stop leaving pictures. I've never stopped leaving notes, though. They deserve to know they were not forgotten or alone. That they were never gone.

Nine

Year 13 of the Loop

Over the next few weeks, spring turns balmy and warm, bringing enough rainwater for actual bathing. The trio explores and maps the surrounding area, trying to decide on a good course of action. Coco's intention to move south was based on surviving while alone. She needed to find milder winters to do the work necessary to stay alive with only Tux for company.

That's no longer an issue. Even without explicit invitations or agreements, Jorge and Tamara have folded Coco into their lives. Or perhaps she's folded herself in. Where they go next becomes a decision they mull over together in the evenings.

Over time, they learn things about each other, though they never speak of what happened during the initial hours of the Looping. That each has a tragedy is obvious in the way they avoid certain details or topics. It's present in the sorrowful gazes they direct toward loops of children or older parents. It's there in a hundred ways. It's there in the fading picture of two children Tamara keeps near her heart.

What they've been doing during their travels is also revealed rather casually in the course of getting to know each other. It's all very interesting, but Coco is more interested in the idea of a community. Now that she's had company, she's greedy for more.

That need is enhanced when Jorge and Tamara inform her that there isn't just one community. There are many. And more are being discovered.

Jorge and Tamara are members of the Solace community and belong to a group called the Seekers—which explains the odd S shape of their hand tattoos. There are other groups. Seekers are those that want to understand what happened to the world. Not everyone believes in that cause. There are different belief systems, independent communities, and even communities who shun interaction with any other group.

Even so, Coco can't wait to visit some of the places she's heard of. There is New Detroit, a name that sounds impressive and populated, but actually has less than two dozen members and is nowhere near Detroit. Other Seeker communities have names like Sooner, Little Rock Two, The Dairy, or Holstead's Farm.

There's a settlement outside Cincinnati inexplicably named Abiding Dude. Even after Jorge and Tamara spend a great deal of time trying to explain the reference, Coco doesn't quite get it.

One evening, while they sort and test piles of underwear and socks to find the few that don't have rotted elastic, Jorge regales her with stories of their travels over the past year. It's become an almost customary activity. Without television, what else is there to do but talk?

As he finishes up a strange story of finding a dead man surrounded by piles of money, gold, and jewelry, Coco says, "That wasn't a good story. He was just a bandit out looting. Give me something good. Maybe something bigger. Or weirder."

With a chuckle, Jorge says, "The weirdest of our adventures was in Washington D. C. last fall. We went there thinking we might find an answer. So, we went to observe the loopers. What a mess."

"So, you just listened and watched everyone to see if anyone saw the Looping coming? How long did that take?"

Jorge frowns. "Well, it wasn't quite that simple, but yeah, that was the general idea. We figured that if anyone had any idea that it was coming, even if only by a few minutes, then someone would have told the bigwigs in government. I mean, it makes sense, right?"

She nods, then tosses a sock onto the growing discard pile after it makes a soft ripping sound as she stretches it.

Jorge drops any pretense of sorting and starts waving his hands while he talks. "Okay, so we figured that with all the loops there, someone would have been caught in the middle of finding out. We also thought it would be a nightmare to get through D.C., so we never tried it. Generally speaking, nobody goes to big cities. It's just too risky. Then one of the newest people in Solace pointed out that D.C. is basically a ghost town on Saturday and Sunday mornings, at least until the tourists get moving. Apparently, no one who works in the government actually lives there. Well, except at the White House, obviously."

Tamara breaks in and says, "Ghost town was definitely an exaggeration. It *was* a nightmare to get through the loops."

"Yeah, but we did," Jorge says, then winks at her. "Anyway, we were there over the whole winter and there were zero indications in the loops that anyone knew anything. The thing is, we still couldn't be sure, and I found this book…" He trails off, seeming to wrestle with how to continue. "Okay, if I admit this, you have to try to look at it from my perspective. Can you do that?"

"*Uh oh,*" Coco says, dropping a sock patterned with hearts into the keep pile. "What did you do?"

Tamara reaches across the piles to pat Jorge's knee and says, "We both agreed to it. It couldn't be helped. That wasn't your fault."

Jorge nods, but Coco can tell he feels bad about whatever he did. She stops sorting and gives him her full attention.

"Right, so here's the deal. We saw a binder. Super fancy. I got a look at it while I was tracking a loop inside the White House. It's not fat or anything, but I could tell it was important. So… yeah, *uh…*"

When Jorge trails off, obviously uncomfortable, Tamara jumps in. "Oh, for crying out loud. It was the President's Daily Briefing. It had his name on it. And he had it close for his entire loop. We took it."

Coco puts her hand to her mouth and gasps, "You broke the President's loop?"

Rolling her eyes again, Tamara says, "Yes. We broke the loop. He went nutso. He died. *Blah, blah, blah.*"

"But didn't the book disappear with him? I mean, if he was touching it during his loop, then it had to have disappeared, right?"

Jorge nods. "Oh yeah, but we had it planned out. His entire loop is in his office. People come in and out, a short meeting, some people reporting stuff. Near the end of his loop, he puts the binder on his desk and talks on the phone. At first, we were interested in the call, but it was nothing. Something about a lunch. Anyway, we charged up our last working camera battery. We were just going to open the binder and take pictures of the pages. There weren't that many. We knew we'd have, at most, about ten minutes until the end of his loop, but if we made noise, all bets were off. We really tried to be quiet."

"That didn't work?" Coco asks.

"Oh, it worked. We got pictures of all the pages. It's just that we also got his attention at the end. I really tried to be quiet, and it was a complete accident. I turned a page too quickly and boom, his head whipped around like I'd just shouted in his ear. I feel bad about it. I even voted for the guy. Anyway, the rest is history."

"Was there anything in the binder?" she asks, genuinely curious.

Jorge nods toward the kitchen table where his computer rests. "I've got photos of it. It's all short blurbs. Some secret stuff. There's even a brief about some conspiracy group that thinks birds are actually spy drones. Nothing to do with what's happened. There's no way anyone saw this coming if not even the president knew."

Coco shakes her head at the bad news. "Did you leave a note? I would have left a note."

With a snort, Tamara says, "Oh, sure, great idea. We should have left a note that says what? Oh, sorry, but we wanted to see what was in his binder, so we killed the President, but hey, it was an accident. No hard feelings."

Coco chuckles. She can't help it. "Point taken. No note." After a pause, she asks, "So, what next? Any idea where else to look for clues?"

Both of them shrug, but after a brief silence filled with sorting socks, Jorge says, "You know, time being all wrapped up in physics is sort of a clue where we should look for answers. Just about everyone who can tolerate it has been studying physics since this happened. That includes me. I had a leg up since I was getting my masters in math at the time, but physics is hard. Like, crazy hard when you get past the basics. It's not something most people are good at when it's forced on them. A person has to want to learn that. You know what I mean?"

Coco does, in fact, know how difficult it is. No matter how hard she studied on her own, having a seventh-grade education and no teachers meant there was only so far she could go. There was no one to ask questions of, no internet to search, and no other mind to bounce ideas off of to clarify her learning. Being self-taught in a world of regular people is a vastly different thing than being all alone in the world and trying to learn.

She's done well on her own. She knows that. While her knowledge level is high in practical areas like biology, medicine, and electrical systems, she gave up on math once she reached the calculus books in the library. It was too much. That also put a stop to most other advanced sciences.

She sighs and says, "Well, I can tell you I didn't get far learning physics. I would have liked to, but, well, I had other priorities."

"Yeah, understandable. Anyway, there are a lot of people… relatively speaking… who think this has something to do with one of the colliders."

"What's a collider?" Coco asks.

"Oh boy, that's a big question." He says, then stops and looks embarrassed.

"What?"

"I don't want this to sound bad, but learning what they do and the various kinds is like a years-long learning process. And that's just to let you know what they do, not how they do it. I don't know how to answer."

Coco frowns, but nods. "Okay, but I need to have some idea. Right now, I'm picturing cars wrecking into each other. If that's not what I should be picturing, then I don't know."

Tamara holds up a hand for Jorge to stop talking. "You are such a nerd, Jorge. Let me. So, Coco, from one non-nerd to another, here's what they are. Colliders are huge places that have loads of nerdy scientists who fight each other for the right to use a collider to do experiments that might, or might not, destroy the world. They have giant tunnels deep underground that they can fling stuff through at incredible speeds. They do stuff like smash atoms or even smaller parts of whatever the universe is made of together at super high velocity just to see what happens. Will it create a black hole? Who knows, let's smash some shit. Will it make an itsy-bitsy big bang? That would rock, so let's smash some shit. You get the idea?"

Jorge looks like he's going to squirm right out of his pants. Whether it's because he's dying to correct the explanation or because he's offended, Coco can't tell.

"Yeah," she says with some hesitation. "Well, not really, but I get the idea. Why do you look like that, Jorge? Is she wrong?"

Tamara's posture straightens, and she looks at him like she's daring him to say yes.

He sighs with exasperation and says, "It's wrong on so many levels, but it's probably good enough for right now. Colliders are where experimentation in serious physics happens, the kind that might help us find out the answers to everything. And yes, they do *collide* particles, but I remain offended at the words 'smash' and 'things'. That was the crudest possible explanation."

Coco tries really hard not to laugh at him but can't help the smile tugging at her lips when she says, "I've read a couple of books trying to explain topics like black holes and big bangs. Books for regular people, not scientists. I know what those are. At a basic level, anyway. Is that what they do in colliders? Mess around with black holes and big bangs? Because even I know that would be dangerous. Do you think they did this? Some experiment went wrong? Or maybe it went right?"

"I don't know," Jorge says. "What I was saying before we got off track is that the few people who've made headway in learning more advanced physics seem to think that's where we should look next. The problem is that most of them aren't in the United States. There are only a couple of reasonable options in this country. And, most people in the communities think it would be too dangerous to even go near one of those places. We have a strict rule that no one gets within fifty miles of them."

"Why?" Coco asks.

"Because what if we disturb something and it catches the rest of us in loops? What if it messes up time even more? What if it destroys the actual world? If whatever happened to the world was in one of those places, then we might very well make it worse by going near it. Maybe whatever would have happened got stopped halfway through. Maybe the planet blowing up is stuck in a tiny loop, so it never happens. We have no way of knowing. You see what I mean by danger?"

She does. Not in a detailed or informed way, but the potential for catastrophe is certainly easy enough to imagine. Coco wonders what a loop like that would look like. What the end of the world would look like if it could be stopped mid-apocalypse and looped back and forth, infinitely appearing and beginning, but never ending. The never-ending end of the world.

It might be beautiful. It might even be worth leaving a note to describe that beauty. Then again, seeing it with her own eyes might mean no one ever sees her notes.

"Yeah, I get it," Coco says. "I also vote no, at least for now. Knowing what happened isn't worth risking what little bit of the world we have left."

Coco's Journal: Age 26

Year 14 of the Loop

I'll always think of that time in Salem as the calm before the storm. Maybe I'll think differently later, but that's my opinion for right now. It was stormy in its own way because I found other people, heard about the communities, and realized I wouldn't be alone forever. That's a different kind of storm, though. A good kind.

Now, as I write this, with what came next so close in the rearview mirror, I wish I could go back. I wish I could have preserved my naïve view of the world, one in which there were a few close-knit survivors who all lived together in harmony. I wish I could vote to travel in a different direction. I can't though. Time is unforgiving, even for those of us not in a loop. We can't change the past.

Ten

Year 13 of the Loop

Coco's eyes keep moving back to the distant column of white rising into the air. It's miles away to the south, but even from so far away, it looms over the horizon. Large, fluffy plumes as bright as clouds coil into the air before currents bend and fold them into the river of the atmosphere. Jorge says it's water vapor coming from a nuclear power plant. As she watches, the loop resets and the clouds suddenly change shape.

"Wow! I don't think I've ever seen that before," Coco says as they watch.

Jorge grunts. "We should be glad places like that nuclear power plant are bound up in hundreds of loops, or else they would have failed long ago."

In all the years she's been traveling, Coco has never once thought about the repercussions of such a thing. Looped industries and power stations were background noise to her. Now that she knows, it's fascinating. And terrifying.

"Forty-two minutes. Not enough. And that's the last boat around here," Tamara says as a looped boat on a trailer flickers, signaling the end of its loop.

Jorge tosses the stalk of beach grass he's been fiddling with and sighs. He stands, looks up and down the shore, and asks, "And you're sure we left our boat here?"

Tamara rolls her eyes. "Yes, I'm sure. I know this is the right place because we tied it to that post. The mark from our rope is still there. It must have come untied and got caught in the tides or something."

Coco says, "Or somebody else came by and took it."

According to Tamara and Jorge, they arrived from the south, detoured well around the nuclear plant and the wetlands, then tied their boat up here. The immediate area is free of loopers, so they can speak without risk.

Coco stays seated, hoping for some sight of a boat bobbing offshore. Their three gear carts—which are nothing more than garden carts with wooden slats added to increase capacity—are overflowing. They have so much stuff to bring with them. They really need that boat.

Apparently, unlooped boats are ridiculously scarce and gas for them is even harder to find. Since Coco can't drive, and it isn't safe to do so on looped roads, she never bothered with gas except in winter, when she needed only enough fuel to power a small generator. A car with a few gallons of gas on a twelve-hour loop was basically perfect. She got exercise twice a day retrieving it and had power and heat around the clock. It was great for a winter headquarters, but too much hassle when simply passing through a new town.

Crossing water is another matter. Every bridge Coco has ever encountered was a nightmare of loops. She walked most of them but rowed across a few narrow bodies of water to avoid the worst ones. Forget swimming. When disturbed from their loops, animals can be just as dangerous as human loopers. Not to mention the added dangers due to the decay of unlooped things. For longer crossings, a powered boat is essential.

Jorge and Tamara join her, both looking at the carts with all their stuff. Tamara says, "We have to find a boat. Agreed?"

Coco says, "Yeah, Tux sure as heck isn't a fan of swimming."

She rises to slip her baby carrier over her chest, then lifts Tux to put him inside. He squirms to get comfortable, then peeks out from the top. His black fur shines under the sun and the white tips of his front toes are curled around the top brace. It's one of Coco's favorite views.

As they walk, Coco can almost trace the exact path the others took when they arrived in Salem. On every visible unlooped surface, there's a spray-painted mark. It matches the mark on their tattooed hands, an S shape with a dot inside each curve. Coco has grown used to seeing it everywhere. When asked, the pair remarked that everyone in their community does the same thing. It's to show anyone passing by that someone has already been there.

Once the trio exits the beach area and reaches the twisting road leading back to Salem, the marks stop. The entire road appears to be looped and there is no signage. It's also too narrow to risk walking on since they have no idea when or where a car might appear. They decide to pull their carts along the side of the road, beyond the safety railing. Some of the road goes over water and marshy areas, but there's a sufficient margin for the entire length. It won't be easy to pull the carts over the muddy terrain, but it's doable.

It takes time to pass back into the city proper, and none of them have been through this part of town. Everything they see now is novel and entirely unmapped, which means they must be silent and cautious. They pass slowly through a housing area. Some have pools filled with inviting blue water. However enticing they may appear, a clean pool means a looper is keeping it that way. They move on.

They camp in a field next to a beautiful house built just off the beach. There is yet another inviting pool close to the house. A child is playing there. Their field is mercifully unlooped and entirely overgrown, so it's safe for them. They make camp in the tall grass as the sun sets in a blaze of orange and pink.

As Coco lies in her sleeping bag with Tux's warm body curled into the crook of her arm, she listens to the sound of a child laughing and splashing, eternally playing with someone who is no longer there.

*　*　*

When they wake, all of them are stiff after a night of cool spring air without even a fire to dry the morning dew. There's little conversation as they pack and ready themselves for another endless day searching for a boat. Almost as soon as they set out, they find a boat club. It's only a few hundred feet down the road, just past a shipping hub lined with containers and a single cargo ship looped in a loading sequence with a crane.

The boats berthed at the club are on the smaller side, but not exclusively. The entire place is tucked into a neat keyhole of water that almost seems carved out for just this purpose. The club is also busy with loops. Coco feels her heart drop at the sight of so many moving vehicles and people.

After a long and frustrating morning trying to pass trucks sliding boats into the water from trailers, or bypass people moving along the piers with baskets and fishing rods and coolers, they realize they will find no unlooped boats here. Most of the loops appear to be short, the boats tied up in loops so complex it would take days to sort and catalog.

Jorge looks toward the bridge, which is less than a half-mile away, and sighs. "We might have to risk it."

"*Ugh*," Tamara groans. "I frigging hate bridges like that."

Nevertheless, that might be their only choice, so they trudge along the side of the road, stopping when the body of the bridge comes into better view. Jorge retrieves a pair of field glasses from his wagon, raises them, then smiles. "Hey! There's a boatyard right there in the middle of the bridge, where it looks like there's an island."

Coco lifts her own glasses. There is indeed a cluster of piers. It looks bigger than the one they just visited, so it might offer more opportunity. "It's not an island, just a bigger spit of land. I see the piers, but I don't see any boats. Also looks like there's a nice margin on the side of the road and it's not all bridge, just a bit elevated off the marsh."

"Could be worse," Jorge says, lowering his glasses and handing them off to Tamara.

The going is slower as they encounter more looping traffic, but the congestion abruptly eases at the intersection leading toward the busier centers of town.

There's a public works facility, then the rusting hulks of old steel buildings that are either unlooped or were long abandoned when this began. Jorge and Tamara go silent, brows furrowed as they look around.

Coco enjoys the respite. They haven't seen a single loop of any kind since they rejoined the road. Then she realizes how entirely abnormal that is. Turning to look toward the public works facility—a water and sewer facility—she watches for movement. There's none. There should be, even on a Sunday morning.

Jorge and Tamara have also stopped. Both are looking toward the bridge. She joins them and understands their furrowed brows. There is no movement visible on the bridge. None.

"Where are all the loopers?" Coco asks.

Instead of an answer, she hears the distant scream of a disturbed loop. It's faint, so distant that if she were walking, the crunch of her footsteps might have covered the noise. Tamara grabs Jorge's hand, her head turning as she searches for the source of the noise.

Another scream rings out, this time from a higher-pitched voice. The first had been a male voice. The second is either a woman or a child.

"What's happening?" Coco whispers.

In a sudden burst of movement, Tamara grabs Coco's shoulder with her free hand and tugs both of them toward the shelter provided by a row of huge pipes stacked nearby. She pushes Coco up against the stack. Crouching, she looks at Jorge and asks, "Chosen?"

Jorge shakes his head, as if wanting to deny it, but says, "It's got to be."

"Dammit!" Tamara says. "We shouldn't have gotten so comfortable. We should have explored this side of town and marked it."

Jorge grabs her shoulders, which have gone tense and tight. "We had no way of knowing they had a group in this area. How could we know that? We've been out of touch for over eight months."

Tamara jerks away, bending and pushing her hands roughly into her hair. Her face is screwed up in an expression that looks like pain. Coco goes silent, pressing Tux's carrier close to her chest, making herself as small and unnoticeable as she can.

"All those people. All of these people!" Tamara says. Her tone holds so much more than anger or fear. There's heartbreak and genuine grief too.

Jorge glances at Coco and holds up a hand. "I promise we'll explain. I promise."

Coco nods, all those bright new emotions brought by being a part of a group fading away. There is more these two haven't told her, and it's obviously not good information. Another enraged scream rings out.

Turning back to Tamara, still bent over with her hands on her head, Jorge says, "Tam, stay calm. Just stay calm. I need to go see where they are and what they're doing. Your family isn't here. This isn't Joplin. No one you know is getting broken."

With a jerk, Tamara stands, her eyes wild. She points east, toward the most populated part of the small city. "They're over there. How do I know? Because that's where the people are. Where they *were*. They probably came over that bridge, straight into town, and started breaking everyone. For fuck's sake, Jorge, there's a damn nuclear plant a few miles from here. This town is within fifty miles. It's fucking illegal for them to do this here!"

Coco hugs Tux to her chest. "Someone is breaking all the loops? Is that what you mean?"

Jorge's face falls, so she knows she's right. "Why? Why would they do that?" she asks.

With a shake of his head, Jorge slips off his pack and retrieves a flare gun from the pouch in front. He slips in a flare and closes his eyes for a long moment. Before pointing the gun at the sky and pressing the trigger, he says, "It's complicated, and I'll tell you everything. Right now, I need to stop them. We have a treaty with another group, and they're breaking it."

Coco's Journal: Age 26

Year 14 of the Loop

I put aside my journals for a few months once I found out about the Chosen. Now I have to play catch up, and that's not easy. It certainly means my entries are less full of pointless detail, but I also miss the nuances of situations as they were. When I think back to what it was like to meet the Chosen, I remember being afraid. Then, I just felt sad. Then, I wanted to kill them, or at least beat the shit out of somebody. Then, I wanted to kiss one person in particular, which felt very treacherous somehow. After that, I realized I knew nothing. Even worse, I was no longer sure I was on the right path. Nothing is clear in this strange world anymore.

Eleven

Year 13 of the Loop

"I'd hoped to get you to the closest community, which is in Kentucky, before you had to hear this," Jorge says. "The law… which is really just a treaty worked out between our two groups… says I have to contact them if we're nearby while in the company of someone who isn't a member of a community. Then I have to allow them to speak with you. It's so you make an informed choice. If I know of a reason the Chosen shouldn't be in a place, I have to contact them for that too. They aren't dangerous like bandits or looters. They won't hurt us." He pauses and looks at Tamara, who is sitting on the ground with her knees to her chest. "I really wanted you to get to a community before you had to hear this stuff. I knew the moment we met that you wouldn't be like them."

Coco only nods, because she has no words. And because she feels a little betrayed. After all this time, people are still keeping secrets.

The flare Jorge fired has completed its arc and is gone, which means that someone from these mysterious others should show up soon. Coco wants to know as much as possible before they do.

"Jorge, who are the Chosen, and why would they want to break loops? And why would you have treaties or laws, or whatever? I don't get it. Why didn't you tell me any of this before?"

Jorge looks past her to check for activity on the road, then meets her gaze. He looks regretful, almost sad. Nudging her a little away from Tamara, he lowers his voice and says, "It's so complicated. This is years of history and we wanted you to be in a community before you had to deal with this bullshit. You know our group calls itself the Seekers, right? Seekers, because we're seeking a way to end this or fix it or whatever, of course, but there's more to it. The way we live is different. We do our best not to disturb things more than we have to. Yeah?"

Coco nods, trying not to look impatient, though she is. "Okay. Fine. The Chosen?"

He sighs. "Well, they're the other major group out there. They have lots of communities, just like us. *But,* they think the world is over and all the loopers are holding things in place for us to keep everything safe as we build a new world."

"What?" Coco asks, shaking her head. "That makes no sense."

"Not to us, but to them, it does. Okay, think of it like this. Take a factory somewhere that's still tied up in a bunch of loops. As long as it's like that, it's safe, right? It won't explode or catch fire or leak chemicals into the ground. The Chosen think that's on purpose, so when they're ready to shut that factory down safely, they break all the loops and salvage it or restart it or whatever else."

"No," Coco says, horrified by the idea. "They just kill people? On purpose?"

"Yeah, but they don't think of it as killing, not like we do. They think of it as freeing the loopers. They don't do it just because they want to. It's all very methodical. Like I said, it's complicated."

A pickup truck loaded with gear roars into view, then slows as if looking for the source of the flare. It's the loudest sound Coco has heard in years that didn't come from a looper. A man's face appears at the open window of the truck. He slows further, then bumps off the road and onto the grass.

When he steps out of the vehicle, Coco is surprised to see that he looks like a normal person, considering what Jorge just told her. In the few minutes since she found out there were people purposefully breaking loops wherever they went, she had enough time to picture them as the deranged supervillains of comic books. Beady eyes, cruel mouths, and wearing all black. Possibly also sporting strange and menacing headwear.

The man isn't a supervillain, though, at least not in appearance. He's youngish, maybe no older than Coco. Certainly, he's within a few years of her. His hair is longish and there are hints of red in the brown when the sunlight hits it. He's wearing well-worn jeans, lace-up boots, and a fleece hoodie over a t-shirt.

He's actually quite nice looking. Handsome even.

When he gets closer, he holds up one hand, showing the back of it and the tattoo inked there. Coco can vaguely make out the shape of a C in dark ink. Jorge and Tamara do the same.

The man glances at Coco when she doesn't hold up her hand, then smiles and says, "Ah, a new Uncommitted. Is that why you shot the flare?"

Tamara jerks her hand down and points at the man's chest. He's still about ten feet away so she doesn't make contact, but the intent is clear. Her tone is dangerous when she says, "Not the only reason, asshole. The law states you can't kill breakers within fifty miles of a nuclear facility. That's the fucking law." She shifts her point to the plumes now barely visible in the distance. "And *that* is a fucking nuclear plant."

The man spreads his hands wide, his stance casual, as if to demonstrate how completely non-threatening he is. "No harm. We aren't clearing this town. As the law allows, we are selectively clearing a path to allow for movement of people and supplies. That's all."

Tamara's mouth twists. "Right. Sure. I believe you because you're just so honorable. Are you limiting yourself to killing only kids and old folks you can be sure don't work at the plant? Have you *selectively* cleared out the restaurant workers and store clerks too? Don't feed me your bullshit. I know what you do."

The man's easy smile disappears. "I know there have been overeager members of the Chosen in the past. We have handled that problem. I *am* abiding by our mutually agreed-upon laws. We have no desire to poison the world with radiation. If nothing else, believe that."

Her rage barely contained, Tamara whirls and stalks away, her lips pressed into a thin, angry line. Jorge watches her for a moment, perhaps worried she might change her mind about walking away and decide to get violent. The man shifts his gaze back to Coco, then glances at Tux, who is peeking out above the carrier and watching the commotion.

"I like your cat," he says. "Boy or girl?"

Coco doesn't answer right away. Nothing about this situation feels comfortable. Everything feels wrought with terrible possibilities and barely controlled feelings. Tamara's natural state is to be tightly wound. Coco realized this within hours of meeting her. She's been an upbeat sort of excited until now, though, and this new, sharp anger feels dangerous. This man feels equally dangerous, mostly because he's so calm, as if he knows he will always win and therefore has no need to get excited about things.

He smiles again, this time showing teeth. He has nice teeth. "Is it a secret?"

"Boy," she says.

He gives an approving nod. "That's good. And he's a good-looking cat too. You should see about getting him into the breeding program. More kittens would be good."

Coco's lips part in shock. "Breeding program? Like the pandas at the zoo?"

He chuckles and winks. "Cats are more precious than pandas now. There are lots of mice out there in farm country. All the communities I know of are part of the breeding program, including us. It's not all yelling and disagreements, you know."

Jorge tires of the charm campaign the man is waging and steps between Coco and the man. "Listen, we followed the rules and now you will too. No more messing with the people. Period. It's not on a major highway or freeway and it isn't a chokepoint that will stop travel if it isn't cleared. It is, however, a few miles away from an active nuclear site, so that trumps whatever excuse you're about to offer. Are we clear on this?"

He takes a moment to consider Jorge's words, then says, "I suppose it won't do any harm to meet the road a bit further north. That said, there's some good farmland nearby that needs to go back to nature, and the marshes are close too. We aren't abandoning this entire state because of a few nuclear plants. The world to come can't get here if we leave everything alone."

"North then. Go north," Jorge says, eyes steady on the man.

The man holds out his hand to shake, but Jorge merely spits on the ground and turns toward Coco. Without bothering to lower his voice, he says, "The law says you can't join a community until you've heard all your options. This asshole is going to try to convince you his way is better. I have to let him do it. You can say no right now, but you can't join a community until one of them has spoken to you face to face. It could mean months of waiting for a contact."

Coco takes in his words and thinks she understands the basics of their agreement. She asks, "And if they find someone like me, they have to wait for one of you to talk to that person too? Exactly the same?"

Jorge nods. "Yeah, exactly. That's the law."

She shrugs, then looks at the man over Jorge's shoulder. He smiles his charming smile again, not reacting to Jorge's disparagements. Coco gazes directly into his eyes and says, "That's fine. So far, I get the impression he's a complete douchebag. I doubt he'll convince me of anything."

Jorge chuckles, but it's a dry one not filled with much in the way of humor. He walks toward Tamara, who has calmed a little. She's wheeled their carts into the open and spread out a tarp, readying herself for a long wait while this man fulfills whatever it is their strange laws require.

The man steps closer, holding out his hand for a shake. There are two white scars on it. Puncture wounds, probably. A dog perhaps. Do these scars show his loss on that first day, like Jorge's arm and her head? Or did these come from breaking loops?

Coco considers ignoring the hand, maybe even spitting on the ground like Jorge did. Instead, she takes the proffered hand. It's warm and dry. She shakes just once before letting go.

"What's your name?" he asks. "I'm Forrest."

Part Two

Forrest

Forrest's Testimony: Excerpt 1

Year 6 After the Choosing

Like every member of the Chosen, I have vowed to write only the truth in my testimonial. That's an easy promise to give and a difficult one to keep. I often wonder to myself: What is the truth? Is there one truth, as there is when it comes to numbers and science? Or does the fact that I'm human mean my truth will differ from what another human may perceive as truth? Does my truth change as each day passes and I view the past with more information to reflect on? Revisionist history is a real thing, so wouldn't my truth naturally change with time?

These are important considerations and I believe they're valid. It's the reason we recently agreed that each member of the Chosen must write a testimonial as their first act, regardless of how long it may take them or how many resources it might use. We must establish our own truth, examine our actions, and then use them to ensure we remain truthful to each other and ourselves. Of course, that means my testimony is many years late, but that's what happens when we make new rules.

We've been given a new world, or to be more truthful, we have been given the old world and that gift includes the responsibility to remake it into a new one. This is a grave responsibility and an unparalleled gift.

As our fledgling group continues to grow and carry out these responsibilities, I want to be sure we act with deliberation and care. We must be respectful. Not just to each other or the world to come, but to those who were not Chosen as well. Sending them into the beyond should not be done with abandon or glee, but with due consideration for who they were. A moment of reflection.

I wish I could say I always felt like that. I just read my entry and I sound as stiff as an old preacher. Is that me? No, it's not. I'm writing like that now because I'm around a bunch of stiff people who act like all of this is some huge ceremony and we get a new world at the end of it.

But it wasn't like that, and I wasn't like that. It's been six years since that day and it's still painful to think about. I'm not blind to the fact that we all have such pain. Some pain is greater than mine. Much greater. It was a shit day.

I was fourteen years old when the Choosing occurred. Unlike some of the others who joined me in forming the Chosen community, I was not surrounded by family that I inadvertently sent into the beyond before I knew what I was doing. I suppose I was lucky. I was asleep during the Choosing, enjoying the one morning a week I could sleep as long as I liked.

When I woke, my family was already out of the house. My father and mother had gone to do errands and shop for groceries. It was their routine. They liked to get coffee and donuts together, then arrive at the store right after it opened. It was the only time they had just for themselves every week.

My older brother was probably with his friends, though I never did find him. My two younger sisters were at a sleepover for a birthday. I found them, but it took quite some time, and I didn't release them. By the time I found them, I understood our purpose better. Releasing them wasn't yet required, so I guess they're probably still with their friends.

When I woke, it was my dog who let me know that something momentous had occurred. The Choosing had placed my dog in a short fragment, one in which he slept, then rolled to his side and snored. It lasted only a minute, maybe less. The strange flickers stopped me from moving, and it took a few fragments of time before I dared to reach out and touch him. He bit my hand, the scar leaving me a visible reminder of him. He transitioned into the beyond right there next to my bed.

I admit that my reaction was not what it would be now. My devastation was real and heartfelt. He was an old dog. His loyal and friendly comfort had been my support for most of the years of my life. I was also afraid, and I didn't yet understand the nature of the Choosing. I didn't know I was Chosen.

The next several unchosen I encountered were not family or friends, for which I am eternally grateful. Unchosen filled our neighborhood, some flickering endlessly as they pushed a running mower, others in cars, or outside playing. It was those that I first studied.

I must also confess that after I had inadvertently sent many of these unchosen into the beyond, I was afraid. I know that many in our group believe I had some great revelation and entered this new world at peace and with purpose. That isn't even remotely true.

I entered this new post-Choosing world in a state of fear, much like a newborn baby faced with light and noise who cries out at it all. I was like that too. I feared. I hid away.

It was only as I watched the grass grow in all the places where the unchosen had been released, only as I saw nature return in those spots while the rest remained frozen in time, that I began to understand. It took years for me to truly absorb what the Choosing meant.

I was lucky that I found others like me so quickly. I don't think I would have survived long enough to understand had I remained alone.

But I understand that purpose now. The old world was irreparably broken. We, the few who have not been stilled by some force greater than we can understand, are the Chosen. We are the ones who must clear away the debris with care and thought for the world to come. These unchosen have been stilled and the processes of decay halted so that we have time to undo the damage, to prevent disasters, to plan for deconstruction and the replenishment of our world so that it is free to become the world to come.

Our duty is not simply to send the unchosen into the beyond. Our duty is to send them on only when we are prepared and ready to correct the things they hold still for us. I get that, but it sure didn't feel like that in the beginning. I must confess here in my testimonial that before I understood our path, I wondered if I might not have been sent to hell.

One

Year 13 After the Choosing

Forrest watches the woman standing in front of him. Her posture is defensive, as if she doesn't quite trust him not to hurt her. He takes great pains to appear unthreatening when he meets an Uncommitted. Many of them have been alone or with only a few people for extended periods. Many have forgotten what it's like to meet a new person. Suspicion is natural under such circumstances. She strokes the cat's head and says nothing, invites nothing.

She's pretty in an unassuming way. With her olive skin and wavy hair, she looks vaguely Mediterranean. Like most people now, she's in good physical shape. Rather than slender, she looks fit and strong. It's hard to guess ages now, but he assumes she's close to his own age.

Skin ages differently than it did in the time before. Now, there are no easy lives filled with pricey creams and salves. She has lines on her face that he doesn't see on the faces of the unchosen. They all do.

"Is your name a secret too?" he asks.

She sighs and glances momentarily at the two people sitting a little distance away. With another, longer sigh, she says, "Coco. This is Tux."

"Coco," he says, liking the way it sounds. "That's an unusual name."

She almost rolls her eyes at him. "Not really. It's a nickname. My brother couldn't say my real name when he was little. So, I'm Coco."

He chuckles. "I wish I could have had a nice nickname. Forrest doesn't lend itself to anything as good as yours. My name was great for getting teased when I was young, but that's about it."

This time, she does roll her eyes. His impression of her being close to his age is confirmed when she says, "Whatever. I don't care."

"Okay, that's fair."

She narrows her eyes. "Can we get this over with? Just give me your stupid pitch so I can go and be with normal people in a normal community. I can tell you right now that I'm not interested in being with a bunch of psychos who go around killing helpless loopers." She stares right into his eyes, the intention in that gaze almost dangerous. Hostility practically radiates off her.

Forrest decides to let it pass. Some of the angriest people he's met since all this happened went on to become happy members of the Chosen. "Well, my *pitch*, as you call it, takes more than a minute. Can we sit down or get comfortable? I won't take up any more of your time than necessary. And if you don't want to hear this now, you can always arrange to meet a Chosen some other time."

She looks down at the ground. The sandy soil is damp from recent rains and the breeze is picking up, still brisk from a long, cool spring.

"We can sit in my truck," he offers, waving at his vehicle.

Again, she narrows her eyes, asking, "Where are the rest of your people?"

Forrest taps the walkie at his belt. "I let them know I didn't need them after I saw your group. They'll stay a few blocks away. We don't like to crowd people."

"Fine. Wait a minute." With that, she marches toward the other two people. They exchange a few words, then she lifts the carrier with the cat off her chest, handing it to the woman. When she returns, she holds out her hand and says, "Keys."

"What?"

"Your truck keys," she says, enunciating clearly, as if he were dim-witted. "I'm not risking you deciding to kidnap me."

He hands her the keys, then follows her to his truck. She takes hard, sharp steps, like she's angry. To be fair, she doesn't seem to be trying to hide that anger from him. She's honest, at least.

When he moves toward the driver's door where she already stands, she waves him away and says, "No. You take the passenger seat."

"And what if you decide to steal my truck?" he asks, not entirely serious. "I like this truck."

Shaking her head, she waves him off again. "The world is full of trucks I can take any time I want."

Inside, she looks much smaller behind the wheel. The truck is lifted to deal with the terrain. It's not the largest or most powerful truck around, but it still makes her look small. She says nothing to him. She just sits and stares, waiting.

Rather than go into an introduction she's clearly not amenable to, he asks her a question. "Have you ever wondered why buildings don't disappear? Or the roads? Have you ever wondered why big things tend to stay behind? Have you noticed that sometimes, just sometimes, things that aren't stuck in a fragment disappear with them? Or that sometimes objects that should disappear when a fragment is released, don't?"

Though her brow furrows at the words fragment and released, it smooths again as she figures out the terminology on her own. Most people do. She shakes her head, but not in negation. It's more of a so-what gesture. That's also fair, because anyone with a brain between their ears has probably wondered those things countless times.

Deciding to press on, he says, "What I'm getting at is that all of this is strange and illogical and difficult. There are things we can never understand. All we really know is that most of the world is stuck and never moves forward. Those of us left behind have to try and survive on what's not stuck. That won't work forever. All the Chosen do is make the world easier for those left behind. That's it. It's also kinder."

Her eyes widen. "Kinder? You think killing all these people instead of finding a way to fix what's broken is kinder? In what universe is that in any way logical?"

"Would you like to be trapped like that? How do you know they don't feel and understand what's going on? What if they do? Can you imagine a worse nightmare?"

Coco shakes her head, clearly dismissing him. "Some of them have really wonderful loops, like walking their dog or meeting with people they love. I would call them heaven. And I don't believe they know. There would be some sign of it."

Forrest thinks about the fragments he's seen, the tens of thousands of them he has personally glimpsed. Yes, there are the occasional lovely ones. Most are mundane, at best. And for every especially lovely one, there is one so awful that it changes any person who witnesses it.

These are not things to be shared with an Uncommitted, though. Talking out the bad things they see in the course of their Chosen work is something only done between those who accept their Chosen status.

"Coco, how about I just tell you what we do and why we do it, and we can go from there?"

She nods, but her arms are still crossed at her chest. "Can I ask a few questions first?"

"Sure."

"You call yourselves the Chosen, right? Who chose you? Are you some kind of cult?"

Forrest smiles, a little embarrassed. Telling the truth is his mandate, but it can be uncomfortable at times.

"Let's just say that was a poor choice of labels. Blame it on us being teenagers when all this happened. We all had way too much drama inside. By the time I understood how ridiculous the name was, it was too late. And no, we're not a cult. We have no religion at all, at least not as a group. Individuals believe whatever they want, but they do it privately, in their own heads and homes. What we have, more or less, is a set of guidelines.

"As for who chose us, that's the mystery. It could just as easily be random chance as anything else. What matters is the result. A few of us, relatively speaking, were left behind for a reason. The fragments outnumber us by tens of thousands to one. They keep the world still so that those who are left can reclaim it without creating disasters. The fragments stuck in their small bits of time give us the *real* time we need to find them all and restore the world."

There is silence for a beat or two. Coco's eyes move like she's taking in his words. She looks calm. That impression is entirely shattered when she speaks. Her voice is as sharp as a blade. "It sounds lovely, as long as you gloss over the people and animals you have to kill to get it. I'm not okay with that. Also, you're full of shit. I know why some things disappear and others don't when you break a loop. Small stuff, like a plate of food or a book they're reading disappears with them, sure. Those are things only involved in that specific person's loop. Bigger stuff is different. I know why buildings rarely go away, and it has nothing to do with magical grandpa in the sky choosing to create your personal garden. It's freaking science, asshole. That means science can fix it."

Forrest tries to keep the surprise from showing on his face. Leaning forward, he asks, "Why do they stay or go?"

"Sometimes love, sometimes hate. All the time, it has to do with intention and history and memory and all sorts of factors."

"I thought you said it was science," Forrest says, not quite able to prevent himself from smiling.

"It is. I don't have all the answers, but things that have a past or are connected to many people or animals don't disappear. Especially buildings. The more people are connected to a building, the less likely it is to decay, even if the loops holding it are broken. Roads almost never disappear. Even though we don't exactly love roads, we *are* connected to them. A house that someone has lived in for years might be totally tied up in their loop, but it doesn't disappear if their loop is broken. Some parts of it might, but never do you see one entirely go away.

"Why? Because of the connections. Everyone who has driven past that house knows that house should be there. Every water and cable TV line connected everywhere else goes there. It has records in courthouses, utility companies, banks… everything. And people in loops are connected to those too. Even if that house isn't actually tied up in those other loops, people who are in loops remember it, or have experienced seeing that house."

She stops, her arms finally uncrossing, and her face animated. Raising her hands to indicate everything that exists outside the confines of the truck, she says, "Everything is connected. And even if I can't write down the numbers that prove it, I do know that's science in some way or another. And that also means the people and animals and bugs in loops are still alive. They aren't fragments, or whatever you call them. They're individuals who are stuck and need help getting unstuck. Everything they are remains tethered to all that exists. That means *they* exist."

The atmosphere inside the truck is loaded, even after she lapses back into silence. The woman fascinates Forrest. She's full to bursting with opinions and life. If he didn't know better, he'd say she was recruiting him. The idea is delightful.

Forrest's Testimony: Excerpt 2

Year 8 After the Choosing

Giving a testimony is important, but it turns out it's not enough. Truthfulness isn't the same as working out a problem. It doesn't equate to coming to terms with the past. Not really. It's been a couple of years since my last testimony, and we've gotten quite a community going. Actually, we've got lots of communities. It's getting bigger and more complicated. We've got more rules.

We also have more baggage. That's the only way I can describe it. Baggage. Mental, emotional, and definitely physical.

We've decided that writing a new testimony every year is the best way to record things. It will prevent us from creating history based on first impressions. It will reflect our changing viewpoints and processes. It will be more complete. It will also allow us to shed some of the baggage we collect over the year.

It's been over eight years since the Choosing. Why did we make up that name? Is it because we were all young and had played way too many video games? It's possible. I tried to raise some interest to change it, but they say it's too late. We've got signs painted everywhere with our radio frequency, all our rules, and it's just what people are used to.

I'd rather we were called something less religious sounding. Live and learn, right?

I'm still absolutely committed to our doctrine of truth—ugh, more religious words—but it's getting a lot harder to actually *be* truthful. The more people I'm around, the more it feels like I can't say what I really feel. It's not that I want to lie, I just don't want to say the complete truth to everyone about everything.

One truth that particularly bugged me this year was the library in town. We've cleared only the parts of town that we can maintain. The fire station, some houses grouped close together, two grocery stores, one gas station, things like that. Then, the council decided we needed to clear the library.

The library has a good number of fragments in it, mostly people who were there Saturday. Some of them were kids, and there's something about those particular fragments that made me want to leave them in place. I don't know why.

When the council brought up that we really needed some of the books inside, particularly the ones on gardening and the entire how-to section, I voted no. But then, they asked me why. According to the rules, I had to tell the truth, and the truth was that I didn't want to because of the way the fragmented kids inside behaved. It was just special in some way I couldn't explain.

Of course, they confronted me in the way the rules say they must. And, putting aside my emotional attachment, which is what we call it, I had to admit that we needed the library. So, we now have the library. I still feel weird about it.

And I'm one of their supposed leaders.

Anyway, we're done for the moment with clearing places like that. We're doing farms and outdoor places now. We've found a couple of geese that weren't fragments, so we've started breeding programs. It seems smart. We need to ensure that humans aren't the only animals left on the planet.

Two

Year 13 After the Choosing

"You are one strange particle," Forrest says. When Coco's brow creases, he adds, "And I mean that in the best way possible. It's a compliment."

"Don't be creepy," she snaps back. "You're only the fourth person I've met since all this started, and it would really suck if you were a creeper on top of being in a giant murder cult."

Forrest can't help it. He laughs.

"What?" she demands.

He waves his hands, trying to negate the laugh. "Sorry, I'm not laughing at you. It's just… I don't know… I guess I'm not used to having jokesters around. I'm not creeping on you. I promise."

As his laughs fade, he catches hold of the meaning in her words. "Wait, the fourth person? I'm only the *fourth* person you've met? In all these years?"

She nods, her expression still shadowed with suspicion, but also some sadness.

It doesn't take much math to solve the equation. If he's the fourth person she's met, and the two she's with haven't been with her long enough to get her to the closest community, then she's been alone except for one other person for thirteen years. That's astonishing. Where is that other person now?

Forrest knows how touchy this topic can be. He can't just jump in with questions that might shut her down or cause pain she isn't ready to bear. He has to consider his words carefully.

Forrest has met many people over the years, and each one handled the Choosing differently. Most spent a good amount of time alone, but rarely more than a year. Sometimes the Chosen or Uncommitted communities come across a small group that somehow remained isolated for years, but those are always *groups*.

Being alone for too long can foster unique behaviors. Some of the Chosen were half-crazed and quite destructive. He's read enough reports to know how bad it can get.

Some grew so lonely they would interrupt a fragment just to have someone recognize their existence, even if only violently and for a moment. Others rampaged through areas disrupting fragments, trying to destroy everything in their anger. Some became so insular that it took time to convince them the Chosen were real people, not hallucinations or delusions.

Still others were so grateful to find people that the Chosen had to develop treatments for cases of extreme separation anxiety. There are still members who grow unmanageably anxious if out of sight of other humans for too long. They live together in special houses until they can handle regular life.

Yet this woman seems quite sane and in no way delusional. How did she do it with almost no human contact? No matter how touchy the subject, he really wants to know what her life was like.

"Coco, this isn't part of the pitch, and I don't want you to hate me or distrust me or any of that. There is no conflict between the communities of Uncommitted and Chosen. None. We're quite friendly, even engaging in trade. Well, a lot of trade, actually. This isn't a situation where you're being asked to pick a side in a conflict. Members of both types of communities have shifted from one to the other over the years. It can make for some messy tattoos, but it happens often enough to be normal. Everyone is welcome to be with who they want to be with. I'm saying this because I can see how tense you are. So, let's put that aside for the moment. Can we?"

Her arms loosen, and her shoulders drop just enough for it to be noticeable. She frowns and asks, "Really? I mean, let's be honest, we're talking substantially different philosophies here. Like, fundamentally so."

Forrest shrugs, because she's right. She also doesn't have the full picture. "Yeah, they are very different. True enough. But the main point each group believes is the same. The *primary* belief is one we all share: That there are so few people not in fragments that every non-fragment life is absolutely sacrosanct. We don't hurt each other. We help each other. Actually, that belief stretches to any non-fragment animal life we find in the wild. It turns out, that's enough to allow for a whole lot of disagreement on everything else.

"That flare, for example. I'm not sure what they told you before they sent the flare, but every single person in their communities and ours carries a flare gun. Usually, it goes up because someone needs help. It's unfortunate that you didn't have time to hear about this before we met. It would have made the conversation far less awkward."

"Okay," Coco says, drawing out the word like she's not sure she believes it. She glances out the window toward her companions. The man is lying down with the cat on his chest, while the woman keeps a close watch on the truck.

"Can I ask you about your time? You said four people, and three of them are here. So, who was the other? Where are they? And how long were you alone?" Forrest asks, diving in despite himself. He hadn't intended to ask all at once.

She doesn't immediately answer. She turns her head and sighs. The sun catches her dark hazel eyes exactly right and, for a moment, they seem to glow in the reflected light.

Those eyes are sad when she returns her gaze to him. "Other than two weeks many years ago, and the few weeks I've had with these two, I've been alone the whole time. Except for Tux, that is. I found him about five years ago. No, not quite five years."

Forrest tries not to show his surprise. That would mean thirteen years of solitude. Or, at least eight of complete solitude and five with a cat who can't talk. He's met no one who survived that. Not a single person.

With a shake of his head, he asks, "How are you still sane?"

She smirks. "How do you know I'm sane?"

He smiles back. "Point taken. But seriously… that's a long time. How old were you when this happened?"

"Twelve. What about you? You said you were a teenager."

He does his best not to react to her age. There are some that age who survived, but they're definitely the exception. Most survivors were adults. The youngest he's ever heard of was ten, but that boy found an adult after just two weeks alone. Otherwise, it's doubtful he would have survived.

"I was fourteen, but I was in a good spot to survive. Most weren't."

She shrugs with one shoulder and says, "I have no idea if I was in a good spot to survive or not. I did okay."

"Why did you separate from the person you found before? You said you were with them for two weeks."

"She died. I didn't do anything to her. She had cancer and was close to the end when we found each other. Part of the time I was with her was spent trying to find her enough morphine and fentanyl to… well. Let's just say she was in a lot of pain at the end."

"That sucks," he says, not actually meaning to say the words. It's pure reaction.

She responds with a grim nod. "Yeah, it did. But it was also good. I knew that if there was one person, there had to be more. I just needed to be patient till I found them."

"Where were you? Can I ask that?"

The suspicion returns, her eyes narrowing. "Why?"

Forrest holds up his hands. "Just curious."

"Manhattan. The New York City one, not Kansas or wherever else they have a Manhattan."

He can't help his reaction. His eyes widen at her words. That's one place everyone agrees can't be visited. Not yet, maybe not in his lifetime.

Perhaps she sees something in his expression than he didn't intend, because she points a finger at him and says, "Manhattan is mine. You people better not go near it."

"Oh, it's yours? You've claimed it?"

Perhaps she understands how that sounds, because she makes a face. "Fine. It's not my property, but it's under my protection. If you want that to sound like I'm the mafia, great, you can take it that way. Just stay away from it."

Forrest nods, because he does understand. Her people are there. Maybe her family. Definitely her friends, school, and history. It's *her* city. She wants to keep her museum of the past.

"No problem. Places like that are off limits, anyway. Too complex. Too much risk. We could damage things that can't be fixed. And we don't actually need it yet. Heck, the art alone would mean we have to stay away. It's safer tied up in fragments."

She nods in agreement. "Yep, it is. Also, the libraries are safe. At least the two I went to are, and those are the biggest."

"Thank you for telling me. If it's safe, it's safe."

She examines him for a moment, her eyes so intent that it's almost uncomfortable. Forrest is more used to being the one doing the examining. It feels strange to be under someone else's microscope.

Right as he gets the urge to shift in his seat, she asks, "So, what are you people? I mean, you're concerned about losing art and helping each other, but you go around killing loopers. What gives?"

Forrest can already tell that Coco won't join the Chosen. Maybe in the future. She definitely has the sharp mind for it. Rather than dance around the subject, he decides to lay it all out on the table.

"I'm not going to give you that pitch. I'll just tell you what we're doing now and that will give you everything you need to know."

He pauses and waves behind them, vaguely north to northeast. "Even in New Jersey, there are farms. Lots of them, actually. There are also loads of wildlife areas. Important ones. Marshes, shoreline, forests… you name it. And, perhaps more vital to survival, there's the river and the path it offers for trade and communications."

She interrupts him, saying, "Yeah, I saw a bunch of it. I came down the 45, then broke off to the 653, meaning to skirt around Salem and just hit the eastern part for supplies and crops."

"You did? I might want you to mark my map later." At her expression, he chuckles and says, "Okay, maybe not."

"So, what about the rivers and stuff? The farms?"

Forrest opens his mouth, then closes it again. He's never had to distill all that they do into one small nugget before. Generally, when they encounter a group, the two groups are together long enough that the knowledge transfers through the normal course of activities and conversation. Even when he meets a new person after being summoned by an Uncommitted community, they already know a great deal and have read the manual each community has for these situations.

How can he sum it up in a few sentences?

"Let me try it this way. Think about fish."

"Fish?"

"Yeah, fish."

"Okay, I'm thinking about fish. I'm thinking that the last fish I had was a can of tuna about five years ago and how opening cans of fish now is super sketchy."

He laughs. "Well, I'm thinking of the swimming kind. They're all fragments now, just like humans, right?"

"Yeah, the ones I've seen seem to be looped."

"So, that means some will be like us, and not be fragments. Unlike us, they don't know how to look for food that isn't wrapped up in a fragment. That goes for all animals, really. They eat food that disappears from their stomachs and don't understand what happened. They just know they're hungry again. They eat more fragmented food. Even if they break the loop of some fragmented creature, any food they get from it will usually disappear when the broken fragment does. It's a no-win situation. Eventually, they die of starvation. With me?"

"Yeah, I know. I've seen a few dead animals. Tux was doing that when I found him."

"So, what happens if we don't get rid of the food that they can't eat? What happens if we don't release the farms that are endlessly growing food that can't be eaten? What happens if we don't sweep the marshes so all the reeds and grass and tiny fish and bugs will return to normal and grow again? What happens to all those who can't understand? The worms, butterflies, birds, and fish? The cats and dogs, deer and wolves, and foxes and everything else?"

Coco looks away from him, her eyes roaming the landscape beyond the truck, perhaps imagining all the small living things that might still be clinging to the edge of survival. Or maybe, imagining all the life that didn't survive.

She looks up at him, her eyes sad. She knows and probably has known for years. "They die. Eventually, they'll all die. I know."

"This trip is to clear a marsh north of here, try to free some of the farmland in the interior adjacent to it, and lastly, survey the river to see what we can do to bring back some life. Yes, we knew that we were within fifty miles of the nuclear plant. We're also very aware that the odds of having a nuclear engineer wandering around in the middle of a huge marsh is approximately zero. We aren't clearing cities just to leave infrastructure to rot. We clear what we need and what will help. That's all. We've actually got an amazing breeding program to get things going again. Fish, bugs, birds… you name it. And yes, cats."

"But you still kill people," she says, as if weighing all the good against the bad.

"We release fragments, yes. Again, animals, fish, bugs, birds… even cats. And people. We do it where it will help. It's not easy to do, but we don't look at it as killing. We look at it as freeing them from an endless nightmare. We do it so that what remains can live."

Coco is silent, obviously thinking. Rather than wait and watch her struggle, he says, "I know you're not ready to do this kind of work. I realize you may never be. I can tell you're a Seeker. That's okay. That's perfectly okay. Maybe someday you'll feel differently, and if that day comes, I'll be happy to see you join us. If that never happens, I'll still be happy to see you when our paths cross. And who knows, maybe someday you and the other Seekers will actually find an answer to all of this. If that happens, I'll be happy for you."

"Really? It's that easy for you to just do what you do and let everyone else do what they do?" she asks.

"It *is* that easy. Everything can be that easy if people are tolerant of differences."

She seems to consider that for a moment, then asks, "Okay, you asked me all those questions about wondering things. Can I ask you one?"

"Sure."

"Have you ever wondered if maybe we're the ones who are dead? Maybe we are. Maybe we see them in loops because that's all we can see anymore. Perhaps breaking loops will leave us without even that glimpse into the living world. Ever wonder that?" she asks.

"I have. I do. I wonder that all the time," he answers.

Coco pulls in a deep breath, then holds out her hand. That surprises

Forrest, but he recovers and shakes it. Then she smiles and snaps her fingers at him. "Okay, I'll mark your map with my info on the trip. But you better give it to me quickly before I change my mind."

Forrest's Testimony: Excerpt 3

Year 12 After the Choosing

Has it really been twelve years? That's what I keep thinking about. Twelve years. In two more years, that will mean that I've been in this new world for as long as I was in the old one. How weird is that?

We had some pretty big celebrations last month. The Uncommitted communities did too. It was nice to be around each other with nothing but partying on our minds. Based on all the people that disappeared throughout the evening, I'm guessing we'll have at least a few babies arriving before next year's celebration. That would be good.

As happens every year, some members of our communities left for Uncommitted communities and vice versa. It's good that it happens. There aren't enough of us left to have children only within our groups. Exchanges are fine with everyone.

It's been a surprisingly easy year. We updated the treaty between the Uncommitted and Chosen, which is good. The cities that are off-limits have been better defined, which is *very* good. We're nowhere close to needing those cities and it's important they stay protected for now. We got some road clearance issues hammered out, which helps everyone.

Right now, we're focused on releasing fragments involving natural areas and farms. Uncommitted survey groups are reporting more animal carcasses, most of them old, but not all of them. That means survivors, but maybe not forever. They've even agreed to release fragments in such places if it looks like there might be food issues for survivors! That's never happened before. It's progress.

I really think us giving them a few dairy cows changed their minds. It took us years to get a small herd going. Now, well, let's just say that milk and butter are hard to pass up. Knowing that other important animals are out there dying of starvation in the midst of plenty probably changed their minds as much as the idea of cream in their oatmeal.

We also need to expand our survey territory. This year, one of the Chosen communities found a group of eleven people in Maryland. They'd been there the whole time. Not once did they see one of our signs or markers, and they hadn't even tried searching for others via radio. They never knew anyone else existed, yet an Uncommitted camp was only ten miles away.

In light of that surprise, we need to put up more signs and expand our radio tower range. People out there need to know others survived. The Council agreed, unanimously, which means the Uncommitted will also be looking for functional towers. Who knows who might still be waiting to be found?

Maybe I'll eventually find my match. That would be good. So far, the longest I've had a girlfriend is five months. They keep ditching me because I travel so much. Everyone wants to settle down and have kids. I want to see everything and find everyone. Sometimes, it really is tough to tell the truth. It doesn't help me keep a girlfriend. Too much truth is awful for relationships.

Three

Year 13 After the Choosing

Forrest takes an informal head count as he pulls up to the convoy of parked vehicles. Everyone is there, still waiting. They've pulled out coolers and food, taking a break in the sunshine and cool air. He's been away only a couple of hours, but he missed his little family.

Tyrone and Kiara gesture at their surroundings in what looks like an animated conversation. They're the closest of friends, but a less matched pair would be hard to imagine, at least in a physical sense.

Kiara looks almost elven, with a petite figure and huge dark eyes. Tyrone towers over her, exceeding six feet by several inches. As gangly as he is smart, he'd once shared that his younger sisters used to call him The B.C., which stood for The Black Crane. An odd nickname, certainly, but it suits him. He's as lanky as it gets, all legs and long neck.

As Forrest steps from the truck, Sven hefts his huge body up from a camp chair. He looks like Thor trying to squeeze out of a kiddie chair. "Hey, Boss. What took you so long?"

Forrest grabs a sandwich and joins the group near the big truck dragging their fuel trailer. The air smells vaguely of gas.

"Found an Uncommitted," he says, taking a bite of his extremely late lunch. The bread has gone stale, but the jam is thick and sweet.

Kiara perks up. "You're kidding. They actually shot a flare for that and didn't wait until they got to a community? Will wonders never cease?"

Forrest shrugs. "They heard us releasing fragments, so they knew we were here. Honestly, it was awkward."

Pam, the oldest member of this expedition by a handful of years, says, "Well, I don't see anyone with you, so obviously we don't have a new member. Must have been *really* awkward." She grins in that way she does, making it clear she's teasing him.

"Yeah, yeah," Forrest says with a smile. "So, what's the word here? Any luck getting a path to the marshes and farms?"

Even as he asks, he knows the answer will be no. The area is still buzzing with fragments driving along paths they have driven thousands of times over the years since the Choosing. He also knows they have to find a way to get where they're going. The marshes are wells of biodiversity. Important ones that anchor the web of life for thousands of animal species. The wilds must be freed from the fragments that hold them in place. It's the only hope for life.

And yet, they have to be sure they don't destroy everything else in the process. Releasing fragments that keep the nuclear plant frozen in time would ruin a lot more than a tract of marshland.

Tyrone shakes his head and points a long arm in the general direction of the road. "We cleared what we could, but this isn't going to work if we keep to the restrictions you put in place. Most of the cars on this road have people of working age in them. We've got no way to figure out which ones, if any, work at the nuclear plant. If we can't clear them —"

"We can't," Forrest interrupts. "That's firm. Unless you can verify that none of their fragments intersect with the plant, we can't clear them."

Kiara clears her throat, then points to the chalkboard propped up against a chair. "We can confirm some. If we camp here, we can clear the shortest fragments, which will give us some space to follow the longer ones. It shouldn't be hard to make sure none of these go near the nuclear plant. Right?"

Pam and Tyrone don't look especially pleased at the idea, but everyone else just waits for a decision. This isn't the best place to camp with so many fragments nearby. It won't be comfortable, and it will delay them, but it would minimize the risk, and that's the most important thing.

Forrest sighs, then asks, "How long do we need? Two days? Three?"

Kiara's lips twist as she studies her board. She and Tyrone share a look, and she sweeps her hands in a quick set of gestures almost too fast for Forrest to follow. It's their own private sign language. Forrest has often wondered if they realize how much of their communication is silent. They were together for a long time on their own.

She sighs. "Two days if we split into groups. The bridge over Route 45 is going to suck. The only real snag will come if we find a conflicting fragment on the bridge itself. Our maps suck balls, so maybe I'm wrong, but it doesn't look like there are many turn offs or detours after that bridge until we get pretty far from the marsh. We're really only looking at a couple of miles of actual road. Then, it's a matter of finding a spot where we can drive the trucks and set up our spring quarters while we do the work. It's your call, Forrest."

He pauses with the last bite of his sandwich on its way into his mouth. "Two days is nothing. Let's set up a barebones camp and get moving. We're burning daylight."

* * *

In the end, it takes four days because of two stubborn fragments. Both are workers traveling south over the bridge and directly across Salem.

Forrest doesn't feel comfortable tracking the two commuters all the way to their destination. Getting too close to the power plant itself would be inviting disaster.

However, they have time. It's the only thing they have in abundance. So, they manage the transits with only the usual amount of complaining and a few choice curses from Pam regarding fragments getting in her way.

Almost as soon as Forrest climbs out of his truck, he can tell the area is perfect for their work. The land is open, without buildings or other obstructions, and they can make noise without too much worry.

Climbing on top of their biggest truck, Forrest scans the area with his binoculars, looking for clues. Pam joins him, huffing and grunting as she climbs the ladder.

"I am getting way too old for this shit."

She says the same thing every time, yet every time they return to base, she immediately adds her name to the list for the next expedition. He hears her unsnapping the binocular case on her belt and decides to give her a minute to get a good look.

It takes closer to half a second.

"Holy shit, that's beautiful!" she exclaims.

"Yeah," he agrees. It is. Fragmented birds swoop in endless, flickering cycles near the water or over the reeds. Marsh grasses wave, forever green. It's stunning. And sad. But freeing it is what they're here for, and that feels good.

The next morning, he wakes up eager for the first day of real work. They plan to be here for months, and it will get hard when the summer heat kicks in, but today feels different. Dressing quickly, he rushes across camp for the morning meeting, looking at this new village that already feels like home.

Pam says their sites look like refugee camps, but to Forrest, they look orderly and welcoming. He's spent most of his time in such places. It's getting harder to imagine life in a house.

The tents aren't the kind meant for casual camping. They have sturdy supports and metal chimneys with friendly looking caps poking up from flaps sewn into the tops. Smoke trickles from the kitchen tent already, the smells of coffee and fried potatoes wafting from the open side. By tomorrow, he'll wake to the scent of baking bread and this place will feel so comfortable that he won't want to leave.

Two sides of the command tent are tied up, allowing for plenty of light. Almost everyone is already there, cups of coffee sending tendrils of steam into the cool air. Sven hustles out of the kitchen tent carrying another big pot. Christmas Trees cover the oversized oven mitts he carries it with.

"Morning. Everyone sleep okay?" Forrest asks, accepting a cup of coffee from Pam, who is closest to the pot. The group returns the normal array of grunts and answers.

He sips and winces at the strong taste. Coffee is a luxury. They have locations with large amounts of it marked on their maps, and only release fragments there as the need arises for a fresh supply. The stuff they have is getting old and bitter. They have no cream or sugar on the road, but Forrest has grown used to taking his coffee black when exploring. Cream and sugar are for more civilized times back home.

Kiara finishes up the last blackboard, and the chalk squeaks against the surface, causing a few people to flinch. Inside the command tent, large chalkboards on easels or stands are lined up along the back wall of the tent, making it easy for anyone passing by to take them in at a glance. They have smaller boards with ancillary information set up on makeshift stands on a table to one side. There are no chairs or furniture other than a single folding table they use for food and morning coffee.

When Kiara is done, she whirls around, shakes the cramp out of her hand, and smiles. "All good!"

Forrest nods his thanks, then takes a moment to look everything over. It's important to get this endeavor started the right way, with the right attitude. This is, when it all comes down to it, the reason the Chosen exist. This farm, this marsh, this land and air.

The flat expanse of terrain beyond the open tent walls is beautiful. Vibrant green marsh grasses sway in the breeze. The gentle shushing sounds of the vegetation permeate the tent. It's so peaceful. Cranes and a hundred other marsh birds swoop and fly over it all. Water glints where the tide snakes inland through a thousand tributaries and streams. It's a sight he never could have imagined when he was young in land-locked Arkansas.

But all of that beauty is a lie. A terrible, hurtful, killing lie.

The greens are those of summer, not early spring, as it is now. The flowers are long gone, replaced with seed heads that should have dropped in fall more than a decade ago. Even as he watches, a heron stutters in mid-air and disappears, only to reappear further away, trapped in an eternal, pointless flight.

That marsh—and all the animal fragments that hold it in place—are dead. They've been dead since the Choosing. But there might still be life somewhere in that tangle of greenery. Even now, some small creature might be dying of starvation, trying to fill a belly with food that will disappear minutes later. There aren't enough living things left in the world to risk losing even one more. Even a mosquito. A frog. A fish.

But that marsh doesn't have to stay dead. If they do their work right, the plants can be freed from the animal fragments holding them in place. Once that's done, they'll bring other life to the area. Birds, fish, and even insects will be trucked from communities where they're being bred. With care and caution, they will shepherd all this new life and leave the marsh a living place instead of a memorial to the long dead.

Their work is too important to do it wrong. This is their duty. To free everything that can be freed and to send the dead into their rest where they can't harm the living.

He thinks of the young woman he met, Coco. She's with the Seekers and he'll probably never see her again, but he wishes he could show her this tragic beauty. He wishes he could explain. If he could only find the words and let her see this marsh as he sees it, maybe she would understand.

Forrest straightens, turning his full attention to those around him. He can only do what he can do. "Alright, here we are, and we've got a lot of ground to bring back to life. Let's get a round robin going." He points toward Sven and says, "You first with mechanical. Then Tyrone with power and comms. Then Pam with survey and life support. Go."

Forrest's Testimony: Excerpt 4

Year 14 After the Choosing

I'm early with my yearly testimony, but it can't be helped. I'm heading off to Ohio, and we'll be gone for months, maybe a year. This time, the Council has called for an expedition of over forty people, equipped to split into two groups, if necessary. Of course, everything depends on whether the Uncommitted council agrees with ours. That's definitely not guaranteed.

I'm heading up to the Powhatan community, which the Seekers call Solace, for our big meetings. Both Seeker and Chosen councils. What do I think will happen? I don't know, but time has softened both groups. I know it has for me.

Only now am I able to look back at my younger self and understand how my dedication was at least partly sheer stubbornness. My desire to see the world set back into motion is what drove me. I didn't understand the complexity of the task.

I believe a good many of the Uncommitted feel the same about their path. Some Seekers have a little Chosen in them and vice versa. In a way, I suppose we're meeting in the middle. Considering how many people swap communities, that's only to be expected.

They have children and a future to worry about, just as we do. It's hard to argue that leaving virtually all the world untouched and fragmented is the right path for the next generation. So now, we have another decision to make, and no doubt, we'll argue for days.

The area in question is the coast of Lake Erie. There's so much there and we have no idea how much is fragmented beyond that coastline. Fish are an excellent source of protein and the number of land animals suitable for slaughter is razor thin. Really, only animals unsuited to breeding are used for food. Beans can only do so much. Some kids are suffering from lack of protein during their development. Fish would be perfect. For all of us.

Apparently, the Uncommitted sent out a survey team to a few places along the coast last year. They stayed far away from Cleveland. Not even the Chosen communities would touch it, given the number of industrial sites there. The reports show coastal areas are simply not improving because everything upstream is still caught in fragments, as are the coasts themselves.

It's not just the many cities along the coast creating the problem. There are also two nuclear plants bracketing the area. If we obey the fifty-mile radius laws, then there is literally no coastline the Chosen could clear. That does neither group any favors.

We have five communities in Ohio and the Uncommitted have twelve. Our populations are almost the same, despite that difference. Over a thousand bodies to feed, clothe, and keep warm during winter. We're ready to send expeditions to clear more farmland. There are cultivated tracts so vast they beggar the imagination. All of it is trapped in fragments, or almost all of it. Crops that never ripen and food that can't be eaten.

Most importantly to the Uncommitted communities, we're ready to clear farms and forests so we can transfer deer from our breeding operation in Pennsylvania. We can't do that until we have land for them to survive on. The Uncommitted are more than eager for that to get started. Again, protein.

Once our game preserve really got going, we harvested a few animals. It's amazing how fast a deer population will grow once you plop them down in a bit of good forest. Trading venison with the Ohio Uncommitted made them eager for the farmland conversion. They don't seem to mind when we take land they consider uninhabited. Of course, it *is* inhabited by fragments. It's just that most of those fragments are birds or animals. There are farmers as well, but I get the impression they don't like to think about them.

It is what it is.

Anyway, I'm kind of dreading the meetings, but also excited by the idea of the trip. We've got two places mapped out that we'd like to explore for access to the lake proper. The best choice is on the west side of Lorain. The route to get there is likely to be absolutely torturous, but there's at least one good marina not crowded by nearby houses.

I've never been to the ocean. Everyone says that the Great Lakes feel like the ocean, so I'm eager to check it out. I have a hard time imagining what it would be like to be surrounded by water. I've crossed plenty of rivers and seen plenty of lakes, but it's not the same when you can tell it's a lake with trees and buildings surrounding it.

I'm also excited for another reason. Whenever we have these big council meetings, we always stay with people in town who have spare rooms. No one has time to take care of a hotel, so I've gotten used to awkward, and occasionally unfriendly, hosts. Maybe not this time!

I got a message on the radio telling me I was going to be hosted by… drumroll… Coco. I really liked her. It doesn't take long to figure out who you like and who you don't in this world. Her, I liked. We disagree on some pretty fundamental stuff, but we'll see what happens.

Four

Year 14 After the Choosing

Not much has changed in Powhatan since Forrest's last visit. They passed a few more grain fields on the way toward town and a couple of barges piled with construction materials on the river, so clearly the town isn't remaining static. Overall, it feels the same. Closely knit, friendly, and industrious.

Once inside the gate, Forrest notices one change right away. There are definitely more people. A good many of them are at the gate for the formal welcoming. Most of the Chosen council has already arrived and are greeting his team with all the rest.

Also, the gate is new. As is the fence.

He tries to keep his smile in place and remind himself of names, but it's been too long for that. Instead, he apologizes and reintroduces himself, distracted as he searches the crowd for the face he's been anticipating.

Coco is there, but not in the front since she's not on the town council. She smiles as he meets her gaze. He gives her a wave, and she nods back.

Forrest recognizes the two people with her. He can't remember the woman's name. Tammy? Samantha? Something like that. It's been months since he met them. Names don't stick that long in his head.

It takes a few minutes for all the visiting members to shake hands, but eventually, he finds his opening. Forrest edges out of the crowd and moves toward the trio.

Holding out his hand, he says, "Jorge, right? And Coco. And…"

The woman takes his hand first, but she doesn't look pleased to do so. "Tamara."

"Right! I'm sorry. I should have remembered."

Jorge is next, and again, he doesn't look delighted. Forrest understands and takes no offense. Not everyone can look past the difference in philosophies. Some take it personally.

"And Coco. I'm glad to see you made it here safely. I had heard, of course, but it's nice to see for myself."

She shakes his hand, then holds up hers for his inspection. The tattoo on it is dark and fresh. "I'm officially a member of Solace. Or Powhatan Point, if we go with old labels."

"So, you're hosting me? Or all of you?" he asks, including the other two in the discussion.

Coco says, "We live next door to each other and, technically, they're still hosting me, but I'm the one with an extra bedroom."

Forrest tries not to look too pleased about the situation, but he is, and he knows his smile is just a little bigger than it should be. "Excellent. I'm glad for the bed. This trip was long and I'm getting too old for sleeping bags."

As they start out, he notices more houses seem to be lived in and asks, "Are you expanding?"

Jorge answers begrudgingly. "Yeah, we are. Once we got the sewer situation sorted, it got easier. We're not piled on top of each other anymore."

Coco nudges Jorge with her elbow and says, "It's not just that. When they left on the trip where they found me, there were twenty-four people here. When we got back, if you include me, there were forty-nine. Forty-nine!"

The fence seems to follow them, then curves behind another row of houses. The Ohio River is only a few blocks away, but it seems distant. "Did you fence off your entire area? That's a bit strange. Is there something going on?"

"Kids," Coco says. "They've got more kids here now. Kids are loud, so, you know…"

"Ah, got it. Say no more," Forrest replies.

The Uncommitted don't release fragments unless they have to, which means some are probably walking around nearby. That would be dangerous for loud children. They could accidentally release one and not realize the danger until the fragmented person attacks.

The houses in this hamlet are older and smaller than in modern developments. In the past, they would have been very modest homes in a village not big enough to merit a decent chain grocery store. Those same attributes are what make the houses so perfect now.

Most have new or newly refurbished metal chimneys for wood stoves, or in a few cases, actual fireplace chimneys. All have garden plots, or more than one garden plot, most with cool weather crops in full leaf. One garden next to the street has a profusion of absolutely enormous collard leaves.

Coco sees him looking and says, "Oh yeah, no one else can get them to grow like that. It's a mystery."

He hears the crow of a rooster and smiles. "That's a good sound, though I guess I'd probably get sick of it pretty quick if I had to hear it every morning. I might start secretly making rooster pies."

She laughs, and even Jorge's lips curve in a smile.

"Yeah, there is that," Coco says. "Breeding is going well. Right now, we only have enough eggs for the important stuff. The rest go to breeding, but they're saying by next year there will be enough hens for people to have a few. They're talking about a lottery for the dispersal, which makes sense because everyone wants some."

He nods. "We did the same where I have my home base. I don't qualify, of course, since I'm never there. I don't even have a house. I shack up wherever they put me. It's a different spot every time."

They stop in front of a small, neat house. A garden still new enough that the borders are sharp rests in the green space next to it. The expected wood stove chimney snakes out of the top portion of a window. The missing pane of glass has been replaced with plywood painted in bright yellow. An enormous woodpile is visible behind the houses, where the driveways are.

"This is it. My house," Coco says, her eyes bright.

He understands that. Most people are like that. They've been lost and once they join a community, they're found. They're home.

She points to the house next door, which is almost the same as hers, only painted a different color. "That house belongs to them."

Jorge and Tamara take their leave politely, but without much in the way of warmth. Coco stands with Forrest, watching them enter their home. She turns to him and says, "I would apologize, but I don't think that would be right. It's just, well, you know, the way things are."

"I do," he says, smiling. "I take no offense."

She shows him around with obvious pride. That someone else who isn't alive anymore is the real homeowner is something both of them know, but don't say. That time is gone, and this one has replaced it.

The house is bright and warm, with a hodgepodge of furniture that fits her personality. A working bathroom is definitely the best part.

Coco catches him gawking at the tub. "Oh yes, it works. It all works," she says. "No hot water from the tap, but water does come out and the toilet flushes. If you want a bath, we can heat water on the woodstove. That's what I do."

After dinner, Coco makes coffee and the smell of it over the hot wood stove is uniquely wonderful. She pours them each a scant cup, apologizing for the serving size.

"We have to parcel this stuff carefully, you know. It's not like we can get new shipments whenever we want, or break loops in a Starbucks for the good stuff like you people do."

Forrest waves off the apology. "We do the same. Only on expeditions do we get bigger allotments. We're just lucky so many people were addicted to it or we'd run out much faster."

"True," she says, returning to the table. "So, what's up? How's life?"

He doesn't answer right away because he isn't sure what to say, or if what he says might not erase the friendliness. He hadn't expected it, especially considering the conditions of their first meeting. It feels surprisingly good to be where he is, just as a person. Still, he wants to know why.

"Coco, I'm not sure I should ask this. I don't want to ruin a nice evening, which is, I must say, very nice, but I'm curious. Why did you volunteer to host me? I didn't expect that."

She toys with her cup, looking into the liquid like it might offer an answer. Eventually, she says, "Well, first off, I didn't actually volunteer to host you. Not you specifically. When the big meeting was being organized, they asked everyone with an extra room to volunteer to host a council member. Most people would only host those from our communities. The list of volunteers for Chosen council members was pretty short. I'm the new kid on the block, so I thought I should suck it up and offer. As to how you were assigned, I don't know for sure, but when I verified that I had the required talk with a Chosen representative, I put down your name. So…"

"Ah, I see," he says, feeling let down by her answer. He smiles, hoping that covers his feelings. "And is that okay? You know, if it's not, you can say so. I would understand."

She seems to consider it, then shakes her head. "No, it's strange, but

I actually don't mind. Once I got here, I read the Chosen manual that has all your rules and stuff. It clarified a few things, helped me understand a bit better. I still don't agree with you, but I do see the advantages of it. I see your perspective. I don't really feel like you're the enemy. I know some do, but I don't."

"What about them?" he asks, nodding toward the house next door. "Me being here won't cause problems for you, will it?"

For a moment, she looks confused. "Oh, you mean Jorge and Tamara? No, it won't. I mean, they aren't going to be coming over and socializing, but we're cool. It's not personal, well, I mean it is, but it isn't."

"Come again?" he asks.

Coco grimaces. "Tamara's from Joplin. Jorge was there with her when… well… you know."

Suddenly, Forrest understands completely. He slaps his hand over his forehead and groans. "Oh, Joplin. That's awful. Did any of her family… *uh*… get involved?"

The Chosen will likely never entirely live down the events of Joplin, despite the fact that it happened before they were even the Chosen. With just twelve people in their entire group, they'd broken up into pairs to search for survivors.

They'd all known something was off with one of their number, a young man named Josh, but they couldn't afford to be picky. He was young, strong, apparently healthy, and though quirky, he appeared sound of mind. Well, as sound of mind as anyone was back then.

He hadn't been. He needed medication, and it wasn't a pill or two for anxiety. He needed antipsychotics, amongst other things. In Joplin, his increasingly bizarre behavior finally descended into a break with reality. He'd been telling his travel partner that the fragments were talking to him, putting thoughts into his mind, all sorts of things.

One night, Josh slipped away from camp during his watch, and it took three days for his partner to stop the boy's rampage. A swath of Joplin was swept clear in a wave, leaving a great deal of waste behind.

Coco doesn't answer right away about Tamara's family, and Forrest's heart sinks. That's a terrible way to have a family member released.

"Me being next door to her probably isn't appropriate, considering," he says.

She shakes her head and pats the table near his hand. "No, it's not like it isn't common knowledge, so I guess it's okay to tell you. Your people didn't get her family members, per se, but it was still awful. Her husband was inside the hospital where your guy wound up in the end. All his banging and screaming apparently disturbed all the loops in the ER. Her husband was just one floor away. I guess it was a close call."

"I don't blame her for painting us with that brush. I really don't. Back then, we were looking for survivors, just like everyone else. We weren't releasing fragments unless we had to do it. Our guy was sick. It doesn't matter though. People remember the bad result, not the good intention. That's how we're wired."

Silence descends for a few minutes, then Coco gets up to turn on the porch lights. When she returns, she smiles and says, "I'm still not used to that. Electricity whenever I want, without having to drag a bunch of batteries and solar panels around. So weird. But a good weird."

He nods toward the refrigerator, which is humming quietly. "I noticed you had a lot more power available. Last time I was here, I think it was just the public spaces, right? Maybe a few lights?"

She shrugs. "I don't know. I wasn't here. I just know the solar farm is pretty sweet, even though nothing matches and it's the most cobbled-together system I've ever seen. We've got enough for lights, energy efficient fridges, and the charging bank for devices. Maybe someday we'll have enough to run houses normally, but who knows? I'm happy with this."

"What's with the porch lights?" he asks. "Seems like a lot of energy."

"They're LED, so it's actually not a big drain, and it's tradition around here. They turn on all the porch lights at night just in case there's a survivor somewhere to see the light. It's kind of sweet, don't you think?"

"Yeah. It's sort of hopeful."

"Yeah, exactly like that. Hopeful."

Forrest's Testimony: Excerpt 5

Year 14 After the Choosing

The most surprising part of being in a position of leadership after the end of the world is the politics. Honestly, I would have thought that stuff would get pushed away in favor of actually getting things done. Nope. Every single thing we debate or vote on requires one-on-one side talks and favor trading. It feels very gross. Dirty even.

Politics. Don't even get me started.

Five

Year 14 After the Choosing

Forrest fills the next few days with private meetings, most of which are tedious and draining. All the voting members of the Councils are doing the same. The same thing happens every time there's a project to be voted on by the inter-community Council... what everyone calls the Big Council.

The Lorain expedition, which might well open up the coast of Lake Erie for recovery, is a contentious proposal and success isn't guaranteed. With two nuclear plants bracketing the area and a major industrial hub just miles away, it's a high-risk proposition. It also holds potential for very high rewards for both the Chosen and the Seeker communities, and the hope of those rewards keeps Forrest optimistic about his chances for approval. Greed isn't good, but it very often wins.

Trade concessions, particularly deer from their preserve, seem to be the most effective tools in his basket. He doesn't mind those concessions since the Chosen already agreed that stocking game would be in everyone's best interest. Even so, it's unpleasant to have to trade for votes. Apparently, politics is still the same after the end of the world. There is plenty of hypocrisy to be found.

The Uncommitted won't release human fragments for farmlands or forests. They've done a wide swath of animal-held lands and even the river, but that's as far as they'll go. Or, at least, that's as far as they'll go with their own hands doing the dirty work.

During each of Forrest's side negotiations, areas kept static by human fragments are marked on a map and slipped across the table. The unspoken part of the negotiation is that the Chosen will clear the marked areas so the Uncommitted can keep their hands clean.

On the upside, Forrest's unofficial tally gives him a boost of confidence that the upcoming Council vote will go in his favor. Lorain, or rather, the marina on the western side of it, might well be within their grasp. With that comes the potential to clear enough water for fish to thrive, if there are any left. They won't know until they get there.

At the end of his third day of negotiations, he strolls along the main thoroughfare toward Coco's house. The light is only just growing mellow with the coming sunset. A group of figures approaches from the other end of the road, still too far away to identify.

The solar field is in that direction, beyond the fence. They must be returning from work. A pair of young children dashes from between two houses at the end of the block, squealing in the course of whatever game they're playing. It obviously involves being chased. An older girl of perhaps nine or ten runs after them. She stops in the middle of the street, yells for the children to stop, then stamps her foot. They pay her no heed, disappearing between another pair of houses.

As the group of adults nears, he sees one of them is Coco. She tugs her hair from its ponytail, then shakes her head and runs her fingers through her hair, laughing at something one of the others is saying.

Forrest stops in front of her house and waits for her to catch up. When she sees him, she waves at her co-workers and jogs the short distance. Her face is still rosy from working in the cool air.

"Good day at work?" he asks as they climb the stairs and enter the house.

"Yeah, really good. One of our groups brought back more panels and hardware. It's not easy getting everything hooked up when the panels come from about ten different makers, but it got done. Every watt counts. Not to mention I got off farm duty to help. Can't complain about that!"

She pauses, then sniffs her shirt. " *Ugh,* I smell like a horse. Do you mind if I heat up a bath before I make dinner? I don't think a basin of water is going to cut it today."

They heat pots of water on the still-hot stove after stoking and fueling it sufficiently to last the evening. The activity is pleasant, filled with small bits of conversation about nothing as they work. He brings in wood. She checks a bowl of dried soybeans that have been soaking all day. He wipes down the kitchen to prepare for cooking. She makes them cups of hot herbal tea to chase away the chill. It's smooth, as if they've been doing this for much longer than a few days.

The bath is a bath only in the most modest sense. Even the big pans of hot water provide only a couple of inches in depth when all is said and done. That this is extravagant in their world isn't lost on either of them. They're both old enough to remember how easy life once was.

Before disappearing into the bathroom, she calls, "If you want a bath, go ahead and start more water. By the time I'm done, it'll be ready."

He does want a bath, though not because the debate was all that physically strenuous. He busies himself in the kitchen, trying to be useful, while Coco bathes. The water is showing tiny bubbles around the pot bottoms when she emerges in a cloud scented by shampoo and soap.

"Well, you look better," he says, then turns back to the counter. He holds up a bundle of cheesecloth, still dripping liquid. "Tofu is almost ready to press."

"Would you look at that? Thank you," she says, peering at the remains on the counter. "Nice. You're a pro."

He laughs. "When most of your protein has to come from beans or tofu made from beans, you get good at it. Also, I love that processor of yours. The handle feels a lot sturdier than the one we have at camp. I always feel like the whole thing is about to fly apart when I use it. Not this one."

"You should grab one. We have a bunch more at the supply depot."

One of the big pots lets out a gurgle of noise as a bubble rises to the top. She glances into the pots. "Your bath water is ready. Are you?"

"Oh, you have no idea," he says, placing the dripping cloth into a strainer.

By the time Forrest finishes bathing and changes into fresh clothes, dinner is almost ready. Coco is humming to herself in the kitchen while cubes of tofu sizzle in a pan that smells of sesame oil and spices. A pot of rice sits near the stove, fluffy and white. Greens and other vegetables, already sauteed, lay waiting to be folded into the dish.

"Perfect timing," she says, giving him a quick smile.

He leans in to sniff the pan. "Damn, I'm hungry."

They fill their bowls and take them into the living room. Coco sits in a big chair, her legs folded beneath her and feet tucked into the gap beside the cushion. Forrest has no idea how people can sit like that. It looks terrifically uncomfortable. He takes the couch, using a pillow as a makeshift tray for his bowl.

Forrest closes his eyes as he takes his first bite. It's heaven. Cooking is apparently another talent of Coco's that he didn't know about.

"You know, today is sort of a first for me," Coco says.

"In what way?"

She looks a little embarrassed. "Today our work group was five people. Five. And while we were wrestling those panels around, we were pretty close together. This is the first day where that didn't freak me out. That's why I'm usually on farm duty. I get panicky when I'm around too many people, but I can't stand being alone. Weird, right?"

"No, not at all. Pretty common, actually."

She sighs, and it sounds sad. "When I was young, I saw hundreds of people just between my building and school. Literally hundreds. Walking, driving, doing whatever. I never thought about it at all. That was just life. Now, if I'm in a room with a half-dozen people, my heart hammers so hard it feels like it might jump out of my chest."

"You're different now. Your situation is different. You were alone for longer than anyone I've heard of. It just takes time."

It seems to take no time at all to reach the bottom of the bowl. Forrest didn't eat so much as inhale his dinner. He glances up and sees he's not alone in that. Coco picks at the last grains of her rice, trying to fish them out with her fork, which isn't easy. She gets one, pops it into her mouth and says, "If you weren't here watching me, I'd use my fingers. Or lick the bowl."

He chuckles. "Me too."

Shrugging, she switches to chasing the last grains with her finger, grinning as she licks off the sauce. "So good. Can't waste that sesame oil."

"Right?" he agrees, abandoning his own fork.

The air is warm and cozy, with the stove sending renewed waves of heat into the room. They sit with their nightly cups of coffee, the only noise the whir of a heat-powered fan on top of the stove. It's good. It's the kind of nice that makes Forrest consider what life might be like if he weren't always on the road.

Coco's eyes are closed, her head tilted back against the plush chair. "You know, if we were loops and I found us, I'd probably consider this scene noteworthy."

"Noteworthy?" he asks.

Her eyes twinkle when she opens them. "It's a pun. If I find a loop that's noteworthy, it means it's interesting enough to leave a note. Get it?"

He laughs softly, too full of food to exert himself. "Did you do that often?"

She pauses for a moment. "More in the beginning, before I left Manhattan. Less since then, but I still did it right up until I got here. It probably seems silly to you, Mr. Chosen."

"No, not at all," he says. Forrest doesn't want her to think of him as some cold-hearted machine who can't see the humanity in the fragments. He does see it. He sees it in every single one of them. He searches for the right words. "We have a different core belief. That's true. That doesn't mean I don't feel anything. Leaving notes isn't silly. Part of me wishes I felt like you. Part of me wishes that someday all those people will wake up. It's just that most of me honestly believes that will never happen."

Her brow creases. "That would make me so sad. To think that way, I mean."

"Yeah, it does."

A thoughtful silence fills the room until Coco slaps her hands on her thighs and says, "Well, that got depressing in a hurry. Change the subject?"

"Okay, tell me something noteworthy. No, tell me your *favorite* noteworthy frag—I mean loop. Your most favorite."

She catches the correction and smiles. "Thank you for that. My favorite, huh? That's a hard one."

"Really? How many are there?"

She snorts and says, "Let's put it this way. If someone were to go count them and tell me that there were a thousand notes, I wouldn't be too surprised."

"Seriously?"

"I kid you not."

He waves his hand for her to go on. "Let's hear it."

She rubs her hands up and down her thighs, her expression searching, then says, "Okay. This one takes some backstory, though."

"I'm all ears."

"Well, there are millions of people in Manhattan, as in something like nine million. I didn't realize this until long after I left, but the loops in Manhattan are shorter than average. Not always, but in general. Actually, the longest loop I've ever seen was there too, but overall, most are shorter. There are a *lot* of static loops there, too."

"Static? The flickering ones?"

"Yeah, exactly. Anyway, I got to see a lot of loops. The notes started because of this one in particular. Up until then, I'd left charts and diagrams everywhere to make it easier for me to get around if I somehow messed up my timing, but I'd never left a note for a looper. With me so far?"

He nods.

"You know when there are two people caught in the same loop?"

"I do. They're pretty rare."

"Yeah. This was one of those. It was less than half a block from my building, so I saw them all the time. After a while, especially as I got older, I couldn't stop watching them. I couldn't quite figure out what their deal was, and it bugged me.

"The loop is short, with maybe ten seconds between flickers. It was a man and a woman. They start out with their feet facing the opposite direction, so you'd think they were passing each other. But, there's something else going on. They're looking at each other and she sort of twirls around to keep his gaze. There's something in their eyes that I can't describe, like they know a joke that no one else does. You know what I mean?"

"Maybe. I wish I could say yes."

She waves a hand dismissively. "It's too hard to describe. I wish I would have printed another picture of them to keep. If you saw them, you'd understand."

"Pictures? You took pictures?"

"Oh yeah, that's another thing I did. Until my printer ran out of good ink, I'd put pictures with the notes. Otherwise, how would they know the note was for them?"

"You had power there?"

"Oh, no. That's another story. I did that myself with car batteries."

"Okay, sorry, go on."

Her eyes defocus as she looks into the past. She smiles fondly at the memory. "Well, long story less long, I simply couldn't figure it out. One day I would see one thing in their expression, the next day something different. In the end, I decided that if they didn't know each other, they *should* know each other. If they did, then they needed to know how perfect they were for each other. Of course, that was a teenager with no social contact talking, so don't judge me too harshly.

"Anyway, I took a couple of pictures, printed them out, put them into a baggie with my note, then taped it on a wall nearby that wasn't in a loop. I used that crazy strong tape, the kind that you can repair a roof with. I'm pretty sure if this ever gets fixed, I'm getting a bill for all the walls and paint jobs I ruined. Seriously."

He grins. "If that happens, they'll have a lot more to think about than paint. So, was that your favorite? Or was it just the first?"

"It's pretty high up there, mostly because I still don't know what the answer is. Were they, or weren't they? You know?"

They grow quiet, her face soft with a pleasant memory. Forrest tries to imagine it. He's never been to a huge city, not even before the Choosing. He tries to imagine Manhattan wallpapered with photos and notes, baggies stuck everywhere and each one filled with some small story of beauty. It sounds lovely.

He doesn't think before he says, "Coco, I think that's probably the most beautiful thing I've heard since all this started. Honestly. You're amazing."

For a long, endless moment, she says nothing. It's long enough that Forrest has time to wonder if he's made a mistake, if he's made this pleasant situation so full of potential into something awkward. Do their different beliefs create a wall too high for her to see him over? He hopes not, because he sees her, and what he sees is something beautiful, inside and out.

Then, she smiles and says, "I like you too, Forrest. I don't like that I like you, but I do."

"You do? Even though I'm a big bad Chosen?"

She chuckles. "Even so. Like I said, I understand your perspective. I just don't share it. And you're more than a Chosen. You're also you." She pauses, grinning. "It doesn't hurt that you're not a million years older than me, either. This town is full of old people."

It's his turn to laugh. She's right. Most of those who kept their wits long enough to survive were middle-aged when the Choosing happened. Survivors in their age group are much rarer.

He asks, "But, what about Jorge? I kind of thought…"

Coco shakes her head. "No. We're best friends. For a while, I thought maybe, but I think he's worried it will mess up our friendship. Maybe he's right. People around here are really careful with relationships. This town is too small to hide from a bad breakup. You can't avoid an ex around here. Anyway, nothing is going on between us."

Forrest feels awkward all of a sudden. What now? It's not like he can ask her out to the movies.

Before he can figure that out, Coco asks, "Do you have any favorite stories? Or would that not be a thing for a Chosen?"

"Oh, I've got tons. But you want a favorite, huh? Let me think for a second."

It doesn't take much searching to find the memory, but he isn't at all sure he should share it. Would she think he was strange? She might. Then again, Forrest likes Coco. For whatever reason, she makes him want to be real. Open.

Before he can lose his nerve, he says, "I never left a note, but my favorite memory is also of a pair. I've never told anyone about this one. It feels weird to talk about it."

Coco spreads her hands. "No judgment here. I promise. Or, well, hopefully no judgment, since I have no idea what you're about to say."

That eases his nervousness, though Forrest doesn't understand why. He takes a deep breath. "Okay, so this was about a year after the Choosing. We didn't even have a town yet, just a bunch of houses we used as a home base. There were a few dozen of us and we spent most of our time in groups looking for survivors. One of our group was pregnant. No, don't look at me like that. I didn't do it."

Smiling, Coco says, "Sorry. Didn't mean to interrupt."

"Anyway, we didn't know how to deal with having a baby. We didn't have any doctors or nurses or anything like that. Plus, we were on the road. She didn't even tell us till she started to show too much to hide it and her boyfriend noticed. We had this big idea that we would all go into hospitals and see if we could find books, or maybe even see loops of babies being born. I was fifteen, so I was an idiot. It made sense at the time. It sounds so bad now."

"Not at all," Coco says. "I probably would have done the same. It's not like we had the internet."

"Yeah, that's true. We went to a hospital, which we'd never done before. They're so busy that they can be dangerous. We split up, and I went for the delivery rooms. We were just scouting this time, seeing what we could without messing up anything. Turns out, this hospital was one where most women had their babies in their rooms instead of going to a special one, so there were a lot of rooms to check.

"The second room I went into had the pair. It was just them, but there must have been doctors and nurses before. For a long time, I just stood there at the door, trying not to get in the way of any fragments that might appear or pass. Eventually, I couldn't help it. I had to go in."

Forrest almost feels like he's there again. The bright sunshine making the shades in that hospital room glow. The smile on that woman's face. The blanketed bundle.

"You okay?" Coco asks.

"Oh, yeah. Sorry."

"Tell me."

"The pair was a woman and her baby, a little girl. She must have just had the baby, like within moments of the Choosing. There was still a mess, and her legs were up and all the rest. But none of that mattered. The baby was wrapped in a blanket, but her hair was still sort of wet looking. The mom was holding her and had spread the blanket a little so she could see her baby. She was rubbing her tiny chest and looking at her baby like she was the only thing in the world. The woman kept saying, 'So perfect. So perfect. You're perfect. Look at you. You're here. I love you.' More stuff like that. Over and over, while she felt her arms and feet and chest and face. It was like she'd never seen a baby before.

"She was so happy. And the baby, she wasn't like I imagined a new baby would be. Her eyes were open, and she was staring at her mother, not screaming or anything like that. She was just looking at her. I don't know. I guess maybe I never understood what that kind of love looked like until that moment. It made me think of my mom, of all the times I felt like she was annoying or sassed her or told her to leave me alone. It made me think about how I could never apologize, because she was gone. I can't really explain. The woman and her baby were beautiful, though."

He pauses then, the tightness in his chest from the memory almost as strong as it was on that day. With effort, Forrest pushes it back. It wouldn't do to cry. Not right now. He's almost surprised to see that

Coco's eyes are shining when he looks at her. He shrugs. "Anyway, that was my favorite."

She nods, running a thumb under an eye to clear an unshed tear.

"That wasn't a good story, was it? I ruined the mood, didn't I?"

Smiling, she shakes her head. "No, not at all. But did you find what you were looking for? Did the girl have her baby?"

"Oh. Well, there are basically zero books in hospitals that are useful anymore. We left there and went to the library, where we should have gone first. I never told them what I found, and as far as I know, the woman and her baby are still in that room, still looking at each other. As for our friend, she had a boy, and everything went perfect. She lives in one of the communities, and last I heard, she has five kids."

"Wow, that's… a lot."

"Yeah, it is, but she's happy. I guess she really likes kids."

They fall silent, the hiss and pop of the fire in the woodstove the only sound in the house. It's not uncomfortable. Rather, it's the exact opposite. That's something he's never had with a girl he likes before. Outside, there's a brief laugh as two people walk down the street. He glimpses them through the window, the friendly porch lights on all the houses shedding enough light to see they're close together, arms around each other's waists.

Forrest wonders if the couple outside knows how lucky they are to have each other.

Glancing over at Coco, he sees she is watching the two people as well. Her eyes meet his and she smiles. Saying nothing more, she stands and holds out her hand toward him.

Forrest glances at it, confused, then back up to her face. Taking her hand, he stands. "What's up? Are we going somewhere?"

Still smiling, she cocks her head toward the hallway. "Not far. Just down the hall."

Forrest can feel his face grow hot. Is she saying what he thinks she's saying? He looks toward the dark hallway and the bedrooms beyond. "Uh, there?"

Coco's smile falters just a little, and her hand drops from his. "Well, I don't want to presume anything. I thought. Okay, maybe I was wrong."

He takes her hand again, then tentatively slides a hand around her waist. When she doesn't object, he pulls her in closer. Her smile comes back.

"Coco, you're not wrong. Presume away."

Forrest's Testimony: Excerpt 6

Year 14 After the Choosing

As expected, the clear routes on roads 148, 9, 147, and 149 are showing signs of damage in places. We recommend organizing patching crews between the Uncommitted and Chosen communities in this area. If this isn't addressed during the next few years, we may find ourselves with impassable roads. There aren't enough good routes through this area to waste any.

Despite our original intention to make further progress north before settling down for winter camp at the selected Chosen community, I have doubts that so much progress will be possible. It's already summer and I think it's likely we'll need to winter in Freeport. That community is tiny and has limited resources, though. It wouldn't be fair to winter there. They would likely suffer under the additional drain on supplies.

We have three decent options to choose from, as I see it. We can split into two groups, allowing one to move more quickly without conducting proper surveys of the areas they pass, while the other trails along and conducts those surveys. Another option is for both groups to speed along, ignoring surveys and clearing roads without proper preparation.

Both options would, inevitably, lead to the release of fragments we are not yet ready for, potentially allowing for significant waste. On the other hand, these areas are thinly populated and appear to be held primarily by animal fragments. A positive outcome of this approach could be the survival of any unfragmented animals still struggling to get by.

Either way, as of this moment, we have cleared roads leading from our current position all the way to the Solace community crossing. We created excellent surveys of materials, way stations, and resources for that route. This leads me to our third viable option. Given the cleared roads, we could, if the council decides that option is best, return to the Solace community for the winter. Our expedition members would welcome a winter in a town rather than a camp. There, we could organize a patching crew for the roads in question, allowing for more efficient use of resources.

Six

Year 14 After the Choosing

Forrest presses his wadded t-shirt into his shoulder wound and tries to steer with one hand. It's not unmanageable, but it hurts. Considering how much sweat came out of him during the day, his shirt is in no way sanitary, either. He'd like to hurry.

Braking at the edge of camp, he steps out of the truck as Pam waves at him from the medical tent. He'd radioed ahead. A few people glance at him as he passes, but he smiles and waves so they know he's alright.

"Okay, Bonehead, let's see the damage," Pam says, pointing him toward a fresh cot. There's a small table with her supplies already laid out on top. She takes the t-shirt away gently, then curls her lip. "Well, that's attractive."

Forrest glances down to see for himself. The cut is ragged and deeper than it first seemed. It wells with blood, which spills over the edge and runs in a red rivulet down his chest.

"*Ugh*," he says, turning away. His head swims. He's never been good with blood.

Pam stops him from falling off the cot, hooking an arm around the back of his neck and easing him down at the same time. She's done this before.

"Okay, tough guy. Just close your eyes and let me get this done." Her tone loses some of its normal gruffness and sounds almost sympathetic.

Forrest screws his eyes shut at the sting as she dabs the wound. Warm, recently boiled water trickles down his sides onto the cot. She calls Sven over, who must have been close by, and asks him to take a look. Forrest feels vaguely nauseated as they discuss how best to stitch a laceration that isn't remotely straight.

When she's ready to begin, Pam covers his shoulder with a piece of gauze and tells him to open his eyes.

He does, relieved when there's no visible blood. "What's the damage?"

"Well, you're going to have a fantastic scar shaped a bit like a lightning bolt. If you decide to woo the ladies with talk of being related to Thor, you'll have an excellent prop.

"If you're asking if you've done something horrible to yourself, then no. It's deeper than I'd like, but you didn't get anything major. No arteries, no major muscle tearing. That said, it's not one of those you can stitch up and go back to work. It will heal, but only if you let it. You're going to need to limit stretching that arm for a good week or two."

Forrest bounces his head against the cot. "I don't have time for that. I simply do not. We've been here for two months and we're still not even close to done with the major work."

"Did you finish with the radio tower? I mean, before this? Wait, don't answer yet. I'm going to give you a shot of local anesthetic. Close your eyes again."

He does, tensing as she removes the gauze. Forrest feels several pokes. "You said a shot. That's more than one."

"Well, it's one syringe full, so sue me for misspeaking. I'll give it a minute to work. Leave your eyes closed. Now you can answer."

"No, I didn't finish the tower, but Tyrone is there with the others, so it'll get done. Let's hope it does the trick and improves Freeport's radio range. Which reminds me, someone has to take the truck to get the others since I drove it back. I left the marker. It's about six miles up the road."

"Is that how you hurt yourself?" she asks. Forrest feels a tug and screws up his face. The tug stops. "Did you feel that? Pressure or pain?"

"Tug."

"Fine, then it's not pain. Go on."

The tugging returns, and he knows each one is a stitch. The mere thought makes him want to vomit. He also knows Pam is keeping him talking so he doesn't focus on what she's doing. That's probably a good thing. He once puked while getting stitches. No one wants a repeat of that.

"I was putting a solar panel in place and tried to keep it steady by leaning it on my shoulder while I put the screws in. I didn't strap it in like I should have. It was hot, and I was rushing. It slipped and got me. My fault."

"You didn't drop the panel, did you?" she asks. Another tug.

"No, I didn't drop the stupid panel. Glad you're concerned for my well-being," he says, trying hard to ignore another tug.

There's a beat of silence and some movement, then Sven says, "Oh, that's a nice knot. You're getting good at that."

Forrest slits one eye open. Sven is standing there, peering down at Pam's work with interest. He grins when he sees Forrest looking, like he's just waiting for him to hurl all over himself.

Snapping his eyes shut again, he says, "Not this time, big man. Not this time."

Sven lets out the kind of booming laugh that only big men with deep voices can produce. Forrest smirks despite himself. Laughs like that are contagious.

"Can you shut up?" Pam asks. "Good grief. Can't you see I'm working here?" She tugs again, then adds, "You can keep talking, Forrest. Only Sven needs to shut up."

Sven ignores the order. "Actually, I came in for a reason. We got a message relayed back from the Council. They say… well, actually, they said a shitload of stuff, so you can read the message I copied when you're done getting stitched up."

"Read it now, if you wouldn't mind. We've been waiting a month."

Sven settles his big frame onto a camp stool behind Forrest with an alarming creak of aluminum and stretching canvas. Paper crinkles, then he starts reading.

Council decision as follows: Expedition will winter over in Freeport. To avoid stress on local area, return to Solace for supplies. Two large trucks will require drivers. To enhance Freeport, expedition will install new water catchment and septic systems. Equipment provided by Council. Return to Freeport before first snow. Minor exploration of area during winter permitted. New instructions for expedition next year. Will brief at Solace.

"*Hmm,* I'm not sure I like that last part," Forrest says.

"I'm not sure I like the part where we're digging septic systems. Or the part about us being out here for at least three more months if we're not returning until the fall," Pam responds.

"What new instructions could they possibly have? I hope there hasn't been some renegotiation."

Pam huffs out a breath. "That does look nice, if I do say so myself. No, Forrest, don't look yet. Let me get it all cleaned and bandaged. Also, what kind of renegotiation?"

"As in someone getting cold feet about us going to Lorain," he answers, then yips when Pam dabs his skin with cold liquid.

"You're such a baby," she says.

* * *

Forrest tries not to look like he's searching for Coco. He is, though. The fall harvest is in full swing, and that makes it look like there *are* more people in the settlement. Or maybe there are more people. As he searches for her, unfamiliar faces greet him. He knows Solace provides a lot of grain, so perhaps nearby settlements sent people to help with the harvest.

Huge bundles of golden stalks are stacked everywhere, each waiting their turn in one of the threshers. They have a few of the machines, but all of them are human powered. Horses are a rarity. Most didn't survive. The air is thick with chaff and dust.

There's no official greeting party or any fuss this time. This isn't a planned meeting of many communities. He's just another member of an exploration team picking up gear and receiving instructions. He's not even counted amongst the Chosen council at the moment, since his vote is proxied out before every expedition.

Finally, Forrest spots a face that might help. It's the informal mayor of the town. His hair is tangled with bits of chaff and his face coated in dust. The man breaks away just long enough to tell Forrest they've set up a house especially for visitors and how to access it. Then, he's back to work.

No one locks doors anymore. There's simply no need without anonymity to hide behind or a crowd of criminals to blend into. Also, the world is covered with things that were once valuable. If anyone wanted them, they wouldn't need to steal. Because of that, all Forrest needs is the address of the visitor house and permission to enter.

Forrest brought only a handful of people with him. The rest headed into Freeport. Sven, as their main mechanic on the expedition, is always a must. Also, he doesn't go anywhere without Pam. Both are excellent drivers, so with big loads in big trucks, they were an obvious choice. Tyrone and Kiara can provide technical and organization support, which is necessary because Forrest isn't at all sure what the Council meant by *new instructions* for the remainder of their expedition.

The house is larger and newer than most in Solace. Paler spots visible on the floor show exactly how much of the interior was altered. The living room has more seating than one would expect, making it look more like a lounge. Four out of the five bedrooms have also been repurposed. Only one has a large bed, while the rest have between two and four twin sized beds, each with a small dresser in place of a nightstand and a number neatly painted on the headboard.

There are two bathrooms, which have been depersonalized to some extent, with shelving added. Each section of shelf is numbered to match a bed and holds a towel, washcloth, and a bar of village-made soap.

Despite the clear indications that the house isn't meant to be a home anymore, it's quite inviting. With the curtains tied back to let in the autumn sun, it's bright and welcoming. In the kitchen, Forrest finds a worn binder containing instructions for obtaining food and where to find assistance for various issues, as well as a page of general community rules.

"Wow," Pam says as she finishes reading the sheet over his shoulder. "They've certainly made a lot of changes while we were gone. I mean, it's been over five months since we were here, but still. I don't remember anyone mentioning doing something like this."

Sven shrugs and opens the refrigerator. Cool air wafts out and it feels like heaven. "Probably because people don't like us camping in their houses all the time. I wouldn't." He retrieves a large pitcher filled with water and tests it with his hand. "Nice and cold," he says, then sets it on the counter to rummage for glasses in the cabinets.

Kiara hands Forrest an envelope with his name on it and says, "I found this on the table in the foyer."

Inside is a short note directing Forrest to come to the administration building and report for instructions. With a sigh, he tosses the note on the counter and accepts a glass of water from Sven. It feels divine after a long trip in the heat. A hot and dry fall might be great for the grain harvest, but it's uncomfortable.

Setting down the empty glass, Forrest says, "Well, I should find out what's going on. If it's bad news, it won't get better by waiting."

Leaving the others to unpack and get settled—and hopefully arrange for a good meal—Forrest takes the short walk to the administration building. Though he looks, he never sees Coco.

The council's representative is ensconced in an office marked with a hand-lettered sign reading, *Chosen Embassy*. That's also new. Five months doesn't seem like long enough for so much to change. It's a little disorienting for Forrest. He shakes off the feeling and takes a deep breath. The door is wide open, as is the window opposite. The breeze trickling through makes the heat less oppressive. At a desk sits an older man with shockingly white hair and equally shocking black eyebrows.

"Dave? Okay if I come in?" Forrest asks as he raps on the door frame.

"Forrest!" Dave says, standing. "So glad you made it. Come in, come in. There's some cool water there in the fridge, if you want. Glasses on the table. How was your trip back?"

"Shorter than the way up, that's for sure. We just have to take it easy where the road is rutted."

Dave frowns at that. "I wish we knew why that was happening. If it can happen there, why doesn't it happen everywhere? Or will it? Even when we release all the fragments on a road, they stay pristine. Or, at least they have until now. Why at that spot in the road? Why now?"

Forrest remembers what Coco told him during their first meeting. It comes entirely unbidden, but it's there, so he says, "I heard a theory once. I'm not saying I believe it, but it fits. Maybe those bits of road are going because all the fragments that remember the road are gone."

Dave, who is substantially older than Forrest, frowns harder, the lines around his mouth deepening. "Oh, that would be bad, wouldn't it? Not at all good for us. I suppose that's an Uncommitted theory? Oh, and pardon my manners. Do sit down."

With a shrug and sheepish smile, Forrest takes a chair in front of the desk. He considers Coco's perspective. "I think she's more in the middle. Not Uncommitted or Chosen, but making her way as best she can."

"Ah, well, I suppose that's a lot of people nowadays."

"Yeah, I suppose it is. So, what are the new instructions all about? For the expedition, I mean. We're taking bets on whether or not this means the Lorain agreement is off the table."

Shifting in his seat, Dave looks vaguely uncomfortable. He fidgets with his pencil.

"Is it that?" Forrest asks, leaning forward.

"Well, not exactly," Dave begins, then places his pencil on the surface of the table. "It's complicated, which is why we didn't put everything in the message. With so many people relaying every communication, it was bound to get butchered, and rumors would fly." He pauses, looking at a huge cork board layered in maps. "It's easier to show you. Come over here."

He flips several maps over the top of the board, revealing a piece of tracing paper overlaying a map with this section of the Ohio River highlighted. There are notations and numbered references everywhere.

Forrest asks, "Is this the survey?"

Dave nods and points to the small red spot labeled *Solace,* then spreads his hands to encompass a long span of the river. "The agreement two years ago was that Uncommitted survey teams would be responsible for the river along this stretch. Because they didn't want rampant releases of fragments, they didn't want us involved. Besides, it's labor intensive and far closer to their settlements than ours. You remember?"

"Of course. I was in on the negotiations."

"Oh yes, you were. I'd forgotten that. I was the one proxied out for an expedition that time."

"I also remember the initial surveys were pretty bad," Forrest says.

Again, Dave frowns, a worried expression on his face. "No, not good at all. The Uncommitted even agreed to release some industrial fragments upstream that might have played a role in the poor water quality. In late spring, after you left, the final report came in, and there are exactly zero unfragmented fish anywhere along this span."

Forrest's mouth drops open. "Zero? How can there be zero? That's… that's…"

"Completely horrible are the words you're looking for. Or perhaps devastating."

"I was going to say impossible."

"Well, you'd think so, but I have to show you a few things. Hold on." Dave grabs a blue pencil from the cup on his desk and uses it as a pointer. "The thing is, their surveys are damn good, as good as ours are. There are fish, but not in the river. Here at the dam, these creeks here—the ones marked in green—even in smaller bodies and tributaries where you wouldn't expect to see a lot of fish."

"Then why aren't they in the river? It's all connected."

"The game of survival has changed, we think. The rules have changed. Every place they've found unfragmented fish, there are *no* fragmented fish. It looks as if it was a numbers game." Dave pauses and points at a blue spot on the map. "Here, for example. Not a place you'd expect to see loads of fish, but there are. Loads and loads. Why? We think because it's fairly isolated. Also, there were enough unfragmented fish that they could survive the violence of the disturbed fragments. And finally, each of these places is far away from the human population. Isolated, even."

Forrest nods, finally seeing. "So, because the river has so many fragments, it's simply too hostile. Those fish that wander out of cleared areas don't make it."

Tossing the pencil onto his desk, Dave sighs and returns to his chair. "Yes, and while this offers a clear path forward when it comes to repopulating the river, it actually raises questions about Lake Erie. The Uncommitted seem entirely amenable to an organized and well-planned clearing of the river in stages, allowing for fish to move naturally in from the small tributaries and creeks and so on. In Lake Erie—"

"In Erie," Forrest interrupts, "we have a giant basin filled with intermingling fish who had no safe spots to get away from fragments. Particularly since there are crowded coastlines where even the outlets and shallows are tied up in fragments by humans."

Dave inclines his head and says, "In a nutshell, yes."

"So, what? We leave the lake alone? Let the last survivors, assuming there are any, die out?"

Leaning back in this chair, Dave's nearly perpetual frown is replaced by something that could almost be a wry smile. His black eyebrows make the expression more pronounced.

"No, Forrest. That's where it gets interesting. You're getting company. Then, we have to figure out how to move living fish—breeding stock—a few hundred miles without killing them. They don't want to stop the expedition. The Uncommitted want to restock Lake Erie."

Forrest almost deflates at the thought of it. The sheer size of the task is unimaginable. He says, "This is going to suck."

With a grave nod, Dave says, "Sure will."

Forrest's Testimony: Excerpt 7

Year 6 After the Choosing

I suppose my biggest concern for this year has been the babies. I mean, there are people not much older than me already pairing up and wanting to settle down. We have many communities now, and some of the other founders are out there inviting more to join. Heck, we've got several more groups scheduled to create new communities next spring.

On paper, it seems like we should start thinking about a new generation. If the Choosing hadn't happened, I might be married or have a kid by now. I get that. I just don't feel like we're being honest and careful.

Having a baby is dangerous, and how are we going to keep up our work if half the workforce stays behind with a baby? That's not me being sexist. We sure as hell can't bring a crying baby around fragments. One good cry and we'd wind up dealing with every maniac fragment released within a hundred yards or more.

Of course, honesty is required, so I said what I thought at the open meeting. To say I'm not popular right now would be an understatement. There I am, at the front with the rest of the council, and every person in the room is staring at me like I just suggested we sacrifice puppies to the devil. Even the other council members.

I don't know. Maybe I'm wrong, or maybe I'm not thinking of the future. I can't be sure, so I abstained from the vote. Self-awareness is a requirement for honesty.

What I *do* know is that the closest thing we have to a doctor is a former phlebotomist. When I first met him, I was what, fifteen, maybe sixteen? At the time, I thought that was pretty close to a doctor. I found out later that meant he drew blood for a living. Well, he also took lab tests like swabs and such, but still, that's not a doctor. Who is going to help if something goes wrong?

Seven

Year 14 After the Choosing

As Forrest walks down Coco's street yet again, he wonders if she's avoiding him. He only has a few more days in Solace before his expedition must return to Freeport for the winter. If he doesn't see her soon, then he won't for a long while; maybe not until next summer, maybe not for two years. He needs to see her before he goes. He wants to tell her how much she's been on his mind in the months since the Council meeting, since he really got to know her.

The fact that he hasn't seen her, that she didn't answer the note he left for her, is making him wonder if she thinks of that time as a mistake. Maybe she does. They are different, yes, but that doesn't mean it couldn't work out between them. Seekers and Chosen get together all the time. Does she regret their time together? Sure, it was only a couple of weeks, but they were probably the best weeks of his life. He really felt something for her and thought she did for him.

Was he wrong?

Her porch lights are off… again. They would be on if she were home since it's past sunset. He glances next door and, sure enough, their lights are on. Forrest considered knocking on Jorge and Tamara's door the previous night but didn't. The last thing he wants is to come off as creepy. Of course, finding excuses to walk past her house so frequently is probably already giving off slight stalker vibes.

Now, well, should he? Coco has to know he's in town. There's no way to escape knowing that when there are so few people in the world. Not to mention that he left her a note. Forrest stands there in the dark, tapping his foot and looking at the small, neat house, the front door framed by two pools of yellow light.

"Dammit," he mutters, then strides with purpose toward the house before he can lose his nerve. If she is avoiding him, or has regrets, then she should tell him so and not leave him wondering.

His footsteps seem loud against the porch boards. The curtains at the big window in front twitch aside, but not enough for Forrest to see more than the vague shape of a head before they fall closed again. He knocks.

Beyond the door he hears the murmur of voices, then a slightly louder, "Come on. You can't let this go on forever." It sounds like Jorge. Finally, steps approach the door.

When it opens, the tall frame of Jorge appears. "Hello, Forrest." It's not friendly or unfriendly, just neutral.

"Is she here?" he asks, then adds, "Coco, I mean."

Jorge looks back briefly, then pushes open the screen door. The squeak of the hinges is louder than it should be. The atmosphere is loaded, and Forrest doesn't know why.

When he enters, he first sees Tamara as she stands up from her seat. Then he follows her gaze and sees Coco. Time seems to stop, and he feels almost as woozy as he had when he saw the blood from his cut.

"Holy shit!"

Her belly is rounded in a way that's unmistakable, particularly considering how trim she is. Her hands rest there almost protectively. Forrest counts the months backward in his mind. One, two, three, four, five… five months and three weeks.

"Holy shit," he repeats, absolutely at a loss for words.

Coco turns her head away, her eyes finding Tamara's. Her mouth is tight when she says, "Well, I guess that answers that question. Problem solved."

Too late, Forrest understands how his words have been taken. "No! No, not that. I'm just… I mean, holy shit." He pushes out a breath and leans against the wall next to the door, bending over to put his hands on his knees. He's suddenly very dizzy.

Jorge is still standing next to him, seemingly ready to open the door and push him out into the night. He lets go of the knob and touches Forrest's shoulder. "Hey, you okay? You're not going to pass out on me, are you?"

"I hope not," he replies.

Jorge pats his shoulder. "Just take a minute. I'll get you some water." As he passes Coco, he murmurs, "Be nice."

The wave of dizziness is already passing, but he keeps leaning against the wall to buy time. He has absolutely no idea what to do, other than make sure he doesn't keep saying *holy shit* and ruin everything. He hadn't expected this. It hadn't even been a consideration.

It should have. He knows that. Even though he'd been careful during those wonderful days with Coco, he knew there was no guarantee. It's not like a fourteen-year-old condom would have done much. He'd used the same methods teenagers used when they were being stupid. Except that one night. That one perfect, crazy night.

Stupid. Stupid, stupid, stupid.

Jorge returns with a tumbler of water and searches his eyes as he hands it over. "You okay now?"

Forrest sips, then nods. "Yeah. Just surprised."

With a shake of his head, Jorge moves toward the couch and says, "I'll bet."

Tamara whispers something to Coco that he can't hear, then Coco says, "No, it's okay. Jorge will stay with me."

With that, Tamara walks toward the door, but edges as far around Forrest as she can. In response to the unspoken request for space, he stands upright and moves away. Her arms are crossed, and she avoids looking at him.

During the brief interruption, the room has changed. When Forrest looks at Coco again, there are clear sides drawn. She and Jorge are sitting on the couch, leaving him with a choice of chairs across from them, the safe demarcation line of a coffee table between.

"May I?" he asks, indicating the closest chair, a wingback thing done in a faded floral print.

She nods, saying nothing and giving away nothing with her entirely neutral expression. At least she's meeting his eyes now. That's progress.

He still isn't sure what he should say, but it's clear they will remain awkwardly silent until he says something. Coco is looking at the coffee table, her hands absently rubbing at her belly. At least Jorge looks sympathetic.

"Were you just going to avoid me? I would have found out eventually," Forrest says, then realizes how that sounds. "Also, you look amazing."

She rolls her eyes and turns her head, but there's a hint of a smile, as well.

Forrest feels all kinds of things, most of them contradictory. He decides to treat this like a testimony. The truth, no matter the cost.

"I'm not sure if I'm allowed to be happy," he says. "I feel it, but I don't know if I should. I'm upset because you didn't tell me. Also, I'm kind of happy you didn't tell me because I don't think I would have been able to keep working this summer if I'd known. I'm worried right now, because I don't know if you'll be safe or if you'll need some medical care that no one can provide. I'm excited about the idea of a baby and terrified of it at the same time. I'm just really confused. Really, *really* confused."

As he speaks, Coco raises her head and watches him, her eyes seeming to search for the truth. When he doesn't go on, she says, "Yeah, all of that."

"I can count the months, but I can't remember exactly how long it takes. I know it's not really nine months, but do you know when you're due? Are you okay?"

"Pregnancy is forty weeks. I'm due in late winter, which is actually good for me. Hot weather is bad after delivery. Cold is good. We don't have enough power to heat all the houses, but they're going to turn on my power all the way when I get close. No wood stoves because of soot particles. Back to central heat and electric stoves for me. So far, everything looks okay. We've got a clinic set up with an ultrasound machine and everything. The doctor is just two settlements over and we have a nurse and a nursing assistant." She looks down at her belly, smiles and asks, "Do you want to know what I'm having?"

"You know?" he asks. "Wait… hold on." He breathes in and out a few times. "Okay, tell me."

"A boy. He looks perfect."

Forrest grins, though he isn't exactly sure why. He hasn't had time to wish for one or the other. Maybe it's the idea of a perfectly healthy baby rather than gender that does it.

"Well, can I ask that we don't name him Forrest? It's a terrible name," he says, half joking.

Coco breaks eye contact, giving Jorge a sidelong glance. He pats her hand. Something is obviously going on. Is the baby not his? Surely, they would have said so by now if that were the case.

"What?" Forrest asks.

Jorge leans forward on the couch and takes a deep breath. "Before you say anything or respond or argue, we need to explain a couple of things and our reasoning. Can you hold on while I talk?"

Forrest's anxiety ratchets up, like an engine with the gas pedal pressed to the floor and the gear in neutral. He has no idea what Jorge wants to say, but their expressions and the fact that they want him to be quiet are clear indicators he isn't going to like it. Or at least, that they think he won't like it.

"I don't know," he answers truthfully.

"Can you try? It's important, and it will help all of us if we know where each of us stands. This is our stance, and you'll have your turn. Okay?"

There's something in that use of *us* and *we* and *our* that bothers Forrest, as if Jorge has somehow taken something from him. Or maybe, as if the three of them, Tamara included, are a team opposing an enemy, which would be him. Feelings aside, this is not a one-person show. No matter what he may want, there are others involved and, in the end, everyone will have to say their piece.

"I'll try," he says, then clasps his hands together, hoping it will keep him contained. He's been told in enough council meetings that his hands say too much.

The other two share one more glance and Coco nods, as if confirming some previous plan, which only enhances Forrest's feelings of being an outsider. Jorge says, "This is new to you. You just found out. We, on the other hand, have had months to think and talk about this. We're ahead of you in that regard, and there have been some decisions made. That said, we can't honestly go ahead with those decisions without you."

Jorge pauses, clears this throat, then goes on. "Given the situation, Coco would prefer if we, meaning she and I, raise the baby as if he were mine. I'm—"

"What? No!" Forrest interrupts without thinking. It's a visceral, instinctive response.

Jorge holds up both hands. "Please, just listen."

Forrest can feel the defensive walls rising as if they were being stacked and mortared right in front of his face. There are so many reasons why this is not a good idea, not the least of which is the law, which is on his side. Fine, if they want to talk, they can. It won't change anything.

He waves a hand as if offering the floor.

Jorge's expression says that he knows exactly what Forrest is thinking and isn't surprised. Even so, he forges on. "I'm happy to raise this baby. More than amenable, really. Coco is my dear friend, and between all of us, I think we can give him a solid, stable, healthy upbringing. It will be better for him in the end. Being raised by two parents on opposite sides of this kind of divide would be confusing and not at all good for him."

Coco stops Jorge with a hand on his arm and says, "It's not just that. Not just politics. It's everything. You don't live here, and even if you moved somewhere close, you'd be gone on your expeditions all the time. Not to mention you'd need to go wherever the Council meets, even when you were home. And… okay, this might sound bad, and I could be wrong… but you just don't seem like a kid person. You're an adult person. Even with all the kids running around here, you never showed any interest."

"That's not fair," Forrest says. "I've never gotten the chance to be a kid person. I've never had a kid."

Jorge must sense an argument brewing, because he gives Coco a look and she raises her hands, as if giving up. After a moment, he asks, "Forrest, can you see our point of view?"

Forrest isn't ready for philosophy yet. He's still trying to get over Coco deciding he isn't a kid person without even asking him first. But he has to say something. He's way behind the curve already. Sticking with facts is safest, so that's what he does.

"The law is pretty clear, so whatever plan you've cooked up is irrelevant. Both communities agree on this. Biological parents must be officially acknowledged because there aren't enough of us. It's too important and the genetics are too narrow for mistakes. So, I'm his father. Period. This isn't a Chosen thing or an Uncommitted thing—"

"See!" Coco interrupts, pointing her finger at Forrest. "That right there is why I want this."

"What?" Forrest asks, confused.

"*Uncommitted.* You call us Uncommitted, even though we don't." She holds up her hand to show the tattoo on the back. "Right here is an S for *Seeker*. It's not like you don't know that. You want to be called Chosen, so we respect that and call you Chosen. We don't call you the Murder Cult. Yet, here we are, and right to our faces you call us Uncommitted and not by the name we have for ourselves. Exactly how does that work for our son? Hmm? Do you simply undermine everything I raise him to believe and call his mother by a label that does more than raise doubts about us?"

Forrest's mouth hangs open. He doesn't know what to say. It's not as if he's insulting anyone on purpose. Uncommitted is the name the Chosen call all those who don't join them. They have since before first contact with a settlement who actually called themselves Seekers.

"It's not meant to be an insult. I… I… it's habit."

Coco shakes her head, pity on her face. "A habit you choose not to change. We call you what you want to be called. We do it on paper, on the radio, in council, and to your face. You call us by a name that implies we're wrong for not being one of you. Lumped in with everyone who isn't you. A lesser class."

Flustered, Forrest says, "I'm sorry. I'll work on that. I'll bring it up in council. I'll talk with the Chosen embassy tomorrow."

Jorge breaks in, his voice calm and even, as if that will bring the temperature down. "That would be great. I'm sure everyone would appreciate that, but it also demonstrates exactly why our plan is best."

When Forrest looks confused, he continues. "You're about to change the rules for an entire population of people, which you can do because you're one of their leaders, one of their founders. If you said you were doing it because the mother of your child, who is not one of the Chosen, asked you to, wouldn't they immediately question your priorities and loyalties? Would anything you do from this day forward be trusted entirely? And likewise, would Coco's suggestions ever be taken at face value with the Seekers?"

The cushions of the chair whoosh as Forrest sinks back, his hands pushing through his hair. He doesn't need to think or contemplate for days to know they're right. It would be exactly like that for both of them. He knows it. Not a single person who switched sides holds a council seat in either group. Sure, they accept swapping camps, and everyone gets along, but deep down, each group thinks that what they believe is right.

Coco's voice is softer, the anger gone and replaced with a kinder tone when she says, "Forrest, I don't regret this or the time I had with you. I liked you then and I like you now. Nothing about that has changed, and I didn't use you or think of our time as a fling. I really did hope for more, but you left. You left and went on with your life as a Chosen. No matter what I might feel, I have to face facts and be honest about the future. I'm never going to believe what you believe. I'll never join the Chosen. Unless you think you can leave them and join—"

"No, that won't happen," he interrupts, his words firm and without thought. It's the simple truth. He doesn't believe what she believes. Her expression shifts, her sadness evident. He wonders if she hoped he would become an Uncommitted... no, a Seeker. Perhaps she did.

"I'm sorry," he says. "I'm not one of you. I don't think that's the way forward."

She nods, her lips turning up slightly, but her eyes shining with tears. "I know."

He thinks about the situation, trying to imagine what a future would be like for a child raised in this world. He tries to picture what it would be like to have that life interrupted at intervals by a distant father who believed something entirely different than everyone else around him. Would he, even if not meaning to, contradict Coco? Would he try to sway his child into his camp?

He would. He knows he would. It would be only natural. He's already thinking of this child as a Chosen.

"I see what you're saying. What about the law? I can't change that."

Jorge takes over again. Back to business.

"Coco and I spoke with one of the council members. Confidentially, we asked him what we should do about this. I'm not sure if you know this, but Seeker law requires that birth records be kept in confidence. The idea is that conflicts will be dealt with, if they arise, but that no one has any actual right to know everyone else's business.

"He told us this problem isn't unique and that there are a lot of births between camps that fall into this general category. It's not just us. It's actually on the docket for this winter's inter-community treaty conference. He says confidentiality is a no-brainer since the Chosen have just as much of this as we do. It's only now coming up because more communities are safe, so there are more children being born and more people to have children with. It is what it is."

"What about him?" he asks, looking at Coco's belly. "You just won't tell him about me? I mean, I don't know how I feel about that. It's a lot to ask of me. I understand it, but that doesn't mean I'm okay with it. Yes, it's new, but I… I really can't describe what happened inside me when I realized you're having our baby."

He stops, tapping his chest with his fist, unable to describe the feeling.

A tear creates a gleaming track down Coco's face. She sniffs wetly and says, "I know. Believe me, I know. As to that, we'll have to play it by ear. When he's ready to understand, we'll tell him. I guess it will be sort of like figuring out when to tell a child he's adopted. We'll have to figure it out."

The trio sits in silence for a while, thinking. Forrest isn't sure what he can bring himself to agree to, but he already knows what the right thing to do is. Right for the baby, anyway. Jorge watches both of them. He seems like such a nice person. He'd probably be a great father. In a way, that makes Forrest feel even worse. He tries to ignore the primal part of his brain telling him to kick the crap out of Jorge.

As they sit there with a clock ticking loudly on the wall, the entire front room suddenly floods with light. It's streaming through the windows behind him. Forrest looks up, confused.

Coco looks around. Her voice is a little panicked when she asks, "Where's Tux?"

Forrest points. "He's right behind your head on the back of the couch."

She reaches over her head to grab the cat, then lets out a breath. "Okay, it's not him this time."

Jorge has already gotten up, hurriedly stuffing his feet into his boots. Forrest stands, not sure what he should do.

"What's going on?" Forrest asks.

Coco levers herself up from the couch, saying, "It means something unlooped is beyond the wall, like an animal. Last time it was Tux getting into the chickens. The time before that, it was a fox, as in a real, live fox. It ate two chickens, but it got away before we could capture it. The lights mean everyone should gather so we can try to catch it."

Jorge reaches for the door, then turns back and says, "No, Coco. You can't go. What if a loop gets broken? It's dangerous."

Coco waves his words away. "Don't be stupid. I'm coming."

"Forget that."

"No way."

Jorge and Forrest glance at each other, having both blurted out their statements at the same time in a way they both know Coco won't respond well to.

Instead of arguing, she puffs out a breath and starts pushing them toward the door. "Fine, fine. Just make sure you catch that fox if it's there! They have two females in captivity, and they need a male!"

"Actually, do you mind if I hang back? I'd like to talk. In private," Forrest says. Coco pauses and looks at Jorge, who then locks eyes with Forrest. *Careful,* his eyes say. Forrest nods, an agreement reached between them.

Once they're alone, Forrest is at a loss for words. Coco opens the conversation for him, saying, "I know this is hard. I do."

Stepping closer, Forrest spreads his hands and glances at her belly. "May I?"

Smiling, she says, "Of course."

Tentatively, he spreads a hand over the rise, not sure what he expected to feel. Some magical paternal connection, maybe? There's only warmth and cotton.

"I can't believe a part of me is there, growing into a whole new human. It's so strange."

Her belly lifts with her laugh. "Oh, I can believe it. Apparently, he likes kicking when I'm trying to sleep. It's not bad, just a sort of a fluttering feeling, but it's hard to sleep when he gets going. He likes it when I hum, though. That usually settles him down, but by then I'm wide awake."

Shaking his head, Forrest lets his hand fall away. Part of him wonders if that will be the last time he'll come that close to touching his child. It's a terrible feeling.

"I'm not sure I can agree to this, Coco. It's not fair to ask me to make this decision at the same moment I find out you're having a baby. It's just not."

Reaching out, she takes his hand and squeezes it. "I know that too. I really do. I also know that you'll see this is right once you've had the chance to think about it. That's not me trying to bully you or force you to agree. That's me knowing that you're a good person inside, that you're the kind of man who will do the hard thing because you know it's right. I hate that it has to be this way, and I really hate that our oh-so-peaceful world isn't quite peaceful enough for us to do this together."

With a sigh, she drops his hand and holds her belly. "What other real options do we have? It's not like I'll give him up for half of each year so you can take him into the wilds breaking loops. I would never allow that for even one day. Would you give up half of each year to live here? Or give it up permanently? Would you be comfortable as the only Chosen in a Seeker community?"

As unfair as it seems, Forrest can see the truth of it. He hates himself just a little for knowing he wouldn't be able to make that sacrifice. He could try, but he knows he would fail.

"There has to be a way," Forrest says, hoping for any lifeline. "Some way to at least be a part of his life."

"And maybe there will be, but we don't know that. We can't bank on it. And, not as his father." At his expression, her tone softens. "I'm so sorry, but think about it from the baby's perspective. He deserves to have two parents who are with him, really *with* him. A distant father who can't even bring himself to live in the same town? What would that be like?"

He knows what she means. He feels it. It hurts.

"Forrest, I know this is hard, probably harder than anything else either of us has ever had to deal with, and you're bearing the brunt of it. But hard doesn't mean wrong. For us, this is right."

That's the worst part. No matter how much thinking he does or time he takes to decide, he already knows the answer in his heart. She's right. He has to let go.

Forrest's Testimony: Excerpt 8

Year 14 After the Choosing

I'm glad these testimonies are private, because I've had the weirdest year possible. Though I'm stuck in Freeport for the winter, digging septic wells in frozen ground and setting up water catchments, I feel like I'm scattered all over the place.

So far, I've gotten no word on Coco and the baby. Jorge promised he would send a message when he arrives, and I believe him, so I'm just waiting. It should be any time now.

I suppose even weirder is that I'm having a child—even though I can't acknowledge that—at exactly the time we're discovering something odd about the children. There were rumors before, but it's not exactly something people would want to test.

Generally speaking, everyone shelters children from the fragments. They're dangerous and children are loud. Not to mention it would be traumatizing to see fragments and know they were once people. As far as I know, no one has ever let a child near a fragment on purpose. Now… well… it turns out the rumors are true.

There was a sleepwalker in Solace when I was last there, the same night I found out about the baby. It's not as if anyone needs to guard the gates from intruders, so there was no one to stop the little girl from walking right out. It was only when her parents discovered her missing before they went to bed that the alarm was raised. Apparently, she was a frequent sleepwalker, but never left the house before.

There was a huge panic, but I really do like Solace's method for calling people. They turn on all the streetlights and flash them on and off. It's brilliant and quiet. I've passed it along via Dave to suggest we use the same signal in Chosen settlements.

At any rate, once people gathered and were told the nature of the problem, there was a real panic. A child out in territory still covered by fragments? What could be worse than that? A disturbed fragment could tear a child to pieces in moments.

The surprise came when she was found. She was curled up in the middle of an uncleared street, the only entirely uncleared street in that town. She'd not only left the fenced area, but also crossed the bridge that splits the town. Fragments walked to and fro all around her. One of them actually began their fragment less than a foot from her sleeping body.

Everyone was terrified, with good reason. Frankly, I'm pretty sure every person there would have happily sent every fragment in the village into the beyond at that moment. They weren't Uncom Seekers at that moment. (I can't believe how hard it is to change to Seekers. Even in writing my testimony. Too bad the only place we still use ink is in testimonies and official records of birth and death. Seekers, Seekers, Seekers. Practice makes perfect.)

Back to that night. Someone had the listing of all the fragments and their times and such, so everyone started trying to find a gap. It was a terrible spot. The parents were too panicked to maneuver the fragment paths and Tamara is slight and fast, so she volunteered. She picked up the girl and we could all see in the light of our flashlights that she was whispering to the girl to be quiet.

But she didn't. The little girl started crying when she was jostled awake, and it was loud. Tamara was ready to run, and the rest of us were definitely ready for a fight. And that's when it happened. As in, *nothing happened*. The fragments paid no attention at all. They didn't seem to hear her cries.

Tamara was in a tight spot, and we were all counting down on watches and what have you, but the girl said she was doing it wrong and asked to be put down. Loudly, I might add. Loud enough that all of us were cringing. Later, Tamara said she told the girl she would put her down if she didn't move away from her and was very quiet. She was put on her feet. Her white nightgown almost glowed in the dark and made her look so tiny.

Then, this girl grabbed Tamara's hand and calmly walked around and through the fragments like she knew where they would be, *because she did*. She said she could see where they would be, and she just led Tamara around them like it was no big deal.

Everyone is testing this. There are no children here in Freeport, or I'm sure they would test it, too. We still hear all about it. News travels fast and furious along the radios. Not every child can do this, but many can. We've spent all these years keeping children behind walls and away from fragments out of fear. It turns out, a good many of them are in no danger at all.

They see the fragments differently than we do. The children say it's like a wave in the air, like a trail of color or an echo of the person, like they leave a mark along their path. And these kids that can see this mark, or whatever it is, are entirely invisible to them. They can shout if they like. None will hear.

Solace tested with a fragmented moth they found and discovered that touch doesn't even make them go crazy. They simply shift, disappear, then start their loop again at the appropriate time, but the children say it hurts the fragments. Hurts them?

I have to wonder what that means. Also, how do the children know it hurts?

Eight

Year 18 After the Choosing

Joey is four years old today. Forrest keeps track, though he's not seen him in two years. He thought he'd be able to handle it, but it's too much. Sometimes he has a hard time accepting that he has a child who has lived in this world for years, a child he doesn't see and can't acknowledge.

Joey was tested with a fragment when he was two, but Forrest hadn't needed to wait for a letter to know he would be at ease in this world. It seemed obvious to him. Testing proved him right. Joey is special.

Coco sends packets with messengers during the twice-yearly supply run to the Lorain Marina settlement. Such regular correspondence is possible because almost everything sent to the marina comes through Solace. Forrest appreciates those in ways he could never have imagined. For a few days after a packet arrives, he feels lighter, like the stress of life isn't really stressful… like he has a son. And this time, there was a photo. His boy isn't just growing and well, he's also beautiful.

He doesn't know how her community managed it, but they can take photos now. He's guessing they got the supplies from a Chosen community who freed fragments and got fresh film or paper or whatever else. He's decided not to ask and break their fragile situation with reminders of their differences.

Slipping on his coat, he leaves the house he lives in with most of his original crew, plus two-year-old Benson, who belongs to Pam and Sven. At over forty, Pam finally became a mother. Many have become mothers recently. Discovering that children are not in mortal danger, or at least most of them aren't, has changed many minds. Even Kiara, who lives with her girlfriend next door, is debating whether they should ask for a donor and have children.

They tested Benson with a fragmented mouse. He is also special. He will walk through the world without fear. That is, he will once he can walk more than five minutes without plopping down onto his butt or flexing his hands and whining for someone to carry him.

Forrest stomps his feet on the porch, testing for slippery spots. It's more than cold outside: It's frigid, and the snow is amazingly deep. Luckily, there's only one road for them to worry about and they have a snowplow to keep it clear.

At the end of the lot, he looks both ways. There's plenty of wood smoke to scent the air. It smells good. Like home.

It's his turn to record the ice levels and inspect the marina. Now that it's freed of fragments, they have to be careful. Maintenance is everything, though so far, it looks like Coco was right about memory.

There are so many ways the marina is tied up in memory, whether on paper or in organic brains, that it remains fresh. Not tied up in a fragment, but still fresh. Things wear slowly, but the winters take their toll even there. It's less than a quarter mile to walk, but the cold is like spears spiking his flesh.

Forrest does his rounds, and everything looks good. Boats pulled out of the water are still firmly on their trailers or chocks. Ice grips the water and makes it look like he could almost walk forever, or at least to

Canada, which lies on the far shore. With a thick coat of unbroken snow, the lake is a blinding white.

In an odd contrast, much of the shoreline is trapped in summer. There are sharp demarcation lines where fragments interact with the water. Ice forms and disappears as these fragments eternally cycle throughout the day.

Despite the climate and terrible winter conditions, the expedition was surprised to find a thriving community already here. They've located another just eight miles away. Neither group is interested in being Chosen. They have something else, a sort of hybrid system that's part Seeker and part Chosen. Something unique they've built up on their own.

They don't have a label for their group, which seems right to Forrest. He wishes he hadn't been so eager to have a group name, an identity. When everything he belonged to went away so suddenly, he'd just wanted to belong again. He's old enough to know that about his younger self. He's entering his mid-thirties and should have figured that out about himself sooner.

After much back and forth, the Chosen council agreed they should drop the matter of classification here in Lorain. It isn't important. The existing communities aren't Seekers, so it doesn't matter if they aren't Chosen. Forrest realized he felt relief, once that decision was made. He still does. They have no labels to divide them.

It's not that he doesn't believe anymore. He does. The basic tenets of the Chosen system still feel inherently right to him. It's only that he's decided labeling such beliefs is wrong.

The sun finally peeks out from behind the clouds. He squints as the light hits the snow and sparkles. A million tiny shafts of reflected light appear on the frozen lake. It's breathtaking.

He wonders if anything is happening beneath the ice. Is there life? So far, there's nothing other than fragments. The expedition was altered to become a joint venture. The Seekers were adamant that their river surveys counseled caution. They came up here and instead of a wholesale net and dump to find live creatures that didn't disappear, they fished.

For two years, they have fished. For two years, every single creature has disappeared.

When he returns home, the house feels like a furnace, though he knows it's set to sixty-two degrees, which would have been unacceptably cool in his pre-Choosing life. Everyone is up and bustling about. The house feels full, but in a good way. Not crowded, just full.

"How's the marina? Buried in a glacier yet?" Sven asks, bouncing a red-faced and angry Benson on his hip.

Forrest chuckles and nods at the child's mess. "No glaciers, but it looks like *he* got buried in oatmeal. What happened? Does he suddenly not like it?"

Sven laughs, bouncing into a swoop that usually sends Benson into giggles. Not today, apparently. With a sigh, Sven grabs a rag from the table and tries to clean the boy's face. He's not having it.

"He's fine. He's just being something of a turdlet today." He raises his voice into a surprisingly high-pitched baby squeak. "Aren't you? Aren't you Daddy's little turdlet today?"

"Toodlet!" Benson shouts.

Shaking his head, Forrest begins the laborious process of removing all his layers. Gloves, hat, scarf, another neck wrap, then coat. "You know, I don't think that's healthy, calling him a turdlet."

"*Of course* it is. Daddy is the big turd and Benson is the turdlet."

Pam breezes in and makes a strange noise with her mouth, a combination of tongue click, raspberry, and exaggerated sigh. "Really? You can't keep him clean for a single minute, can you?"

She plucks the child from Sven's arm and sets him on her hip without so much as breaking her stride. Through some mysterious alchemy that only Pam seems to have, she tickles her finger under Benson's chin, and he laughs in delight. All the anger is gone, just like that.

Forrest and Sven watch her bump open the baby gate into the kitchen with her hip and disappear with the child.

"How does she do that? Why doesn't it work for me?" Sven asks.

"Magic," Forrest says.

From beyond the wall where the laundry room is tucked, they both hear Pam yell out, "Because you're a big turd!"

He laughs. What else is there to do?

Part Three

Coco

Coco's Journal: Age 34

Year 22 of the Loop

Sometimes, when I watch Joey, I can't help but wonder what it all means. Is he—and are all the special children like him—a signal that there is some way to correct what's happened? Or is it what the Chosen say it is, an adaptation of some sort? Rapid evolutionary change. Is it, as they insist, proof that we are meant to create the so-called new world?

I have such a hard time accepting their explanation that I cling to the Seeker version. It's when I watch him, so young and free and utterly at ease, that I wonder if I'm somehow hampering him by believing as I do.

Then again, we were all young and free and utterly at ease once upon a time. The world didn't care. The looping happened anyway. I suppose all I can do is try my best to let his childhood last for as long as it possibly can.

And this strange gift he has. What is it, exactly? How is his small body able to hold such an ability? How are any of the children able to do what they do? I'm not sure we'll ever know, or how we could even begin to understand it. It's not like we have scientists in modern labs overflowing with cutting-edge equipment. We're lucky we've got indoor lights and cold-water plumbing.

Not knowing why this gift is showing up in children doesn't mean we have no information. We have some, and it's important. A census done after the discovery of this strange phenomenon provided tantalizing hints as to which children might see the looper paths and be ignored by the loopers. There are two known factors that will increase or decrease the likelihood of a child being born special.

The more time the parents have spent in close proximity to loopers, the more likely they are to have children with the gift. That means people like me, with my thirteen years spent in the midst of loopers, are primed to bear children like my Joey. Forrest, too, since most of his time was spent on expeditions rather than in settlements.

The other factor is time since the looping began. As more time passes, more gifted children are born. The current consensus holds that, in time, all children will be born this way. Of course, the Chosen grabbed onto that nugget as proof they were correct about creating a new world.

As it stands now, the oldest children we have found with the gift are sixteen years old, which means they were born only five or six years after the Looping began. There are only three of them in the Seeker communities, which means it was very rare then. Their gift doesn't seem to be as strong as it is in some of the younger children, but strength is difficult to judge when there are no adults capable of seeing what the children see.

It's remarkable to me that this momentous change was happening without us recognizing it. I suppose it shouldn't be such a surprise. Isn't that the nature of parents and children? Our instinct was to protect our young, to keep them away from the dangerous loopers. Only secured behind walls could they play and be loud and do all the things children need to do in order to grow up strong and healthy. It was only when we lost control of that division and a child went into danger that we found out there was no danger after all. How strange life is.

One

Year 22 of the Loop

Coco watches the children as they play during recess. School is less haphazard than before, which is good for keeping schedules and working. It also means she misses Joey during the day. He may be eight years old, but he'll always be her baby.

He's running around with the other kids, playing some game that makes little sense to Coco, but it's clear they're having fun. He has Forrest's good looks, but there's a lot of her in him, as well. The way he looks up at her from under his brow with those long lashes reminds her of her little brother, whose face she hasn't seen in over two decades now. Sometimes the reminder is painful, but it's also good. She doesn't want to forget the faces of her family, no matter how many decades pass.

Tamara plops down on the bench next to Coco. She's grown so much older in the past few years that Jorge and Coco worry for her health. Tamara claims it's only menopause, but there's something else going on.

It sometimes seems like Tamara is being honed or whittled, small bits of her removed so that her features are sharper, her bones somehow more prominent. Even the fit of her clothes is different, despite the fact they aren't loose or tight or anything specific. The fit is just different.

It's that and a thousand other small things. Each one is a worry tugging at Coco's heart.

"You ready?" Tamara asks, then glances at her watch. "We're supposed to be at the gate in about twenty minutes." A couple of children holler her name and Tamara waves, a wide smile on her face.

For a moment, Coco says nothing as she looks her friend over. Is her complexion less tan? A hint of something pale or gray in the tone?

When there's no response, Tamara turns to look at her. A look of irritation quickly replaces the question in her eyes, which she rolls. "Seriously? I'm fine!"

"Something is wrong. I know it," Coco says. This is territory they've traveled too many times lately. Tamara is losing patience with Coco's incessant worry, and Coco is losing patience with Tamara's avoidance.

Sucking in a deep breath, Tamara closes her eyes for a moment. When she opens them, she shifts on the bench enough to take Coco's hands in hers. "Listen," she says, using that overly calm tone that signifies she's really irritated, "I promise that I have no information on any specific thing that is wrong with me. Period. Dot. End of story."

Coco narrows her eyes. "That's oddly specific."

Tamara releases her hands with a frustrated noise. "You're impossible."

There are so many paths forward in the conversation, most of which Coco has taken in the past without a lot of success. The practical aspect of losing one of the community's most capable members. The heart tug of what losing her would do to Joey. A hundred more.

Instead, Coco says what's in her heart. "I can't lose you, Tam. I don't know how to live in this life without you. I can't lose one more person. Not one more. Your face was the first one I saw after all those years alone, and the very idea of you not being in this world makes me want to crawl out of my skin. If there's something wrong and I don't do everything possible to fix it, I'll go crazy. Completely crazy. This world takes everything, and I won't let it take you, too."

Her expression softening, Tamara squeezes Coco's shoulder. Understanding seems to pass between them for a moment. No words are needed. Then, the moment is over. Coco knows something is coming when one of Tamara's eyebrows shifts upward and her lips quirk. She says, "Control freak much? Damn, Coco, I mean, it's good to be loved, but context is everything. There was a vibe there, like a distinct stalker vibe."

Coco pushes away Tamara's hand with a sigh. "You're terrible."

"I am," Tamara agrees with a grin. "I really am."

They sit together in the sunshine for a minute, watching the children play, then Tamara slaps her thighs and says, "Okay, enough of that bullshit. We've got less than fifteen minutes till we have to be somewhere, so I'm going to be straight with you. Once I do, then I want you to promise me that you'll believe what I tell you and you'll stop worrying so much. Stop wasting time and enjoy the ride. Agreed?"

Coco nods. "Yes, agreed."

"It's completely true that I know of nothing specific wrong with me. I wasn't lying to you. The catch is that I have no way of knowing if there's something really wrong with me outside of a few basics. No one does anymore. Those days are over. We can't even do most blood tests. The only women getting mammograms are the loopers stuck getting their boobs squished in the machine over and over."

Pausing, she waves a hand at the playground and all the children. "Everything we do is so that they will have those luxuries again. So that they can expect to live as long as our parents did before the Looping began. You and me? No, we don't have that option. Well, maybe you, because you were a kid when it started. But everyone my age? No. We've had too many untreated illnesses, eaten too much old, bad food, and had way too much panic and stress. On top of that, not one of us had even the most basic preventative care. Do you get it now? Do you understand?"

It's a lot to take in. It's not as if Coco never thought about all that. She had, just not in the context of how it would affect her friends. "Yes," she says, then makes a face. "What I don't get is how you're okay with it. So... I don't know... casual about it."

Tamara snorts. "Oh, I'm not casual about it. Not even remotely. Unlike you, I won't let it run my life. Whatever I have left is mine, and I'm not giving over even one day to worry and fear."

"I see."

Tamara shakes her head, and they fall silent for a moment, watching the children play. She smiles as she turns back to Coco. "I know it's hard to understand, but maybe this story will help.

"My grandpa died of a heart attack when he was sixty-two. It was in front of all of us at a big family gathering in his backyard. Keeled over while he was laughing his ass off in front of the grill, turning the meat and filling the air with drool-worthy smells. He had a bottle of cold beer in one hand and his tongs in the other. Until that moment, it was a perfect day. The sky was so blue people remarked on it. Clouds so detailed and sharp they looked fake. The air was just right, not too hot or humid. People were splashing in the pool, and everyone was laughing. The tables had nets over them for the flies, but us kids kept sneaking under the table and reaching up to snatch deviled eggs. Perfect."

When Tamara trails off, Coco frowns and says, "That is an awful, traumatic story. Is this supposed to make me feel better about you?"

"Sorry, got carried away. And yes, it was horrible and traumatic at the time. You don't need details, but the important thing is what happened later. My great uncle, my grandpa's brother, died just one year before the Looping began. He had cancer... twice. It took years, and for the last few of those years, he was genuinely unhappy and unwell most of the time. During a visit, when his wife left the room, he said something to me that matters here. My grandpa was the lucky one, he told me. He died too young, but he died so fast he never even knew it was happening. He died happy, with everyone around him laughing and having a great time."

Coco understands. Smiling, she says, "So, you want us to be happy. To party at the grill and not worry too much about the end of the party."

"Yes. That's exactly what I want. So, can we go now, or do you need more therapy?"

"You're still terrible," Coco says, then stands to scan the playground. Her eyes find Marla, the housemother who watches the children when their parents are gone. She has the most glorious head of curly, unruly hair. Coco always wanted hair like that when she was young. Raising her hand in a wave, she calls out, "Marla!"

The older woman smiles and waves back. "I've got it," she says.

They don't need more than that. Coco will be gone for a few days on a supply run—maybe more, depending on how quickly they proceed—and Joey is staying with Marla.

Tamara is silent for a moment as they walk, but she finally says, "You know you can stay back."

Coco shakes her head. While she technically could, she *can't*. She's one of the fastest and most agile of the adults. She's also had more experience than anyone else getting through loops, thanks to her thirteen years alone. It's a no-brainer that she should make this trip.

Jorge could stay, but he's incredibly fit and strong for his age. It's hard to believe he's in his late forties. No one believes it when they meet him. Tamara is going as their medic. She's the only field medic not out on some other expedition, and the two nurses they have need to stay behind for the community.

And they definitely need to bring a medic. Half the people going on this expedition probably shouldn't because of age-related problems. The age imbalance of the surviving population is one of the oddest things about the post-looping world. Most are either very young or a senior citizen… or approaching it, anyway. Most who survived the looping were mature enough to remain calm. Young people like Coco rarely made it. The old, who often needed too much medication, didn't survive.

The population of the unlooped skewed early middle age, which means virtually all of them are getting up in years. It's been twenty-two years since the looping began. The settlements are graying but are also filled with children and adolescents born to women almost too old to bear them.

Coco and Tamara are the last ones to arrive at the gate. Everyone else is standing around, looking uncomfortable. Expeditions like this are necessary, but no one likes the idea of breaking loops. Sometimes, it can't be helped. Medications are usually the items that tip the scales, and if they go to a pharmacy or grocery store to break a loop for medicine, they might as well take it all.

Sometimes, Coco wonders how much Seeker the Seekers still have in them. It seems the lines they won't cross grow blurrier every year. But the decision has been made, and she can't deny that being useful out in the world is something she has missed. A lot.

She consoles herself with the knowledge that they don't break as many loops anymore. That's because of the gifted children. The oldest of them in Solace, a sixteen-year-old named Malia, will go with them on this supply run. What she and the others like her can do has changed everything. They can see what will stay behind when a loop is broken.

It's easy to see what items aren't looped. Coco just looks for the dust, the dirt, the faded wrappings. Looped things appear new, because in a way, they are. Each loop, they reset. Sometimes those looped items stay behind when a loop is broken, and sometimes they disappear.

Until they discovered the gifted children, no one ever knew what would stay behind and what wouldn't. It was a wasteful, terrible guessing game. No longer do they have to guess. Malia can tell them before they break a loop.

Yes, they will still have to break loops. Yes, under the Seeker definitions, that means they're killing people. It's not anybody's first choice or even their fourth choice. At least this way, they aren't doing it on a guess and hoping to get the items they need. This way, nothing is wasted… especially not lives.

Pushing away grim thoughts, Coco focuses on the good they'll do. Someday, it might be Joey that needs what they'll liberate from the grocery store pharmacy today. That makes it worth it.

Coco focuses on the group around her, watching Jorge give the standard speech he gives every time a supply run departs. He's so incredibly competent and comfortable in his role. She loves him for that, and for a thousand other reasons. It took some time after Joey was born, but suddenly the love was there, and he wasn't just a best friend, but something much more. He sees her smile and winks.

Once a few questions are answered and last-minute hugs and kisses dispensed, the group exits the gates and heads for the ferry. Coco smiles at Tamara, giving her a one-armed hug.

"Ready for another adventure?" Coco asks, still smiling.

Coco's Journal: Age 34

Year 22 of the Loop

Something that keeps surprising me is how clean and smooth loopers are. I get used to the way we look now, see it as normal, then find myself shocked when I see a looper. Usually, I wind up staring into the mirror and scrubbing my face when I return home. They have such shiny hair, such beautiful skin, such clean clothing. They even smell good. Maybe that's why I always look at people's hair first. It stands out on the loopers. Salon smooth, freshly cut, dyed, curled. Now, someone with amazing hair is a rarity.

We're not savages or anything. I realize that, but I can't deny we're different. All the little niceties just don't exist for us. If given a choice between bringing back a bag of flour after a loop is broken or a few bottles of face cream, we'll always choose the flour.

Well, mostly we will. I admit to a fondness for Oreo cookies. No matter what, I'll find space for a package of Oreo cookies.

I was reminded of this recently. We broke two loops to get to a grocery store and pharmacy. I felt awful about it, but the real news is that we didn't break any of the other loops in the store. Those people are all still there, still looped and doing the same things they've been doing for twenty-two years.

All because of the children. It's so strange. It's taken years to understand their gifts. And right about the time we think we've got it, some new facet shows up. Something else for us to wonder over and, at least for me, fear a little. My Joey has such a strong gift. I know it will make his life easier, but I worry for him.

Jorge tells me we'll probably keep seeing new aspects of their gifts as they grow up. He thinks it's like any other part of their body and will change as they grow, like baby teeth giving way to permanent ones or stronger arms and legs. I'm not sure I'm ready to see what that will mean.

Two

Year 22 of the Loop

"Why does he shove the socks under his bed?" Coco mutters as she lays flat on the floor to reach for the sock in question. "It's not like the hamper isn't right there."

"Did you say something?" Tamara calls from the bathroom across the hall. It's her turn to scrub the tub. Coco doesn't envy her that.

"Nothing. Just talking to myself," Coco calls out, grabbing the sock. It's filthy. Of course it is.

Getting back to her feet, Coco tosses the sock into the overflowing hamper and sighs. Joey's room is a mess and his idea of cleaning it up is kicking all the evidence into the corners. With him playing outside and her off work, it's time for a real cleaning.

Eyeing a suspicious lump under his bed covers, she flings back the coverlet to find the clean sheets she gave him two days ago at the bottom of his bed. The old sheets are still in place. And this is after insisting that he's old enough to take care of his own room. She shouldn't have agreed.

"You have got to be kidding me!" she exclaims, grabbing at the bundle.

Tamara comes to the doorway this time. "What now?" she asks, smiling.

Coco holds out the sheets and shakes them. "He told me he was old enough to do this on his own."

"And he is. That doesn't mean he's going to do what you say when you say it." Tamara laughs at her expression. "It's part of growing up. All kids do this kind of stuff."

Rolling her eyes, Coco looks at the bed. "Fine. Okay."

"Want help?"

Coco sighs. "No. I'm just irritated." As Tamara turns away, she says, "Wait. Tam, will you help me turn this mattress? I might as well go whole hog."

"Sure thing. Actually, we should do them all. Mine hasn't been turned in a really long time. I don't even want to say how long."

Whipping off the sheets, Coco grips the edge of the mattress and says, "Okay, here we go."

Even as she hoists the mattress onto its side to flip, she sees the collection of items secreted underneath. It's too late to stop the toss, and as Tamara pushes the bottom back toward Coco, it shoves dozens of candy bars off the edge of the box spring to land around Coco's feet.

Tamara must hear the noise, because as Coco takes in the sight, the other woman walks around the bed to get a look. She chuckles. "No wonder he wanted to take care of his own room."

Coco stares at the candy, but there's nothing funny about what she sees. Bending, she picks up one of the candy bars. The wrapping is bright, smooth, and undamaged. She picks up another. The same. They're all the same. There are at least three dozen of them.

"Oh, no," she whispers.

Kneeling to join Coco on the floor, Tamara gathers the candy bars. She nudges Coco with an elbow. "It's not the end of the world, Coco. It's just a thing kids do."

"You don't understand," Coco says, eyes still glued to the candy.

Her tone must cut through the humor, because Tamara puts her handfuls of candy on the bed and touches her arm. "What's wrong, Coco? What don't I understand?"

Coco holds the candy so that Tamara can see the label. "Don't you see? What's wrong with this picture?"

For a moment, Tamara looks confused, but it clears. Her hand rises to her mouth. "It's new! It's fresh from a loop." She pauses and looks at the collection of candy. "It's all new."

Coco feels like her heart has an anchor on it. Joey can see what breaking a loop will leave behind, including candy. Which means…

"Wait," Tamara says. "Even if he broke a loop to take the candy, where would he find it? There's nothing like that inside the walls. The loops here were broken before anyone settled here. Did he go beyond the wall? Out into the rest of the town?"

Coco hadn't even thought that far ahead, but Tamara is right: He would have had to go into the uncleared parts of town, and he would have had to do that by himself. Or, maybe with other children. This situation was going from bad to worse.

Without a word, Coco marches out of the room toward the front door.

Running after her, Tamara says, "No, Coco. Maybe you should wait to calm down. Maybe talk to Jorge first."

"Not happening," she says, flinging open the front door. The children are playing in a clearing across the street. It takes only a moment to spot Joey, kicking a ball with some friends.

"Joey Christopher Wells! Get in this house right now!" Coco shouts from the porch.

Joey stops immediately, and Coco can hear the chorus of "Ooh" and "Somebody's in trouble" from the kids around him. Head hanging, Joey walks toward the house. He does it much slower than he needs to, but Coco is already regretting the yell, so she crosses her arms and waits. She's yelled at him no more than a handful of times in his life.

Her heart almost melts when he precedes her into the house and stops in the living room, avoiding her gaze. As she closes the door, he says, "I'm sorry, Mom. It was an accident."

That surprises her. The candy was an accident? Or something else? "What was an accident?"

"The picture frame. I didn't mean to break it." He looks at the wall over the couch where a print hangs. Sure enough, there's a badly done patch she hadn't noticed, bubbles of dried glue all over one corner.

Shaking her head, she points toward his room and says, "March."

Shoulders drooping and head bowed, he shuffles off. As Coco follows, Tamara mouths, *Stay calm.*

As they enter the room, Joey is already rushing to pick up the candy bars strewn all over the floor. He looks up and says, "I wasn't going to eat them all at once. I *promise.* I only have one a day. Just one."

Sitting on the bed, Coco pats the space next to her and Joey drops the candy to join her. Taking a deep breath, Coco says, "Joey, this isn't about eating candy bars. It's not even about hiding candy, though that's bad enough."

Pausing to find the right words, she plucks one of them off the bed. Coco can't help but wonder if this is all her fault. Did she minimize what happens to loopers when they're broken to avoid talking about death with her child? Probably. It's too complex a subject for a kid, too heavy a load to bear. Perhaps he just doesn't understand what he's done. And that's saying nothing of the danger a broken looper represents.

She pushes her hair away from the scar on her forehead. "Joey, look at my head. Do you see my scar? Haven't you seen the scars on all the other people? Loopers don't seem dangerous to you, but if one breaks while you're around, you're still in danger. And my scar is nothing compared to what can happen. Do you understand that?"

He nods, eyeballing her scar. She's never told him how she got it and isn't sure she ever will. He doesn't need details. He knows she got it when a loop was broken, though. That's enough.

"Speak up," she says.

"I know, Mom. Loopers can hurt me if they get broken, no matter who breaks them."

"I'm glad you understand that." She pauses, readying herself for the next part. "Joey, you know we don't break loops to get candy. We don't break loops unless we have to. Do you understand that loopers are real people? They're stuck in a loop, yes, but they're still real, just like you and me. Honey, we can't break their loops unless we absolutely must. Do you… do you understand what happens when a looper disappears?"

Joey almost looks annoyed, which is not what Coco expected, and it doesn't make her happy.

"Mom, I know. They die, just like Mr. Ferrell down the street who died and then we had a funeral and he got buried under the ground and he can't ever come back. I *know* they're real."

Coco is appalled. How can he possibly be this casual about what he's done? She holds up the candy bar. "So you thought it was okay to do that to a looper for a candy bar? I don't even know what to say to you right now."

"Mom—"

"No, don't you Mom me. And where did you get it? Did you go somewhere beyond the wall?"

"I went to the place with the magic gas."

For a second, that brings Coco up short. Magic gas? Then she realizes where he must mean. It's one of the few places he's ever been beyond the wall. There's a large gas station and convenience store that has gas on a fourteen-hour loop. They use it for generators and big equipment when they clear fields. Eternally refilling gas—magic gas. Joey went with Jorge once to fill up the gas trailer. Then she remembers where it is.

"That's more than a mile away! Across the bridge! How did you get there? Who else did this with you?"

"No one, Mom! I walked. It's not that far. And you can see fish in the stream when you go over the bridge."

"Honey, I just don't understand why you did this. If you know that loopers die when we break their loops, then—"

"Mom! I didn't break any loops!" Joey shouts.

Tamara and Coco share a glance, both confused. Either he doesn't understand or something else is going on. Did he just happen to go inside the store after the loop was broken? No one mentioned the gas station getting unlooped, and Coco is certain that would have been news.

"Mom, I didn't. I promise. I didn't have to. You don't understand."

"No, I don't," Coco says. "Explain it to me."

He looks up at her, then away, like he really doesn't want to tell her whatever he's about to say. "Sometimes when the farm is busy, some of us kids go to the bridge and sometimes we go to the gas station to smell everything and look at all the stuff."

Coco can feel her blood pressure going up, but she purses her lips and says, "Go on."

"You know how I can tell when something will go away or not? Like the colors. Stuff that will stay is brighter, right?"

She nods.

"Well, a few of us noticed that if you put your hand close to things, you can sometimes feel a tingle, like when you brush your hair and it crackles. You know, like…"

"Static electricity? Like the blankets in winter that make sparks sometimes?"

"Yeah, like that. So, we liked to see what things would tingle and what didn't. Then one day, I just took a candy bar. A tingly one. I don't know why I did it, but I did. They dared me to eat it, but you told me I could get hurt if I ate something that disappeared, so I didn't. I hid it instead. The next time I went back, it was still there. It didn't disappear. I was by myself, so I ate it. It was so good."

"Hmm, I bet. But I don't understand. If it was looped, why didn't it disappear?"

Joey shrugs. "I don't know. But if you feel the tingle, then you can take it. It makes me really tired though. And sick sometimes. I threw up once when I tried to take too many. So, I only take a few every time." Glancing at the candy bars strewn all over, he adds, "I went a lot of times."

At this revelation, Coco's mind switches gears from mother to survivor in the span of a heartbeat. "So, there are other kids who can do this?"

"I don't know. I know some can feel the tingle, but I went by myself to get the candy. I was kind of afraid to tell anyone because they might tell on me. I wanted to keep my candy."

Tamara and Coco look at each other. Shaking her head, Tamara says, "This could change everything. I'll go get Jorge."

Coco nods, and Tamara takes off without another word. She wishes she could keep this a secret. This new twist of the gift doesn't make her happy. It makes her even less happy than knowing her son is gallivanting around in uncleared territory by himself. If he can do this, if other children can do this, then the burden placed on them will be far heavier than any child should have to carry.

But if he can do this, it isn't her secret to keep. The best she can hope to do is understand it.

"Can you show me? When your father gets back, if we take you to the gas station, can you show me how you do this?"

"Yeah! Can I get more candy?"

Coco's Journal: Age 36

Year 24 of the Loop

It's strange what a person can get used to. Good things and bad things and incredibly weird things. We just got back from a scouting and supply run, which is normal. What shouldn't be normal is that I brought my ten-year-old son with me.

Watching him run his little fingers over rows of items and plucking out a few without them disappearing has become almost unremarkable. He can actually take something out of a loop and it will stay behind. Not disappear. It was hard to accept that new reality, but now, it's the new normal. At first, he couldn't take anything heavier than a few ounces, but yesterday, I watched him take an engine part that weighed well over a pound. We needed it for the farm equipment.

Some of the council are making noises about sending children into the busiest places, like the home improvement stores that have hundreds of loops inside. They insist it's safe for them, but I'd pack us up and be gone from Solace if anyone tried to pressure me into letting Joey do that.

Even so, it's weird to watch him do what should be impossible.

Sometimes, I feel like I'm raising an alien, not a child. The irony is that I very distinctly remember my mother saying the exact same thing about my older brother. Maybe all children are aliens to their parents at some point.

Three

Year 24 of the Loop

At ten years old, Joey no longer wants to hold his mother's hand. When she reaches to take it, clasping his hand in hers, he makes a face and says, "Mo-o-om."

Coco pats his sticky fingers, then bends to kiss them before letting them go. She smiles, though it really breaks her heart. She wonders if this will be the last time. He's growing so fast.

He runs ahead, short legs pumping through the tall grass of the large field. When he catches up with his current best friend, they squeal and run together, leaving their mothers behind. Within moments, they stop to tussle in the grass, laughing wildly.

Noises like that still make Coco's belly clench. It's an almost instinctive reaction. Not so for the children. They can make as much noise as they like. The parents are the ones who must remain silent. She catches up to Marla, who was also left behind by her child.

"It must be nice to have knees that can take that kind of abuse," Marla says, smiling after the two kids.

Marla was forty-four when her son was born, so she's one of the oldest of the moms. Her hair is still a wild profusion of uneven curls, but it's grayer every year. It's still beautiful, though.

They walk in companionable silence for a while, then Marla reaches out to touch her arm. Quietly, she asks, "How are you doing, Coco? You holding up? I know it's been a few months, but I haven't asked since the funeral."

She means Tamara. Has it really been a few months already? For Coco, waking up and realizing she wouldn't see her ever again is a fresh pain every single day. Her death is still a mystery, but their best guess is heart disease. She'd been getting tired more easily, her face growing strained at effort she would have laughed off a year earlier.

One night, she went to bed, and the next morning, she didn't wake up. She was just fifty-eight years old. Oddly, that story Tamara told her about her grandfather and the heart attack at the grill kept running through Coco's mind. She didn't get that death, but it wasn't that far off. It didn't make her absence easier, but it was something to cling to.

"I'm okay. The house still seems empty, though. Tam was a big presence. She filled up a room."

Marla pats her arm. "It will for a while. That just means you loved her, and that's good."

As they near the border of the field where it meets the forest, the children stop at a post with an orange flag and wait, though Coco can hear the complaints even at this distance.

The field west of town has been clear for years. It's lying fallow this year, but in other years they grow crops on it. Bordering it is a forest that seems to stretch forever. The Chosen cleared parts of it ages ago, then stocked deer and other species once it was safe. Not all of it is cleared of loops, though. It's not a place for adults to go without caution.

This particular section is also a training ground for the children. Here, they can learn to trace loops without the confusion of looped people. They can hone their skill at spotting the strange echoes they can see in looped animals and insects. They can grow more comfortable using the gifts they were born with.

It's also a good way for the adults to measure that gift, because not every child has it at the same strength. Some see the trails of light dimly, while to others, it's as bright as a beacon. Tracing loops and seeing paths takes practice for some, while others do it as naturally as walking. Joey's ability is on the stronger side. That's not to say he doesn't need practice. He does.

For a long time, Coco tried and failed to imagine what the world looked like to Joey. It just wasn't something she could fully grasp. Two years ago, another settlement sent word that they'd discovered the answer. Someone found a book of artistic, urban photography. The settlement intended it for use in their school, so children could see what cities once looked like.

Inside, there were a few long exposure shots of people crossing a street at night in a brightly lit city. One of the gifted children asked if they could take pictures of the loopers like that, too. It turned out, the image captured almost exactly what the children saw every single day: Loopers leaving a trail of ever-fading images behind them.

Once the book made its stop in Solace for everyone to see, she'd felt almost frightened at the idea of Joey facing a world where people were visible echoes of themselves. Would he grow to believe they weren't people? Would he only see them as remnants of something gone, or would he continue to believe as the Seekers did?

Only time would tell.

At the flag, every pair is teamed up with their armed guide. Calling their escort a *guide* is a nicety. What they really do is make sure the parent and child are safe if something happens and a loop is broken. Each is armed with a bow and arrows, which are relatively silent and safe to use. Each also carries a gun as a last-ditch weapon. Those are used to signal an immediate and terrible danger, so everyone can run. Today, they are assigned to Rafael, who is just a few years older than Coco.

He was a teenager when the looping began, but fortunate in that he found another person quickly. He was alone for only a few days. Coco likes him, and so does Joey. She lets out a quiet laugh when the two high-five.

The forest is thick, and the light dims almost the moment they enter. A guideline hung with small strips of colored fabric marks their intended trail. The guides change these regularly so the children don't memorize or share the features of the paths.

As they walk under the canopy, Coco relaxes a little. Shafts of light filter in, making some areas seem to glow in vibrant color. The heat and grassy scent of summer fades, replaced by cool shade and the smell of trees and old leaves.

Joey chatters on, pointing out looped animals and insects with excited squeals. The adults are silent. He spots a rodent and a host of insects. There are some birds in trees, but not many. Even without people to disturb them, the remaining loops in this part of the forest are disappearing as the stocked animals take over.

Joey stops. His brow creases as he frowns into the distance. Coco sees nothing except trees and more trees. She glances at Rafael for an answer, but he shakes his head. He points in another direction, where a hawk is stuck in a static loop, forever suspended about twenty feet above the ground.

Leaning close, he whispers, "Nothing else big right here. I walked it yesterday. Just that bird."

Stepping closer to her, Joey almost leans against her hip. He used to do that during his shy years, when meeting new people made him nervous. He hasn't done it in a very long time.

Coco squats and tries to see what he sees. Nothing. Leaning close to his ear, she whispers, "What do you see, honey?"

He looks at her like she's the one seeing things. "The snow. It's right there."

"Snow?" she asks, confused. She places her hand on his brow. The warmth of a boy in summer is all she feels.

Joey pushes her hand away and shouts, "Hey! Can you see me?"

Coco stands and grabs Joey's shoulders, pulling him close as if to protect him. She knows nothing will hear him, but she can't help it. He tugs away, jumping up and down and waving his arms.

"I'm right here! Right here!" His shouts are nearing excited screams.

Suddenly, he rips himself away and ducks under the guide rope, running headlong into the forest, still shouting. Coco stumbles after him, Rafael doing his best to hold her back. Her foot catches as she tries to leap over the rope and she goes down hard, letting out a grunt on impact.

A looped squirrel begins a mad and dangerous chirping bark from somewhere close, but she can't see it. Rafael follows, his bow up and searching. A squirrel or a deer might not be traditionally dangerous, but one on a broken loop is a clear hazard. There are hundreds of viciously scarred faces in the world to testify to that.

Joey is already at least forty feet away and still running. He yells, "Yes, I can see you!"

As Coco scrambles after him, her feet tangling in the underbrush, the hawk suspended in the air lets out a strangled scream. She's making too much noise. It flaps but can't leave the spot where its static loop held it for almost two and a half decades. The wingbeats stop as the bird dies, then flickers out of existence.

Coco stretches her hand out toward Joey, even though he's far beyond her reach. She wants to scream, but a lifetime of silence stops it in her throat. All that comes out is a hoarse, gasping noise.

"My mom is here! Wait! I'm real!" Joey shouts.

As Coco watches in horror, he leaps forward, then seems to bounce backward, as if he's just run headlong into an invisible wall. He sprawls on the ground, entirely still. There's a strange disturbance in the air where he impacted, almost like a ripple or a shimmering heat haze above a long highway.

This time, she screams. A chorus of noise washes over her as untold loops break.

She falls next to Joey, her hands going everywhere at once. His eyelids flutter as she cups his face, so glad to see that small sign of life that she forgets the loops and their noises. A gunshot rings out somewhere else in the forest.

"Joey, Joey!" she exclaims, patting his cheeks.

She's shoved aside as Rafael reaches them. In one swift motion, he slings his bow over his shoulder and scoops Joey up into his arms. He growls, "Move! We have to move! The whole forest is broken!"

He's running before Coco can even get to her feet. She follows, her hands reflexively reaching for Joey's bouncing head. Behind her, the broken loops wail in rage and die.

Coco's Journal: Age 36

Year 24 of the Loop

I used to wonder if maybe we, the unlooped, were the dead ones. I thought maybe we were ghosts, and all we could see of this world was a snapshot. I thought maybe it was the loopers who were alive, and we simply couldn't reach them.

As I grew up and saw more, I almost stopped wondering about that. The proof that we were alive seemed so clear. Now, I have to wonder again. Are we an afterimage? Are we stuck on one side of a line, and beyond that, the world goes on? Am I Coco, or am I only the fading memory of a girl who died long ago?

Four

Year 24 of the Loop

"He's describing hunters. The orange vests and orange hat. The puffy suits for staying warm when you sit in the cold. Even the cooler and the long guns. There's absolutely no way he could know what they were and describe them in such detail. No way," Jorge says, his hands chopping the air. The other local council members nod their agreement.

The meeting is full, but most are silent observers now. So many people asking questions and talking over each other had required intervention. As Coco and Rafael sit in chairs across from the town's current council, she feels the others behind her. She can feel their eyes on her back.

She touches the bandages on her hands nervously. Bird pecks and a nasty squirrel bite. Getting out of the forest quickly came at a price. Rafael got the worst of it since he couldn't even fight off the animals with Joey in his arms. The angry red of new stitches marks one temple.

Joey is still in the clinic, though that's merely a precaution. There were no bumps or cuts on his face to indicate he hit anything solid when he bounced off clear air, but he got a good lump on the back of his head when he hit the ground. He was questioned briefly, but the nurse eventually pushed everyone out, giving them dirty looks in the process.

Another council member cuts in. "And the snow. Don't forget that. Deer hunting season, I'm betting."

The oldest of the group of five councilors nods at Coco. "And he's positive they saw him? Positive?"

"Yes," she says, her throat still sore from the scream, the first in her life as far as she can remember. Her throat didn't like it. "He said at first, they looked around, then one of the two men said a bad word and pointed right at him. He said the thing he saw them through was sort of like a loop trail, but different. It was just hanging in the air, and he could see right through it to wherever those two men were. He doesn't understand it."

"And we don't know if it's gone?" the man asks, glancing from Coco to Rafael and back again.

Rafael shrugs. "No idea. He was out like a light when I picked him up. We cleared out of the forest immediately. I know I didn't see anything."

"No," Coco says when the man looks at her for confirmation. "I also wasn't looking. I was looking at my son. But there was something..."

When she trails off and glances at Jorge for guidance, he nods slightly. She's already told him this part. Coco isn't sure if it was real, or if perhaps panic skewed her senses.

Clearing her throat, she continues. "I'm not entirely sure if I actually saw anything, and I didn't see any hole or snow, but when Joey impacted whatever it was he ran into, there was a sort of... I don't know what to call it... maybe a disturbance? It was like the air sort of rippled. It was a fraction of a second at most, and I can't be sure."

Silence greets her words, then murmurs break out in the crowd behind her. The oldest counselor taps the block of wood they use as a gavel against the table and says, "Quiet, everyone."

No one has to yell for order or anything like that. This world isn't like the old one. The murmurs die away.

"And what about the other children?" Jorge asks, though he knows the answer to that. He's prompting for the benefit of the other counselors.

Rafael's brow creases momentarily, then he understands what Jorge is looking for. "Ah, well, the gunshot alerted everyone in the area. All the guides know to evacuate their team immediately when that happens. There were no other children in sight when it happened, so I doubt any of them would have had any opportunity to see it."

The oldest counselor breaks in. "And how long until we can go back with some of them and see for ourselves?"

Rafael considers a moment, then says, "Probably tomorrow. Most of the loopers in that part of the forest are small. Birds and squirrels high up in the trees, loads of various insects, a few deer. We keep that part partially tied up in loops just for training. Today's incident probably cleared most of the immediate area. The loops are pretty short and tightly routed. Technically, it's probably safe now, but I would wait until tomorrow and go during daylight."

There's some tense and eager discussion amongst the council. They agree to inspect the forest the next day, then the meeting is adjourned. Coco tries to wait for Jorge to join her, but her nerves get the better of her as he talks with another counselor. These after-meeting side talks are the way things really get done in their community, but they're annoying. Now, it's unacceptable. Joey needs her.

Jorge must sense her frustration, or see her nervous pacing, because he waves her on and calls that he'll catch up later. Coco hurries toward the clinic as fast as she can go without running.

The bell hanging over the door tinkles as she enters. The nurse, who is usually at home by now, marches out of a side door as if ready for a fight. Her mouth is already open to castigate the visitor when she sees Coco, then her expression shifts into something more friendly.

"He's finally sleeping," she says. "I put a cot in his room for you, since I figured you'd be staying with him."

"It looked like you were ready to do battle there for a second," Coco says, joining her in the corridor flanked by treatment rooms. "Everything okay?"

The nurse waves her hand dismissively. "Oh, you know, the usual paparazzi."

Now that Coco is here and mere feet from her son's bedside, most of the tension that gripped her during the meeting falls away. She sags against the corridor wall. "No, really, is everything okay?"

"Everything is fine, Coco. I promise. You know how many of the counselors tried to get in to see him before the meeting. While it was going on, we had a few more visits for, quote unquote, clarifying questions. I told them to eff off."

"And no sign of concussion?" Coco asks. It had been her primary concern due to the size of the bump on Joey's head. It was why he was staying overnight for observation.

The nurse shakes her head with confidence. "Not even a little bit. His eyes are clear and tracking. He was hungry. He went to the bathroom twice. His headache seemed to improve after a cool compress, and he says it barely hurts when he presses on it. I finally let him go to sleep."

"Can I?" Coco asks, pointing to the sliver of light shining out of his door. The hallway is dim, with just a nightlight to make it safe to walk at night.

"Sure thing. Do you mind if I pop home for a moment? I'd like to say goodnight to Malia and grab my nightclothes since I'm staying."

The family lives next door just in case of medical emergencies. If Joey is sleeping, then it seems a shame for her to leave her children at home alone. "If Joey really is doing well, and I'm certainly not leaving him tonight, why don't you sleep at home? I can come next door if something happens."

The nurse points to a small rectangular box at the end of the hall that looks like a doorbell. "Actually, you can push that, and it will ring in my house. I'll know what it is and come running."

"Perfect."

"Are you sure, Coco? I don't mind staying."

With a firm nudge, she urges the older woman toward the door to reception. "Go on. The dragons have been slain, so go enjoy sleeping in your own bed."

Silence descends once the bell stops and the door closes. The only time Coco has ever been here at night was during her labor with Joey. Then, the clinic had been active and bustling, with all the lights on and people ready to step in should she need help. Now, it's quiet and dim and it feels strange, like she should whisper and walk only on tiptoes.

There's just one light on in Joey's room, and it's dim. It's enough to see that he's sleeping peacefully, curled on his side as usual, with his hands tucked under the edge of the pillow.

For a few moments, she simply watches him. She has no idea what it must be like to live inside his head. The things he can see and sense are not the same as what she can. The gifted perceive the world so differently that they might as well be a different species.

She smooths his wavy hair away from his face and presses a kiss to his forehead. It's warm from sleep, but it's a good warm. A child kind of warm. He smells of antiseptic and boy. He needs to wash his hair.

Coco retracts her hand when he stirs, but he doesn't wake. As promised, there's a cot made up next to the narrow bed, complete with a pillow and a fresh sheet. A colorful blanket is folded down, ready for her to slide in and rest.

She won't though. There's no way she could sleep, and she knows it.

Before the council meeting, she'd rushed to pack a satchel for the night. She rummages until she finds her book, then moves the chair closer to the lamp. As long as she can look up and see him sleeping, see him breathing, she'll be fine to sit here all night.

An hour or so later, Jorge joins her, and they hold each other as they watch Joey. Coco urges him to go home and sleep in their comfortable bed, but it's useless. Like her, he can't bear to let Joey wake in a strange place without him. There's no room for two in her cot, so Jorge takes the chair next to it. As Coco drifts off to sleep, she feels Jorge's hand clasp hers.

She whispers, "I love you, too."

* * *

The next day, all the gifted children except Joey are led back to the spot. None of them see the disturbance or even any hint of it. There's nothing out of the ordinary. Two days later, when the nurse clears Joey for regular activities, Coco and Jorge take him to the spot. The entire council joins them, each of them eager to be on hand if Joey sees the disturbance again.

Coco's skin almost crawls as she watches Joey tentatively walk the area where he saw the hunters through a gap in their world. Jorge grips her hand while they follow Joey to the spot, all of the council trailing behind them. There's no evidence of the shimmering air she saw before. This is now just a forest, though it's a far quieter one than before with all the loops broken.

After a few moments, Joey returns to his parents. Coco can't tell if his drooping posture is because he doesn't want to disappoint everyone, or if he's still not quite himself after his injury.

Jorge bends to look Joey in the eye. "You okay, buddy?"

Joey nods, his eyes darting to the silent council members arrayed along the path.

"And did you see anything?" Jorge prompts when Joey doesn't offer the information.

"No. There's nothing there anymore."

Coco isn't sure if the council members are disappointed or relieved. Probably a bit of both. There's no denying something happened. The way he bounced off some invisible barrier in the presence of two witnesses is proof of that.

The questions left behind are many, and each is unanswerable. What was it? Why was it there? Why is it now gone? What does it mean?

Using their robust radio network, the news spreads. The big Seeker council requests information, then the inter-community council does the same. There are rumors and counter-rumors. There is hope for some and fear for others.

What there isn't is some sort of repeat of the situation. No one else has seen such a thing, or if someone has, they haven't recognized it. Jorge theorizes that the reason Joey noticed it was because of the difference in seasons. Winter snow against summer's green is hard to miss. Add in that he saw people who looked quite different from the ones he knows, people talking and laughing and dressed for winter, and it becomes a more plausible theory.

Joey is tasked with providing a full account. A rather talented artist from another settlement makes the journey to Solace, using detailed questions to draw Joey's descriptions. It takes time, but once the drawings are complete, Joey says they look just like what he witnessed.

Coco sees the drawings right after Joey pronounces them correct. There's no question these are real people, two men with flaws and quirks a child couldn't dream up. The hunter's orange is just one aspect of that. There are other things, like the way their hair is cut and the hat logos. Coco is sure that Joey has never seen a NASCAR logo in his life.

The portal or tear—which are the two words most often used for the phenomenon—is not what Coco imagined it would be. The drawings show depth and ragged edges that look almost like broken glass, except without the shine.

The council enacts changes to procedures faster than Coco feels comfortable with.

The age of majority is sixteen, requiring a meeting of the local council to ensure the child is actually mature enough to be declared an adult. This has always been an important rule because no child is permitted on expeditions or supply runs. That's been true since before Coco joined the Seeker community. Even the Chosen have that rule. It's common sense.

It seems common sense is no longer enough, however. A child of thirteen can now be allowed on excursions as long as they demonstrate a sufficient level of maturity. On top of that, *all* excursions will now have one of the gifted with them, if possible. They're supposed to be on the lookout for other such phenomena.

But that isn't all of it. Already unsettled by the rapid changes to the rules the Seekers have always lived by, Coco is called for a meeting with a few council members. As she walks into the council room, wondering why she's being called for a private meeting, a council member tells her what they're going to say is confidential.

This makes her nervous. "What do you mean by confidential? And where is Jorge? He's on the council, so why isn't he here?"

The lead council member, a man Coco doesn't particularly like, answers. "This is a conflict of interest for Jorge. And confidential means you can't discuss what we tell you with anyone outside this room."

"Not even Jorge? Are you telling me that I can't speak with my partner, who should be in this room, about what the rest of the council says to me? If so, then we're done here."

Another council member puts out a hand to stop the leader from answering, which is a good move on his part. He's a much better talker. He says, "No, that's not what we're saying. Let me start over.

Confidential means we need a promise that you won't speak about this with non-council members. Not because it's something nefarious, but because the project itself is sensitive. Very sensitive."

Coco narrows her eyes, but nods. "And Jorge?"

"This is a conflict of interest for him. And you'll understand why once we explain the situation. Jorge will be asked the same thing we're going to ask you, but as a person, not a council member. Does that answer your question? And if so, can you keep the information to yourself?"

For a few seconds, Coco thinks about it. It still sounds sketchy, but then again, she hasn't actually heard what they want yet. "Okay. I can do that."

With that, she listens, and she almost can't believe what they tell her. They describe a plan for a joint expedition with Chosen and Seeker members to Texas. Specifically, to a huge complex where one of the world's more powerful colliders existed. It was built ages ago, abandoned by the government before it was completed, then mothballed for some potential future project. Decades later, they resumed work and changed the original plans to incorporate every current technological advance. It opened only four years before the looping.

Like every other place that might cause irreparable harm if loops inside were broken, it's been avoided. The Texas Expedition to the collider will go forward only because they finally have gifted who can make the trip safer. They can get inside without potentially blowing up whatever is there by disturbing loops. The expedition is likely to last a year, perhaps longer.

And they want Joey to go with them.

She is horrified they would even ask this of her, of Joey. She holds up a hand to stop the flow of words. She's done her part and listened. Coco doesn't need to hear anything more.

"Wait," she says. "Let me be sure I have this right. You want me to send my ten-year-old son with a bunch of random people, on an expedition taking him hundreds of miles away, through who knows how many loopers, to a place that might have ended the world, and let him go for over a year on top of all of that? Is that what you're saying?"

A council member holds up a finger, as if pointing out a flaw in her reasoning. "Technically, he'll be twelve when the expedition leaves."

Coco shoots an icy glare at the councilman, who looks down, suddenly very interested in the papers in front of him.

"Well," she prompts. "Am I right?"

The lead council member nods. "Not quite, but yes. The people won't be random. These are experts we're gleaning from a dozen different communities. We need to keep the numbers as low as possible, or the expedition logistics would become unmanageable, but we're all agreed that you could accompany him. Or Jorge, if you decide he should go instead."

Rather than answer this absolutely ridiculous request with anything that might be construed as agreement, Coco stands and walks toward the council chamber door.

"Coco?" calls the lead council member.

She turns toward them, all lined up at their table and looking her way. "Let me be clear. The answer is no. It will always be no. If you ever ask anything remotely like this of my family again, we will pack up and leave. Not just this settlement, but the Seeker community entirely. And if I hear of any other child going, I will tell everyone the kind of absolute bullshit you people are planning. I wish you luck on your expedition, but the fact that you want to take a child... a *child* ... says a whole lot about your priorities, and what it says is not good."

With that, Coco leaves the building and heads straight for home. Before she's finished explaining everything to a shocked Jorge, the council sends a message retracting their request. That the council backs down doesn't ease Coco's mind even one bit. If it takes that kind of threat to protect her child, then how safe are they? How safe is anyone?

Quietly, Coco begins to make contingency plans. She also slips a packet to one of the drivers bringing supplies north. Jorge is always sad when she sends packets to Forrest, but this time, he adds his own letter to the mix. Coco doesn't read it, but she knows he's asking for a promise to keep Joey safe if the worst happens.

When the supply caravan leaves Solace, Coco watches them go, wondering what the future holds in store for any of them.

Coco's Journal: Age 44

Year 32 of the Loop

Jorge and I have always had trouble deciding when to tell Joey who his biological father is. It appears we waited a little too long. Joey is eighteen now and, as hard as it is to believe sometimes that I have an adult child, I do. And he's smart. He knows he doesn't look a bit like Jorge and has only hints of me on his face. He may not know Forrest, but he knows he must look like someone.

As the years passed and Joey grew, it got easier to avoid the subject and simply pretend we didn't need to address the issue. If we told him, then he would be burdened with keeping the secret as if it were shameful. Either that or decide to tell others and risk the bias some would show toward him.

We were right in believing there would be stigma, because we see it in other families and with other children. There's no stigma if the parent shifts camps and joins the Seekers, even if they spent a lifetime with the Chosen first. It's only there for those who have parents on opposite sides of the line.

Stigma wasn't the only reason, of course. Jorge loves Joey and genuinely views him as his son, which is entirely natural. They are so close that I feared, perhaps more than Jorge, this knowledge might mar that wonderful relationship somehow.

Strangely enough, it was Joey who told us in the end. He simply asked if there were any girls in Solace he shouldn't want to date. At first, neither of us understood why he asked the question. It was shocking enough to think I've got a son old enough to date that my brain might have fritzed out for a second. Joey very matter-of-factly pointed out that since Jorge wasn't his biological father, he needed to know if he was related to anyone in town via his unknown biological father. We should have realized he knew.

Honestly, I think Jorge was crushed. He covered it well because he's the kindest person I've ever met, but it was there. I could feel it. Joey is our only child. When we truly became a couple so many years ago, I hoped we might expand our family. No one can say Jorge and I didn't try. For whatever reason, Jorge never managed to get me pregnant. Not in all these years and now, well, it's pretty much too late to hope for that. I think Jorge felt like he was losing his only child.

He didn't need to worry. Once the shock was over, Joey's steadfast love and devotion erased any doubts. Jorge is his father, and that's that. All the rest are details that don't matter.

In other news, I think it's time for our little family to leave our life in Solace behind. We're making our plans to go north now. If we go, we won't come back. I can't believe I'm writing those words. I genuinely thought I would live here forever, or at least until the Looping was fixed. Of course, the words I just wrote are part of the problem. Forever or until the Looping ends.

The Seekers weren't supposed to end up accepting forever. The goal was supposed to be that we end the Looping, or gather as much information as possible so that future generations might end the Looping. Living forever in a small town, generation after generation, simply living our lives and nothing more wasn't what we were supposed to do.

But we are.

I don't think there are any more real Seekers, not in any organized way. We've settled. There are no more expeditions to find clues or information. Not for a while now. To me, it's become clear that the leadership of the Chosen and the Seekers are more alike than different. They both just want to go on and live in this new world. Of course, we have kids and even grandkids now, so who can blame them? We have a pretty beautiful life.

It's because of this that we have to leave, but not *only* that. Yes, we need to return to being Seekers in a general sense, but there's more to it. Jorge found out some things about the Texas Expedition that went out so many years ago, when Jocy was just a boy. The same trip the council wanted Joey to join. And it isn't good news. It throws everything I thought I knew about the Seekers into doubt.

I can't write more about it. Not here in a book anyone might pick up. I shouldn't have written this much. What he found out means we have to go someplace far away from the centers of Seeker or Chosen power. We need to fade away and hopefully, be forgotten.

As for me, I'm torn, and I feel bad about it. I'm also scared, which is so strange. Leaving Solace is a big step and, oddly, I'm frightened. I'm terrified of everything beyond these gates, and I don't know why. It makes me feel so weak, and it's embarrassing.

The other night, I finally broke down and told Jorge how I felt. I was ashamed to admit how afraid I was. I spent thirteen years alone, other than the two weeks with Ruth and the few years I had with Tux. Even thinking about doing that again makes my stomach clench into knots.

I'm not sure what I expected him to say. Maybe soothe me, or encourage me, or something equally supportive. What I didn't expect was for him to say that he was afraid, as well. So, we talked. We talked about what we were afraid of and how we could help each other get through it. It was a good talk, and just what I needed.

I've always been anxious, a bit tightly wound. I know this about myself. It's a good trait when you're young and in the thick of it and need to think fast, but it's not great when you're comfortable and contemplating an unknown future. My mom was the same way, so I came by it naturally.

Jorge said one thing that really stuck with me. He said I could do all that I did when I was young because it's easy to be brave when you have nothing to lose. Or if not brave, then foolish enough to do things that look brave.

Now, I have everything to lose. I have a child, a comfortable life, a home that's been mine for seventeen years, and a job I'm good at that makes life better for the people I care about. I have so very much to lose and giving all of that up for an unknown future takes actual bravery, not just bravado.

Maybe he was laying it on a little thick. He probably was. It doesn't matter, because it helped me understand why I'm frightened, and that will help me do what needs doing.

And then there's this: When we told Joey that we were planning on leaving Solace and asked if he would join us, he didn't answer right away. I thought he might decide not to go. After all, he's an adult.

For several minutes his expression was intense as he considered the information. I got very nervous. Then, he just smiled and asked if they had more girls where we were going than here in Solace, because he was having no luck, and everyone was pairing up except him. Jorge busted up laughing, and that was that.

Five

Year 32 of the Loop

Coco has read enough of the reports to know that the north is a harsh place, but as they approach Lorain, the mellow summer makes those reports seem like lies. It's beautiful, and only a little cooler than Solace. Even five miles away, she can smell a tantalizing hint of water in the air.

Joey is driving, which is a hair-raising experience for both Jorge and Coco. He learned to drive in a world without a memory of traffic laws, so it's more about efficiency than comfort. At eighteen, he's at that age where he feels immortal, and his driving reflects that.

Coco leans over the front seat to tap her son's shoulder and says, "Slow down or you're going to give your father a heart attack."

That's not just dramatic talk. Jorge is fifty-six and his blood pressure medication is a scarce commodity. Most of what's been liberated was used up long ago. There are still endless stocks of it tied up in loops, but finding it isn't exactly easy. His pressure has been inching up over the last five years, and despite being fit and eating primarily vegetables, he's not been able to get it down. Coco worries about him every single time he works in the garden—or when Joey insists on driving.

Joey taps the brakes at her words, glancing at his father. "You okay, Dad?"

With a laugh and a dismissive wave, he says, "Oh, I'm alright. Your mother would wrap me up like a toddler if she could. I'm fine. But, really, you don't need to go so fast."

"I'm only going thirty-two miles an hour."

Coco tightens her seat belt. "Which is, what? About ten times as fast as we walk? Believe me, it feels fast from back here."

The truck was liberated from a loop last year, so it's quite fresh. The gas is likewise from a recent liberation. Being a hybrid, it's an excellent vehicle for them to use for the long haul. That it's one of the last models produced, with the added ability to charge with electricity rather than running purely on fuel, has made it doubly useful.

Coco knows they will need such a versatile vehicle. They aren't going back to Solace.

"Oop, there it is!" Joey exclaims a few minutes later.

A slight rise reveals a vast expanse of gleaming blue water. It disappears again as they traverse the crest and follow the curve. Thick trees line the road, but once they hit the straightaway, the blue returns.

"Oh, my," Jorge says, leaning forward. "That is a lot of water, isn't it?"

Joey laughs. He's always laughed so easily.

It's obvious when they're in the right place. The houses look lived in, with gardens everywhere and a huge, cobbled-together, radio tower looming over everything. A sign on the side of the tower reads, *Lorain Settlement.*

Coco radioed once they got within range, so they're expected to head directly for the marina. She points and says, "Okay, we're supposed to follow this street to the end. He told me the entrance is off to the right."

"Yep, I see the marina," Joey says.

The instructions seemed more complicated on the radio, but the entrance is easy to find. They bump over the railroad tracks inset into the pavement, then onto the marina proper. Once the glare of the sun shifts, Coco sees people. So many people.

Jorge is peering out the window as well, leaning so far forward his seatbelt reaches its limit. "Wow, look at that. The whole settlement must be here."

A man jogs along the back of a massive building, waving them forward. Joey creeps along, never shifting his foot far from the brake pedal, his eyes darting toward the boats in slips to their left. They turn between two buildings, then the lake is back, filling the world with luminous blue.

Coco touches Jorge's shoulder in support. The waving man is Forrest.

There's a big awning that looks like a recent addition to the building. Smoke from barbeques billows into the air and is swept away by the breeze. A huge crowd mingles between a small building further away and the area under the awning. Boats bob on the water just offshore.

When Joey turns off the engine, Forrest approaches. He motions them out, smiling all the while. Coco's heart swells when Jorge hurries to shake Forrest's hand. They exchange a hearty greeting with no awkwardness. The two men stand together, both full of smiles, while Joey helps Coco from the truck. The back seat is a tad cramped when it comes to leg room, so she appreciates the polite gesture.

Through their letters and packets, Forrest knows the status of things. He is aware that Joey has been told he's his biological father. Joey knows that Forrest has two other boys, both much younger than he.

Even so, Forrest hasn't seen Joey since he was a toddler, and Joey has no memory of Forrest at all. Coco is prepared for this to be uncomfortable.

As they approach, her anxiety falls away. Forrest looks Joey up and down, grinning all the while. "Well, you're taller than I remember," he says with a wink. "I've waited a long time to see you, you know." He holds out his hand and they shake. It's a warm gesture, with Forrest gripping both his hands over Joey's. It's sweet.

It's done so naturally that it isn't even remotely like a bomb going off. Forrest is right about Joey's height. He's at least four inches taller than Forrest, and is even an inch taller than Jorge, who tops six foot one. Coco knows it comes from her side. Both her parents were tall people.

Height aside, it is glaringly obvious that Joey is Forrest's son. From their hair to the set of their chins, they are obviously cut from the same genetic cloth. Oh, there's enough of Coco in her son for her to see it, but far more of Forrest.

Once the initial greetings end, Forrest gets right down to business. "I know we've all got a lot to talk about. I've read all the letters and your recent packets too. I've briefed a few of the others, but not in much detail. We'll be able to talk on our own this evening. My boys are staying with Pam and Sven tonight, so we'll have some privacy. That's for later, though.

"Right now, the whole settlement is here. We don't get a lot of visitors, and they're very excited about getting three new folks. This cookout is a sort of tradition. Well, it is when we're not buried in snow. That okay?"

He told Coco some of this on the radio the day before, so it's not a complete surprise. She also understands that he's really asking if they can handle it, if Joey can handle so many new and strange people.

When she glances up at her son to gauge his level of overload, he's staring at something with his lips slightly parted. Following his line of sight, Coco suppresses a smile when she sees a long-legged girl in bright pink shorts disappear between two buildings. Yes, he can handle this many people. No question.

Placing a hand on Joey's arm, Coco says, "Joey's been looking forward to meeting your sons quite a lot, so it would be lovely."

Forrest leads them between the two buildings and into the sunlight. People are talking and laughing. A line of them stands alongside a narrow channel leading from the docks to the lake proper, yelling and waving. When they get closer to the smaller building, which must have been a restaurant or clubhouse in the past, Coco sees a few boats in the water, pairs of people inside all rowing furiously as they race along.

The whirlwind of faces and names makes the time pass swiftly. Plates of crispy-skinned fish and grilled vegetables find their way into her hands. Chilled water flavored with slices of strawberry or cucumber ease her throat after too much laughter and talking. Wet children race past as they squeal in play, their bare feet slapping against the ground and leaving footprints behind.

It's a lot, and after some time, Forrest finds her again and says, "I think Jorge might need to rest, and Joey looks like he's at his saturation point. Are you ready to go?"

She puts her cup on the table meant for dirty dishes. "Oh, you have no idea. This is… a lot."

"Oh, we're a lot for anyone. Nice, though, right? I mean, we might be a bit loud and boisterous, but they're all good people."

She nods and smiles. "Yes, it's very nice. I like them."

"Good!" he says, then leads her out of the crowd. There are a lot of waves and goodbyes, many of them quite loud, but it's exactly as Forrest described—nice. Jorge looks tired, so she slips her arm under his for the short walk to their truck.

Forrest drives them to a small, neat row of attached houses. He pulls into the driveway of the end unit and hops out. "Home sweet home! Bring your bags for tonight and we'll worry about the rest tomorrow."

Coco's Journal: Age 44

Year 32 of the Loop

Despite all the letters and packets and planning, I really wasn't sure what to expect when we went north. I really wasn't. I was picturing Forrest as he was, all intensity and gorgeous looks. Some part of me worried that I might feel the same as I did so long ago. I was worried Jorge would be resentful, or maybe Forrest would because Joey is biologically his. I wondered if Joey might not see his brothers and feel he belonged with them and always had.

It *was* strange, but it was nothing like I imagined. Forrest is just… well… Forrest. It was like seeing an old friend, but nothing more. His boys are wonderful, and they looked up at Joey like they were being visited by someone they'd always missed. He, for his part, seemed entirely at ease. I don't know if that was real or if he was trying not to hurt Jorge's feelings, but when he went to bed and left us to talk, he hugged us exactly the same way as he did every other night of his life.

All told, I think coming here was the right decision. We took a big chance, but I think it's all going to turn out well.

Six

Year 32 of the Loop

With Jorge still wide awake after a long nap and Coco far too wired for sleep, Forrest suggests they use the private time to talk. She wants that, too. There are so many things that need to be hammered out, and she doesn't want to do it in front of Joey. He's too much a part of what needs discussing.

With fresh cups of tea in front of them, Coco says, "I know I sent a letter when it happened, and it's been a few years, but I want you to know I was very sorry to hear about your wife. We both were."

Forrest smiles, but it's tinged with sadness. "Thank you. That's kind of you. I've had some time and I have the boys, but it never entirely goes away." He pauses and looks down for a moment. "It's not my place to say anything, but I hope you'll be careful. Pregnancy so late in the game isn't safe, but she wanted to go through with it. No one should have to go through that kind of pain."

Coco pats Jorge's hand, knowing he must be feeling the sting of infertility. "We are careful, but thank you."

There's an awkward beat, but Forrest recovers quickly. "I've got questions, of course. This is too big to talk about in letters that only come twice a year. Can you tell me exactly what you meant by Joey's differences? The changes with the Seekers. And… well, all of it. I really don't hear much anymore."

"What happened with that, anyway?" Jorge asks. "You leaving the council, I mean. The Chosen rep at Solace just said you'd retired. I mean, I sort of get it. You proxied your votes out more than you didn't because you were always in the field, but retire?"

Forrest chuckles. "Retired? So, that's how they decided to handle it. I never knew."

"You didn't retire?"

"Hah, no. Well, maybe they *retired* me, but it was more like I got kicked off the council entirely."

"Why?" Coco asks. "I mean, you're one of the founders. How does that even work?"

"What else do you do with someone who doesn't believe anymore?" Forrest says with a shrug. "You can't have a Chosen founder who doesn't believe they're Chosen. And it's not like it popped up out of the blue. It was building up in me for years. A lot of years, really. But, with me out of the way up here, busy with a wife and kids, it was easy to push under the rug for a while. My heart wasn't in it. I never liked the politics, and I didn't like sidelines leadership. I grew out of it, but others still believe."

"Then why didn't you come to the Seekers?" Jorge asks.

"Because I don't believe that either." At their confused expressions, he sets down his cup and explains. "All I believe now is that I don't know what the heck happened or why it happened or what we're supposed to do about it. That's all. If I have any label at all, it would be pragmatic. I'm cautiously pragmatic."

"What does that mean, in practice?" Coco asks.

With a sigh, Forrest turns his head, as if he's examining the world beyond the walls. Coco remembers this. It's what he does when he's searching for words. Some things never change, apparently.

Spreading his hands, he says, "I don't know what the people and animals out there are. Are they fragments? Are they alive? Are they echoes of something we can't see? Are they looking at us from some other reality and wondering why we're stuck in little snippets of time? I have no idea. No one knows, as much as they might want to.

"All I know for sure is that every time we release a fragment—or looper, or whatever label you use for them—we do something that we can't *undo*. Not ever. Whether it's a good thing or a bad thing, we can never know. All we *can* know is that it's permanent. It should be done only when there's no other option. I'm pragmatic about what needs to happen and the cost, but I'm not eager to do anything irreversible. I suppose almost everyone in Lorain is like that. Not all, but most."

The official position regarding this settlement has always been that it's a joint Chosen and Seeker venture. It's always been a point of pride that the two camps can create a long-term, successful settlement with both belief systems. Coco wonders if that's really the case.

She asks, "So, this place isn't part Chosen and part Seeker?"

Forrest shrugs again. "Well, technically, it is. There are a couple of folks who still believe the Chosen stuff, for the most part, anyway. A few strict Seekers. But there was already a settlement when we got here, and they weren't either. Most of us just sort of migrated to the middle, then… I don't know… we just lived our lives. We're very isolated up here and our population is just high enough to be all that we really need. It's good. And that means we get news twice a year when the supply missions come to trade, which also means I know bupkis about your situation. Tell me everything."

Coco and Jorge share a look. They'd expected Forrest to have the same knowledge they did, more or less. Coco holds out her hand in invitation toward Jorge and says, "Be my guest, Mr. Science Nerd."

Jorge makes a face at her terminology, but Coco can tell he secretly likes it. "Okay, so you know about the rips, the windows like the one Joey saw when he was a kid?"

Forrest nods, then hedges by saying, "I know all about Joey from your letters, but the last I heard was that there was only one other child who saw a rip. And I know there was something special to do with math from your last letter, but I don't actually understand what Coco meant by that."

Jorge exhales loudly and says, "Wow, you really are out of touch."

"Like I said, neither side is particularly happy with our town, or me in particular. Solace disabled some of the radio tower relays between us, so no one can even reach us by radio until they get to Freeport. With Freeport recently disbanded, I don't know how long that will last."

Coco knew there were tower problems, but not that it was purposely disabled. This is just another reason to be glad they left. The Seekers have been changing for years. The emphasis has shifted from finding a solution to living their lives, which is natural, but even after their settlements were steady and comfortable, the seeking hadn't resumed.

Instead of working to fix the world, the Seekers now seem geared towards the status quo. Building a new world and expanding their reach. They're becoming Chosen in all but name.

"Just tell him everything," Coco says, knowing they'll all be sitting for a while if Forrest knows so little of the state of the world.

Jorge sips his tea, then says, "Here it is in a nutshell. You can ask me all you want later, but this is as short as I can make it. There are two other gifted kids who spotted these windows, but there's a catch: No one can verify the sightings. The windows are gone before another gifted can get there. They don't last.

"For all three of the kids who saw the rips, the parents were young when the Looping started. Both parents spent extremely long periods beyond the settlements. And when I say extremely, I mean like you and Coco. Not only that, but your day-to-day existence was right in the mix with the loopers, not closed off behind walls. Close contact, like Coco in Manhattan. Finally, all three of the kids have some sort of affinity for physics, and the mathematics used to describe physics, that isn't in any way expected or the result of specific training. In Joey's case, we discovered it just a couple of years ago when he was introduced to the basics of the subject at school. It was uncanny. With me so far?"

"Yeah, I guess. Keep going," Forrest says.

"Here comes the interesting part. When I brought up Joey's physics skills during a council meeting, thinking we might add more schoolbooks to the next salvage list, the result wasn't even remotely what I expected. Instead, they said they were aware, and deemed it irrelevant. And he cracked that course in less than a week. Instead of offering him a more challenging schoolbook, which is what we do for any other subject, they said that was all the physics they offered, period."

"Uh, no offense, Jorge, but why would a town council care about one kid's schoolwork? I mean, seriously, why would they?"

Spreading his hands like the answer is obvious, Jorge replies, "We're Seekers, remember? For the first ten years of this thing, all we did was try to find scientific answers to what happened. *Everyone* tried to learn science and math, but it wasn't enough. We needed someone genuinely gifted in the field, a Hawking or an Einstein. So, I was showing them a potential candidate, someone who might be able to help in a real way, someone who, with proper tutelage and resources, might help bring the Seeker dream to life. Not by himself—I wasn't saying he was some math savior or anything—but every mind counts, and minds gifted in that kind of science are rare."

Forrest holds up a hand to stop him and says, "So, what, they just don't care anymore?"

"No," Jorge says and shakes his head. "It was more like they didn't *want* him to learn more, and I got the impression they'd stop him if he tried."

Forrest lets out a long, low whistle, his eyes wide. "So, that would imply they know there's something important he might learn."

"Bingo," Jorge says, touching his nose.

"What about the other two who saw those windows?"

Coco answers with a grim smile, "Both are Chosen and are being held up as some sort of oracles, like maybe they can see the future through the rips or something."

Forest's eyes move quickly over the table, as if he's shuffling a bunch of random pieces together and finally seeing a picture begin to develop. His head bobs in tiny nods to himself, like he's checking off blocks or filling in blanks. When he looks up, there's a small, knowing smile on his face. "The Texas Expedition."

"Yep," Jorge says.

Coco asks, "Do you know what happened with them? Were you out by then?"

Forrest gives a rueful shake of his head. "Oh, I was out long before I was *actually* out. I know they were lost or died, but that's the last I heard."

"That was the expedition they wanted Joey to go on, the one I wrote you about. He was just ten! He would have been twelve when they left. And they were..." Coco pauses to gather herself, then says, "You tell him the rest, Jorge. I can't."

Jorge reaches over to squeeze her hand briefly, then says, "There's more to it, and lots of breadcrumbs to follow on this trail. And yes, that means Joey would have probably died like all the rest of that expedition. When I figured out what happened to them... well... that was the last straw. That's a big part of why we're here now.

"Here's what we know: The closest settlement to the collider is Chancy's Hand, about a hundred miles from the collider. The expedition made it that far on their return trip. They stopped there, spent two days inside the radio room, and used the secure frequency to the main council, the one for both the Seekers and Chosen. Then, they left Chancy's Hand for the Seeker settlement at Russellville, which is another two hundred miles away. They never got there. The only substantial affiliated settlement between those two places is—"

"The first Chosen settlement," Forrest interrupts. "My settlement. The town that I came from."

His expression grim, Jorge says, "Yes."

"You think the Chosen did something to them? To stop them from telling anyone what they found?"

Jorge shakes his head sadly and looks down for a moment, then says, "No. I think they both did, the Seekers *and* the Chosen. It's only when I look back that it makes sense. Whatever it took that expedition two days on a radio to relay, it went only to the inter-community council on a secure channel. And while all that excited reporting was going on, I didn't know it. No local councils knew about it. Not a peep got relayed through to the other settlements."

Forrest breaks in and says, "I got a few lines in a message that said the expedition was lost, but nothing about a report."

Jorge nods. "Just another clue that something isn't on the level. And there's more evidence that whatever happened to that expedition was at the behest of both Chosen and Seeker. Almost all the big council members now live in the same place so meetings can happen faster and easier. Most were already living in one spot by then, so one side couldn't have decided something big like this without the other knowing. I think they decided, jointly, that whatever the expedition found was too dangerous to get out. I think they got rid of the expedition to keep what they found secret."

Jorge makes a face, as if he doesn't want to believe what he's saying, but he keeps talking. "It took me a while to sort this out, but I had over three years to look for answers. I had to be careful, because if they killed an entire expedition, they wouldn't hesitate to add one more body to the pile. It took time to plan something that wouldn't raise suspicion. Eventually, I submitted a proposal for refining oil. Told them I wanted to create a system we could use after we eventually ran out of gas stations. They gave me permission to visit some fellow science nerds and do an on-site examination of a small well.

"I really went down there to find some answers. Only one of my cohorts felt the way I did about the situation, and he helped me break off long enough to hurry my ass to a meeting with a contact in Chancy's Hand. The fact that we have all this skullduggery is proof enough things are getting sketchy. I met with the contact and found out the expedition didn't find an answer in Texas, but they found out where one might be and how to get to it. He'd been keeping his knowledge secret and was almost too scared to talk to me. I'm not the only one who guessed that the expedition wasn't lost by accident. However, the guy came through, and now we know exactly where we need to go to find answers."

"Really?" Forrest asks, surprised.

Jorge smiles. This is his area, and Coco knows he's had to hide his excitement from everyone for an awfully long time. "Yeah, but you're not going to believe where. Coco almost crapped her pants when I told her."

"Where?" he asks.

"Upton, New York. There's a collider there, and they were in the middle of something big right about the time this happened. A looper inside the Texas facility spends her entire loop going around and making sure they're ready to monitor an event happening in the Upton collider. Half the report relayed by the Texas expedition was, apparently, details on this upcoming experiment. They got transcripts and analysis of every loop inside the Texas collider. My contact didn't understand the science, but he listened to enough to get the basics. They were analyzing data on some imminent experiment in Upton. As in, happening right that moment. The place is called Brookhaven."

Forrest glances at Coco and raises his eyebrows. "Does that mean it's close to Manhattan?"

She can't help laughing. Only someone who's never been there would ask that. "Nothing off Manhattan is close to Manhattan." When he doesn't get the joke, she clears her throat and says, "As we would measure it, it's not too far. It's on Long Island, but it's still a universe away in terms of traffic."

"Yeah, true," Jorge says, then pushes on. "I didn't want to talk weird science, but there's more. The Chancy's Hand contact said something super important, though he didn't realize it. The gifted that went on the expedition could *see* things inside the complex. They did some cutting-edge stuff there, relativistic stuff that I don't understand entirely, but the gifted could see the remains of those experiments. They said it looked like snakes of light running right through the ground. It's all over the tunnels, miles of it. I don't think either council wanted that knowledge to get out."

Forrest looks as if he might deny that possibility, then asks, "You think they killed them to stop it from getting out? Why would the Seekers do that? I mean, I can almost see the Chosen doing that, but not the Seekers."

Coco doesn't wait for Jorge to answer, because she knows this answer in her heart. "Because they have too much to lose now. *We* have too much to lose now. The Seekers haven't actually sought for a long time. People have grandchildren. Children and actual grandchildren. We have towns and lives and our own history. No one wants to fix this because fixing it might erase all that we have. It might erase all those we love. I understand their viewpoint. I really do. When I look at Joey and think about someone erasing him from existence, or at Jorge and think that we'll go back to our time and never meet each other, I feel like I would kill anyone who tried that."

She stops talking. Her voice is rising with each word, and she doesn't want to wake Joey. He shouldn't ever have to hear what she's about to say.

"But," she begins with a sting in her throat, "that's what I feel in my heart. My head knows that this world can't go on like it is. Not indefinitely. What happens when the loops inside nuclear plants inevitably decay? Because that's happening, no matter what we want to believe. Things are decaying and those loops will be broken at some point. What happens in coal plants, in industrial hubs, in cities full of pollution-causing materials now kept at bay by the loops?

"I know in the hard part of me that understands reality that we must find the solution. It won't matter that we have children and grandchildren and towns and lives once the rot sets in. Yes, we might erase ourselves by fixing things, or erase our children, or our entire lives after the Looping, but we might not. We don't know for sure. What we *do* know for sure is that when hundreds of nuclear plants go belly up, humanity will be erased, along with everything else in this world. And not easily, either. Not in some instantaneous cosmic reshuffling of time. No. We'll all die painfully and horribly and over dreadful years of suffering. We have to fix this, no matter the personal cost. We have to. There is no choice, only the illusion of choice."

Jorge places his hand over hers, his touch warm and comforting. She knows he understands her, understands entirely how hard it is for her to say what she just said. He also knows that it's true. That's the worst part.

Forrest clears his throat and says, "I know you're upset, and I understand what you're saying, but I have to ask the obvious question here. Does that mean you want to go to Upton?"

Jorge cocks his head. "That wasn't clear?"

"And how exactly are you going to do that?"

Jorge looks confused. "I'm not sure what you mean?"

Forrest leans forward, clasping his hands on the table. "First, you're not going alone. You won't make it. Even with Joey to help you navigate around the fragments, you've got a thousand miles of territory to cover, and most of it hasn't been touched since this started. You need a group, a dedicated one. Second, we're old and beat up. If we don't have a very good plan and about a thousand contingency plans, we'll all die.

"And that brings me to the most important part. My team is here, and I'm pretty sure they'll want to go, but we've all got kids. Small kids. Heck, my youngest still gets cranky when he needs a nap. Most of the kids are still training to get around fragments. We can't do this without time to let them grow and gain some skill with their gifts. We'll need them out there. I could go on. I can create an endless list, but you know I'm right."

Frowning, Jorge says, "I do know, but how can we wait? We have a clue. It's out there. We just have to get to it. And what if the council finds out that I know about Upton? They won't take the risk of me telling someone. They'll probably come for me. You're talking about years of waiting. Years!"

Forrest nods in acknowledgement. "I am. I'm also talking about getting there at all. As of now, the council is unaware that you know about Upton, and I'm sure not going to tell them. We need the time. The kids need to grow and train, the routes need to be scouted as far as possible, and supplies need to be cached. We can't do that quickly, not if we want to do it right. If Upton is the place we need to go, then we need to arrive there alive."

Coco's Journal: Age 48

Year 36 of the Loop

I'm not sure I'll ever understand entirely what Jorge is talking about when it comes to all this. I try, and I'm not stupid, but I'm just not him. I don't get warm and fuzzy when I think about all this crazy physics stuff. Not even remotely.

What's weird is that Forrest isn't like that either, but the two of them are constantly discussing it, hands moving as if they're flying invisible paper airplanes at each other. They like to talk with their hands. Both of them.

Jorge says that the gifted kids aren't actually seeing things like trails of light in a spectrum we can't see. They don't have some intuitive understanding of vectors we don't possess. He says it's different than that.

He says we see in three dimensions. We see the dot, the line, the box. X, Y, and Z. Three dimensions. We reference those three dimensions using time, but we don't really possess time, it possesses us. We are time's passengers.

Jorge believes what the gifted kids are seeing is a glimpse beyond our three dimensions. Not fully or completely, but they are seeing time overlaid on objects. Like we see the box, they can see beyond that into time. What was in the box… what will be in the box… where the box was and where it will be.

To me, that sounds insane. But apparently every time I remember something from childhood or even yesterday, I'm engaging my three-dimensional brain to access an extremely rudimentary knowledge of the fourth dimension. In short, my memories are me accessing what *was* in the box. The gifted are simply better at looking inside the box.

Totally bonkers.

The proof is in what the gifted saw at the Texas collider—the light trails of past experiments. More proof is in those rare glimpses through those windows, like the hunters in the snow. Jorge thinks those weren't some other reality or parallel world or the future. They were glimpses into the past. A small, temporary overlay of the fourth-dimension bridging into our own, if only through sound and light.

It also explains why the gifted can move or push a looped person or animal. Just as I can push a box out of the way because it's a physical object in three dimensions that I understand, the gifted can interact with time in unique ways. For them, it's like pushing a statue to the side, with the looper remaining entirely rigid. They don't react. They simply wink out, then reappear to start their loop at the correct interval. It's the gifted influencing time in ways we can't.

The gifted can also see what objects tied to loops will go or stay. Jorge says that mystery is related to the reason Joey bounced off that window into time as if it were a concrete wall, and why some of them can pluck objects tied to loops and the object doesn't disappear. To them, time is a real and movable thing. Not always, perhaps, but sometimes. The more powerful the gift, the more control and interaction is possible.

It also explains the strange way Joey understands physics and absorbs the math like I would a cake recipe. It's just something he already knows that he needs to be reminded of, nothing more. It's like that because he lives, at least partially, in a world quite different to ours. A world in which non-gifted people glow a little because all our time is wrapped up inside us and is still moving and playing out. Because our potential paths are so varied, our lights are thin, gossamer strands too distant to see, but there, all the same.

Jorge also says he better understands why the gifted vary so much, and why there are so few like Joey. The younger a person was when the Looping began, and the more time in proximity to loopers a person has, the more it changed the person. Whatever happened to the loopers sort of rubs off on us, or maybe infects us. And the younger a person is, the more it matters when it comes to reproduction later. He says it changes our genes somehow, or the way the genes are expressed. The gifted children are born of those changed genes.

For Forrest and me, who both have more time among loopers than anyone else I know, that meant we had a child like Joey. The other two were born to people much like us. Both were explorers who spent most of their time out in the world.

People who stayed in settlements, or avoided expeditions, or cleared an entire area and then refused to leave that space, rarely have gifted children. A few, but not many. It's predictable enough that younger people now want to go and be amongst the loopers to ensure they get a good "dose" of whatever it is.

I'll never tell Jorge this, because I know it will hurt him. It hurts me to think it, but when I consider what other effects Joey might someday have to deal with, or when I imagine possible negative outcomes related to this strange change, I'm glad we couldn't have children together. Not because I don't love him, but because I fear for the children who are now growing up with this inside them. Who knows what might come of it?

In other news, I feel like our long years of planning, working, and waiting might be coming to an end. We've been here over three years now, and Lorain feels like home. It's wretchedly cold in the winter and the wind that comes off the lake seems to slice right into my bones, but there's also that blue sky so sharp and clear it can lift any bad mood. As much as I loved Solace and never wanted to leave, I think I love Lorain even more.

For lots of reasons. The people, the settlement itself, the lack of politics. And, we've been happy here.

When we first arrived, no one knew the information we brought with us. We were just new people for them to get to know. Over time, the knowledge of Upton has spread as we worked to gather a large enough expedition. First to Forrest's inner circle, then beyond. At this point, I'd be surprised if anyone here doesn't know most of it.

We fear the news will spread beyond Lorain. Without radio contact, someone will have to travel over a hundred miles without anyone noticing just to reach the next radio tower, or maybe slip a packet of letters to the driver during the next supply run.

Sadly, I think the only reason this hasn't happened yet is fear. Everyone who knows about Upton also knows the council had everyone who knew about it killed. It would make anyone think twice about telling on us. After all, whoever tells our tale is also admitting to knowing about Upton and makes themselves a target.

I think the part of this whole situation that bothers me the most, the part that really cuts deep, is that I can't deny the world isn't as good as I thought it had become. Despite our differences, the Chosen and the Seekers live in peace. Violence is rare and individual, not pervasive or systematic. With the whole world held still like a fly in amber, there's no need to steal or rob or extort or anything like that. Most of the reasons for violence in our past just don't exist anymore. It's actually easier not to be violent or criminal. When there are only fifty or a hundred people in your day-to-day world, why would you alienate one of them by robbing them of something you can easily get some other way? It's also hard to be a criminal when anonymity is impossible. You can't get away with anything.

I should have known this peace wouldn't last. I should have known that where there are humans, there will be a justification for harm at some point. There's no question that the main council, the leaders of both the Chosen and the Seekers, killed an entire expedition of innocent people who were simply doing the job they'd been sent to do. And when Jorge went to Chancy's Hand, the only one left who knew anything of the expedition's findings was an eavesdropper who'd been wise enough to remain silent about what he'd heard. Everyone else who might have had knowledge disappeared shortly after the expedition did, including two children.

Such an act, or series of acts, wasn't done on impulse. It was done with thought and intent and planning and power. The council had people to act as their agents in the actual killings and disposal of the bodies. Perhaps even more people to act as investigators in locating those who interacted with the expedition. That means there is a system of power and influence capable of enacting such heinous plans and, ultimately, that the world is not what I thought.

If anyone in the council finds out what Jorge knows, then not only will he be in danger, but so will everyone he might have told. Joey and I would be included in that number without a doubt, but also the people of Lorain. There's no way they could let what we know get out into the wider public. Whatever peace might have existed would be shattered if they knew their own council was killing people for uncovering hints of what caused the Looping.

I can't end this journal entry on such a low note. It won't do. And there is happiness in our world. So much happiness. I can't do anything to push away the bad in the world, but I can bring forward the good.

Joey just celebrated three years with his first love, Layla. I know I've written about her before, but I have to say, I'm genuinely happy about this match. She's a wild and brash girl that I can't help liking a great deal. Three years together! If things keep going as they are, I foresee them moving in together. Most people don't bother with official marriages, but wedding parties still occur now and again, so it could happen. With us leaving Lorain in a matter of months, and no end date for our travels in sight, I don't know when they'll be able to settle down. But once it's all over, who knows?

Seven

Year 36 of the Loop

"So, here we are. It's time," Forrest says, rubbing his hands together as if in need of warmth. Coco can tell he's nervous, which is entirely understandable given the situation. "Just hang on for a second with the questions and let me get this out. Can I get some quiet?"

The room is crowded, the air stuffy from so many people breathing at once. There are a few chairs pushed to the sides of the room, but no real room to sit. Fifty people make for an efficient barrier to seeing if one doesn't stand tall. Upstairs, the smallest of the children are being tended by a volunteer. The murmurs and side conversations finally fade, and the room is as quiet as it will ever be.

"We knew it was only a matter of time," Forrest says, with a rueful gesture. "The entire Heinz family is gone, and so is a truck. They're dedicated Chosen, and they left in secret, so I think it's safe to assume they've decided they have enough information to take to the council and that the potential reward is worth the risk.

"Now, the road to Freeport is a mess because no one has cleared all the deadfall from the winter yet, so that gives us some time. Also, they'll have to get much further south before they reach a working radio tower to Solace. If I were them, I wouldn't say anything on the radio, which means they'll probably have to get all the way to Solace and see if they can get in touch with someone on the council in person. Make a deal for their safety, probably. All in all, that gives us a few days, but only a few days. We hadn't planned on leaving until just before the next trade trucks came, so now we have to pack about a month's worth of work into a couple of days. It won't be easy, but we can do it."

A hand shoots up, and Pam's voice follows. "The new settlement isn't ready. Not completely. Do we have time to strip this one for parts?"

Coco knows she means the solar, the precious wood stoves, and all the accoutrements that make life possible in a world like theirs. They have moved some of those items to the new settlement, but not enough. Everyone thought they would have more time. They don't.

As Coco looks around at all the tense faces, she feels their fear permeating the atmosphere. This is a new thing for the people of Lorain. It's new for most of them. Until recently, no one had any real reason to be afraid of anyone else. She feels guilty for bringing this with her. They took in her family over three years ago and have become family. Now, they're afraid and potentially in danger because of that.

To remain safe, the people of Lorain must leave their homes. Given that the council wiped out a few dozen people in an expedition, then more in a town simply because those people *might* have overheard information about Upton, the council will have no choice but to continue their path of elimination or confess what they've done. And given that there's been no release of information or handy confessions, the people of Lorain are certain what's in store for them.

Tyrone floated the initial idea of relocation. He called it "going Roanoke," which Coco hadn't understood until someone explained it was a colony that disappeared without a trace hundreds of years ago. Now, Lorain is going to attempt the same.

Or, at least part of Lorain will. The town will actually split into three sections. The largest part of the population will relocate to a new, hidden settlement, leaving the Chosen and Seeker worlds behind them.

A small group who refuses to believe they're in danger are staying behind in Lorain. No amount of pleading or reason has been able to sway them. It saddens Coco, and she fears for them, but it is their choice.

The final group consists of those who will travel to Upton. Unsurprisingly, many of them are the same people who spent their youths exploring the world after the Looping began. More surprising is that most of them started out as Chosen. It's strange to consider that the Seeker dream of finding the cause of the Looping might be completed by former Chosen.

The new settlement was carefully scouted and lies further west along the Lake Erie coast. It's close to a nuclear power plant, which means the area is avoided by both Chosen and Seeker groups. Hopefully, the isolation will allow the residents of Lorain who aren't going on the expedition to live in peace. The world is large, and with no clues where the new settlement might be, finding them will be unlikely.

A rumble rolls through the crowd as concerns about the limited time to prepare are discussed.

Forrest raises his hands, asking for patience. "I know we meant to strip the town of useful stuff, and I know we thought we'd have more time, but we don't, so we can't. We've got a few days, but we can't wait to leave until we see them coming. Before any search parties arrive, we have to be gone. We know what the new village will need for critical functions, so we focus on that first. Solar and woodstoves are primary. Then, all preserved food and tools. If we have time, we'll go down the list further."

Joey's arm shoots up and Forrest nods in his direction. Joey stands taller and asks, "What about the other people here in Lorain, the ones not going to the new settlement or on the expedition to Upton? There's no way we can hide what we're doing. What's stopping them from following and telling any scouting parties where the new settlement is?"

There are murmurs in the crowd, which can only mean many others are wondering the same thing. At twenty-two, Joey is a fully functional and independent member of this group. He also inherited Forrest's easy way with people, coupled with being influenced by Jorge's keen mind. Coco can tell he asked that question because he knew others wanted to, but likely wouldn't because of how it would sound. Smart. The people need to be reassured that those leading them have thought about that problem.

Forrest waves for Sven to stand and says, "Sven has been handing security, so I'll let him take this."

Sven, who remains a giant of a man despite his gray hair and lined face, raises both hands to quiet the murmurs. "Security is important, yes, but the ones we're leaving behind aren't our enemies. They simply don't believe there's any real reason to worry. That's okay. They don't mind the Chosen or the Seekers in their lives, and that's their choice. They don't think the council would hurt them to get rid of a rumor. Again, that's their choice. *We're* the ones who are choosing to leave all that behind. That said, we *will* have a watch, and as it stands right now, the choke point we've set up will make it obvious if anyone follows. Just be cautious with what you say and we'll be safe."

Another woman raises her hand, stretching tall to be seen, then says, "Do we have enough houses yet? Can we all fit?" There are more murmurs from the crowd.

It's a good question, and the fact that so many people are packed into a single room reinforces how big the Lorain settlement is. Lorain is now one of the largest settlements outside of the initial camps much further south. It's certainly larger than Solace by a mile. There are one hundred and twenty eighty people in this settlement, and it isn't a surprise more than half of that population was born after the looping.

Forrest pats the air for quiet again. "If you don't mind some crowding, there's plenty of room in already cleared houses in the new settlement. That's not due to a lack of cleared homes, but because there aren't enough wood stoves installed for heat. Once there, everyone will make quick work of it. And yes, the area we chose is more than roomy enough for those who are relocating. It's got room for generations of expansion. Truly. The garden space alone is going to make many of you very happy."

"What about the fish? We can't take transplants until the ice melts," a man Coco can't see over all the heads between them says.

His expression rueful, Forrest says, "That's true, but you also can't transplant any until you clear some loops there. On the upside, there are two marinas, big ones. The set up for a new fishery is perfect, including good spots for tending transplants. By the time you're ready, you can either return and trade for transplants or fish from the water yourselves. Either way, you'll get them."

That seems to satisfy a lot of people, because there are tentative smiles and head nods all around.

A heavily pregnant young woman raises her hand and asks, "How long will you… I mean all of you going to Upton… stay and help us get ready?"

"As long as we can," Forrest says.

* * *

With the meeting over, they fill the rest of the short day with dismantling lives. A few houses are stripped bare, and the former occupants crowd in with families who still have heat. By the time they're done for the day, it's late and Coco's hands are chapped and sore. She warms them around a cup of hot tea.

Forrest's small home seems crowded with Coco's family camping in the living room. A handful of the core leadership cluster around the dining room table, chairs close together. Behind her, Joey and Layla are leaning against the back of the couch. Layla's mother, Chantelle, is squeezed in next to Coco.

"Well, this is a shit show," Pam says, then sips from her cup.

"Sadly, she's right," Forrest says. "It is kind of a shit show. Sven, what are the numbers?"

The big man extracts a wrinkled sheet of paper from his pocket. "Sixty-three total are going Roanoke. That includes kids. Out of that, only forty-four are full adults. Six are teens that can pull their weight, which makes an even fifty. Staying here are thirty-one, with twenty adults and teens. That leaves us with a group of thirty going to Upton, including us geezers. We also have kids going with us under the age of fourteen."

Coco thinks about their long journey and the hazards it represents, then asks, "Which kids are coming? How old?"

"Mine," says Forrest with a smile. "I know I said I might leave them behind to keep them safe, but we could be gone for a year or more. I can't do it. David and Richie are both strong on the gifted spectrum. And even though Richie is twelve, I think he can handle it. David is fifteen and close enough to an adult to make his own choice. He wants to go."

"Kiara, you still bringing yours?" Pam asks.

She nods. "Darrell is an adult and Aliya is close enough. Honestly, she would probably come on her own if we tried to leave her behind. She's at that age. Both are very gifted, so that's a plus. As for my wife, she can't come because of her health, as you all know. She really wants me to go and says the kids are old enough to decide for themselves. I don't feel good about it, but… well… you all know the situation. We've got her care in hand."

Coco's heart breaks for Kiara. Her wife has developed severe rheumatoid arthritis. At least, that's the best they can diagnose it. They all know there's no way she could make this trip. It would be torture.

"So, who's the youngest one we're bringing?" Coco asks, moving away from the subject.

"Richie," Forrest says.

With a glance at Tyrone, who has kids at home, she asks, "What about yours?"

He shakes his head. "My wife and I are at odds about this. Sadie, my oldest, is coming. She's grown up and can make her own decisions. My wife is keeping the others at home. She won't come. She understands why I have to, but we have agreed to disagree."

Kiara, sitting next to him, pats his hand. "And I thank you both for your decisions." To the others, she says, "My wife is going to move in with his wife, in case it gets worse for her."

Once they're done with the roll call of who's going, they grab plates of casserole, fully intending to take a break. Instead, they stand around talking between bites. Small side debates and negotiations take place regarding everything from how many vehicles they'll bring to routing considerations. It's a lot, almost too much.

Coco finds Jorge chatting with Layla and Joey. They both like her. She's wonderfully blunt and strong, with an underlying sweetness she covers with humor. She also has the most enormous hair when she lets it go, and Coco has always been a big fan of wild hair.

At the moment, she has it tamed into three thick braids close to her head. It makes her look more adult somehow, the planes of her face more pronounced. Joey calls them her warrior braids.

As she watches, Layla slips her arm under Joey's, laughing against his shoulder at something Jorge says. The three of them are so comfortable with each other. Coco wishes more than anything that it could last, that they could stay here in this settlement and forget everything beyond it.

She almost wishes she could stop time once again so that they could be happy forever. At least, part of her does.

Time has run out for all of them, or at least, it's getting there. Early signs of loop decays were noted some years ago, and it's gotten worse. Loops are being broken by crumbled masonry, buckled doors, or rotten roofs. The world's slow decay is breaking the loops simply by falling apart around them.

Joey and a few of the other very gifted say that they can see some loops thinning, as if they're being worn away somehow.

Recently, a supply group claimed to have seen a pack of dogs, wild and dangerous looking ones who were never anyone's pets. They said the pack targeted a looper at a convenience store door. One attacked the looper, keeping his attention, while the others slunk into the store. No doubt, they also freed the loops inside and ate the food released when they were broken.

In short, the animals that have survived are learning. They are breaking loops to feed themselves. It's an alarming development.

Eventually, something critical will break. They always refer to the easiest example, nuclear power plants, but there are more dangers than Coco can list. Risks abound. Stored munitions could fire off, oil could spread from tankers into the oceans, or toxins from innumerable factories might soak the land. All of them represent a hazard. All of them are vulnerable.

When that happens, and it will happen, those left behind won't have the option to run and hide. They can't hide from the air. Everyone will suffer, Chosen and Seeker alike. No living thing will survive once it all goes boom.

There's no guarantee that those born after the looping will disappear if they fix time, just as there is no guarantee they'll stay. Part of the reason so many are willing to take this trip is the notion that if they discover how to correct time, they will be on hand for the discovery of how to stay present afterward. Coco doesn't know the answers. All she knows is that she's glad this group of people is willing to try and that, in the end, no matter what happens, she will have given her best effort in the company of those she cares about the most.

Coco's Journal: Age 48

Year 36 of the Loop

I don't like feeling like a criminal. I really don't like my boy being labeled as one. That's what this feels like. As Lorain prepared to disband and the people to scatter, I already felt responsible. Now, we've gotten news that the council is calling us criminals. They turned our intention into something bad so that everyone would be on their side and wouldn't believe us about what Upton really is. It's smart on their part. Very crafty.

We'd all wondered if they would hunt down everyone in Lorain like they did the members of the Texas expedition, but we'd also considered how difficult it would be to kill everyone who knew about Upton. After all, Jorge found out. Who's to say one person wouldn't survive and start the entire cycle over again?

I guess the council figured that out as well and decided on a much more effective tactic. Instead of telling the truth or trying to kill us to cover it up, they simply changed the story. Now, rather than being people with a clue about where to go to fix time, we're a group who will put all the world in deadly danger by interfering with the collider's experiment. Propaganda apparently works just as well now as it did before the Looping.

Because of that, I'm packing up an entire lifetime, or what I can take of that lifetime, into the bed of a truck in a hurry. I'm leaving behind a lot, but I'm taking all my notebooks. I have a feeling that I won't be coming back. Whether that's good or bad remains to be seen, but I think this is my last adventure. At least I'm taking this final trip with everyone I love.

Eight

Year 36 of the Loop

Coco has a hard time believing this mature woman in front of her is the same Malia from so many years ago. She'd been a small child when Coco arrived in Solace, had babysat for Joey many times, and had been Joey's first crush. That shy, coltish teen has been transformed entirely by the years between then and now. She's married, has children of her own, and is Solace's primary scout. And now, she's here in Lorain giving them terrible news. News she's brought at significant risk to herself.

Her color is high, and she's breathing heavily, but she waves aside all offers of rest, settling for taking great gulps from a jug of water Forrest hands her.

"I have to start back, and I have to hurry. I'm supposed to be scouting a new settlement location sixty miles south of here. I ran the last mile over land in case someone was watching the road. My vehicle is back there, and I have to hurry before I'm out of comms range long enough for people to notice."

She stops to drink again, then wipes her mouth with the back of her hand and returns the jug to Forrest. She unclips the canteen from her belt and hands it to Richie, Forrest's youngest child. "Can you fill that?"

He runs off, and she immediately unleashes a rapid-fire barrage of words. "Listen, you need to leave, and you need to stay away from the settlements on your way to Upton. Everyone knows about that now. The inter-community council has riled everyone up and the communications channels are filled with bulletins about it. They're saying that you intend to disrupt some big experiment in Upton, and if you do, it will destroy everything. As in, the entire world. It's a joint statement from both the Chosen and the Seekers, so people believe them. Right now, there are flyers with some of your pictures on them being driven all over the place. We're being told to stop you, no matter what it takes."

Frowning, Jorge asks, "As in, violently stop us?"

She nods. "Yeah, though they don't specifically say to kill you, that's the implication. I'm quoting the radio speech here when I say they called you 'a clear, present, and ultimate danger to life on Earth.' I'm not shitting you."

Coco thinks of all the wonderful people in Solace, people she called friends and family. "Surely, people don't believe that. I mean, they know us. They know me. They know Jorge. Half of them helped raise Joey. And if you're here, you clearly don't believe it."

Malia waves her hands in front of her face, as if to deny or push away the idea. "Oh, people do know you, but it's been a long time since you left. Trust me, a lot of them believe it. My mom, Marla, might be one of the few who doesn't. She's still on the town council, but won't be for long, I don't think. She's the one who said I should come up here." At Coco's expression, she adds, "And no, I don't believe it either. It's bullshit. It's because everyone is afraid that if you succeed, we'll all disappear. I don't think that will happen. Neither does my mom."

Joey makes a face of disgust and says, "So much for being Seekers."

Jorge puts a hand on his shoulder and says, "It's easy to be a Seeker when life is crap. It gets a lot harder when you have kids, grandkids, and a whole society. People believe what they're told, especially when it's what they most desperately want to hear. It's human."

With a nudge to make some room, Joey steps out of the cluster and walks away, shaking his head as he goes.

"Did you hear anything about a family from here arriving in Solace?" Forrest asks. "I only ask because I'm guessing that's why this is happening now. I'd just like it confirmed."

Malia frowns in confusion. "No. I've been scouting for weeks. I knew nothing until I got that first bulletin on the radio. Now, it's constant updates. If that family did arrive, then they haven't been seen in public. That doesn't bode well for you. There's a team coming here to take you, Forrest, along with a few others for questioning. I actually came here for you, not Coco. I didn't know she was still here."

Jorge immediately responds, "I think that's why Solace hasn't been sending people to look for us. We've got too much history there. It's hard to be cruel to someone you know and care about just because someone tells you to."

"Maybe," Malia says, then shrugs off her small pack to retrieve an oversized, soft-cover book. It has curling, worn edges. Paper maps were uncommon by the time of the looping, but these huge road atlases still existed. They're now used by scouts and heavily annotated. The amount of intelligence a person can glean from one is staggering. Coco knows how precious the volume is.

She shoves the book toward Jorge. "This is my scout book. I'll figure out an excuse for losing it. They'll be pissed, but they'll believe me. You take it. Every settlement we know of is in there. *Every single one.* Radio channels, relay stations, places where we don't have radio coverage, all of it. Supply and fuel depots too but be careful with those."

He takes the book and holds it as if it might break. "How much time do we have?"

She shakes her head. "Days at most. I parked a mile away because I was worried they might already be here. My mom told me on the radio —and don't worry, it was a secure channel—that they're collecting a party from a nearby Chosen community to come here. Organizing that will slow them down some, but like I said, not much. If I were you, I'd be gone before daylight. Seriously."

Richie returns just then, the canteen in one hand and a small sack in the other. He hands her both and says, "Cake and chowder to eat."

She smiles, takes the parcel, and ruffles his hair. "Thanks, cutie!" She looks back up and says, "I have to go. Just, keep what I said in mind."

Within a few minutes, she's gone, her trim form disappearing into the trees as she runs for the safety of her car. Forrest turns away and says to the few people who happen to be there, "Get everyone. We go tonight."

It feels like someone lit a fire underneath the world and everyone is hurrying to keep their feet from scorching, Coco included. There's so much to do that her head spins trying to decide what to take care of first. Jorge finally wraps his hands around her upper arms and tells her to breathe with him. It helps clear her mind, and she gives him a quick kiss in appreciation.

Forrest informs the Roanoke group, dashing from house to house as darkness falls. It's early spring, and the ice has melted enough to make the trip, but no one expected to leave this soon. There's still much to do, and there's no time to do it. Instead of an orderly migration, they will have a rushed exodus.

As Coco brings load after load to the truck for Jorge to sort and pack, unhappy voices rise as others along the street try to pack up their lives in a few short hours.

They're lucky to have fresh vehicles already liberated from loops. It was done with great regret and as much care as possible. All the trucks are from a dealership, so they're new and, hopefully, reliable. New generators and other necessities were also gathered, so it's the food and personal items that matter. Those are difficult.

Forrest rushes over as Coco drops off two big duffels of cold weather gear at the truck. He's flushed with exertion despite the cool air. He plops onto the tailgate for a breather and says, "The Roanoke group leaders are taking over their prep, so we only need to worry about ourselves. Some of those that were staying are scared now. They don't want to be caught in the crossfire if people really are going to be questioned. Who knows what that means? Torture?"

Coco clutches a duffel to her chest and asks, "What are they going to do? Go with the Roanoke people? Us?"

"The Roanokers don't want to take anyone new because they're not sure if they can be trusted. And honestly, I feel the same way. How do I know one of them isn't joining just to betray us down the road?"

"Then what?" Jorge asks, stopping his work. "We can't just leave them. These are your people, our people now. That's not right."

Forrest waves off the notion. "I gave them the map marked with one of the other locations we scouted before we chose the final one. It's in a different direction and it's a good spot, but it will take a lot of work. We didn't choose it because it wasn't big enough. They can manage it with their numbers."

With an exasperated sigh, Coco drops down next to Forrest. "This feels so wrong. All of it is wrong. People splitting up, not trusting each other."

"It is what it is," Jorge says. "Hand me that duffel and keep moving, Coco. We don't have time."

Coco's Journal: Age 48

Year 36 of the Loop

I honestly never considered the notion that we would actually be on the run. As in, running from the law… whatever that is now. But we are, and frankly, it sucks. I've gotten so used to a comfortable life with a bed and a pillow and meals cooked on a stove that I'm no good at this anymore. It's a little hard to believe I lived like this for over a decade and thought that was normal. I think I'm officially old, or at least too old for this kind of life.

Nine

Year 36 of the Loop

Despite the actual distance being no more than fifteen miles as the crow flies, it's taken four days and over one hundred miles to reach a decent spot to rest and plan. The entire group is rather uncomfortably camped on a baseball diamond in a park smack dab in the middle of the endless suburbs between Lorain and Cleveland.

It's a no-go zone for anyone not gifted or in the company of a gifted. While there was never an official exploration in this region, a few of the Lorain gifted came this far to check out a wildlife refuge nearby. That's how this small oasis was discovered. The path required for their trucks was both torturous and long, but they made it without disturbing a single loop, which means their back trail is invisible to any gifted search parties.

Their first morning is beautifully sunny, which is a nice change from the gloomy weather of the past two days and nights. Coco shifts coffee pots on their camp stove, making sure finished pots stay warm while the others bubble and brew. Already, people are emerging from tents and looking her way.

"Please tell me that's ready," Joey says as he walks over. "Mom, I gotta say, I forgot how awful it is to take a piss in the cold air."

She clucks at him in disapproval but smiles anyway. "Don't be disgusting. Your girlfriend is ten feet away."

His grin widens as he snags the cup. "Oh, Mom, everyone pees. Even you."

Layla reaches them and takes his cup. "Oh, I don't know. For years, I thought my dad didn't fart. Then I found out that he went outside to do it so my mom wouldn't know."

Coco waves both of them away. "No, no, I do *not* want to hear that. No way. Both of you, scoot! You're savages and shouldn't be anywhere near food preparation."

The couple walks away, laughing. There's no question the two are perfectly matched. The kind of barriers Coco associates with normal civilized behavior simply don't exist for them. It's not that they aren't civilized, it's just that it's less showy somehow, less superficial. Maybe they're simply more comfortable with their humanity.

When Jorge returns with a huge bowl filled with freshly peeled and sliced potatoes, he stops short at the look on her face. "What?" he asks, looking down at himself as if he might see something wrong.

She takes the bowl with a little more emphasis on the taking than necessary and says, "Nothing."

He eyes her for a moment, then his eyes shoot toward Layla and Joey giggling near the tent. "What did they do?"

"Like I said, it's nothing. They're just trying to shock an old lady," she says, sliding a couple of big frying pans onto another camp stove.

Still obviously not understanding what's going on, he says, "Alrighty then. I'll just leave that alone. Can I get my good morning kiss?"

That suggestion lifts her mood considerably.

"How about two kisses?" she asks, smiling.

* * *

Supplies are an issue. They spend that first day taking a final tally. The situation reflects their hurried departure. Things were missed. Important things like some of the food, the water filters, and, of all things, the trailer with the fuel tank on it. Coco has a hard time believing anyone could forget something so vital, but then again, she didn't notice it wasn't among the trailers being towed, either. Perhaps most important to Coco, Jorge has only enough medication for another eight days. His blood pressure won't tolerate missing many days of medication.

Fortunately for them, and unfortunately for nearby loopers, they are within a quarter-mile radius of just about anything they could ask for. Aside from a slew of high-end luxury car dealerships, which set Jorge and Forrest on a streak of wishful thinking, there are fast-food franchises, large drug stores, service and gas stations, home goods, and pretty much everything else. Some of it is visible from their little spot on the diamond.

Once a plan for the next morning is decided, the group crowds into a few larger tents to conserve heat while they sleep. Between Jorge's rumbling snores and Joey's outstretched limbs, Coco barely catches a wink. She climbs out between everyone into the weak, gray pre-dawn light. She's surprised to see Chantelle, Layla's mother, already stoking the coals of last night's fire.

Tugging her coat tighter, Coco approaches, hoping for coffee. Chantelle sees her and waves a stick, then points to the camp stoves. Yes, coffee.

Steaming cup in hand, she joins Chantelle as the first flames lick the air. It feels divine. Coco doesn't even mind the smoke from the firepit as long as she can keep feeling that delicious warmth.

"I don't know how you sleep at home," Chantelle says, smiling. "I could hear Jorge snoring right through the tent. Between him and Sven, I don't know who's worse."

"Sven," Coco blurts out. "Definitely Sven. He does that weird hiccupping thing at the end."

The other woman chuckles, then adds more wood to the fire. "Want to help me get breakfast ready? Maybe the smell will get them all up."

They work well together and prepare the food in no time. The only fresh vegetables they have are potatoes and onions, and those won't last being bumped around in vehicles day after day, especially not since they've been in storage all winter. So, once again, it's a meal of fried potatoes and onions.

All the other foods they brought are dehydrated, which is a specialty of the Lorain settlement. Canning isn't safe in places where the winters are harsh. Jars explode or the tops shoot off if they freeze, so they dehydrate most of their summer produce.

Between the smell of coffee and frying food, most people are up early enough to see the sun rise over the treetops. A few of the teens resist until Forrest shouts that they won't get any food if they don't hurry. That brings them running.

Breakfast over, the work begins. They've got to get their supply situation in order, and they don't have time to waste. Given their numbers, the gifted are divided up and sent in pairs to scout. Each older and more practiced gifted is teamed up with someone younger and not as experienced. Joey is matched to his youngest half-brother, Richie.

As Joey so bluntly put it when Forrest suggested teaming up a gifted and non-gifted, "Let the old folks rest. They can't do much, anyway."

It rankled to be lumped in as old folk, but he had a point. If the gifted had to wait and lead non-gifted through the mazes of loops, all the while remaining silent, it would take forever to scout even one location.

Less than an hour later, Joey and Richie reappear, both of them racing down the street. Joey is shouting and raising his arms for their attention. Loopers don't notice, but Coco's heart leaps up into her throat all the same. Have they been found already?

It seems everyone else has the same idea, because Forrest races for his bow and Sven picks up his. Everyone goes tense in a heartbeat.

Perhaps Joey sees it as he approaches, because he yells, "It's okay! But holy shit, you have to see this!"

Reflexively, Coco says, "Language." He can't hear her, but it's habit.

Joey slows enough for Richie, then lopes to a stop, gasping for breath. He's smiling. Richie is too. They must have found something good.

"What is it?" Forrest asks, grumpy after being scared without cause.

Joey gulps down breaths with his hand to his chest, then finally says, "I moved a loop. I *moved* it."

Richie nods emphatically, not quite as winded, and says, "He totally moved it. Just… boop… and it moved."

Coco has zero idea what's going on. She looks to Jorge, and he shrugs, equally baffled. "Honey… Joey, you move loopers all the time. It's creepy, yes, but we know you can do that."

Finally catching his breath, he waves his hand as if waving what she said away. "No, that's not it. I moved *the loop*. The actual loop. The path the looper takes. It bent. I saw it. Richie saw it, too. It bent!"

Brows furrow all around the pair, coupled with a few "Whats?" and one "Check for fever." There are no gifted in camp at the moment other than Joey and Richie. No one in the small crowd knows what it's like to see a loop trail. Coco has a hard time imagining Joey being able to move something that's invisible.

"Joey, are you okay?" she asks, moving to take his arm. She's perilously close to checking his forehead to see if he actually does have a fever.

He shakes her off, but not unkindly. It's more like he's so excited that he can't possibly wait for other minds to catch up. He looks at Jorge and says, "I did, Dad. I really did."

As usual, Jorge is the only one who seems to understand all this. "I believe you, son. Now, we just need to figure out how and why."

Part Four

Forrest

Forrest's Testimony: Excerpt 9

Year 36 After the Choosing

Every few days, I see Coco scribbling furiously in a book, usually after dinner when things settle down for the night. I knew she'd always kept a journal when she was alone, and for a little longer after she went to Solace, but I didn't know she was still at it. Decades of it.

It makes me feel like a loafer. Once I was well and truly booted out of the Chosen, I kept my own sort of testimony. It was useful, a sort of purge of all the things I see and do that stuck to my brain.

I don't do it annually, but whenever something that needs purging happens. Or sometimes when there's something good. Milestones for the boys, unusually funny situations, or even good things that aren't spectacular, but manage to stick long enough that I actually go find my not-exactly-a-testimony book.

Tonight, it isn't one of those bad things or good things. It's more of a weird thing. Coco has been furiously writing for long enough that I figured I should probably do the same. After all, what's happened is definitely strange enough that it merits a mention.

It's not that Joey has somehow moved a fragment's path that my mind keeps turning toward, but the way Coco looked when she realized it happened. It was like she was watching her son get diagnosed with some horrible, fatal disease. She was scared and heartbroken and it looked, for all the world, like she was saying goodbye to her boy… our boy… for the last time.

I realize that seems an odd way to put it, but that's exactly what it looked like from my perspective, and I didn't understand it. Why would discovering some new facet to Joey's gift make her feel like that? Now that I've had time to think about it, I think I understand. Mostly because Richie just came up to me and could barely contain himself, hoping out loud he'd get that "superpower" too. I felt a tinge of it in that moment, and a part of me immediately hoped that Richie would never develop that ability.

The reason she was frightened is because it's another step away from being human, at least human like us. It's a step into being something different and new and perhaps not meant to be in this world. When I understood what she saw, when I felt that same momentary fear, I finally understood Coco better.

Since she came to Lorain, she's been different. The young woman who strode through the world alongside the fragments and survived alone is barely there anymore. I hate to admit it, but a few times, I really thought she was being weak. Not brave. I was completely wrong. I had it backwards.

By understanding that expression on her face, by feeling it myself, I think I know what's really going on. I won't know for sure unless she opens up to me about it, but if she's kept her feelings secret this long, I doubt she'd do that. I feel like I'm right though, and I think only a parent would understand.

Our gifted children are different. They're something that could never… would never… exist in our old world. Every single time that gift grows stronger or some new part of it shows up, that difference grows. If our children could never exist in our old world, what happens to them if we fix time? It's all fine to say we might just go on, but the more powerful the gifted get, the more like reassuring nonsense that sounds.

I think Coco has been living for a long time with the certainty that her child could not exist in our old world. Despite her love for him, which no one could ever doubt, she still searches for the truth. That's brave. She's not weak, though she is afraid. And now that I've seen it, I'm afraid too.

One

Year 36 After the Choosing

With his fists shoved into his coat pockets, Forrest tries to keep his mouth shut and hands still. It's difficult.

It's not just that Joey is his biological son, though there is some of that. He kept his distance and never let on who he was to the boy, but that didn't mean he felt nothing. For over twenty-two years, Forrest has felt the dull ache of something missing. It passes into the background, sometimes for long periods, but it never entirely leaves him.

He only realized it was there and what it meant when David was born. Suddenly this slimy, purplish, cone-headed bundle of angry screams came into the world and was plopped into his hands. It should have been gross. It should have made him want to hold it at arm's length and ask for a refund.

Instead, it felt like his heart was literally trying to crawl out and hug this new human. Like tentacles he couldn't see were emerging from all the vital structures of his body and wrapping themselves around this screaming creature, forever entangling them into one extended being.

Only later that night, with his wife finally resting and the baby—no longer purple or slimy, but still alarmingly cone-headed—finally quiet, did he understand how much he'd missed with Joey. He understood the constant, inexplicable ache in his heart.

It's that old ache which makes it difficult to stand still and not interfere. It's also that his youngest son is standing there looking up at Joey with hero-worship in his eyes while he tries to figure out how he can perform this new trick as well.

Though most of the gifted have returned to find out what all the yelling was about, a few are still trickling in. Their questioning began before Joey had a chance to regain his breath. The gifted are excited by this new ability.

The interrogation is too chaotic to be productive. Everyone in camp, gifted and non-gifted alike, pepper him with questions that he's almost entirely unable to answer.

After letting it go on long enough for people to know they won't be getting answers, Jorge holds up both hands and says, "Okay, everyone. We're not going to get anywhere like this. How about we stay in camp for the rest of the day, and I take just a few of us to talk to Joey? A crowd is no good for this."

"But we deserve to know too!" exclaims a young gifted named Trig.

Layla, who must have taken lessons in snark from Pam at some point, shoots a level look his way and raises an eyebrow. "Really? Because we want to keep it secret and make sure no one else knows how to do something so incredibly useful."

Trig must be too hyped up to get the sarcasm. Before he can speak, Layla holds up a hand and says, "Yes, we all need to know about it and hopefully figure out how to do it. We can't do that until we figure out exactly what it is. Do you learn best in front of a crowd?"

His lips move like he's trying for some smart remark, but he finally relents and says, "Fine."

Jorge looks around, spots Forrest, and waves him over. He does the same for Layla. Jorge moves the group to the edge of the park, where there are a few picnic tables. They're still in sight of the group, but not within earshot. The small party is uncomfortably family-centric: Coco, Jorge, Layla, Joey, and Forrest.

As he reaches Coco, Forrest leans close and whispers, "Maybe I shouldn't be here."

She makes a face. "Seriously? Don't be an idiot."

After Joey drinks from a canteen, he plops down onto a bench and asks, "Can we sit? My legs feel like noodles from adrenaline and you're all looming over me."

They sit, with Forrest taking the far spot next to Layla. Jorge reaches out and pats Joey's hand. "Take your time, son."

When Joey nods his readiness, Jorge jumps right in. "Okay, let's go from the top. I want to be clear and make sure I understand what happened. When you say you bent 'it,' you mean the trail you see behind all the loopers that shows their path, right?"

"Yep."

"Right. We all walk through the trails all the time. So, what was different this time?"

Joey shrugs with every part of himself. "I have no clue, Dad. *No clue.*"

"Did you try to do it again? After that first time?"

"Yeah, and nothing happened."

Jorge nods as if this makes sense. "I want you to really think about this question. Even if it's embarrassing or uncomfortable, I want you to tell me what you were thinking when this happened. What was your exact state of mind when you bent that trail?"

Joey glances at Coco, his face reddening. "I guess I was worried."

"Explain."

Joey pushes out a breath, which makes him look young and tired, then he says, "Before I left, Mom told me that no matter where I'd been assigned to search, I needed to get into one of the pharmacies and find your meds. It was essential, and she didn't care what else I had to do, I had to get those meds. That if I couldn't find any at either of these pharmacies, she wanted me to come right back and tell her."

With a disapproving glance at Coco, Jorge says, "Coco, come on. I won't explode if I miss a day or two."

Without even a second's worth of delay, she responds, "Oh, really? All we know is what we see in the medical books we have, and yes, you might explode. Or your heart, anyway. I have every right to be worried. You could stroke out, have a heart attack—"

Joey puts his hands up to stop them from arguing. "Mom! It doesn't matter right now. And I *will* find his meds, even if I have to go search every house in that subdivision over there."

Visibly suppressing his irritation, Jorge says, "Okay, so you were worried. How did that play into what happened? Be as specific as possible. Also, was there anything else prominent in your mind?"

Joey looks down at the table's battered surface for a moment, then closes his eyes. After a brief silence, he says, "I was looking at all the loops. There are so many on that street. They crisscross all over and there are cars everywhere on really confusing loops. Every door is looped to hell and back, too. I kept picturing Dad getting sick or dying, or us staying back because we couldn't keep going. I thought that even if I found some meds, would I be able to reach them to take them out of a loop, or would they be locked away where I couldn't reach them?"

He pauses and cocks his head, eyes opening as he catches the memory he needs. "I was standing there and thinking that we'd have to map for days to find a path for the trucks, or I'd have to break a lot of loops. I remember that I didn't want to break all those loops. There was this one, a lady who reminded me of Mom. She's going into that fried chicken place, and she obviously works there. I just remember looking at her and wishing I could somehow make it so that the loops weren't in our way."

His eyes widen, and he smiles. "That was it! That's when I passed through the loop trail, just like always, but it felt… I don't know… gooey or something. I looked down and saw it was bent."

Both Layla and Coco say, "Gooey?"

Joey nods.

"Right," Jorge says. "All the gifted say they feel something when they walk through a trail. You've described it as a quiet buzz, like what it feels like to walk into a house with electricity versus one without power. Is that accurate?"

Both Joey and Layla confirm this with nods.

"So, what exactly is the difference between buzzy and gooey? Be specific. Do you actually mean sticky?"

Joey searches for words. Forrest can see him discarding descriptions and searching for more, his expression shifting as he tries to find the perfect word. He can't imagine what it must be like to try and explain a world none of the older people can even perceive.

It reminds Forrest of a story he heard when he was young, about a kingdom of the blind where a one-eyed man is king. Except, there are no kings and the poor guy with an eye has to spend his life trying to describe what the blind cannot possibly comprehend.

Finally, Joey snaps his fingers and says, "You know that honey candy Pam makes? The one that goes in the big pans and has to dry in the air for days and days?"

There are nods all around because everyone has eaten it. It's an annual tradition after the honey harvest. It's delicious, supremely sticky, and probably very bad for their teeth.

"It's like when the kids try to sneak some before it's ready. When they try to take some, it stretches out. They make a game of it, seeing who can get it to stretch the furthest. It was just like that. Not sticky feeling really, not gooey exactly, but more like the way it looks when something is sticky. Like the candy stretching. Do you understand?"

Forrest does, but it's obvious that Jorge and Coco don't. They've probably never seen what Joey is talking about. Forrest breaks in. "Like pizza cheese on the commercials. When it stretches. That's what he's talking about."

That seems to get the idea across. Everyone looks to Jorge, who seems deep in thought.

Forrest asks, "What is it, Jorge?"

"I'm not exactly sure, but… well… I'm thinking about the day Joey saw the tear, the one with the snow and the hunters. That day, you ran into something that wasn't visible to the rest of us but was to you. You impacted it. Based on what your mother said later, you were in an excited state. Correct?"

Joey nods, glancing at his mother with a blush of guilt. Coco looks tense.

Shaking his head, as if pushing away an answer he doesn't like, Jorge says, "I could be wrong."

"What?" Joey prods.

"We've always theorized that the gifted are changed in some physical way, in a real biological way, by changes in their parents. We were exposed to the loopers, and our children's skill levels with the gifts reflect those levels of exposure, right? The more loopers we were around, the more gifted our children. More or less, anyway. We don't know exactly what this change is since we don't have genetic labs anymore. The assumption is that you see time. Not in everything, but in living things."

Warming to his words now, Jorge talks faster, looking from Layla to Joey. "Some people think the glow you see inside of us—those of us not in loops—is because our time isn't foretold or set in stone. We have too many choices. You see the loopers differently because their time is, at the moment, a set thing with a specific path.

"Also, you can move a looper without disturbing them or destroying their loop. That means you can, in some sense, interact with time. You can even remove small items from a loop, and it doesn't disappear.

Or sometimes you can, anyway. What if, and I'm really reaching here, what if our theory that you can glimpse time as a physical object is more pronounced than we thought? What if it takes a different kind of concentration or state of mind to achieve that level of interaction?"

Joey leans back and says, "You lost me on that last part. Concentration is what it is. What different kinds are there?"

Layla nudges Joey. "I think I know what he means. It's like those other two gifted who saw the rips like you did when you were a kid. They were super excited and scared. Is that what you mean?"

"Yes, like that," Jorge agrees. "Joey, you saw the rip, but when you bounced off it, you were in an excited state."

"So, what does that mean? Does that mean I have to… what… stay amped up or something?"

"No, I think it means you need practice. Anyone in a total panic might be able to shove a crashed car away from their trapped child, but an Olympic weightlifter practices for years to lift a fraction of that weight reliably. You have done the former… now you have to do the latter."

Forrest's Testimony: Excerpt 10

Year 36 After the Choosing

It's a lot to take in. The very idea is bizarre. Instead, I found myself worrying over my boys… my other boys. Joey is their half-brother, and he's admittedly more gifted than they are, but what if this thing is in them, too?

Maybe I should be as excited as everyone else at the potential. They're all happy and smiling and talking about how much easier it would be to get around if they can move fragment paths instead of timing everything or destroying them.

I'm not, though. Not at all. Every time I hear someone at the fire give another example of what they might accomplish, I think about how much weight this new skill puts on Joey's back. How much weight it will put on the back of anyone who learns to do it. That's not fair, and I feel selfish for saying I don't want my boys to have to deal with it, but it's true. I don't.

Jorge came over to talk to me for a bit. I think he could see the worry cloud over my head. When Joey was first born, I resented Jorge. I really did. I knew he and Coco weren't a couple at the time, not like a real couple, so I managed my resentment. Once I found out they'd become an actual couple, it came back briefly. I wasn't around him during those years, so I doubt he even knows I felt that way.

As time went by and I grew up more and found love and all the rest, the negative feelings went away. I don't know exactly when, but they did. Mostly, I felt grateful that Joey had a father who loved him so much. My boys made me understand the importance of that kind of love from the moment David was born.

Once they moved to Lorain, I guess I was surprised to find how much I liked Jorge. He's smart and helpful. He's good company and the man can grill a fish like none other.

When he came over this evening, he asked if I had anything I wanted to talk about. At first, I said I didn't, but after he sat down, I let it all pour out. He gave me a nice pep talk, making sure I understood that if this was really a skill that could be taught, then it would be something they all did as naturally as they do anything else.

He was right about the learning. All the gifted have to practice when they're young. In the beginning, they see trails as giant blobs if there are multiple fragments around, unless they're very gifted. We teach them, even though we can't see them ourselves. It becomes natural to them, so maybe this will, too.

I feel a little better about things. Jorge is back with Coco now, probably doing the same for her as he did for me. She's got her arms crossed with her hands on her shoulders, like she's protecting herself or can't get warm. I really do feel for her.

Two

Year 36 After the Choosing

"Okay, Joey, now concentrate on the trail as a solid thing. It's no different from a bag of rice. It's got weight and it can be picked up and moved. Focus on it and look at it, really look at it," Jorge says in a smooth, low tone. With a fragment mere feet away, he's got to be careful with his noise levels.

Joey stands in the middle of the street, slightly crouched. He looks, for all the world, like a movie superhero about to take flight or launch a fireball. Only Joey and Layla can see the trail we're using as a test. To Forrest, it looks like an empty street with a man on the opposite corner. Apparently, this is the only spot nearby where there is only one fragment trail and enough clear space for us to experiment.

The fragment is a man with his hand out like he's holding a leash. We've watched him go past twice now. Coco had the brilliant idea to dump buckets of soil onto the path he takes across the street. The center of that big spill of dirt disappeared when the fragment reset, clearly defining the man's path and providing us non-gifted with a reference. Joey is supposed to try to move the trail just enough so that we can see a difference in the man's path.

So far, he's tried twice, and nothing happened. He says his hand passes right through.

Jorge keeps his voice low even as he instructs Joey. "Now, take a deep breath and hold it. Good. Now let it out slowly. Do it again."

Joey does, and his shoulders sink, his whole body seeming to relax into the task.

Jorge's voice drops even lower, becoming barely audible to anyone except Joey. The fragment is beginning another cycle, so it's test time. "It's there and you can see it. Feel the buzz shift as it turns solid. It must be moved, so you will move it. Now, move it."

Joey's fingers inch forward smoothly. This time, his face isn't tense. His body isn't tense. He is simply there. There's no visible indication that anything happens, but Layla bunches both fists to her smiling mouth to keep quiet and not disturb Joey's flow. Something is obviously going right.

Suddenly, Joey smiles and steps back. He nods toward the fragment, who is about to cross the street for probably the millionth time in the past thirty-six years.

It's not much. Maybe a few inches, but the change is as clear as the gorgeous day around them. The scattering of soil on the ground loses a few inches in a slight curve above the cleared lane.

Coco clasps her hands over her mouth to contain a gasp. Forrest isn't sure, but it's possible some sound may have escaped from his own throat. They're back far enough that the noise isn't obvious to the fragment. The man continues his eternal walk. At Jorge's signal, the group moves back down the street to the clear area where there are no fragments to disturb.

Layla, who doesn't have to worry about noise, starts jumping up and down, fist-pumping the air, and shouting silly things that make no sense, like, "You effing sexy beast-slaying boom baby boom!"

Nearby, Coco whispers, "Layla, language."

Jorge remains focused, staring at Joey. He reaches out to touch

Layla's arm and still her. She stops jumping, but she's practically wiggling out of her shoes in excitement.

"Tell us what it was like, Joey. Exactly," Jorge says.

Joey nods. "You were right about thinking too hard. When I did it the first time, I was thinking about what I wanted to happen, not doing it. The other tries we did today, I was thinking about doing it, but with part of me knowing it was impossible, if you know what I mean. This time, I focused, but it was different. I thought about the end result, not the doing. I felt pretty relaxed, but also… I don't know… determined?"

Smiling, Jorge grabs Joey in a hug and squeezes him tight. Quietly, he says, "You did it, son. You did it."

When he releases Joey, he looks to be sure the group is inside the clear area designated as the talking zone. Since they are, Jorge launches right in. "Okay, so I think it's safe to say that it's not just emotional, but that's probably the gateway for it to happen accidentally. Equally important is understanding that what they see is real, despite us not seeing it. A real, solid thing. It's knowing that it can be done and being clearheaded."

Coco asks, "But how do you feel now, honey? Are you tired? Does it hurt?"

Joey shakes his head, but his expression is less certain. "Not tired, exactly. It's like when I learned something new in school. Like that. And it doesn't hurt. Also, I didn't get the idea that it hurt the looper either. When we push them out of the way, you can tell it hurts, like we're forcing them. This time, I didn't feel that."

"Well, that's good," Layla says. "I hate that feeling."

Forrest agrees with her on that. One of the main reasons he's been so reluctant to let David go on supply runs is the habit of asking the gifted to move fragments out of the way to clear a path. He doesn't want his son getting too used to the idea of hurting others for convenience.

It's just one of the many disagreements that eventually led to his departure from the Chosen.

Coco still looks worried and asks, "Okay, so what do we do with this? I hate to be the one to ruin the fun, but we really do need to get supplies and your father's medication. It wouldn't hurt to get more first aid supplies, either. We took so little from Lorain. And, not to mention the obvious, but we really aren't that far from Lorain. We shouldn't stay here long."

While he's out of his depth when it comes to nurturing these new gifts, the local geography is entirely inside Forrest's bailiwick. "Coco, I agree we need to secure supplies, in particular medication. Not just Jorge's, either. Pam needs medication as well. I'm not dismissing that and do agree with you."

"Okay," she says, eyeballing him like she knows his words mean he doesn't agree with her at all. "And?"

"We don't need to leave here. Not in a hurry, and not yet. In fact, we'd do better to stay here and get well supplied, then wait to be sure we won't get trapped by spring snowstorms during the trip."

Coco points vaguely westward and says, "We're too close to Lorain."

"*Eh*, close is relative," he says, looking for an example. He finds it in her own story. "Okay, look at it like this. Try imagining someone searching for you in Manhattan. I've never been there, but I've seen pictures. Imagine you trying not to be found and someone trying to find you. This is kind of like that."

She waves him off. "No, it's nothing like that. This isn't a mega-city with millions of people in skyscrapers. Also, to find me, all someone would have to do is climb to a different window on a different block every night until they saw my light. It's doable. Not likely, but doable. Or they could just follow my trails of broken loops. Or my signs. Or—"

"Okay," Forrest interrupts her flow with his hands raised in surrender, smiling because he knows from experience that Coco can absolutely continue running through examples until night falls or they all die of thirst. "Here's my point though. We don't come to big cities. Not Seekers or Chosen. Why?"

"So we don't wreck things we can't fix."

"Yeah, which means no one has been here, either. This place was explored off book. The only people who know about this park are here with us. Sven, Pam, and Kiara."

He can see she's about to argue, so he hurries on. "And this place has industry. Cleveland and all the surrounding areas are like giant red flashing lights screaming not to enter. Between biotech, manufacturing, and shipping, any broken fragment could mean disaster. No one will search here."

Coco looks around, growing visibly nervous. "Maybe we shouldn't be here, then. If one of these loopers belongs to a biotech place, then who knows what we might do if we break one. We *definitely* shouldn't be here."

"No, we're fine. We just shouldn't get any closer to Cleveland. Here, we've got a measure of control and awareness. And there's probably most of what we need for our trip within sight of this street. We should get what we need, then get everyone well rested and ready for the road. The gifted can train and maybe even learn how to do this new thing. If they can, life will get easier. Imagine not having to break fragments just to drive safely? That would be huge. And good. What do you all think?"

Jorge slides his arm around Coco's waist and says, "You both have excellent points. I vote we stay, but let's make some rules to keep visibility down. No fires during daylight so we don't put smoke into the air. A taller barrier around the fire at night to keep the light from shining too far. Fewer lights at night… that kind of thing."

"Agreed."

When Forrest turns around to check with Joey and Layla for their agreement, he realizes they've wandered down the road toward the fragment he moved. They appear to be deep in conversation, and Joey is motioning toward something in the trees.

Waving his arms over his head to get their attention, Forrest motions them back to the group.

"What's up?" Jorge asks as Joey approaches. "Is something wrong?"

"No," Joey says, sounding uncertain. "Not wrong, but different. I can't tell for sure, but I think some part of that tree... the leaves there on the street side... aren't looped anymore. I don't know for sure."

Layla explains further when the only response is confusion. "Leaves and trees and grass and stuff like that are different, not like people or animals. They don't really glow like you do, probably because they don't do anything on their own. Leaves don't decide anything. They just hang there. Objects, like that trash can over there, are different. They look less real if they'll disappear when a loop is broken. I mean, you know that from supply missions, so I'm not saying anything new. Plants are different."

"I'm lost," Coco says.

Joey pats Coco's arm and says, "Sorry, Mom. We're not trying to be cagey. I just can't explain it properly. If Dad agrees, I think we should test it out. If changing a trail can actually unloop a bunch of objects at once without breaking the loop... well, that would be everything. Yes, I can take a few small things from a loop, but I can't do that with everything, and I can't do a lot of things at once or I get sick. This, this could change everything."

Forrest can't stay still and let the parents take the lead anymore. This idea sounds too good to be true. If it is true, then it would be amazing. It would mean his boys could avoid ever breaking a fragment. No guilt.

"Wait, Joey, just a second," Forrest says, moving closer. "Are you saying that you think you can do stuff like... I don't know... liberate food or medicine *en masse* by changing the fragment's path? Not breaking it?"

With a shrug and a smile, Joey says, "Maybe. I'm pretty sure that part of the tree used to be looped. I'm almost positive. The leaves are a slightly different color on part of the tree. You can see that for yourself, right? I'm saying we should test it."

Forrest's Testimony: Excerpt 11

Year 36 After the Choosing

When I think of all the fragments I sent into the beyond, believing with the arrogance of youth that I somehow knew all the answers, I can hardly stand it. Faces come back to me now that I'm older, and if I'm not actually wiser, then at least I'm less foolish. I remember so many faces. Children, old people, workers of all shapes and sizes, dogs, cats, deer… the list is endless.

How can one person deal with knowing they caused so much pointless death? Maybe I'm being harsh on myself. I know I'm not considering all the bellies that were filled with the food we set free when we released a fragment. The water, the farms, the seeds, the homes, the medicine… all of those things were essential at the time. I'm trying to remember why releasing fragments made sense.

Trying isn't really working, though. In the moment, I acted because I didn't want our people to starve. Now, with the comfort of a belly full of potatoes grown on a farm and a warm coat on my body, I find it's much easier to engage in revisionist history. It's hard to see it from the perspective we had back then. I know we had no way of knowing this strange turn of events would happen, but still… what a waste.

Three

Year 36 After the Choosing

It takes two days, during which Coco repeatedly reminds Jorge that he's running out of pills, to find a place that will work for the test. Forrest hears her and feels bad for her, but also for Jorge, who has to placate her. Even Layla starts in on Jorge, urging him to sit down, or watching him too closely while he works. Forrest is glad when they eventually locate a fragment that won't cause too many ripples if the experiment fails.

Layla still can't do what Joey can, but she said she felt something on one of her recent tries, so everyone remains hopeful that all the gifted might learn this skill. Eventually, anyway. Joey, for his part, has spent the last two days practicing. Though he's careful and only nudges trails, he can do it reliably.

In a nearby house, Joey and Layla have found a fragment for the test. It's tricky for Forrest and Jorge to follow them inside, but once they get there, Forrest can see how perfect the setup is even without being able to see the trail. The small foyer seems crowded with four adults.

The fragment works at a hardware store, as evidenced by the name tag on a shirt hanging from a door. His entire path is limited to the house, and it involves objects they can test.

The group stands out of the way and watches while he completes one path. The young man stutters into existence in the hallway, walks to the kitchen, and prepares a bowl of cereal. Then, he walks to the living room, sits in a recliner, and watches the blank TV while he shovels in his breakfast. It takes less than seven minutes. Joey and Layla both confirm that the bowl he uses is looped and will disappear with the man, but the cereal box is brighter and will stay behind. Likewise, a glimpse into the fridge shows the milk will stay, but other things will go.

It's perfect for a test. While Joey and Layla could probably take something else in the house, they can't take anything essential to the fragment. They might take what he sees, but not what he touches. The man touches the bowl, so they couldn't take that. And they would only be able to take what they could get close to. If they feel a tingle when their hands get close to an object, they can take it.

But that skill drains them terribly. After a few items, they feel like they need to sleep. If they continue, they grow pale and ill looking. If they persist beyond that point, then comes the vomiting and the days in bed trying to recover. Since they discovered some of the gifted can take items from loops, it's been reserved only for the most important things… primarily medications.

Joey holds up a finger as the man prepares his bowl again. The moment the man passes, Joey hurries to the kitchen and braces himself as if he's about to do something strenuous. He pushes out a slow breath, rolls his shoulders, then closes his eyes.

To Forrest, it feels like the process takes forever. He keeps glancing toward the man eating his breakfast and then back at Joey. With one final deep inhale, Joey slowly opens his eyes and, using both hands, pushes at the air.

There's nothing for Forrest to see, but it seems like Joey is pushing against something with resistance. Without breaking his hold, Joey shifts his feet and twists, like he's shaping something into a circle. He looks at the air, his eyes following an invisible line, then nods and steps back.

When he reaches them, he says, "I did it, but I'm not sure what's going to happen."

When the fragment repeats, stuttering to life in the hallway, they all watch intently, looking for change. The man walks into the kitchen, but not like he did before. His hands come out, just as they did when he reached for the cabinet, but stop mid-reach. He walks in a tight circle around the far end of the kitchen, then sits in his chair, hands still raised.

Layla startles them all when she says, "Dayum, that is some freaky shit right there."

She's lucky Forrest and Jorge are steady enough not to make noise when startled. Even so, Jorge reaches out and tugs her sleeve, miming for her to be quiet when she looks at him. It's evident to Forrest that Layla has spent way too much time with Sven and Pam. Her language choices are like listening to the script of a teen movie from his childhood.

Joey grins and points to the cereal box on the top of the fridge. Jorge motions for him to check. They'd discussed this part of the test. They need to see if the food has been released or if it will revert. Up until now, when a fragment is broken, some things are left behind and some things aren't, but everything that is left behind is exactly as it was at the moment of the choosing. Fresh and new.

Now, there is the question of what time will do to something that's *untied* from a fragment. Jorge has suggested two options: Reversion and release. If it's released, then it will be the same as it was on the day the Choosing happened. If it reverts, it will be stale by more than three and a half decades. Will time release it, or will time catch up?

Readying their scavenging bags, Joey and Layla enter the kitchen to check and take everything. Inside the cabinet, Joey points to the bowl. It's still there. That's big, because the bowl would have disappeared if the fragment were released. That's huge. It means shifting a trail is actually more profitable than releasing a fragment.

Joey whispers, "Cross your fingers," before opening the fridge. He grins like a fool when the door opens. "It's cold." It takes a few minutes for them to empty the fridge, and they have to stand by while the man begins his new path once more. When Joey hands him a bag, Forrest can feel the chill right through the fabric. Fresh groceries.

After they leave the house, Layla retrieves the cereal box and holds it in the center of their little cluster. She grins and says, "Time to test."

"You first," Jorge says to Joey.

He digs into the box. There's the sound of crunchy balls that will supposedly taste like peanut butter. Forrest used to love this cereal, but it only hinted at peanut butter in his memory.

Joey takes out a single piece. The round ball looks normal to Forrest, and he grins when it crunches just like it should. Joey's smile brightens, and he says, "It's frigging awesome!"

They all test, and yes, it's fresh. Memories flood Forrest's mind like a punch to the gut. Sleepy mornings before school and after school bowls of this sugar-laden treat while he played video games instead of doing his homework. Arguments with his mom about putting empty milk cartons back into the fridge. Unloading groceries with the poor grace of an adolescent who thinks they have much better things to do.

Jorge nods at him, bringing Forrest back to the present. "Totally fresh. Just like when a loop is broken."

Layla digs in and retrieves a fistful, saying, "Only, we didn't break a loop. We didn't!"

"How do you feel, Joey?" Jorge asks.

Joey flexes his hands. "Good. Really good. It was a lot easier that time. It's sort of invigorating, like I got my batteries charged or something. It's almost the opposite of when I take things from a loop. That drains me, but this feels good."

"That's probably the sugar rush from the cereal, but I'm glad to hear it," Jorge responds.

They still have to be quiet because there are fragments within earshot, but Jorge takes a moment to peek into the grocery bags. For one moment, he looks less like a sixty-year-old and more like a kid. "Oh my gosh. We have almost a full gallon of milk. We have butter and cheese!" He looks up, grinning. "Actual cheddar *cheese*. I say we go back and celebrate."

Forrest's Testimony: Excerpt 12

Year 36 After the Choosing

We've been here a month, and it's a good thing we have, though each delay felt like we were taking a risk. I've picked this book up a few times but wound up getting called away or doodling stupid things instead of writing. Every night, or almost every night, I see Coco bent over her journal. Seeing that makes me think I should write something down too.

The thing is, Coco has always been sort of prim, sort of self-contained. Not in a bad way. It's more that she's very controlled. It's something we used to see in people who spent too much time alone. If they don't develop some serious self-control, they don't survive. Unlike most, she never shook off those habits. But, when she gets into her writing groove, I see her change.

At first, it's like a mad scramble to get words onto paper, but after a few minutes, she relaxes. I would never try to peek, but I'd bet money... or maybe something of actual value like toilet paper... that inside her books is the only place she lets go and is simply herself.

I envy her that. I'm trying to do the same thing. Maybe I can write enough thoughts that I won't spend half the night with my brain racing, worrying about the boys and tomorrow and what comes next. It's worth a shot.

First, the delays, because that's a big one in my brain bucket full of worries. We needed supplies in a big way. Then, before we even got that handled, we needed to delay so other gifted could learn to move trails, if possible. It turns out that the more Joey does it, the more tiring it is. At first, he said he felt great, but it takes a toll. While that was going on, we also got a full week of some truly epic spring snows, which melted into slush during the day and froze into jagged and slippery ice at night.

We got a couple of really bad falls out of that. Tyrone's left arm looks like someone went after it with a baseball bat. He's still our very own Black Crane, tall and skinny, without an ounce of fat to cushion a fall like that. There are no bones out of place, but Pam is fairly sure it's fractured. It's so swollen and dark it looks shiny. Bruises that vibrant even at a distance have got to hurt like hell. He's splinted up and complaining about being side-lined. He's also over fifty, so he has to take time off or he could wind up with complications. Bones do not heal as quickly as we age.

Delays are bothersome, yes, though I'm glad we weren't on the road when the snow started. Being someplace new where we didn't know the area would have been tough. The gifted found us a decent house that we could camp in, so we're crammed in there, but it's not that bad. Cold, but not freezing with that many bodies producing heat. I'm surprised the floor didn't cave in with so much weight on it.

This thing with moving fragment trails is probably what bothers me most. The very idea that they can move something that isn't even real is simply weird. To them, it's real, but it's not to me. It's a concept, not a thing. It's time. Just time. I look at my boys and wonder if these two humans that I love so much are really, all the way, entirely human.

It's a terrible feeling. Guilty and shameful. I wonder how many other people here are secretly wondering the same thing about their kids. You know someone is. Or maybe I just hope they are because if someone else is, then I'm not a monster for doing the same.

I have to admit, there are benefits to this bizarre new skill. We're all profiting from it. So far, Layla, Joey, and Benson—Pam and Sven's son—are the only ones who can move trails reliably, though it took a couple of weeks of hard work before they could. They have to be taught the skill, but watching someone else do it seems to help them learn faster. Most of the young ones, including both my boys, still can't do it. A few, David included, say they can feel the trail there, waiting to be moved, but it won't budge. I can't see it, so who knows?

As to the advantages, I'm on watch tonight, so I can turn my head and see it for myself. Our watch is stationed on the roof of a Kia dealership. There are better places, but this one is convenient and open enough that it works. No lights, no fires, and no smoke anywhere nearby. So far, there's no sign anyone is looking for us within line of sight.

Instead, what I mostly see are relocated fragments. Cars that once zipped up and down streets on eternal repeat are now idling and still, lined up neatly along the side of the road. One of the two fragments from the chicken place now paces in tight circles in the parking lot. A dozen from the drugstore now walk in a staggered line far enough behind the building that we can safely move in and out without disturbing them.

Even weirder are the ways they have further manipulated this skill. The drugstore and pharmacy are good examples. Joey and Layla simply moved all the fragments in stages, stretching their trails like taffy until they went out the door and away from the building. Once they were done, it released everything inside the store. It's much better than when a fragment is released… or broken if I use the Seeker word for it. Or killed, if we're going to be honest with ourselves.

The difference is that moving them releases *everything*. All of it. Nothing goes away, maybe because the fragment is still alive. It's simply not held up anymore. They don't see it, touch it, or sense it, so it's released. After we found the medication we needed for Pam and Jorge, we were left with a completely stocked drugstore that looked exactly the same as the day of the Choosing.

It was surreal. The coolers were powerless, but they were still cold. As we always do when fragments are released, people went for the cold stuff first. Usually, there's only so much of it left because a lot disappears with the fragment. Not this time. There was so much ice cream, so many frozen snacks and cold sandwiches, that we couldn't actually eat it all. Not even with thirty people shoveling plastic spoons into cartons of creamy goodness as fast as possible. Most of it melted. Warm soda and beer are fine, but warm ice cream? The milk alone was enough to make us cry, especially since we had no way to preserve anything.

Pam and Kiara had the bright idea that we should see what happens if they adjust a trail so that a fragment never loses contact with the freezer in the chicken place. Two workers were inside. One was obviously closing up from the night before, while the other was making biscuits, probably for the Sunday morning customers.

The first one didn't work. Joey miscalculated how the turn would alter what the fragment saw. The second one did though, and it's the weirdest thing. She still makes biscuits, still works the oven, still goes to the cooler and freezer, but her trail isn't a couple of hours long anymore. It's over eight hours long. Joey stretched it out so that instead of starting again, she walks to the office and turns in circles for almost six hours, making eye contact with the fridge on every cycle.

What did that do for us? Well, it means a lot of good things. The last tray of biscuits has to be pulled out of the oven before they burn, because the oven stays hot for longer than the old loop. It also means we have refrigeration despite there being zero power. It's weird and inexplicable, but there it is.

Also, the biscuits smell amazing. Unfortunately, we can't eat them. Not unless we want the pain of them disappearing after being digested all the way down to the small intestine. Not worth it. Close, but not worth it.

During one of my turns to take out the woman's last tray of biscuits, I watched her walking around in circles over and over. I realized how much that horrified me. Maybe I haven't shed all my Chosen beliefs. We'd worked on the assumption that the fragments weren't people, but some sort of echo… a *fragment* of the person they once were. We'd also believed that if there were any part of that person still alive, it must be hell to be trapped like they are. That was why it was easy… well, relatively easy, to release them into the beyond. We felt like we were freeing them.

I thought I'd stopped believing that, but maybe not. When I saw that woman in a tiny office walking in circles, all I could think was that Joey had just made this woman's hell into an even worse hell.

Four

Year 37 After the Choosing

"Welcome to Pennsylvania, everyone!" Jorge exclaims as he exits his truck. "Home of yours truly!"

The vehicles are clustered together on a dirt track leading to yet another farm, this one obviously still held by a fragment. The fields contain machine-precise rows of abundant summer growth, despite it being September.

There are a few back slaps and welcome home sentiments, but they aren't especially hearty. Everyone is tired and weary of the road. It took over four months to get this far. Just ninety miles of progress as the crow flies. For their group, it's been hundreds and hundreds of careful, excruciating miles.

Forrest's back cracks as he stretches, and he winces at the pain shooting down his left leg. He doesn't need an MRI or whatever they used before the Choosing to know that his lower back is a hot mess. They found a book with the very direct title, *Heal Your Own Back,* in a clinic over the summer. He's been using it and, sure enough, it helps. The catch is that he has to do the exercises every day. Driving under stress or creeping about on tiptoes does not help him keep his gains, either.

Everyone has gotten used to his strange exercises, so while the boys unload the vehicle with their camping gear, he plops down onto the ground and twists his legs to the side, keeping his back flat to the ground. The relief is immediate, and he sighs.

"You okay?" Pam asks from above him. "How's the back?"

"Like guitar strings," he says, which is his usual code for the tightness and pain being particularly bad.

Her lips twist to the side in thought, then she says, "Let's spring for some heat on that tonight. Don't give me shit about it being too hot for a hot water bottle. Just do it."

He nods, then twists his legs to the other side, letting out a grunt as his muscles stretch just far enough to be painful in a good way.

By the time he's done, the others have set up most of the camp and a crowd surrounds a portable table. Planning time. Still shuffling, Forrest joins the crowd in the back, not pushing forward or trying to butt in. The gifted are the ones who need to be in front. This is their show.

Joey peers at the map, which is getting ragged, then straightens. With a shrug, he says, "So, if we're saying that all of Interstate 80 is out, fine. It's obviously the quicker route since one lane has been cleared for trade between settlements. It's also watched, or at least it was where we scouted. We have to choose between heading much further south and giving every settlement a wide berth or taking a chance pushing through these two-lane highways. Either way, it's going to take forever."

Jorge grunts. "Everything is going to take forever. That's just how it is. Pennsylvania is heavy with settlements, but most of them aren't original Chosen or Seeker. Mostly, they formed on their own and kind of folded in with the crowd for convenience. It's possible they won't give us trouble."

Pam shakes her head and says, "No, no way. We tried that already, and look what happened. Every single settlement in contact via radio has gotten word about us and no one has contradicted the bullshit the councils are spreading. If we hadn't left half the group out of sight and ready to intervene, who knows what would have happened at the last settlement. Those people were in the mood to capture first, ask questions never. And they knew who I was before I said my name. They've got our pictures."

Forrest's belly still flips when he thinks about that day. The group contacted a small settlement to see about refueling. It should have been safe. The settlement was only loosely associated with any faction, and well off the main travel routes. The people tried to capture Pam and the others who approached the gate. It had required a show of force to escape, followed by two weeks of going the wrong direction to avoid search parties.

Joey nods as if in complete agreement. "What she said."

Sven, whose age is catching up with him after months on the road, says, "At this rate, it'll take us years to get to Upton, let alone figure out if there's anything inside that might help."

"Then it takes years," Joey replies.

With a sad smile, Sven says, "A lot of us might not have years. We might, but we might not. I'm just saying that we need to pick up the pace. I know we're trying not to leave a trail that a gifted would notice. A road cleared of fragments is a dead giveaway, yes, but not every cleared road is always being watched by a settlement."

He stops talking and tugs the map a little, turning it so that he can show them his thoughts. He drags his finger along the interstate, then shifts to a lesser road to the south, making little taps at the marked settlements.

"The interstate is out, I agree. It's too easy, and they probably have some sort of monitoring at likely spots. Fine. But here we have another cleared road, and all of these, here. These larger ones are supposed to connect the settlements to the interstate. All these little ones aren't like that, though. Those are probably the roads cleared before there was a settlement, or when it first started and no one knew about anyone else.

They're all over this entire stretch. If we go out of our way now and hit these first cleared roads, we can make it most of the way across without ever going near the Chosen or Seeker infrastructure. We might get close to settlements, yes, but if we time it right, we can get past without so much as raising an eyebrow."

Most of the surrounding faces look dubious, and Forrest understands that entirely.

Sven holds out his hands, as if offering a tempting deal. "Or, we can go further south and head east at the same pace we are now. We should get there within a decade or two, assuming the fragments don't keep getting disturbed by cockroaches and mice and we all die in a fireball by then. Your choice."

While he might be laying it on a little thick, Forrest also knows he's not wrong. They've noticed a lot more animals over their months on the road, mostly small ones like squirrels or other rodents. And while they can't prove it, it looks to Forrest like the animals have learned how to get by in this world. There are gaps in the fragments that can't be ignored. Most of the time, those gaps are near food.

It looks as if the rodents of the world have discovered that if they find delicious food, they must bite or bother the humans or animals nearby. They have learned to clear fragments and take their stuff. It sounds strange, but it was bound to happen. Animals learn to get by. They always have. They don't have to know why they're doing it, only that it works.

There are other undeniable signs. A silo half-full of rotting corn, a warehouse with pallets of flour, the plastic nibbled open and spilled flour half turned into a solid block, but still carrying innumerable mouse footprints in the mess. They've seen other, similar signs in grocery stores, restaurants, and even feed lots. No human would release fragments and leave so much behind. Animals do that. Sooner or later, they'll release the wrong fragment. Something will go boom.

"He's right," Forrest says, despite his desire to remain silent. "Sven is right, and we all know it. If we travel at night, we're a lot less likely to meet a trade convoy or anything like that. No one travels at night, so let's do that. We can get through if we go fast and quiet. It won't be fun sleeping during the day and staying up all night, but no one promised us fun. It will give us more time for the roads that aren't marked as cleared on the map. Yes, we might go right past a settlement. Yes, they might see us if that happens. But if it's at night? Less likely."

Everyone's expressions grow less uncertain, more thoughtful of the possibilities. Tyrone asks, "What about winter? It's going to get super shitty out there in a couple of months."

Forrest smiles grimly. "All the better for us. Once it snows, we'll know exactly when we reach any stretch of road that's caught in a loop. It will be summer on that road, so we won't be able to miss it."

That settles it, and heads turn back to the map. Forrest doesn't need the details. What he really needs is a hot water bottle and some ibuprofen.

Forrest's Testimony: Excerpt 13

Year 38 After the Choosing

I never once considered that we might be in actual danger. Not really. Might we be captured and detained? Sure. Prevented from reaching Upton? Yeah. I never really thought they would try to kill us, though. I never thought they would commit acts that can only be described as atrocities. To believe humans had become better than that was stupid.

I suppose I feel it more now because Joey is going to be a father. Layla is pregnant. The timing couldn't possibly be worse, but accidents happen. Joey was, himself, an accident. Layla was probably an accident, too. Accidents are probably how the human race survives tight times. But it adds to this feeling I have, this sense of foreboding. We are bringing my future grandchild into danger.

Five

Year 38 After the Choosing

Jorge holds Coco close while she tries not to fall apart. Her eyes are wide and streaming tears. Most everyone else is silent, dumbstruck by the sight in front of them.

The Verrazzano-Narrows Bridge rises above them like something from another world. It has been racked by explosions. Massive, warped chunks of metal twist where it just rises away from the ground. Forrest can see pieces dangling near the superstructure that anchors this side of the bridge. As the summer wind blows, it groans as if in pain.

It took almost a year to cross Pennsylvania and New Jersey, most of that taken up by the cities. They planned and prepared for the eventual necessity of going on foot. They parked the vehicles a few miles back, knowing they couldn't get a convoy through densely populated New York City. Forrest, along with everyone else, knew something bad was coming almost as soon as they started walking. The number of fragments decreased as they left the vehicles behind. There were a few crashed cars, a few suspicious gaps in traffic, and far too few people. It wasn't what they'd expected from New York. Then, the gifted reported that they could see no more trails of light ahead. There were no fragments at all.

They prepared for this entire area to be a potential chokepoint.

There are only so many ways to get to the finger of land known as Long Island. There's the water, of course, but getting a boat can be tricky, and none of them wants to risk a long trip across a bay peppered with debris and who knows what else.

What none of them expected, especially not Forrest, is what they're seeing now. What has been done is painfully obvious. A crashed tractor is askew on the road. Not a small tractor either, but one of those huge ones. A little further down, two more are blackened and burned. It looks as though they were used as enormous bumper cars.

This tactic was one Forrest used in the beginning, before he'd tamed himself and his beliefs into what became the Chosen system. To clear a road fast, find the biggest thing on wheels you can and go full speed ahead. Crash into the cars, and their fragments go away. About half the time, so do their cars.

Whoever crashed these tractors likely cleared hundreds or thousands of fragments on approach to the bridge, then either planted enough explosives to destroy the asphalt, or tried to actually bring down the bridge. That the bridge is still there almost doesn't matter, because no one will ever cross it again, not even by foot. Not without serious climbing gear and a younger body than he possesses.

As the wind picks up, groans reverberate from the rubble. It sounds like the bridge is asking for help. Coco cries louder. It's grief. This is her city. Layla, her pregnant belly rounder by the day, tries her best to comfort the older woman.

Pam stomps up the line to stand next to him, those hard footsteps a reminder of her younger and angrier days. "What the fuck, Forrest? What the actual fuck? Was this our people?" she says. It's not really a question.

"We're not the only people in the world, Pam. It could have been entirely unrelated," Forrest says, but he isn't as confident as he tries to sound.

Sven plucks a piece of greenery from the ground and hands it to Forrest. "This didn't happen all that long ago. We'd see more growth if it had. This couldn't have happened more than a few months ago. And why would anyone else destroy a bridge? What's the point?"

Crumpling the bit of weed in his fist and dropping it, Forrest says, "And what reason would the Chosen and Seekers have for destroying a bridge? Why? What does it get them?"

Sven and Pam share a look, like they can't believe how dense he's being. Maybe he is.

Pam moves to stand in front of him, making him look her in the eye. "Forrest, think. When there are only so many ways to get someplace, why would someone destroy paths to that place? Duh. They're herding us. It's been almost a year and we've had only one close call, but we've seen evidence they're still looking for us. Looking hard, too. They're using resources for scouts and staffing frigging watchtowers and all kinds of crap. But they haven't gotten us. This," she pauses, eyeing the destroyed bridge, "is because we're close. They only have so many more chances to get to us before we get there. We need to think, and then do the smart thing."

Forrest looks back at the sound of snapping fingers and sees Jorge mouthing something over Coco's head, but Forrest can't understand him. Looking irritated, Jorge whispers into Joey's ear, then waves him toward Forrest.

Joey approaches, leans close, and says, "My dad says that if they did this here, they probably did it to other bridges. He says he will not let my mom see that. He wants to cross over water."

Scanning the surrounding area, Forrest sees not a single fragment. Not a single moving car. He asks Joey, "Do you see anything? Any trails at all?"

Joey scans, but his eyes never linger on any one thing. He shakes his head. "It's like a giant crater or something. There's nothing. No looper trails at all. Not even on the bridge, but I can only see so much of that. Beyond that big metal thing holding it up, I really can't tell. There might be some there."

Forrest sighs but isn't surprised. The noise of all the crashes would have had a snowballing effect around them. The explosions alone had probably disturbed fragments in a one-mile radius.

They don't go far, but by evening they have a small camp set up near the shore on an overgrown bit of field that was probably a nice lawn not too long ago. The trees are enough to obscure Coco's view of the destruction, if she doesn't crane her neck to see it.

Based on how much foliage has grown, the destruction is recent, just as Sven first suggested. Probably no earlier than spring, meaning mere months since somebody released all the fragments here. There's almost no doubt in Forrest's mind that this destruction was meant to stop their group. Or send a message. Pam was right. He just didn't want to believe it at first. Who would?

After Coco falls asleep, Jorge joins Forrest and a few others at the shore. The wavelets make soothing sounds. They could all use a little soothing.

"She okay?" Forrest asks. "I mean, not okay, but okay enough? You know what I mean."

Jorge's expression is all the answer they need. He faces the sea and says, "She just kept saying there are almost a thousand bridges and tunnels in New York, and everyone is within hearing range of at least one bridge. What's left of her family is on that island, you know. If they blew the bridges… well… I think any of us would be upset."

"Shit, I should have realized what upset her so much. Noise travels," Pam said.

Forrest is surprised at the number. Everyone else must be as well because Sven says, "Holy smokeballs, is that true? That can't be true. Where would you even put a thousand bridges?"

Jorge shrugs. "No clue. Anyway, we need to talk about what to do next. Why here? It's not like we can't cross the water in a boat. What's the point of so much destruction?"

Sven answers, "To send a message or herd us toward a specific path, like Pam said. And this is a good place for it because it's the obvious point for us to cross. They could be sure we'd see their message if they left it at one of the big bridges."

"What the hell message does this send other than them being assholes?"

Forrest takes a deep breath and says, "That they're serious and they won't let us get to Upton. That's pretty much it. They're letting us know that they don't care what they have to destroy, they won't let us get there. They won't let us fix anything."

With a hard kick at the wet sand, Joey says, "We don't even know if we can fix anything. We're looking for information, for crying out loud. We don't know anything yet, just that we should look there."

Jorge drapes an arm over Joey's shoulder, squeezing him in a half hug. "We'll figure it out."

Pam has been standing to the side, silently fuming while staring out at the dark waters. With a sharp shake of her head, she turns back to them. "All this means is that we're on the right track. That's it. It means the snippets of information we got about the Texas expedition weren't everything there was to know. That expedition disappeared because of what they found. Whatever the information was that they were killed for, we obviously don't have all of it. There's more to know, and it must be really frigging important if it's worth doing all this to stop us."

She pauses and waves her hand toward the bridge. " *No* doubt, given that whole shit show over there. If they're that determined for us not to reach Upton, that means we absolutely *must* get there. They got the full report from Texas before they killed the expedition. The only thing they don't know is that we don't know everything that they know."

Forrest has to think for a second before the words make sense, but it clicks when he repeats it a few times in his head. She's right.

The Chosen and Seeker councils must know what his group will find at Upton. It must be something definitive. It might even be what they need to fix this whole mess. The only thing the council doesn't know is how much Forrest and his people know. They probably think Jorge knows everything that was in the report.

Sven, always with his mind on security, says, "Okay, I get it. But now, we have to figure out how. If they did this, it's entirely possible they've got more planned if we make it across. If I were them, I'd set up a temporary settlement in an area we would have to go through. Something well stocked and full of true believers—"

"They won't go near the facility," Jorge interrupts. "No way. If any of them actually believe that disturbing whatever is going on there will destroy our world, or mess up this timeline, they'll stay far from it. More than likely, they'll be completely paranoid about any loopers within miles and miles of it. Maybe the whole island. Thousands of people work at the facility, and they might live anywhere nearby."

Sven nods. "Good point, yeah. Very good point. I'm going to need a map and some coffee. Since everything around here has been cleared out, can we manage some supply runs? It's not like we'll be hurting anyone."

"Yeah," Forrest says. "Let's get the kids on that, because I have an idea, too. I don't like it, but I don't like any of this. Jorge, you and I need to source a local map and find a marina."

"Oh, joy," Jorge says.

Forrest's Testimony: Excerpt 14

Year 38 After the Choosing

If there has been a least favorite part of this entire two-year trek, it would be this most recent part. A tourist map pointed out a nearby Coast Guard station. Jorge and I went there first to find a big enough boat. Sure enough, the whole place had been burned, including the boats. All the fragments in the vicinity were gone, as well. This wasn't some surgical or careful operation. It was meant to destroy, period.

It took forever to find a decent boat. It's not like we had current local street maps or anything. Eventually, we found a few cartoonish walking tour maps, but they didn't exactly point out where boats were other than what we already found.

Pam had the bright idea of taking one of the big vehicles from the Army Reserve base and traveling along the beach. We checked, and sure enough, there were no more fragments, but the place was still fresh. A few months isn't long enough for gas to go bad, and there was a lot of it.

Noise was a concern, but we tried out a few until we found a vehicle with a suppressed enough rumble that it was worth the risk. It turns out, driving down the beach is a great way to avoid traffic. We had to stop and wait a few times for fragments as we got further away from the bridge, but there were surprisingly few. Jorge thought maybe the opposition had gone down this beach to be sure there weren't any available boats the same way they did at the Coast Guard station.

I'm sure he was right, because after a stretch of beach containing a disheartening lack of anything resembling a boat pier, the fragment density suddenly picked up dramatically. A bit further, we had to abandon the vehicle. We had Layla with us, which is good because without her, we never would have made it through. So many people. I didn't care how long it took. I was just glad these fragments hadn't been killed off.

Layla dragged us along like ducklings, weaving and twisting through a confusion of trails we couldn't see. We kept hold of each other's arms or walked close together in her wake. Her brow was creased hard enough that I thought the lines might become permanent. We were all sweating.

We passed several entirely fragmented beaches and a boardwalk, then Jorge shook my arm from behind me. When I turned my head, he was smiling and nodding ahead, but more toward the water than shore. Sure enough, there was a single boat glinting in the sunlight.

Layla was so focused on the people that she hadn't noticed, so I squeezed her hand and repeated Jorge's nod. She looked, and I swear when she turned back around to smile, a thousand pounds of weight had dropped off her shoulders.

The opposition, or the Chosen-Seeker army, or whatever we call them, had obviously given up, going only so far down the beach before calling it quits. What we found wasn't a simple marina. This was a giant basin scooped out of the coast. It was huge and full of boats. Big boats. Expensive boats.

I gotta say, the other half lived pretty darn well before the Choosing. Coming from some Podunk town in Arkansas where the 'other half' consisted of people like me who actually lived in a house, I'm consistently surprised by how well some people lived and how poorly others did. The world before the Choosing was decidedly skewed, and I'm glad I didn't know about it when I was young.

I'd always felt lucky as a kid. My parents had a house in a good neighborhood. I had nice clothes. I got upgrades to my game systems when they came out. In my school, I'd been a kid from the good side of town. Not rich, but not like most. What we called 'well to do.'

I've discovered over the years that I was simply unaware of how much others had, so I was happy. My life compared better to most in our area. Coming through Jersey and into New York was an eye-opener for me. And this place… well, this marina was something else altogether.

We had to spend the night there, which was fine and expected. Given the number in our group and how long our journey might take, especially if we brought supplies, we looked at the yachts first.

Eventually, Layla redirected a few fragments to release a boat big enough to do the job, but simple enough for Sven and Jorge to manage mechanically. Several more fragments had to be redirected in order to release the fuel pumps, but she managed it. It was weird watching her wave and push at the air, her face creased in concentration. Often, it's graceful, like a dance. At other times, like this one, it's surprisingly impersonal and brusque, like shooing away a fly.

Once it was done, I felt intimidated stepping onto the boat. It was so big, and it looked mean and ready to roar, all swoops and curves. It actually had more than one floor, but Jorge called them decks or levels. It was definitely nice.

I suppose I expected more bedrooms considering the size, but there was no question this thing was deluxe. There were also a few crew berths, so we could sleep a few more. Also, I really expected a bigger kitchen considering how many lounge areas there were. Then again, what do I know about the lives of the rich yachting set?

Getting the boat ready wasn't so much about actually getting it ready as it was figuring it out, which was practically Christmas for Sven.

Layla redirected the trails for the marina store. Sven said we needed to empty it because we have no idea what we might need. One thing on his list was paper charts, which was tricky because people mostly used electronic charts, according to Jorge.

Tomorrow morning we're supposed to take this bad boy for a test drive here in the cove. There are a couple of fragments in our path, and we're concerned the boat might be noisy enough to break them, but there's no help for it. We'll do our best.

Six

Year 38 After the Choosing

The yacht has a small boat on a deck in the rear, a nice surprise which will come in handy as a ferry to the shore. Forrest steers the little boat as close to shore as he dares and everyone in camp runs down to greet him. Scanning the group, Forrest sees Coco joining the throng. That's progress. She'd still been crying off and on when he left. She still looks wan and tired, her arms crossed up high as if she's cold. Even so, she smiles when he sloshes through the last bit of water, dragging the boat's line with him.

Tyrone and Benson splash past him to retrieve the small craft. Forrest's wet pant legs slap against his shins. His boots are tied together and flipped over his shoulder, so at least they'll be dry.

Pam claps her hands quickly under her chin, grinning. "Oh, goody, goody! Look at that big, beautiful beast!"

Layla had hurried back to camp ahead of them, retrieving the vehicle on the way, so everyone knew they'd found a decent boat. She must not have fully explained how big it was based on their reactions. Everyone is absolutely delighted.

David and Richie push to the front, both of them grabbing him for a hug at the same time. It feels wonderful, even if both his boys could really use a wash.

Coco looks at him in question, then asks, "Where's Jorge? Isn't he coming?"

"We can't leave it unmanned," Forrest explains. "Jorge and Sven are keeping things running and figuring out the systems."

She nods, but it's clear she's disappointed.

"Jorge asked if you might not be willing to go to the boat early. He says he could use your help. If we hurry, I can get you back tonight with your stuff."

She brightens just a touch at his words, immediately turning away. Over her shoulder, she says, "I'll pack and let Joey know."

Once in camp, Forrest washes quickly and changes his clothes, which he's been wearing for a few days now. Bringing his old clothes outside, he asks Pam, "Are we washing or tossing?"

She waves in the general direction of an enormous pile of boxes they amassed at the edge of camp while he was absent. "Tossing, unless it's something you really want to keep. If it is, then you have to wash it yourself. There are some buckets over there, but water is tight. Bottled water only. Unless you want the ocean, but that's going to leave everything salty."

He considers it for a moment. These jeans are some of his favorites. There's a veritable mountain of bottled water piled nearby, but they might need all of that for drinking soon. He tosses his clothes onto the discard pile with reluctance. The pile reeks. He wonders, not for the first time, what people will think of the messes left behind if the world and time are ever fixed. He can't imagine.

Coco is ready to leave sooner than he would have thought, even before he has a chance to eat. She has boxes and boxes of stuff, far more than she brought with her in their two wagons when they left the vehicles behind.

"Been shopping, I see," he says as he approaches her tent.

With an embarrassed little wave, she says, "No, it's not that. Joey took me back to the vehicles so I could get what we left behind. It's personal stuff that I don't want to let go. If we can't take it, I understand, but if there's any way to bring it, I'd like to."

He thinks he knows what's in those boxes. He saw her pack her journals back in Lorain and saw her carefully transfer the boxes from vehicle to vehicle. For whatever reason, they're too important for her to leave behind. Maybe it's simply her history and she won't let it go.

He grabs the first box. "No problem. There's plenty of room. We just have to get it all over."

The boat is loaded to the brim and bobbing in the water in short order. At least this time, he's wearing khaki pants loose enough around the legs to roll up above the knees.

Coco steps in, hopping a few steps to keep her balance. "Oh my, I do have too much stuff."

"No, they added some canned goods," Forrest says with a chuckle. "Don't worry. We've got to stock as much food as possible."

He watches her as he steers the small boat. The wind whips her hair back and he can almost see her stress fading. It's good to see that. It reminds him of what she was like all those decades ago when they first met.

With the sun dipping low, Forrest doesn't linger at the yacht. Leaving the boxes on the platform Jorge calls the poop deck, he speeds back across the water toward camp. Jorge waves goodbye, one arm around Coco's shoulder. They look happy.

There's a lot to do, and they start the next day. While Forrest can't say that he's glad all the fragments in such a large radius were cleared, especially not the way it must have happened, it is undeniably convenient. There's none of the normal discussion required regarding what fragments have to be released or, as is more often the case now, rerouted.

The group has had so much travel time together that organizing work is a breeze. Everyone knows what everyone else will do best, will ask about, will suggest, or will argue about. After four days of backbreaking work, the group decides they need to tally up their assets and have a meeting of the minds. Once they leave this place, stopping to gather supplies won't be possible. At least not in the near future. Messages from the boat crew pointed out some very obvious problems that none of them considered, each of which needs to be solved before they leave land.

Forrest waits for the morning coffee and breakfast to do its work. Faces clear of sleep and morning grumpiness, especially after David and Layla start cooking. The entire camp smells of sizzling pork and fried bread.

Luckily for them, and very unluckily for the local fragments, the explosion on the road freed almost an entire apartment complex adjacent to the freeway. The pantry goods inside included a rather shocking number of cans of spam and corned beef hash. No matter what anyone might have thought of those foods before, they are treasures now.

When it looks like everyone is awake, Forrest sets aside his empty plate and says, "Okay, we've done well, but we really need to talk for a minute. Brainstorm some solutions. On the boat, Jorge pointed out something we all missed. Specifically, he noted that we have one very loud, small boat to get people and supplies to shore when we get where we're going. This will not work, particularly if they have anyone watching for us to pass by in a huge boat, which they will. I would. We need to figure out a better way to get all of us to shore quickly."

Pam's hand shoots up like she's been waiting for an opening. At his nod, she says, "Okay, I've heard some good ideas for that going around, but that's not really the biggest issue. When I was on the boat yesterday, Sven brought me up to the bridge and showed me some things none of us had even considered. We need to talk about that before anything else."

Forrest hasn't been back to the boat since that first night, so this is new. The last thing they need is another problem. "What is it, Pam?" he asks, trying to keep a neutral expression.

"Right, so you know those charts you guys snagged at the marina?"

He nods. "Sure. What about them?"

"They've been figuring out how to read them and what all the notations everywhere mean. The discussion led to some ideas about why the opposition busted up the bridge." She pauses, looking around as if to be sure Coco isn't nearby. "We didn't go look for ourselves, but we know they must have blown up more bridges because of all the debris washed up around here. Hell, there's part of one of those big green signs sticking up out of the water fifty feet away. Right? With me?"

There are nods all around, so Forrest motions her onward.

"Here's the thing. On the charts, it looks like there are only so many places on the island to bring a big boat. Jorge says there are bays and inlets and miles of marshes and boggy bits on the southern side. Originally, we were just going to cross to the nearest spot, then make our way to Upton over land. He says we can't do that. Most of the marinas on this side are meant for small boats. Jorge and Sven both say it's risky to go through any of those because they're shallow. We don't know the area and, really, none of us are good with boats. He—"

Joey looks antsy as she talks, eventually interrupting her and asking, "What does this have to do with the bridges?"

"I'm getting there. Keep your pants on," she snaps, scowling a little. "It's not like this is a short frigging thing here. I'm summarizing, but I can only squish it so much."

"Sorry," he says.

"As I was saying, Jorge and Sven both think that they blew this bridge, and any others, to make sure we decided crossing by boat was the best decision. They—meaning the opposition—*want* us to do that."

"How does that help them? I mean, there's a lot more water than roads," Layla says.

Pam holds up her finger like a professor about to make her point. "Exactly, but that island is like a maze of cities and swamps and farms and everything in between. There's activity all over it. Fragments moving everywhere. It's hard to see a few people moving around when a million more are moving around, too. Plus, I looked through those big binoculars on the boat. I can see every boat to the horizon with them, which means they could see us from land. They could track us easily and know exactly where we stop. They can pinpoint our landing spot and they won't have to search for us on land. So, yeah, they want us to cross by water. It's a no-brainer."

Forrest feels like an idiot. Of course. If he were on the other side, he'd do the same. And he fell right into the trap. He says, "So, basically, you can set a few people to watch the water and see us coming, then know exactly where to find us and attack. All they need to do is radio in a sighting and they can have all their forces waiting to greet us."

She nods, a grim smile on her face. "Bingo."

"So, what do we do?" he asks. "Do Jorge or Sven have a solution?"

"Yeah, but it sucks. They say we should take the ship far away from shore, like ten or more miles, and then go all the way around the island to the other side while staying out of sight of land. It's the only other option. They plotted it out and yes, it's a long ass trip. Also, if that's what we're doing, we need to go shopping. We need inflatable swimming pools. A lot of them. That's how we're getting to shore."

Forrest's Testimony: Excerpt 15

Year 38 After the Choosing

I gotta say, I could get used to this kind of life. This boat is more ship than boat, but it's designed so that a small crew can operate it, with one extra crew spot for whatever people need when cruising on their yacht. Seriously, this is the life.

Of course, we're not using it like it's meant to be used. We're jammed in like sardines. There may be four full suites, but there are also over two dozen of us. We make do, but sharing a bed with both David and Richie spread out like starfish almost makes me want to bunk in the lounge. At least there, we have an amazing view.

I'm glad everyone with even the slightest mechanical and electrical aptitude came on board as soon as we got the boat. It's scary complicated. Just looking into the mechanical spaces makes me put my hands into my pockets.

Between Sven, Jorge, Tyrone, Kiara, Brian, Garrett, and all their assorted kids—who really aren't kids anymore—this place has been ticking along nicely. Getting fully fueled was a bit of a fiasco, but once that was done, our range is over a thousand miles, even with all the electrical running. Amazing.

Technically, we could make this trip in twenty-four hours, even including our long, detoured version that requires we stay beyond sight from the shore. This boat can haul ass if we push it, but we won't. Practically speaking, we know just enough to know we don't actually know anything. We're going as slow as molasses.

All the navigation aids along the coast don't work, obviously, but the radar on this ship is pretty sweet. Sven is using the shape of the land to approximate where we are. Tyrone says it almost feels like he got his hands on a computer game again, only a very boring and slow one. To me, it all looks like gibberish, but then again, my expertise is all from the ground. Navigating through a forest is more my speed.

There have been hiccups, but they're all hormonal. Maybe it's the sea air, like Coco says, but my goodness. It's embarrassing. David is an adult and has been on the road for over two years with Aliyah, who is Kiara's youngest. They're the same age and they've always had a thing for each other, but really? Seriously, Kiara and I are within spitting distance, no matter where we go on the boat. It's not like they can hide what they're doing. Being a parent can be super awkward sometimes.

And they aren't the only ones. Joey and Layla recently declared themselves married while we were eating dinner, which shocked no one except Coco, who started crying because there was no wedding. They claim that with a baby soon to be born, it's best to be officially married. Pam's son, Benson, and Tyrone's daughter, Sadie, are also a couple now.

And finally, there's Trig, whose parents couldn't make the trip, and Darrell, Kiara's son. I'm pretty sure Trig came along because of Darrell. His parents approved and wished they could go, but honestly, neither of them would have survived the first winter on the road. They knew their son wanted to be with the one he loved.

I'm not saying it's scientifically proven or anything, but I definitely think there's something to the whole romance of the sea thing. I just hope no one else winds up pregnant.

As for me, well, I'm trying not to seem as anxious as I am. Inside, I'm conflicted about everything. Should we do this thing? I love my boys and I can't bear the idea of losing them. And the more I think about it, the more I doubt that we can keep this world if we fix time.

My doubts solidified because of the cereal we took from the man when Joey first altered his loop. We'd known that it would either revert or be released, and if it reverted, it would be stale. All the decades since the Choosing would catch up and that cereal would be inedible. If it was released, it would be the same as it was on the day the Choosing happened. It was released.

Why would this cause me to doubt?

When Joey detached that cereal, he fixed time for that box, and it went back to the way it was when it all started. If that happens to the whole world when… and if… we manage to fix time, then what happens to everything that came after the Choosing? If we're released, along with everything else that's fragmented, then these decades of our lives will simply never have happened.

That includes my boys. That includes all the young people on this ship and everywhere else that people have survived and made a life for themselves. It's a terrible thought.

Seven

Year 38 After the Choosing

"Do you still see the light?" Forrest asks, looking from Layla to Joey and back again.

Almost everyone is crowded on deck, most of them trying to see whatever light it is that most of the gifted can see. Forrest sees nothing.

Both young adults nod, their eyes fixed on some point in the darkness. Joey raises a finger toward the dark land to the south of them. "It's right there. It's not bright, more like a smudge. It's miles away."

"And you're sure it's not a fire?" Jorge asks.

That was everyone's first thought. Had this combined resistance force actually set fire to the facility, or perhaps the land around it, to prevent an approach? Such a thing would disturb countless fragments and surely defeat the purpose of preventing interference at the lab. Plus, the non-gifted may be getting on in age, but at least one of them would have been able to see the light if it was a real fire.

Layla shakes her head. "It's not a red light like you'd see from a fire. It's more, I don't know, *pure* light. Sort of all colors at the same time."

Joey says, "Yep, that's what I see."

Sven looks down at the chart they've brought from the bridge, then out at the land. Stabbing a finger at a red circle inked onto the chart, he says, "Upton isn't on this chart, but we estimated its position by comparing it with our regular maps. If that was correct, then that's really close. That light might be the facility."

Forrest glances at Jorge. "And this is what you said the Texas expedition reported? Light right through the ground at the collider? Like snakes of light left over from the older experiments?"

With a grim nod, Jorge says, "That's the info I got, yes. That's got to be the facility."

Sven, who has become the de facto captain of the vessel, says, "Well, that settles the question of where to go, but now we have to figure out where to park. Our options are pretty limited."

Sven and his cadre of quasi-capable chart readers leave for the bridge, already talking about mysterious water things like draft and tides and channels. Forrest, like many others, has tried to make sense of all these new concepts, but he's a land mammal and always will be.

A few of the others drift off, either to their duties or to their beds. Those remaining are mostly those assigned to sleep in the lounge, including Forrest and his boys. He couldn't take the stateroom anymore and let another group have it. Coco and her family are assigned to the other lounge, so they remain as well.

Forrest tries to collect his thoughts and go over their tentative plans. Plans they have made, then altered, then altered again. Originally, their intention was to sail to the eastern part of the island, then enter through the series of bays toward the interior. That would have put them approaching from the east with just a few miles of land to cover, most of that marked on the atlas as swamp and parkland.

What they hadn't realized was how many boats would be inside those bays. Not just dozens, but chaotic dozens, popping in and out of existence as their fragments of time reset. The group knew immediately that path wasn't for them. Between each of the bays are tight channels. If the outer bay was that chaotic with fragments, then the channels would be impossible.

Regretfully, they'd turned the ship and looked to the more open water of the Long Island Sound. It wasn't the choice they'd hoped to make. The sound was all good water but had fewer spots to approach the shore.

All the ideal spots were too far west, which would require a long, overland trek through dense populations. Now, they would have to settle for getting close enough and hoping no one was stationed on the north side of the island and watching for them.

"Do you ever wonder if maybe we shouldn't do this?" Jorge asks.

Forrest starts a little. He hadn't even heard Jorge come stand next to him at the rail.

Should he be honest? Should he say the things that will bolster Jorge's convictions? He opts for the truth and says, "All the time."

For a long time, the men are silent, listening to the engine's hum and the soft shushing of water sliding against the hull. The ship is traveling north while they plan, away from the island and out of sight. Despite the silence, Forrest can tell there's more coming. The atmosphere is full of whatever Jorge hasn't yet said.

At last, Jorge turns his back to the water and leans against the rail with a smile. "We have one hell of a boy, don't we?"

It's the first time he's ever used that word in reference to Joey. An inclusive *we* that acknowledges their joint parentage of the son who isn't Forrest's son, but is.

"Yeah," he says, then adds, "You've done an amazing job raising him, you know. You're a much better father than I am, I think. You were right all those years ago. It was hard to accept, and for a long time, I didn't accept it. But you were right."

Jorge pats his shoulder. "Thank you."

Again, there is silence, but when Forrest glances away from the water, he sees Jorge's face is wet with tears. "Are you okay?"

Jorge has never been one to cry. He's always been too busy finding a way to fix things. Of course, Forrest wasn't a part of Jorge's life on a day-to-day basis before this mess, so perhaps he just wasn't around to witness it.

Wiping his face, Jorge takes a shaky breath and says, "Layla felt the baby move today. I've never felt less sure of what we're planning than after she said that. That baby is a real person and will be born in a few months. And we're going to do what, take away that time? Take away all time? Maybe erase them?"

Jorge sniffs, but before Forrest can respond, he goes on. "I don't want to lose this life, not one day of it, not even the really shitty days. I realize we don't know what will happen, but I don't want to risk losing any of this. If we fix time, we might end up right where we were when time stopped. Most think we'll be young and with the people we love and none of this will have happened. We won't miss it because we won't remember it. Maybe that makes some people feel better about it, but it horrifies me. This was my life and I want to keep it, and all the people in it. I know we have to do this, but I don't want to. Not one bit of me wants to."

His head swimming, Forrest leans heavily against the railing. His belly twists, like it did when he first boarded the ship and the motion made him queasy. He breathes through it, his mind running a mile a minute. The baby is moving. It's not an abstraction anymore. Should they do this? What if it does erase them? Erase all that's been and happened since the moment of the Choosing? What if they are all like the box of cereal?

No, he can't think like that. They don't know if anything will be erased. They really don't. It's just as likely, perhaps even more likely, that time will simply resume, leaving them all standing around in the middle of a bunch of people who can't understand how a crowd of dirty savages suddenly appeared in their midst. This is what he has to believe. If he doesn't, then he can't keep going on this mission.

Shaking his head, Forrest says, "It won't take away time. I can't believe that. I won't believe it. We have to remember what will happen to all of us if we don't fix this. If we don't find a way to start the clock, then all of this will end, anyway. We have to try."

Jorge nods. They remain silent, both gazing out at the dark water, both worrying about things no one about to become a grandparent should have to worry about.

After a while, Jorge says, "I don't know what you want, specifically, but Coco and I want you to know that we'd love it if you were also the baby's grandfather. Layla and Joey would like that as well, but it's your choice. More grandparents are always better. It means more love and kids can use all of that they can get. What do you say?"

Forrest feels his own eyes sting now. He'd wondered about his place in the baby's life but hadn't hoped for this. He nods, looking out at the dark sea and says, "Yes."

* * *

At least a dozen inflatable pools in many shapes and sizes litter the beach. Forrest keeps the small boat from the yacht as steady and slow as possible as he drags two more pools on a line behind him. They've overturned a few by hurrying. If everything isn't loaded evenly or if the water surges even a little, the pools flip and send their treasures to litter the sand beneath the waves.

Despite some in the group complaining they were losing time by being overcautious, Forrest is glad Tyrone and Sven insisted they wrap the valuables in plastic. Boxes also sport long lines with brightly colored floats at the ends. Even now, several of their group are hauling in lines attached to precious boxes of canned goods or equipment they desperately need.

This run turns out well and Forrest slows the boat gradually and gently, allowing the line to slacken and the pools to drift shoreward for retrieval. Coco and Joey splash out to take the line from him, both of them quick and quiet. They hand him the line for some empty pools to take back for loading. It looks almost festive as he returns. A handful of brightly colored, puffy pools bouncing along behind him.

When the last loads are packed and ready, Sven joins him on the boat for the last trip to shore. Some of their group stay behind on the yacht to keep it safe in case it's needed again. None of them have to say that would mean they failed, or only found another clue and not a solution. It's unspoken, but there.

Those on the ship will also patrol up and down the coast, using their vantage point to scan for threats. The secure handhelds they found onboard will allow them to communicate with the shore, yet not be overheard by the Chosen-Seeker group they all know are here somewhere.

The ship crew also keeps the rifles, which can, if necessary, be used from the ship against targets on shore if they pull in closer. No one wants that because of the noise, but if it must happen, they're ready.

The ten people remaining aboard wish them good luck, but their faces are grim and their expressions tight. No one is really sure what good luck actually means. Forrest isn't the only one who half-wishes they won't be able to fix anything. Everyone probably hopes for one thing and then another by turns throughout each long day. He does. With so much still unknown, it's difficult to be certain what he wants.

At the beach, which is bordered by thick forest and a huge industrial complex, Forrest cuts the engine for what may be the last time. He savors the feel of it, just in case it is.

The beach is free of fragments, probably because of the ugly complex and thick forest. It's a nice beach, he supposes, but he really wouldn't know. So far, they've all seemed nice to him. Being from the Midwest means a distinct lack of beach access other than a small lake with a beach made mostly of mud and leaf slime.

They drag the small boat to the edge of the forest, a feat of no small effort, leaving it hidden for later use. Soon after, farting sounds and giggles flood the beach as the young stomp on the pools to hurry the deflation process. Before the older people even have the various goods sorted into big-wheeled carts, the pools are wrapped and secured inside the boat.

The carts they will drag this time are larger, and a few even have trailers behind them created from another cart. Some of them came with them all the way from Lorain, while they cobbled together others during their time preparing the yacht.

Once everything is packed, Forrest can't believe how much stuff they have. Then again, they have no idea how long this endeavor might take or how much food will be available. They can't stop to search for supplies. They know that. And once there, what will they find? Does a place like that even have a cafeteria? Is it like a college campus, or more like a factory with a lunchroom and vending machines? No one knows.

It's late afternoon, but the sun is still high, and the hours of darkness are shorter this time of year. Forrest makes his way through the clusters of carts and backpacks toward the main group.

Once there, he taps Layla's arm and asks, "Do you see the light yet?"

She shakes her head with an apologetic expression. "Nope. It's not obvious in the daytime."

They've previously described it as a glow on the horizon from the ship. Not really bright, but quite large and diffuse. In daylight, they've never spotted it. He'd hoped being closer might make it more obvious, but apparently not. Sunshine is a hard thing to match for brightness.

Hands pressing into his lower back, Jorge stretches and says, "Thank all the stars for solid ground."

Layla's mother, Chantelle, gives a quiet but fervent, "Here, here!"

Forrest scans the beach again and sees nothing. Not a single fragment. That might be suspicious, but they saw a good many on the other side of the big industrial complex where a row of houses crowds the beach. Small boats dot the waters in front of the homes, so it doesn't appear as if anyone has been clearing fragments. This one spot just happens to be clear.

Checking his watch, Forrest says, "Well, we've got about four hours till it's fully dark. Take a nap if you want. Definitely relax and stay off your feet if you can. We'll eat before we head out. It's going to be a long night of walking. First watch is Pam and Darrell. Are you both okay, or do you need to rest?"

Pam nods her readiness, already slipping a quiver of arrows over her head and shoulder. Darrell hops up and grabs a pair of binos and his own weapons. No one likes that they need weapons, but it is what it is. They have no idea who might be close and what their intentions really are.

Forrest doesn't know if he can sleep, but even if he can't drop off, he can at least rest with his eyes closed and hope his mind drifts. That's rest of a sort. David and Richie can sleep anywhere, so he's not worried about them. They're already settling back on a blanket when he reaches them. As he lies down and looks at the deep green trees against a brilliantly blue and cloudless sky, Forrest once again wonders if he's doing the right thing.

Part Five

Coco

Coco's Journal: Age 51

Year 38 of the Loop

Now that we're here on Long Island, with Upton just a few miles away, all I want is to go back. I want to forget about time and loopers and all the things that will eventually go wrong. I want to see life play out until my last day. And when I die, I want to go knowing that life will go on and on and on forever.

One

Year 38 of the Loop

"Six miles never seemed this long before," Coco whispers to Jorge over her shoulder. He's trudging along behind her cart, next in line.

He grunts softly in response but says nothing. Ahead of her, Joey's cart wobbles just a little. It's overloaded. Coco feels guilty that most of her cart is weighed down with her journals, but they've come this far, and she's not leaving them behind now.

Everyone has something they can't leave behind, so she's not alone. Pam has her photo albums filled with her family as they were before the Looping. Brian has his deceased wife's knitted blanket, the last one she made. Chantelle has her husband's fishing tackle and hat. For Sven, there's a collection of laser etched crystal blocks, images of his family on annual vacations floating forever inside. For Kiara, it's a bronze casting of her mother's hands created by her artist father. For Tyrone, his father's briefcase filled with mementos.

Even Forrest has something, though Coco doesn't know what it is. He keeps it tucked away in a wooden box wrapped in plastic.

She stops as a raised fist travels down the line from hand to hand. With a sigh, she waits. It's been like this the whole way. Six miles may be the distance from point to point—or at least, that's their best estimate—but the trip itself is much more than that. They have to pick their way through the loops over roads they don't know, between swatches of spongy forest and trails that dead end.

After a few minutes, Layla awkwardly jogs down the line while holding her growing belly in place. She informs everyone of their status as she passes. There's a tangle of loops ahead on the road. The shoulder is still safe, but Benson is going to clear some space. Apparently, their path narrows to almost nothing just ahead.

As Layla moves along the line, everyone sits, including Coco. Moving the loop trails is not a quick process, especially when it involves cars. No mistakes can be made, or a gifted might find themselves flattened by the car they're trying to move.

Joey comes first to her, then Jorge, asking if they're okay and peering at them as if he'll be able to see the truth of their answers. He seems so mature for twenty-four. Coco doesn't remember being as thoughtful as he is at that age. Well, she was alone then, so maybe that's why she was different.

She glances back at Jorge, and even in the dark, she knows he's breathing too hard. He's been taking his blood pressure meds, but there's something wrong and they both know it. In a rare moment of fear the night before, he whispered that he could feel his heart pounding in his neck and ears even when he was resting.

In the dark, he shakes his head at her, silently letting her know she should say nothing to Joey.

The rest is short, but good. Her feet feel less like blocks of wood when she stands and grips her cart handle. The forest to one side of them is thick and very dark, full of rustling noises that make her nervous. It's probably just the night breeze, which is lovely and fresh, but she can't really know, so her ears remain perked.

The road they walk along is a divided four lane with a wide, smoothly paved shoulder. It's a major road, which they found only after bumbling along a smaller one cut through the forest. That had been a nightmare. They started and stopped, alternating between hurrying when the gifted made a gap in the loops and stopping for long periods while they created more.

There are occasional large houses set back from the road, but mostly, it's just trees and more trees. Joey and the other gifted say the light they see is almost directly ahead, but there's only the darkness of night for Coco.

After another ten minutes, they stop again, but this time for a real break and some food. It's early for that. Coco wonders why until Forrest gets everyone huddled together.

Standing in the center of their group, he says in a lowered voice, "Big intersection up ahead, the kind with a cloverleaf and overpass. It's wide open but covered in fragments. Benson scouted and said there's too much traffic. All the gifted are going to have to work together to make a clear spot to cross the road."

Sven asks, "Does that mean we're camping here? This is a shit place to camp. The forest sounds like it's swarming with fragments. I don't think anyone has been through here since all this started."

"No," Forrest says, then scans the faces in the crowd until he sees Benson. "Tell them what you found."

Benson leans in. "Before this road curves off to go into… what did you call it, Forrest?"

"A cloverleaf. It's because the roads look like a four-leafed clover from the sky."

"Right," Benson says, but his expression makes it clear he has no idea what Forrest means. "Before the cloverleaf, there's this track into the forest. No loops on it. I peeked in and there's another whole road there, but sort of like a half-road, like they started and gave up. There's a big open spot of asphalt. No loops on it except small ones, like from animals. We can camp there."

Forrest takes over, saying, "It's tight and there are a lot of fragments on the road next to it, most of them going fast. Just keep moving and hug the far end of the shoulder. No lights in camp, either. Just a quick cold camp and sleep."

When they get moving, Coco sees what Forrest meant by a lot of loops. As the cars whip past, she can feel the push of air against her. Her cart is harder to drag in a straight line when the big trucks go by. It's quite noisy as well, but at least that will cover their own noises.

She lets out a sigh of relief when she sees the cluster of people against the trees. Only a few of the cars have headlights on and there are no streetlights, of course. Even so, the moon is quite bright. The people are deep shadows lined in silver light. She wishes she still had a camera.

At the trailhead, Coco sees the reason for the delay. Carts are lined up along the trees, a few people digging through them for sleeping bags or whatever else they need. Coco and Jorge are almost the last in line tonight. Only Sven and one more person are behind them.

As Coco follows Joey along the line of carts to park, there's a soft *whoomp* of noise. At the same time, Trig, who is searching his cart, spins like someone might spin a top. He grunts and hits the ground with a dull thud.

"Trig? You okay?" Pam whispers from the cart next to him.

Another of those strange, soft *whoomps* comes, but this time it's accompanied by an odd sensation near Coco's head, almost like motion, but not quite. David, Forrest's older son, shrieks and grips his arm.

Before she can even process what's happening, Pam shouts, "Shooting! Someone is shooting!"

Too much happens too fast. The noise around them rises as people knock over carts or cry out in dismay. David groans in pain. In the forest, a legion of screaming animal sounds rise like a chorus of hellsong.

Before she can unfreeze herself enough to move, there's another *whoomp*. This time, it's Joey who reacts, screeching as he claps a hand to his ear.

Jorge grabs her arm, probably intending to drag Coco into the trees, but then stops and releases her, reaching for Joey instead. His eyes wide, he glances down at an unmoving Trig and then back at Joey. He shouts, "They're aiming for the kids!"

This unfreezes Coco and she races for Joey. With Jorge on one side and her on the other, they drag him back into the trees, heedless of whatever loops might be there. As the trees close in around them, there's another soft sound, but this time, the target was clearly meant to be Aliyah.

Instead, Chantelle is hit while shielding Aliyah and Richie with her body. She arches her back, her arms flying wide. She falls, unmoving, but both kids race for the trees.

There is mayhem as Coco reaches the open asphalt area. People are tucked into the trees around the periphery, but she can't see who is where. Coco and Jorge tuck themselves into a dark spot not already occupied. Joey isn't screaming, only making tight noises of pain with a hand pressed to his ear.

Jorge yanks their son's hand away and looks, almost wilting in relief after a moment. Under the silver light, Coco pulls Joey down so she can see for herself. His ear. It's ugly and bleeding. She pushes his hair away, fingers searching his scalp. There's no wound beyond his ear.

Around them, people are frantically doing what they can or must. Pam has David behind cover, examining his arm while he cries in pain. Many of their group have weapons out, shooting futile arrows into the dark or searching for anything they can aim at. Others push those not in ample cover further behind the trees. Layla appears, crawling through the underbrush, dragging her mother's body into the clearing.

Coco gasps at the sight. Chantelle is entirely limp. Her neck and body bend unnaturally against the obstructions of underbrush and uneven ground. Joey shouts, then breaks away, hurtling himself toward Layla and her deceased mother.

He falls to his knees and grabs Layla. Never releasing her grip on her mother's wrist, she lets him enfold her there on the ground. The sounds that come out of her shatter Coco's heart.

Forrest rises from a squat next to David, Kiara quickly kneeling to take his place. He backs up a few steps, his bloody hands still out, as if reaching for his injured son.

Jorge taps Coco's shoulder and says, "Go. Get Forrest back. He needs to keep his head. We are not safe. I'll take care of Joey and Layla."

Racing for Forrest, Coco grabs his arm and asks, "Is David alright?"

Silver tracks line Forrest's face. "Pam says it's in the muscle of his arm. She says she can stop the bleeding if I leave her alone. Coco, they shot my boy!"

Shifting her grip to his shoulders, she shakes him hard and says, "Mine too." When he looks up again, suddenly stricken once more, she says, "He's fine. His ear. You have to ignore all of that right now. We all do. We are not safe. At least one person is shooting at us, and we don't even know where they are! We need to do something."

Suddenly, Sven appears from the shadows. Within a few seconds, everyone who isn't tending the wounded gathers near the trees, except Joey and Layla. Layla cradles her mother, softly keening a wail almost inhuman in its grief. Even Richie leaves his brother's side and crowds in, an angry fifteen-year-old ready to avenge his brother.

Everyone talks at once, some calling for an immediate response, others for caution. The angry voices of broken loops in the forest begin to fade, so Coco hisses, "Be quiet! You're just telling them where we're hiding."

The noise dies immediately, a few fearful faces scanning the trees for foes. Sven's voice is low, but no less full of fury for the lack of volume. "That was a silenced weapon. That's why it sounded so soft. Suppressors on the guns. We should have known. The overpass is the perfect spot. They've probably got a shooter at every decent approach. All those fragments in vehicles made cover noise. The shooting definitely came from the overpass and—"

Tyrone interrupts. "Were they really aiming for the kids? Why?"

Jorge says, "They were. No question. There were better shots to be had. As to why, it's obvious. Without the gifted, we can't get into the facility. It wouldn't be safe to go to Upton. It wouldn't be possible, and we'd never do it without them."

An appalled silence falls over the group, then Forrest asks, "How many shooters were there?"

Sven shakes his head. "Probably two. Probably with spotters. That's what I'd do. And they're long gone or setting up a new kill zone nearby. No doubt they've already radioed our location to their leadership."

Brian curses and says, "We have to get out of here, and we have to do it fast." The man looks frantic, like he might start blindly running to any place that isn't this one.

Sven grabs his shoulder. "Calm down and think. No matter what, they're spread thin. They've probably been covering all the main approaches twenty-four-seven for who knows how long. If they'd known we were coming to this spot, there would be a lot fewer of us standing here right now. It's going to take time for them to organize, but someone is probably watching from somewhere right now. Maybe one spotter and one shooter, or maybe just a spotter to relay information. Whoever they left behind, they would have had to move their shooting spot. They wouldn't stay where we can find them and shoot back."

"Then let's search and kill them," Benson says. At that moment, he looks a lot like his father, Sven. Icy and dangerous.

Forrest keeps looking back at David, who is no longer whimpering. Pam is winding bandages around his arm. They need Forrest to be in this conversation, so Coco snaps her fingers near his face. "Forrest! Help us here. You were on the Chosen council for ages. What do you know about this kind of thing? Since when does the council have weapons like that?"

His head whips around and his expression flashes momentary guilt. He swallows hard and says, "Okay, okay. I'm here. In the beginning, before we were sure how things would go down, the early Chosen gathered things. Silencers, ammo, and all kinds of shit. We were teenagers thinking this would be like Mad Max or whatever. They have some serious equipment stocked away, but this tactic? No. We never did anything like this. We were at peace."

Coco is shocked, but she should have known people would collect dangerous toys. It should probably surprise her more that it took this long for someone to find a reason to open the stockpile and play with all their weapons.

Sven nods. "Right now, at this moment, we have time. Not much, but some. They're going to rely on our need to tend the wounded and not go into the open. They're going to collect their forces, but in case you didn't notice, they aren't disturbing fragments. That overpass and the roads here are a nightmare to get through. They didn't clear anything. It's too dangerous for that since it might disturb fragments at the facility. That means a little time for us. We have to leave, but we need to be smart about it."

"So, what do we do?" Coco asks.

From behind her, Layla says, "I've got an idea."

Everyone turns at the sound of her voice. It's hard and rough, a combination of fury and grief. The young woman carrying Coco's grandchild is arranging her mother's limbs, making her look as if she's lying down for a rest. She is no longer crying.

Coco's Journal: Age 51

Year 38 of the Loop

Leaving our dead behind? It's just too much. In what world do we leave our loved ones unburied? In what world are we forced to in order to stay alive? Not this one. The new world is full of peace, civility, and shared hardship. Or it was. Or maybe, I only thought it was. Watching Layla leave her mother's body was one of the hardest things I've ever had to watch in my life, and I've seen a lot.

Our world is so beautiful. The lives we live in our communities are so peaceful, good, and full of purpose. I thought maybe the Looping had freed us in some ways. With nothing to fight over, we didn't fight. It seemed wrong to erase it in favor of the bitterness of our world before the looping. Back then, it was all fighting and hatred and climate change and endless deception and too much badness to catalog.

It turns out this world isn't so different after all. It just needed something to spark the fire and here we are, fighting once again.

Two

Year 38 of the Loop

Though they've carried it for the two years they've been on the road, never have they transmitted on the community radio. They used it to listen, to learn of activity around settlements or trade convoys. It's nothing more than a souped-up mobile version of something called a CB, which Coco didn't even realize existed before the Looping began.

Apparently, truckers used CBs, but so did many others. They charge theirs up every few days, getting new batteries as necessary, but they've never talked on it.

For the Chosen and Seekers, these radios have always been the most efficient means of communication with limited towers. Channel nine is, and always had been, the emergency channel. Every settlement monitors it. Even scouts do, since most radios will monitor two channels.

Now, just twenty minutes after Layla said she had an idea, Coco covers her ears as a looped car careens directly off the road and into the big triangle of land between the petals of the cloverleaf. The car is on fire. The poor looped woman inside is no more.

Forrest pushes the button on the radio and says, "That was a warning. You've killed our people. You've killed our children. We're backing away, but if you come for us, we'll burn everything. We'll break every fragment on this island. We'll burn it to the ground. If it ends the world, so be it. This is your only warning. If we see you, we burn it."

It's a terrible threat, but an effective one. What the opposition fears most is disrupting the experiment at Upton. That they've taken such pains to disrupt no loopers on this crowded island is proof. Any loop disrupted could be one that interacts with the Brookhaven Lab in Upton, and that would be bad.

Time seems to drag as everyone stares at the silent radio, then there's a crackle and a rough voice says, "You can back away. Do not come any closer to the facility. Retreat and leave the island. We won't fire."

The terrible thing they've done by sending that burning car into the open has meant the loss of at least one person. Hopefully, it will save many others.

Forrest tucks the radio in his belt and shrugs. "That gives us some room, but they're going to expect us to leave. They can't see us now with the trees, but eventually, they'll get more people in the area. They aren't breaking fragments so it won't be fast, but they'll come. Layla, I hope your plan works."

"It will. I know it. We'll need as much of our stuff as we can, though. And this needs to look like a retreat if anyone can see us. Grab all the carts and move."

Layla and Joey hurry everyone back in the direction from which they came, only now they're on the access road on the inside of the tree line. Next to Coco, Jorge's breathing sounds like an overworked bellows about to explode. She glances at him, but he's focused ahead. Even David is doing this hurried walk better than Jorge, and he got shot in the arm.

They return to the road's shoulder when the access road ends, once again bordered by traffic but too far away for a shooter to even guess their location. Further on, the only residential street on this stretch joins the road. Layla calls for everyone to hurry, then tells them to be quiet. She can be loud, but the non-gifted have to hold in their exhausted gasps.

She calls out instructions as they pass her. "Wait right here. Benson, get everyone off the road. If we lose control of the truck, I don't want anyone in the way. Sven, stand ready at the entrance to the street right there. Aliyah, you're with Joey. Everyone, this might suck, so get ready to move quickly."

With that, she gives Joey instructions, one hand under her belly for support, and the other waving in the air as she sketches out what she needs him to do.

As soon as she stops talking, Joey lets go of his cart and starts running, Aliyah hot on his heels. Coco is terrified he'll get himself killed. Layla seems to droop, exhaustion taking over now that her part in her plan is over. Coco waves her over and puts an arm around her, offering what comfort she can.

Her plan is a good one, but it requires precision and the right vehicle. A loop they passed on the way here was a big panel truck, one riding high and labeled with an online megastore's logo. It turns into this street and stops at a house before returning to the road.

There are loops everywhere in this small housing area. Benson and Darrell bend a few, hands swooping and dragging the air. Benson yells for them to line up their carts in the yard and stand still. It takes a few minutes to do as he commands and remain silent in the process.

There's a teenage girl flirting with someone who isn't there a few houses down. Her head cocks and one leg turns so her heel rests on her other foot. It's a coquettish maneuver made awkward by her age. A man drives a car into his driveway and gets out over and over. A kid plays in a yard across the street. Someone exits an RV that looks like a permanent installation next door.

Coco feels her heart hammering as she stands in line, one hand firmly on her cart and the other draped around Layla. She's waiting for the noise and hopes she doesn't hear it. Suddenly, Joey reappears at the end of the street, his hands stretched to the side as he pulls the invisible trail. He curves around, then seems to bundle something in his hands. Then he takes off running again, pulling whatever it is behind him.

It looks insane, but what he's doing is stretching the loop trail, a skill he has perfected over their years on the road. He can slow them, speed them up, make them go in circles. If he messes up, then the loop might interact with another and break them both, but being able to see where loops go means he rarely does that. He just avoids crossing trails.

He said that he was going to slow the loop, giving Sven just enough time to do the unthinkable. Coco mourns the coming loss, but there's no alternative. Whoever this person is, they will owe him their lives.

The truck comes, but instead of the quick turn it normally takes, it slows and wobbles, as if the person at the wheel can't steer straight. Aliyah is almost weaving back and forth in place, ready to jump.

Joey yells, "Go!"

Aliyah glances at Sven, who has raised his bow in steady hands. She leaps for the sidestep, yanks open the truck door, squeezing her body behind it, and Sven fires. There's not a single peep of noise. It's over that fast.

The truck careens wildly. Sven catches the door even as Aliyah is flung off the step. She tumbles, but rolls to her feet, eyes on the vehicle. It's clear when Sven has it under control. The truck rumbles to an idle and the brake lights brighten the darkness behind the truck.

Joey holds up a hand toward those in line and yells, "Hold!" To Sven, he yells, "Turn it around."

Now that the truck isn't looped, it can break loops with noise. Staying at the end of the street, Sven pulls the truck in a tight turn without going into reverse. Everyone knows never to reverse a commercial vehicle without disabling the warning system first. Those beeps have gotten too many people attacked by loopers.

Joey gets the cargo area door up, taking great care to lift it quietly. He illuminates the contents with his flashlight and Coco sighs. It's not full at all. This must have been a loop from Saturday evening, probably after most of the deliveries were made. That's good.

It takes a good half hour for them to remove cargo and transfer supplies from the wagons to the truck. Before everyone loads themselves, they huddle for one last talk.

Joey asks, "Are you all sure? All of you? I'll try to miss as many loopers as I can, but we'll break more than a few loops. It's possible we might break something crucial. Is everyone sure they want to risk this?"

Coco knows no one is really sure, but there's no other viable choice. Yes, they can go back to the boat and leave the island, never to return. That's an option, but it's not a viable one. It would also surprise Coco if they even made it back to the boat alive. The council won't give them the opportunity to sway a community to their side with the truth.

If they don't reach the facility before this night is over, they never will. Their only path is the most direct one, the one that the enemy won't expect and won't be able to deal with in time. They must barrel through, no matter what it disrupts or who gets hurt in the process.

There's a long moment of silence, of people looking at each other for support. It ends when Forrest takes Joey's hand and holds it in both of his. "There's no other option. Not really. You do what you must, and know that we're all sorry you have to be the one to do it."

Joey's eyes shine a little, but he nods and turns away, leaving them a free path to pile into the truck. There's barely enough floor space in the truck for everyone to crowd inside, sitting so close together they are literally squeezed in. As she tries to get her legs to fold sufficiently for the small space, Coco sees the carts outside. It seems wrong to leave them behind, all parked in a yard like lost children. Bits of baggage litter the area.

When Joey pulls the big door down, he pauses and looks them over one last time. The bandage over his ear is dark with blood, but it's his heart that's really breaking. Coco can see it and hers breaks with his. He's grown into a kind man, one who would never choose to hurt anyone. He will have to hurt many people before this night is done.

A battery-operated lantern fills the cargo area with just enough light to see each other, casting stark shadows on the walls. The truck lurches and at first, but everything seems alright. Then, the sharp twists and turns begin, and they grip each other for support. Around them, boxes and bags shift, some sliding off piles and onto other piles. Or onto them. Cries fill the air as airborne belongings pummel the passengers.

Coco tries to imagine what it must be like for Joey up front. She tries to imagine what it must look like. Gold-tinged streaks of colored light twisting and turning in bewildering patterns from so many loops on the roads. She knows he's using what he sees to avoid breaking loops when he can, scooting between and around them. It must be so confusing.

It's hard to hear anything other than the rumble of the truck and the clatter of gear. Almost every face is intent, listening for any noises that might mean danger. Jorge has Layla cradled next to him, securely held while she leans against his shoulder and cries.

Coco glances to her other side toward Darrell. His face is stiff and stricken. He lost Trig, and worse, he never got to say goodbye. Trig's body was too near the front of the line, exposed to the overpass because of the way he fell. When they retrieved the carts, he could only look and see Trig sprawled out, nothing more.

Shifting to make enough room for her arm to move, she rests her hand on his back. It's a question. He answers by leaning in, tucking his head against her shoulder. His body shakes with sobs, and she holds him close, so he knows she's there. That she has him and she won't let go.

After a series of sharp jerks and turns, of hard braking followed by equally hard accelerations, there's a crash of glass shattering, followed by screams from disturbed loopers. The ride gets worse, bumping up over obstructions that create alarming sounds beneath them. Even Darrell lifts his head, his tears temporarily halted by more urgent fear.

A sharp ping above makes Coco look up. The gray light of the coming dawn shines through a small round hole in the wall. Another few pings follow, scattering holes all along the wall.

Jorge's voice is sharp and tight. "Turn off the light. Everyone get down as flat as you can!"

The darkness returns, but there's little room for anyone to get lower than they already are. Almost without thinking, Coco pulls Darrell to lean into her lap while she curls over him. They can afford to lose her, but not the gifted. They can see what she can't.

Noises of alarm rise as the truck leans hard. She's almost lifted from her spot as it bounces over more obstructions. The noise beneath them changes suddenly. The hollow, roaring whine of the road lessens into something that almost sounds like a frantic slapping against the undercarriage.

"What is that?" Coco asks, thinking it might mean something has broken in the truck.

Jorge's voice comes out of the darkness. "I think we're off road. Maybe a field or grass or something."

Once he says it, she can feel it. Innumerable stalks sliding along under the truck. Another jerk and swerve, then the road returns, but it's not smooth. They're all slammed to one side as it swerves into what must be a U-turn. There's more twisting and turning that feels never-ending, until the truck jerks to a sudden and disorienting stop.

David pukes, splattering those next to him and filling the space with the sour smell of bile. Pam's voice murmurs soothing sounds. Coco's heart is about to climb out of her throat. Have they stopped because they made it, or because they didn't?

The truck starts moving again, but slower, more cautiously. A few minutes that seem to last an eternity pass before the truck stops again. This time, the engine is turned off, and she feels the slight shift of weight that must be Joey getting out.

Very slowly, the cargo bay door rises and the opening frames Joey's face. The pre-dawn twilight is enough for her to see that they're surrounded by a complex of buildings. They don't look especially impressive. Utilitarian is the word she'd use.

Apparently, this is just another thing she can't see. All the gifted around her make soft sounds of wonder and their faces turn to look in the same direction, to the left of the open truck door. Joey nods in that direction and smiles grimly. He whispers, "We're definitely in the right place. You should see the light."

Coco's Journal: Age 51

Year 38 of the Loop

In the few weeks we've been here, we still have no clue how to stop the Looping, or even what caused it. None. Yes, there's the light that all the gifted can see, but it's just light. Or, to be more accurate, bundles of light so dense they seem to fold in on each other. All of it is coming from the heart of the facility. Clearly, this place is the source of it all, but how and why are critical questions we can't answer.

I asked Joey what the light looked like. He says it's like tiny, illuminated strands of all different colors, as if someone walked into a hive of bees that were looped during a frantic moment, only billions of times denser. I can't imagine it. Not really. It sounds lovely, though. Also, frightening.

This place is a lot different than I thought it would be. The building isn't showy, but it's solid and we can make it secure against the opposition forces. Other, equally utilitarian buildings cover the area, all with specialized functions. Surrounding it all is the collider itself, though we can't see it from above ground.

The opposition is all around us, with armed spotters in ever-changing positions. So far, they haven't managed to get any shots off at us. There are too many loops and they're likely afraid to disturb them. We've caught glimpses of the people who tried to kill us. There are a few recognizable faces. Some are Seeker and some Chosen, but none are particular friends or former travel companions that we know of.

Forrest has been speaking with whoever is leading the forces on the emergency channel. They've each made their positions clear. They can't get us out without breaking the very loops they want to remain intact, and we can't leave without getting shot. Not out the front door, anyway. This building has basements leading to tunnels and rooftop access. We can get out if we need to, at least in small groups or pairs.

Forrest told them we wanted to know why the looping happened, and that was our primary goal. That's a lie, but who knows if they believe us. Given how little we know, maybe they do. After all, the gifted embedded with the opposing forces must see this light the same as ours do. They must have explained what they see to their leaders. Perhaps they also wonder what it means.

Our time here is limited, no matter what. We've got five or six weeks of food. If we ration, then we can stretch it, but only so far. As long as we don't get too long of a dry spell, we'll be fine with the water we collect when it rains. But not food.

There's a cartoonish map of the complex downstairs depicting important points of interest… like where food might be. Some of our gifted are going to sneak over to the cafeteria and coffee shop. It's not even a mile away, but they'll have to plan carefully and wind their way through the dense loops between buildings to remain shielded from the snipers.

Here's another surprise. We don't think the opposition knows the looper paths can be moved. Why do we think that? Because of the way they move around. They're cautious and careful and never move faster than a slow, considered walk. If they could move paths, then they would.

I suppose I never considered the possibility that other gifted wouldn't also accidentally discover that ability. Joey didn't until we were on the run, during a moment of high anxiety, and no one had heard of such a thing before that. I merely assumed it was something they might all learn eventually.

Of course, not all our gifted can move the paths, even after years of working on it while on the road. Those with moderate gifts can't seem to shift their perception enough to allow the paths to become physical.

I spoke with Jorge about why the opposition might not have discovered this new ability. He pointed out that the other two children who spotted the time tears were Chosen. Both were sheltered and looked on as oracles of a sort. They were taken around to try and spot tears all the time, but they went with groups of protectors. They didn't interact with the world so much as view it from the pedestals they'd been placed upon.

In a way, I suppose that makes sense. The most gifted Chosen never needed the skill, and it takes practice to be useful. Our other gifted learned how only after Joey trained them. To believe one can do it, one must first believe it can be done. That's what Joey says.

For my part, I'm trying to be useful, but I often feel like I'm in the way. My anxiety is too high to sit around and wait for something to happen. I have to keep busy. Those of us who survived the looping have spent our lives being protectors, the ones who get things done and figure out how to operate in this looping world. Our children are the ones we protect. They've followed our lead.

That's no longer the case. Only they can parse out what's going on in that huge ball of light that I can't see. I'm not comfortable with that at all.

Though it seems strange to have happiness, we have that, as well. There's a baby to think about. Layla is really showing, and I finally had to ask her about her timing. She's in amazing shape, but she's tall and well-muscled, with an athlete's frame. She shouldn't look like she's got a basketball under her shirt if she's really five and a half months along.

It turns out Layla was guessing her dates. Apparently, she's one of those women with terribly uneven and unreliable cycles. Missing a month—or even two—isn't unusual and sometimes going only a few weeks between cycles happens as well. After some rather embarrassing math, Pam and I both think she's actually more like seven months along.

So, that means in roughly two months, we will deliver my first grandchild. It's bizarre to think of it, because here we are trying to find the answer to the riddle of time. If we're successful, all of this might never have happened. Maybe I'll wake up as a twelve-year-old with no memory of any of it. Or maybe everything will start right up again, and Layla will deliver her baby in a bright, clean hospital, in a world populated with billions of people.

It's almost unspoken now, all these possible outcomes. Most people seem to believe that what exists now will still exist. Time will restart and we will be here. I suppose that's how they manage to go on doing what they must.

For me, it's not so easy. I want to see this grandchild come into the world, grow, fight with siblings, and drive his or her parents crazy like Joey did with me in his time. I want to see them happy and safe and secure until I die of old, old age and Joey has gray hair and lines on his face.

I'm not sure I can actually bring myself to do anything that could erase that possibility. Not sure at all.

Three

Year 38 of the Loop

Coco opens the refrigerator once more, just to see the light click on and feel the rush of cool air. It's delightful.

"Mom, the food's going to go bad if you keep doing that," Joey says, his voice amused.

She closes the door and turns around, still smiling. They've set up a more permanent camp in a part of the building that only had two loops nearby. Neither appeared to be involved in whatever experiment was going on, or if they were, their loop doesn't show them doing so.

One looper was on the phone, forever repeating an aggrieved conversation about funding and why knowledge was an appropriate gain for the money spent. The other appeared tired. Exhausted, really. She was standing by herself, head tilted back and her back stretching in an arch so pronounced it produced pops.

Joey moved both loops, but only after careful consideration. It was odd to watch him work. His hands waved in the air like he was doing tai chi, or maybe stretching their loops like taffy.

Both of them are now safely tucked away in a janitorial closet, leaving the group a selection of offices and open space for living quarters. When Coco passes the closet, she can sometimes still hear the tired voice of the woman trying to get another round of funding. What a depressing loop to be on. Even knowing there are two people in a closet nearby, Coco and Jorge both agree that they have lived under far more onerous conditions.

All the portable solar panels they brought with them have been set up, and most of the power is being routed to batteries for use by the refrigerator, a modest one with a freezer and an excellent energy star rating. The LED lights are also in use, but they have to be cautious with that, ensuring the light doesn't give away exactly where they are inside the building.

Coco joins the group going through papers once she's done with the general morning duties organizing their so-called camp. It's tedious, but it has to be done and Coco is a fast reader. Despite computers, there are literal mountains of paper in this place and in a few other important buildings on campus where they've searched for clues.

Jorge, Joey, and a few others read journals, proposals, plans, and other technical data Coco can't begin to understand. As Joey and Jorge talk over the contents of a binder, Coco watches from the corner of her eye. They're so engaged and so utterly of one mind.

At least today, Joey is here where she can see him. Safe. Benson and Joey have developed an excellent method for freeing up looped food around the campus. Their secret night trips make Coco's hair stand on end. But the trips for food, no matter how risky, buy them time. If they're efficient, they can last this way for months.

All in all, things are moving slowly, but they are moving. No one has breached the lower chambers where the source of the light is. Not yet. Beyond the steel entrance door lie the tunnels, and somewhere in that maze, the ball of light that's connected to the Looping.

Their three most gifted often sit near the door, examining the light when it's dark outside, talking quietly together. This morning, Joey informed Coco that he wanted Layla to stop doing that with him. He's not sure what being so close to the collider might do to the baby. He says they can both feel the baby responding to the light, maybe even becoming aware of it. It's an unnerving possibility.

As the afternoon shifts to evening, work ends and Joey heads off to sleep for a few hours before returning to the light. Jorge looks tense, for whatever reason, and Coco only manages to get him alone once everyone starts eating dinner. It's almost dark and her eyes feel sticky from reading small print all day long.

"What's wrong?" she asks, not bothering with niceties. She knows he understands. They've been together far too long for him to take offense.

He sighs. "Joey is ready to go down. He says he's had long enough to feel the character of whatever the light coming from below really is. He didn't tell me this before, but apparently, he and Benson have been interacting with the light for some time."

"Interacting? What kind of interacting? I don't like interacting of any kind. He should wait for all of us to decide." Coco's tone is more agitated with each word. What she really wants to say is that they should stop and go home because she loves her boy and none of this feels safe.

Jorge holds her upper arms and says, "He can feel it, Coco. Really *feel* it. After he told me this, I asked Benson and Joey to show me what they meant and… I saw it."

"Saw what? It? Do you mean the light?"

His expression seems uncertain. "Not exactly. It's more like I saw what happens and what they can do, and in that, I saw the light."

Coco moves his hands away from her arms. "What are you talking about?"

He gazes into her eyes, as if trying to gauge how much she can handle hearing, then says, "The reason Joey didn't want Layla down there anymore is because they've learned something new. When they focus on the strands that make up the light, they can make themselves *not* interact with the light the same way they can make the light of looper paths physical to move them. They can alter it, making it solid or not."

Coco has no idea what he's saying and shakes her head.

"What I'm saying is that they can pass through it."

"We walk through loop trails all the time. We have been since the beginning. They can too."

"No," he says, his voice gentle, "not like that. Those little lights are like endless small loops. If one of us stands on the start of a loop trail, we'll get smashed when the person reappears, and their loop starts again. That's just how it is. That's true even for Joey and all the other gifted. They just don't because they can see the start and they walk around it. That light is made up of endless, infinitesimally small loops no one could walk around, and they can pass *through* it. They can become different, not purely physical. It would be like you or me walking along a freeway and all the cars passing through us instead of hitting us. Like that."

Coco tries to imagine it but can't. In her mind is an image of Joey like a static loop, there and not there, eternally flickering into and out of existence. It's such a terrible thought that her body tenses.

Jorge sees and grabs her hands. "It's okay, Coco. It's not bad, or ugly, or scary. And I think it's because whatever those loops are made of, it's not something we would normally notice in life. Like light from the sun comes down and interacts with us all the time, but we don't run into it like a wall. We pass through and around it. I think it's like that."

She still doesn't understand, but she gets the gist. "What's it like when he does that?" she asks.

"He glows."

Coco's Journal: Age 51

Year 39 of the Loop

It seems the opposition has decided that the eleven weeks we've been here is enough. They want us to leave, and they've made their point in the cruelest way. Brian, Garrett, and beautiful, bold Aliyah are dead. It happened days ago, but I couldn't bear to write about it until now. They were on a food run just like we've always done, but they didn't come back.

Benson used a different route to reach a roof access on another building. He saw their bodies. He also saw two people tucked tightly between a series of loops, well-hidden if one came from our normal direction. A trap for anyone who came to find the missing people.

He returned immediately and reported it. The killers would have had to be gifted to be where they were. Kiara is broken now. Her daughter, gone. She simply lies on her pallet and stares at the wall. Aliyah and David—Forrest's oldest son—were in love. They were so young and had the potential for such a long life together. It's all over now. Forrest does his best to comfort his son, but how can he? Can a father, no matter how loving, ease the pain of a murdered love?

We can risk no further harm to our gifted. From now on, that means we're trapped here with what we have. Candy, dried food, our canned goods. We can last for a while.

Everyone except Joey and Benson is now on security duty. We've barricaded the front entrance as best we can. It's the only glass entry into the building, just in front of the small lobby area. Conference tables, desks, and even divider panels meant to break up open floor plans into cubicles have been put to use covering the glass. Guards at the steel doors on the ground floor are sufficient, we think, so we can use almost everyone else to man the barricade.

Joey says we can't break any more loops here, and they've moved all those they can, but he can't move them all. Some of the loopers have to keep doing what they're doing or we risk breaking the experiment. We have to protect those loopers as well as ourselves now, so we've barricaded areas where they are.

We can't shoot back. All we have are bows. Those aren't much use against gifted soldiers armed with silenced weapons, especially since we'd have to open a door and expose ourselves to even attempt a shot.

We're all just watchers now, protecting this building and the door to the light beneath us. That's all we do. Watch and sleep.

Two days ago, one of the shooters shot right through an office window where many of us were sleeping. It didn't hit anyone, but we understood they weren't going to let us be, even if we stayed inside. We're all jammed into a windowless meeting space now. We use no light at night.

We've emptied a storage room adjoining the meeting space of audio-visual equipment and supplies, converting it for Layla when her time comes. I hate that she has to deliver her child in what is, essentially, a large closet.

Things have been changing so quickly. After Joey went below and into the light four weeks ago, he began to change. I suppose I thought once Joey went to the source, he'd know what to do and we'd do it, but it's not like that. He says he has to understand what's down there, to untangle the tangle. I don't understand a bit of what he's talking about, but I do know how much he's changing... becoming something not entirely human. It's frightening and I've tried to write it down as it happens, but I know it makes no sense.

At first it was small things, like him standing still and looking at his hand, turning it this way and that like he'd never seen it before. Then, he would reach for something and miss. Sometimes he shuts his eyes for a moment like he's concentrating, then grabs for whatever it was. A cup, a plate, a book. He looks at people differently, like he's reading a sign just beyond their heads. Sometimes, I catch him watching me, or maybe the space behind me, and smiling like he's discovered something wonderful and new.

Sometimes, when the light is just right, it seems as if I can see past his skin, like he's not entirely physical anymore.

Once, when I was bandaging a cut on his hand, he brushed back my hair with his other hand and said, "You had such beautiful dark hair when you were little. You were so sweet. I never thought about what you were like as a child. You've always just been Mom. I hope my baby is like you."

That scared me right down to my bones. It was like he actually knew what he was saying was true. Like he was there. I have no pictures from my childhood. None. I never went back to our apartment to get photos. I couldn't tolerate going there again.

There are other things, too. They're small things, but they add up. Jorge looks as worried as I feel, but Joey says there's nothing to worry about. He says he's perfectly fine. He said he's having a girl and that we should get ready, because she's coming very soon.

Four

Year 39 of the Loop

Her name is Domino, and she's small and wrinkly and perfect. She even has the beginnings of what Coco hopes will be Layla's hair. It's wild from the moment she's dried and bundled. Her skin is as soft as anything Coco has ever felt and she smells of newborn baby. It's the best smell in the world.

"Why Domino?" Coco asks. She hadn't wanted to say that isn't a real name, at least not for a person. Maybe a hamster or a tuxedo cat with crooked markings at a stretch.

Jorge shifts in his seat and looks uncomfortable. Layla merely grins. Joey actually laughs.

"What?" Coco asks, obviously the only one not in the know.

Joey, who is sitting on the edge of the pallet holding his daughter, kicks out his foot just enough to tap Jorge's leg. "You want to confess this one, Dad?" he asks in a teasing tone.

"Uh, not really, but okay," Jorge says, then grins sheepishly. "You remember when that Solace salvage crew got all those comic books and movies on disc? The ones that were accidentally released when they freed up that big farm?"

Narrowing her eyes, Coco nods. "Yeah, I remember us deciding he was too young for… no, you didn't. You let him see that movie?" Lowering her voice, she hisses, "He was twelve, for mercy's sake!"

"Mom, I really wanted to see it. I'd never seen one like that before, and you know I was big into comics then, and—"

"*Deadpool* was a filthy movie, especially for a kid," she interrupts, keeping her voice low for the baby.

"You watched it. Also, technically, I saw all three of the movies. Domino came into the picture in the second movie. Plus, the spin-offs," Joey says, grinning.

Coco shoots a glare at Jorge. "I saw the first two, but I never watched the third one. It was all too dirty for me. I didn't even know there was a spin-off. And I was what… forty? Or close to it. My goodness. You're naming my grandbaby after a comic book heroine who hangs around with a potty-mouthed superhero who kills everybody?" Coco stops, sighs, then realizes it actually doesn't matter. It's a good name. Certainly, no one else has anything remotely like it.

Jorge shrugs and smiles like he knows he's in the doghouse. Coco shakes her head and says, "Never mind. She's adorable. She'd be adorable if you named her Crabgrass."

The baby stirs, so they all go quiet. Layla takes her back for nursing. Coco remembers how strange that was for her when she first had Joey. It's natural, yes, but it's not simple. Both baby and mother need to get used to it.

She taps Jorge on the shoulder and says, "Let's give them some peace. Do you need anything, Layla?"

Layla shakes her head, still smiling. She had a pretty easy labor, all things considered, but she's sore and her body needs rest.

Joey follows them out, then asks Coco to stay for a moment. Jorge leaves to take his turn on watch. Other people filled in for him while he visited his new grandchild. Coco and Layla have been off duty for two days to get through the ordeal.

"What is it, honey?" Coco asks.

Joey smiles and says, "I want to show you something."

With that, he takes her hand and guides her toward the steel door leading to the tunnels below the facility and, eventually, the collider. It's the path to the light she can't see. She stiffens and stops, her body going cold.

"Where are we going?" she asks, even though she knows.

He squeezes her cold fingers. "It's okay, Mom. I need to show you."

At the entrance, he stops her and says, "I have to carry you from here. Don't let go of me."

"No," she says, not wanting to see whatever it is he wants to show her.

"Mom, it's okay. I promise."

She lets him pick her up like she used to pick him up to put him to bed. He does it so easily. He's so tall and strong, but she really hadn't understood how strong. He smiles and says, "Just be calm. Put your arms around my neck so your hand touches my skin. You have to touch skin."

She does. It feels awkward. "Did you show your father this?"

"No. I don't need to. He understands. You're the one who needs to see it. Don't be afraid."

She's terrified, but she nods anyway.

He walks toward the entrance and uses his leg to open the big door, which he'd already propped open. He stops, closes his eyes, then breathes slowly. She can feel him relaxing, despite her weight.

Opening his eyes, he says, "Close your eyes, Mom. Breathe. I'll get you there and then you'll see. Keep them closed. It's too much otherwise."

She does, but it's hard to keep them closed as he moves. It seems to take a long time, lots of steps. Steps against metal, then padding, then more metal. He takes every move slowly and deliberately. There's something in the air. The hairs on her arms rise, like she's surrounded by static.

When they stop again, he goes still. He takes steady breaths, as if readying himself for effort, gathering himself. He says in a voice that sounds distant, like he's moving somewhere beyond her, "Open your eyes, Mom."

At first, she doesn't want to. She doesn't want to see whatever it is. The feeling of being surrounded by electricity, of the air almost sparking with potential, is so much stronger now. Joey is patient, just holding her and waiting. She's amazed his arms aren't tired yet. She slits open her eyes, looking up at him. They widen of their own accord at the sight that greets her.

Joey is there, but he's not really Joey anymore. Just as Jorge said all those weeks ago, he is glowing, but not really. It's like the light is bending around him, leaving him surrounded by bright bands of luminescence.

Something about the way he looks is familiar, and he smiles as she cocks her head, trying to recall where she's seen it before. Maybe he knows what she's searching for already. For a moment, nothing comes, and just as she's about to ask why he looks as he does, she remembers.

She was with her father, a self-proclaimed star nerd, watching the first imaging of a black hole. To her very young eyes, the result hadn't seemed so impressive, but the simulation had. Her father told her the black hole wasn't what she was seeing, but all the light around it. She hadn't understood, but she researched it later, during those years alone in Manhattan. That's what Joey looks like now. It's the light of an event horizon, an infinite reflection of a universe filled with light. It's not white, not colored, but all colors blending and separating and moving.

He's smiling down at her, but he doesn't look solid, or at least not all the way. She has no words for what this is. She can see the tiniest pinpricks of light shining from his skin, then shifting to shine from another infinitesimally small spot. It's beautiful.

"What is this?" she breathes.

"You asked why I named her Domino. This is the answer. The woman in the movie was special because she was the luckiest person in the world. Even the worst things would always work out fine. That was fiction, but my Domino is the real thing. She will never know fear. She will never know death." His smile is unnaturally serene, as if he were suddenly relieved of all doubt and worry. "She will never know pain. All she will know in this life is the love of those around her right now. That makes her the luckiest person who ever lived."

"No," Coco says as she realizes what he's saying, her tears blurring him until he's merely a shape made of light. "We can go back. We don't have to do this."

"Yes," he says. "You taught me right from wrong. This is right. I can see and feel trillions of lives all over the world. I can see them from here. All of them. Every insect. Every blade of grass. They'll all die if we don't do this. And we, the humans left behind, won't survive for long. I can see that too. The loops are fading. I see them even now being interrupted by decaying buildings, animals, and the shifting earth under their feet. Once they go, everything goes.

"But there's more to it than just our world and our lives now. I've learned much since I learned how to read the light here. The looping is expanding. It travels ever outward, binding more inside it. It will go on forever until the whole universe is inside it. Unless we stop it. And we can."

She rubs her leaking nose against her sleeve, keeping her hands around his neck. Blinks away tears. "But we'll have time. We can fix some things. We can find a way."

He shakes his head full of lights, an event horizon in the shape of her son. "No. It's more complex than that. We live because they do."

"What? Why? I don't understand. Who are they?"

"Time," he says. "Time is everywhere, and something is happening to me. I can glimpse it. Sometimes, I can't see beyond it. I can see what's happening to me will happen to Layla and all the others like me. It will be in Domino before she can make sense of it. I saw this moment with you, your life before—you alone in Manhattan and with your parents at a roller coaster and you so scared when you were having me. I see too much, and I can't stop. It will happen to all the others. We won't be able to survive like this. Humans weren't meant for that. No organic being is meant for that. We are too fragile to carry so much time. When I look at you, I see all the faces you have worn and all the people you have been in your life. I can't see *just* you anymore."

Her voice is thick and shaking. "I can't let you die. You're my baby. You *have* a baby."

"We won't die. I can't explain it other than to say that our existence is its own force. We have existed, we do exist, we will exist. These lives have been, so they will always be. We must change, true, but we will never end. We will become something else. I just don't know what."

"How do you know?" she asks, trying hard to stop crying. Her nose is running.

He nods toward her face and says, "Use one hand. Go ahead. Keep the other on my skin."

She scrubs at her face with her t-shirt, then quickly puts her hand back.

"Aren't your arms getting tired? I'm not a featherweight, you know."

He smiles again. "I just picked you up a few seconds ago and I've been holding you forever."

She shakes her head, and the moment of relief is gone. Her son, appearing in this moment to be made of light, or consumed by it, sees and knows things she'll never comprehend. It seems for him, this moment and all other moments are the same thing. She can't even begin to wrap her head around it, but there's no going back from this knowledge. "How do you know you'll survive this?" she asks again.

He looks ahead to something beyond them. His eyes reflect the moving light. Dark, infinite pools surrounded by light. "Look," he says.

Coco turns her head and almost can't see the enormous, complicated equipment, the racks of mysterious things, and the huge pieces of metal all arranged in ways that probably only make sense to drunks and physicists.

All of that is secondary to the ball of light and the infinite arcs of luminescence surrounding it. Part of it seems trapped, like a static loop. Other parts are spinning, circling, and moving. It's beautiful chaos.

"What is that?" she breathes, her voice almost too soft to hear.

"It's the point when time matters. What they were doing here… well, they understood, but they didn't. The universe is sensitive. These things can't be overlaid or pushed aside. This is the result. This is what happens as time starts. It can't move. It's hard to explain."

"That's *time*?" she asks, knowing she'll never understand what he sees.

"In a way. It's time asserting itself onto time. Not exactly that, but there are no words."

All the pinpricks of illumination she sees on Joey are coming from the ball. It's so dense it looks like one solid, infinitely compacted light. "Those are loops, right?"

"Yes, but they're unconstrained by distance. They are continuing, moving outward, entangling and splitting into more loops and threads. We're harming others. It will continue on and on, extending further and further. It must be put back where it belongs, then time will flow."

"That's why you want to fix it? Because it's spreading?" she asks. For just a flash, Coco realizes how significant his words are. So casually, he'd just confirmed there is life beyond Earth. It's like he's looking out of a window and can seem them, all of them, all across the universe. She looks up at Joey, at his calm, serene smile and the unnatural glow surrounding him, and she realizes her worst fears and greatest hopes have come true. Her son has achieved more than she could have ever dreamed, but he has also become something beyond human comprehension. Beyond human.

Again, he smiles as if he sees her words even as she thinks them. He nods, seeming to confirm that notion. "It's taken me all these weeks to understand how to escape the limitations of our perception of time. Yes, I see the irony. As I witness time, as I learn to see more, I change. The observer is influenced by what it observes, and also influences what is observed. I see it, and I see what needs to be done, but not yet with perfect clarity. Only as I interact and leave observation behind will I truly understand all the possibilities.

"What I do know is that I can make things right, or more right. I see many paths, and I can choose one that will correct time. I think I can choose more than one, but only if they align. Some paths fold and fit together, others are prominent, and some are weak and distant. I could even turn it back to the moment it began, but that path is singular, and it would begin all over again. I must choose something else. What I don't know is if I can choose a path where you remain and still correct time. I may have to lose you to save others."

She looks away from the light and back to the shining, glowing face of her son. The relief she feels is as big as this world. If he can find a path to staying alive… whatever that means for him… then all else is secondary.

"That's perfectly okay, Joey. Truly. When a house is on fire, you save as many as you can. You don't walk past people who need to be saved because you love one of them a little more. I believe what you say. This house is on fire, so save as many as you can. I know everyone out there would say the same thing. It's the way we're wired. We've lived our lives and we love our children. If you can find a path that will save you and all the other kids, then do that. That's how the living live on. We live on through our children. It's always been that way."

Coco's Journal: Age 51

Year 39 of the Loop

I'm going to write until it's over. I tried to stand watch at the doors with all the others. I really did. I kept shaking so hard my knees were hitting the barricades like rattles. Finally, they sent me up here to be with Layla and Domino. I've said goodbye to my son, and I'm a wreck. That's not the right word. There is no word for how this feels. How does a mother survive saying goodbye to her child? I know they do, but how?

I knew it was time for him to go. I hate writing that down, but I did. He could barely walk the last time he came up from a session at the source. His eyes were distressed as he tried so hard to focus on anything in the here and now. It must have been so confusing for him, seeing time unmoored so completely. When he finally recognized me, he squeezed his eyes shut and tucked himself against me like a small child. He barely made sense, his words a running commentary of everything he sees. Of snippets of past events and objects. Of glimpses of the future. Of worlds beyond our own.

For a few minutes, he was petting Tux, although our cat died almost two decades ago. It calmed him some, then he jerked his hands away and started crying, saying we'll all rot away like that. We had to give him one of the last, precious sedatives to calm him. As he fell asleep, I held him. I knew it would be the last time.

As much as I wanted to keep my son, I knew he could no longer live in this world as he was. It was becoming a torture and eventually, he would die. His only chance for life is to change into whatever he's becoming. So when he woke and his eyes drifted toward the light, I kissed his cheeks and told him I loved him, and I let him go.

I feel like I might die from it, but I can't yet, because we still have to deal with this world until Joey is done with whatever it is he's doing with that ball of misplaced time.

Almost everyone is guarding an entrance. Even Kiara is there, her face grim and marked by grief. No one will sleep or go off shift. It's time to watch and keep the doors shut until the end. The enemy is outside, mostly clustered at the glass doors of the main entry. When it got dark, they melted out of nowhere, threading through loops toward the doors.

Our gifted say the light is getting too bright, that it's been expanding and growing, filling up the ground floor and spreading beyond the building and the collider outside. They say it started when Joey went down yesterday. Their gifted must see it and know something is happening. They're all standing there at the barricades, searching for some gap and whispering through the wood and glass that we must stop what we're doing. That we must please, *please* stop, because we'll destroy the entire world and everyone left on it. They're not even trying to kill us anymore. They're just begging.

Layla is so calm, and Domino is quietly sleeping. We moved her pallet out of the storage room so she could be in open space where the air isn't so stuffy. She's propped up using rolled sleeping bags as a backrest. When I look at her, she smiles serenely, but her gaze always returns to the light.

I swear I saw the baby looking as well when she was awake. Just like with Joey, I saw the golden light in her eyes. A new event horizon reflecting an entire universe.

Earlier, I asked Layla if she could see through time like Joey can.

She said she glimpses things, but not like him. She says she can feel it there but can't quite grab it the way he can. I asked if she could see Domino's future. I asked what she would be like growing up.

I shouldn't have asked, but I was too afraid to ask Joey before, and now it's too late to ask him anything. He said goodbye to me, and now I can't ask him. So stupid. I should have said so much more to him.

Layla smiled at me like she knew what I was thinking. She reached out to squeeze my hand and told me Domino wouldn't grow up in the way I thought of it. She would expand into herself. That's how she said it. *Expand into herself.* What the heck does that even mean? I can't think about it anymore. It's more than I can handle.

I know what I most need to write. It's the only thing I never recorded in my journals. I try not to think about it. If this works, someone might need to help my older brother, so I have to write it now. I left a note for someone, asking them to help, but I never wrote the story. And who knows if the person I left that note for will even be alive when all this is done? So many loops have been disturbed.

Corey might wake up from his long sleep and be alone. He was a pain in the butt, but he's my older brother, and I love him. It's hard to imagine that he'll be fourteen years old when he wakes up. I'm over fifty and have a fourteen-year-old older brother. It's been so long since I wrote his name, or even spoke it. It's time to do that now. Just in case.

Joey told me he can't be sure what will happen to all those whose loops were broken. He said he wouldn't know until he fully explored time to see what paths would work together. He says it would be very difficult to choose a path that would bring the broken loopers back, because they all died at different times over the decades. Their losses were not singular events with a single path. That sounds reasonable to me. That means there will be losses which I caused. My brother should know what happened if he's alone when this ends. I owe him that.

The morning the Looping started, my mom was making breakfast.

Sundays were always good breakfast days. Pancakes with the works. She told me to go wake up my younger brother, Chase. He was three and a sleepyhead. My older brother, Corey, was at the opposite end of the apartment in the room they called the mother-in-law suite. Sounds fancy, but it was because he was a teen and becoming annoyed by everything. My mother told me to let him sleep.

I went into Chase's room, and I knew something was wrong. He was flickering. Now I know he was in a static loop, but at that moment, I just saw my brother sleeping in bed with his chubby foot kicked out from under the covers like always, and he was flickering. I don't know what I was thinking, but I reached out and touched his foot.

Because he was in a static loop, all that happened is he went rigid, and then he was gone. Completely gone. The sheets collapsed into the space where his little body was, and he was gone. The teddy bear next to him in bed disappeared with him.

I was twelve, so I wasn't exactly prepared for this level of weirdness. I actually looked for him, tossing his bed covers and even looking under the bed. No kid is ready to see that and believe it. He wasn't there, so I ran to the kitchen, panting and freaking out so much I couldn't talk. My mother told me to go wake up my brother, then flipped the pancakes… then she flickered too.

I froze. I wanted to scream, but all I did was freeze. She did it again. Told me to wake up my brother and flipped the pancakes.

Something finally unstuck me, and I ran over and grabbed her. I know I called out for her. I know I did, but it must not have been as loud as it was in my head. I only realized that later. When I disturbed her loop, she made this horrible noise and swung that frying pan right at my head. I can still remember the pancakes flying into the air as she rounded on me. The pan hit me, and that's how I got the scar on my forehead.

When I woke up, she was gone. I was lying face down in a huge puddle of blood. The cut was bad. My head hurt and I was confused, but the strange thing is, I didn't think of my older brother at all. In hindsight, I'm sure I had a concussion, so maybe that's why my thoughts were so jumbled. I couldn't stop the bleeding and I was incredibly frightened, not to mention entirely incapable of dealing with this surreal change in the world.

I stumbled out the door and went for the neighbor, the one who always watched me when my mom had to work late or take a business trip. That's who we were supposed to go to if there was ever an emergency.

When I knocked on her door, I heard her scream like my mom did. It was exactly the same. There's nothing else like it. It's a sound so full of fury that it makes your hair stand on end. Then there was a crash. Then nothing.

I ran back to our apartment and got the key for her place. It was there in case I ever needed help. I went in and she wasn't there, but there was a huge mess on the bathroom floor where everything was knocked off the shelves. Her dog was still there, sleeping in his little bed in the kitchen. He was flickering, too. I didn't touch him. I just said his name. He snarled and disappeared.

I think some part of me understood the rules already. People are like that. Humans figure out the rules quickly when bad things happen, even children. Maybe especially children. The vulnerable need a more attuned sense of danger and there was suddenly danger everywhere.

In the hallway, I saw Mr. Holidae getting his paper. Our building allows the Sunday paper to be delivered right to the doors. I waited, holding a soaked kitchen towel to my head. In a minute or so, he repeated the entire sequence. The paper reappeared right before he opened the door. Just reappeared. Not there, then there, folded neatly and lying as it had been before.

When I went back to the apartment, I tiptoed to my older brother's room. He was sleeping, but not flickering. For a minute, I thought maybe he was like me. I sat on the floor and watched him. His loop is longer, that's all. All my growing hope was dashed as the minutes stretched and he flickered at last. His loop lasts sixteen minutes. I crept out and never opened that door again. Never once.

As far as I know, my brother is still sleeping in his bed. Like a fairytale princess, he's been asleep for almost forty years. It's time for him to wake up. I hope. I hope, I hope, I *hope*.

So, he'll need help when this ends. He'll be alone. And now, if whoever reads my journal passes on the message, he'll know why. Tell him how sorry I am. Tell him I've spent almost forty years wishing I could go back and simply walk out of the apartment.

The first thing I did when the Looping began was kill two of the people I loved most in the world. I didn't mean to, but that doesn't change that it happened. It's a terrible thing to live with, and I think it will be terrible for him to live with too. He won't be able to understand what it was like. I think he'll probably hate me, so please, tell him how sorry I am.

I know all of us who were alive when the looping started have a story like this, or one close to it. Most of us were near people we loved. I don't know most of their stories. Most can't talk about it. I know some. Tamara's daughters. Pam's entire family. Sven's parents. All the people down there keeping the doors closed are hoping right now that all those people come back. I hope so too. I want that more than I want to survive.

There. I've written it. I've confessed the bad thing. It's done and, strangely, I feel marginally less frantic. I don't feel like my skeleton is trying to rattle out through my skin. Maybe it's just that I got it off my chest before it was too late. Or maybe it's only the writing that soothes me. I've been doing it for so long. Possibly, it's the only thing that ever really soothed me. It's my teddy bear or my blankie or whatever other thing people cling to when they're scared of what might crawl out of the dark.

The baby is awake, her big eyes looking up. Layla is smiling and looking around. One of her hands rises to sweep the air. It's like she can see something beautiful and strange that she can't resist touching. I can't look at her. There are rattling noises from below. The barricade. They're going to break through, I think.

Before Joey went down for the last time, everyone brought the special things they've kept up here. Pam's photo albums, which are all ratty now. The crystal blocks with pictures. The blanket. All of them are here, arranged like silent goodbyes. No one had to say anything. We all understood.

Even Forrest brought his box up. I knew I would never have a chance again, so I asked him what was inside. He smiled and said it was *the meaning of life.* I know it was stupid, and maybe it was just my nerves overcoming my brain, because I actually asked him what it looks like. I know, stupid.

He didn't laugh at me. He just took my hand, looked into my eyes, and told me that inside were all the letters and packets I'd sent him over the years about our son. All the pictures of Joey I'd sent to him. Even the envelopes were inside. He told me that was the meaning of life.

I felt weird about that, because really, I'd kept Joey away from him for most of that life. Maybe he could see that, because he told me that if I hadn't been alone and miserable for so long and if he hadn't been a young and arrogant asshole, then the world would never have a chance to be fixed like Joey is doing right now.

He said we made him by accident, but it was the only thing that could right the world's wrongs. He said that's the meaning of life. He said that if he could give one thing to the people who are left when this is over, it would be that one bit of wisdom. He wants them to know that no matter how many bad accidents happen, good can come from them. Sometimes, even really big, good things. I suppose that's a nice thought to leave behind.

All my journals are piled here with everyone's stuff—my whole life from the age of twelve—like bricks I could build into a wall and hide behind, except I can't hide behind them. Layla is sitting up now, her face almost lit by joy, one hand still reaching for something I can't see. I really want to build that wall. It's coming. I can feel it like static in the air. There's nowhere to hide, and—

Five

The End of the Loop

Coco senses so much moving past her, in flashes of light and movement. Is she in the dark, or is it only that she isn't anywhere physical at all? It's hard to tell. The flashes of colored light are moving so fast, all around her, but it's not random. There's order within the confusion, and it's meant for her in particular. It tugs at her. Without understanding why, she knows she can stop the motion. She can see what hides inside the colors. She reaches for it. She stills the chaos and images resolve from color into life.

Immediately, she understands. She smiles, but can't feel the smile, only the emotion of it. She knows she isn't really Coco anymore, not the way she was.

There is Chase, her baby brother. He's in his special booster chair. Pancakes falling apart from too much syrup. Their mother laughs while she tries to wipe his face. The air smells of breakfast and happiness.

This is the pancake breakfast they would have had, the one that the Looping stopped from happening. At her urging, the flashes of light zip past again. Coco knows she can stop it anytime and see all that might have been. Would have been. She stops the colors again.

Corey is older now, almost a man. He's standing still in his graduation cap and gown. Chase stands behind their mother, making faces while she tries to get a picture. Coco is older, with plumper cheeks and no scars. Taller and unmarred by starvation and cold. She's making faces too. Corey finally cracks up and the picture snaps.

Chase is a young teen still awkward in his new growth. He's dancing in awkward shuffles with their mother and dressed in a dark blue suit. There's a pink flower on his lapel. Then, Coco is swept around the dance floor by a beautiful man she has never seen before. He leans close and whispers that he loves her more than anything in the world. This is Coco's wedding. Her wedding dress is covered in lace.

Mother's eyes are wet behind a black veil. Two small children stand with a sad woman next to her: Corey's children and his wife. The coffin containing Coco's older brother is lowered into the ground. A motorcycle accident. Corey is gone. He was just thirty-four.

Now a full-grown man, Chase has dark circles under his eyes and a big smile on his face. He's holding a baby bundled in yellow next to the hospital bed of a woman glowing with happiness. He says, "Coco, look at my boy." Coco lifts her daughter, full of toddler eagerness, to peek at the bundled newborn with her. The girl's hair is dark, with rainbow barrettes holding back her curls.

Coco stands in front of a room filled with young adults sitting in theater seats. She points at one of her biology students and asks a question, a confident smile on her face. She is a professor.

Their mother, old and so, so wrinkled, sits in a wheelchair. She pats Coco's hand and tells her that it's okay. That it will all be okay. Chase is bald and has a little paunch. They are both crying.

A front porch with a wicker loveseat, cushions in bright green. The day is beautiful. There is a crowd of people on the lawn. They are playing flag football. Young children cheer at the wrong moments in the game. Coco sits down next to Chase and rests her head on his bowed shoulder. They've grown so old he doesn't seem like a baby brother anymore. A dog with a graying muzzle slaps his tail against the porch boards. They are both too old to play and have been for many decades. His hand shakes with palsy as he gently clasps her age-swollen knuckles. With an old man's voice, he says, "We did good, Coco. Mom would be proud of us." Like Coco's husband, Chase's wife is dead, but they didn't leave the world without adding to it. All of the people on the lawn belong to them. Children, grandchildren… and the baby one woman holds is Coco's first great-grandchild.

There are four old people surrounding her bed. Coco doesn't know their faces, but she sees herself in each of them. Sees her mother and Corey and Chase and her father in the features of these people who were once her babies. They are with her because she is going. Because it's time to go. She tells them that it's okay, just as her mother told her, because that's what mothers say. It is the last thing a mother can do to protect her children. She can tell them it's okay.

The motion picks up again, the colors sliding past in a blur. Coco reaches out with her thoughts to stop it again, but it doesn't respond. The life moving by her with so much color is no longer hers.

Coco can sense Joey somewhere. There and not there. Words and feelings, but not. He showed her the world that would have been. An interrupted path. In the blur of passing time, she catches his regret. There is a question there.

He can restore the past. He can choose the path that will erase all that has happened. He can bring back her life and erase all this pain. Coco knows that if he chooses this path, then he will erase all that came from it. Himself, Layla, Domino… all of those who have moved past being human.

He offers this because he loves her. Perhaps he never really understood what the world once was. Only now that he has become something more can he see and feel all that was lost. Whatever he and the others are is beyond her comprehension, but he's still young. Seeing time is not the same as living it. Pain and joy are intrinsically bound in a marriage that defines life. It defines the very act of living. At life's very core is the knowledge that it ends. That is something Joey can never understand, will never understand.

Coco's life was hers. Perhaps it wasn't the one she could have had, but it was hers entirely. She was there when the web began to spin out the days of her life and there to shout in defiance as the web was torn away by the winds of time. Her time belonged to her, and it was precious.

There are no voices in this strange non-place, but everything is full of meaning. She shows him, pushing away the thoughts of the life she might have had. She shows him her father pointing into the night sky, his eyes shining as he whispers that she is made of stars, that all living things are made of stars and the endless light between them. The moment she saw Ruth and realized she was not alone. How her pain fell away and her heart felt like it might burst from her body when she saw Joey's newly born face. His hair shining in the morning light behind the safe walls of Solace as he ran and played. The moment she realized she loved Jorge entirely. Her fear and awe as she watched Joey become something new and far, far beyond human.

She tells him, even without words, that it will be okay. Joey accepts that reassurance. He chooses a path, and time obeys.

As it happens, Coco needs no signs or words to tell her. She can feel it. There's a tugging that wants to take her away, to someplace else, or maybe into nothing at all. Joey is there, and somehow, he is keeping her in place. He doesn't want to let her go. The swirling world of chaotic colors returns. This time, the lives are not hers, but she senses she can stop them and look. Perhaps only for the briefest of moments, but she can see what will come.

Reaching out with her thoughts, she once more stops the swirling light. It is a miracle.

Earth is covered in infinite strands of moving light. She's so high above the world she can take in the blue marble of it in one glance, surrounded by a web of golden light and so, so beautiful. She wants to see closer, and suddenly she is lower, able to see the strands of light retreating away from the core in the collider at Upton, moving in their complex paths as if being reeled in like celestial fishing line. This is what's happening now. This is Joey cutting away the loops and restoring time. Her perspective shifts so rapidly that she isn't sure it's her directing the shifts at all. It's as fast as thought.

She sees the strands retract as they approach those loopers who made an impact on Coco. The woman and the dog. The homeless man. There's Sophie, smiling as she jauntily climbs the steps in Ruth's house, the golden leash of time swirling around her as it shortens. The twirling woman, her golden loop illuminating her face as she makes the last twirl in her near-endless apocalypse. Corey, shifting in bed as the last inch of bright light disappears into his body. His future is no longer tied to a golden leash. It belongs to him again.

And she sees different lights go out. Clusters of them, tiny and blue, winking out all around her. She knows each of the names that go with those lights. Jorge, Forrest, Kiara, Pam, Sven. All of them… gone. Is her light gone too?

A memory comes to her then. Jorge, still young and vibrant, without a strand of gray in his hair. He's sitting at the table in the house where they first met. He shrugs and tells her that maybe they aren't in loops because they just don't fit in the pattern. Coco thinks he was right. The lights of those who didn't fit have finally gone out.

It's over. However Joey held on to her for this last gift, he can hold her no more. Time is moving on, and Coco is no longer a part of it. She doesn't know what happens next. Heaven? Nothingness? Inside, she senses Joey saying goodbye. He is so large that he fills this strange eternity. There, but not there. Stars and the endless light between them.

The motion of things moving past continues, but Coco can no longer stop it. Those sights are not hers. They are the ever-after of people she will never know. It's fading, or she is. She looks down the endless, blurring line made of life and time. Forever. It lasts forever.

Epilogue

Corey, Sarah, Charity, & Sophie

Epilogue

Corey

For the hundredth time, the 911 line is busy. His dad's line is busy. The cellphones are charging, and he's tried calling every contact in his phone. Busy circuits. Nothing.

He tries not to look at the apartment. It's all wrong. His room is fine. He woke up late, and at first, he was happy they let him sleep in. They never do that. Chase or Coco or his mom always bang on his door and tell him to get up. Not today. He woke after ten and wanted breakfast, then he opened the door to everything being *wrong*. The apartment smells like the school basement.

No one is here. Chase's room is covered in dust so thick he choked when he opened the door and sent it all flying. Coco's room looks like someone robbed the house. It smells terrible. Their mom's room is the same as Chase's. There's a big black stain on the tile floor in the kitchen that's freaking him out even more. There's a blank spot in the center of the stain that looks like a face. It looks like old blood.

What's beyond the windows is scary too. Everything is a mess outside. Crashed cars and pieces of buildings are all over the street. People are running, but he can't hear anything from so high up. There's not a single piece of food in the whole house. There's a huge pile of empty cans and boxes that look a million years old in the corner of the living room.

And the light. Why is there so much light? He can almost feel it brushing his fingers as he moves his hand through the air. Tiny charges that frighten him because they also comfort him. They are warm in the wrong way.

He tries to reach 911 again. Busy. He tries the TV, but it doesn't work. The whole thing is completely covered in grime. The plastic feels almost sticky, like it's breaking down into whatever goo plastic is made from. The remote has no batteries, and when he hits the button on the bottom of the TV, the screen just crackles weird and goes blank.

He tries to connect to the internet with his phone again. No Wi-Fi. He's getting a signal, but it times out. All lines are still busy.

Corey wants to leave, to go somewhere and ask someone what's going on. He tried the intercom, but the doorman never answered. He can't bear opening the door again. Once was enough to see that it's not just his apartment that got wrecked. He went to the neighbor they always go to when there's a problem. Her door was unlocked and the keys that normally hang in the kitchen were inside the lock. He can tell these are their keys because Coco made the keychain from a picture. The whole apartment looked like his.

Plus, people are shouting and running on the street, and this might be the zombie apocalypse. He sees cop cars racing. Ambulances dodge all the chunks of concrete that have made craters in the road. It's definitely the zombie apocalypse. He's been awake for twenty minutes and he thinks he might have actually slept through the zombie apocalypse.

He jumps when there's a knock on the door. Running for it, he peers through the peephole. Zombies? No, it's a pretty lady with mascara lines on her face.

"Who are you?" Corey asks, so terrified that his voice shakes.

She looks at the peephole. Her hair is a mess, and her nose is red.

"My name is Sophie," she says. "Coco sent me. She said you might be alone, and she didn't want you to be afraid. I'm going to help you, Corey. I'm going to help you get safe."

Corey almost sags against the door. Finally. Someone.

He opens the door and rushes to this stranger who knows his name. They hug each other, both of them crying. Neither of them is quite so afraid anymore. The light is all around them.

As darkness falls on the first night of this new and unwritten world, they both look up to a heaven filled with stars. Endless stars and a universe of light between them.

Epilogue

Sarah

Dr. Sarah Swanson stretches, then stops with a jolt. Instead of a wall of windows, she's facing industrial shelving and a dingy wall. Where is she? She did the checklist, went upstairs, stretched her back, went to the bathroom, and returned to her computer. They did the final checks and… what?

There's a flashlight on a shelf, shedding dull light through a dirty lens into the cramped space. Next to her, the director in charge of funding, Mira Parker, stands with her hand near her ear, her eyes wide. They are in the janitor's closet.

"What the…" Mira says.

Something feels wrong. Sarah was in one place, now another. She turns around and opens the door, peeking into the hallway. The overhead bulbs are flickering. Even with the overheads, the light in the hallway is wrong. It's usually flooded with sunlight and overheated from the glass doors. Now, it's tinged with gold and far too dim. There's a bad smell.

"Don't go out there," Mira says.

Sarah ignores her, emerges from the closet, and utters an expletive. Something very bad has happened. Barricades hide the glass doors and frontage. It's made of desks and bookcases and everything else that can be moved or torn from a wall.

Mira peeks out from around her and says exactly the same word Sarah did. "What's happening?" she asks.

The overhead lights are steadying, the hum gone. They illuminate a wide space that shouldn't be this way. She walked through this spot when she arrived early this morning. She passed it again on her way upstairs twenty minutes ago. The whole place looks and smells like a badly run refugee camp. The air is thick with the odors of sweat, raw sewage, and dirty socks. She holds a hand over her nose and looks, really looks.

"Don't go near it!" Mira yips, still hiding behind the door.

Sarah waves her back and steps carefully around the debris. Rolled up sleeping bags. A box of candy wrappers. Jugs of dirty water. A battered lantern that looks like it's been used for a hundred years. As she gets closer to the barricade, she sees bundles of clothes. No, not bundles, piles.

They are lined up at the barricade. The clothing looks as if they've been shed like snakeskin. There are bows and quivers of arrows mixed in. She tentatively touches a pile with her foot. Underneath is a pair of very worn boots, still laced, with socks inside. As she toes the pants away, an empty sock is drawn down the pant leg. It flops over the boot.

At last, she sees the message. It's scrawled on one of the posters on the wall. It reads, *Read the books upstairs. Last one first. Explains.* Below that, scrawled in a different hand, are the words, *We were here!* Around those words are signatures. Varying wildly in style and form, there might be twenty names, maybe two dozen.

She gapes at the scrawled names, the barricades, and the empty clothes. Her heart thumps like a hammer.

Sarah is a part of this team, a scientist riding the bleeding edge of knowledge. She knows what the risks are. No matter how low any one risk might be, it's still there. The kind of experiments conducted by her and those like her are meant to decipher the universe's secrets, and there is always a risk of something unexpected. As unlikely as it seemed when she walked upstairs to stretch her back, it seems this time, the unexpected really happened.

This project is the most advanced and technically precise ever conducted in the history of humanity. This entire facility was renovated specifically for it, mountains of money and time invested to obtain knowledge in an experiment so complex it would have been unimaginable not long ago. It was designed so that they might glimpse, maybe even someday understand, what came before the sticky beginnings of the universe. Her stomach drops as she looks at the devastation around her. Sarah runs for the stairs to the collider, shouting at the top of her lungs as she does.

Epilogue

Charity

Charity keeps the young man in sight, swinging around to be sure he knows she's looking. Almost every Sunday, they pass each other, and every time she says that will be the day she stops and says hello. She's going for her morning tea and grain bowl at the kosher-vegan cafe. He's going for his coffee and bagel at a place known for its bacon. She knows this because she saw him go inside. Today, she will make it clear that he should stop and chat. And if he doesn't, she'll just have to hope the coffee place has decent kosher-vegan tea. They'll probably laugh at her. Their sign has a pig on it.

He's smiling. She's about to stop, to say hello, to tell him her name. Then the light changes. Golden light, like the rays of the sun slanting into a dusty room, suffuses everything. It glows. For one moment, they smile at each other in the inexplicably golden light.

Then he's not smiling. His expression goes blank as he looks past her. Charity looks too. Something is very wrong. Trash, dust, and debris are everywhere. None of this was here a second ago. The man drops his case and puts his hands to his head, turning in a circle to look. Everyone around them is doing the same. Brakes squeal. Shouts rise from everywhere. She turns in a circle too. This circle is very different from the flirty one of mere seconds ago.

There's a car on the street that looks a hundred years old, all rust and filthy, brown glass. The tires are flat and almost seem to be crumbling away. There are pieces of masonry lying on the ground, some of them big enough to have dug divots out of the asphalt. She can tell they came from the building across the street; they're carved and fancy. An enormous scaffold that was perfectly fine a moment ago is scattered across the street in disordered piles. It looks ancient, all rust and dents.

The disorder... the weirdness... is everywhere. Every place her eyes stop there is something else that wasn't there when she saw that man and caught his eye. Some things look fine, but many things definitely do not.

She turns when she hears the man gasp. He's pointing at the wall near them. He looks at her, then back. Attached to a sign on the wall with an extraordinary amount of wide, curling tape is a scarred and battered piece of plastic. Behind it, she can barely make out two photos. They are of her and the man she's been dying to speak to. She recognizes the images. She just did that. That twirl. She is wearing that dress. He is wearing that shirt. Behind the photos is a piece of paper with writing on it. They can see the first line. It's bold and big and reads, *For You Two*.

They look at each other, then together, begin tearing at the tape.

Epilogue

Sophie

"You'd better hurry or…" Sophie trails off and blinks her eyes a few times. Her mother was standing right there. She was just at the island, turning on the kettle and getting the coffee ready. The tray is there. The coffee press is there, but now, it's covered in dust and lying on its side.

She makes a soft sound, not at all understanding what's happened. Did she faint? No, she's still standing here with her hand on the door. Stroke? Maybe. That would be bad. She's way too young for a stroke.

"Mom?" she calls out. No one answers.

She walks through the kitchen, looking. She checks the floor, but her mother isn't lying somewhere she can't see. Looking back at the island, she gets the feeling something is wrong with it. She walks back, puts her hands flat on the granite, looking around.

Now she sees it. On the floor is a line, two lines. A path along the floor is exactly as she remembers it, gleaming and spotless. Beyond that path is… what? She taps the toe of her shoe against it. It depresses, or maybe compresses. Squatting, she touches it. It's dust, but a layer so thick she can't even see through it.

Rubbing her fingers together, she stands and shouts, "Mom!" Her voice reverberates with the panic building inside her chest.

For a moment, she feels enormous relief as the swinging door to the laundry area opens. Tammy rushes in and the relief ends. "What is it, Miss?" Tammy asks, brow creased.

"My mom was right there. She's gone. Did you see her?" Sophie asks. She wants to point to the dust on the floor but freezes as she sees the crazy vines covering the rear window that looks out onto the little garden.

Tammy scans the room, then frowns. "She was just here. I went in to shift the laundry." She pauses, eyes stopping at all the oddness juxtaposed over the normal. "What happened here?"

Sophie doesn't answer. Tammy's confused expression is enough to know that she didn't have a stroke or imagine the strangeness. Panic rising, Sophie races through the rooms downstairs. Some are normal, while others are decidedly not. Blasting through the service pantry and the short, wide hallway that connects the service areas to the living areas, she skids to a halt.

Her slick-bottomed heels slide in the dust, and she falls onto her rear, scrabbling back from what she sees. The entire rear living area is in a state of serious decay, a long-abandoned place subject to damp and rot. Stained wallpaper hangs in curling strips, exposing mold-blackened plaster behind it. Even that is crumbling in some places, scattering chunks and piles of itself onto the discolored furniture. The big windows to the rear garden are nearly obscured by vines.

Regaining her feet, she races through the rooms. Everything is a disaster. All the decay stops in a razor-sharp line near the big foyer. She can see it perfectly. A tiny cliff of dust creates a border between order and chaos, between decay and normality. She steps out into the light streaming through the immaculately clean glass surrounding the interior entry door.

The entry hall is perfect. The stairs are perfect. The ceiling is perfect. The service hall door opens with a bang, slamming against the stops as

Tammy rushes out. She's well past confused now. Tammy looks as terrified as Sophie feels. Her hands are twisting together at her chest.

"What happened?" Tammy asks in a shaking voice.

Shaking her head, Sophie tries to be calm, but her entire body is shaking. "I don't know."

They both look toward the door. Despite the heavy wood and iron bars and everything else, they can hear the squealing of brakes, the crash of metal on metal, and people shouting.

"My mom?" Sophie asks, knowing the answer, but asking anyway.

"Nothing, miss. No one is here. Something is very, horribly wrong."

"Wait there," Sophie says, then counters that. "No, I'm sorry. Do you have family? Where are they?"

Tammy pulls her phone out of her pocket. "Just my mother in New Hampshire. My phone is dead. I called on the house phone. It works, but all circuits are busy. It says all circuits are busy." She glances again at the door and the noises coming through it. "I don't think we should go outside."

Sophie squeezes her eyes shut, trying to order her thoughts. Order. Yes, be ordered and things will fall into line. "My grandma. I have to check on her."

Tammy starts at that, as if she's forgotten something important. "Oh, Ms. Ruth!"

They both take the long curving steps two at a time. Everything is clean and perfect until they reach the landing.

"Oh, my God. It's like downstairs!" Tammy exclaims.

It *is* like downstairs. The carpet along the center of the floor is worn so thin Sophie can see the woven base. It's also gone almost entirely brown near the center. Like the first floor, the upper hall is decayed, only it looks slightly less damp and more abandoned. There are hundreds of cans of food lined up along one wall, most of them rusted through and slumped into piles. There is a smell. Musty and old, but there. Something not good.

"Grandma?" Sophie calls weakly, but she can see the door to her grandmother's suite from where she stands. She can see the big, time-yellowed sheet of posterboard on the door. She can see the tape and the bag.

Tammy's hands rise to her mouth, and she gasps, "No. What has happened here? What is happening?"

The poster bears a slightly crooked message in letters so large they can be read from thirty feet away. *Don't open the door until you read this.* Below that is an arrow drawn and colored in, pointing downward toward the mass of tape.

Not sure if her shaking legs will carry her, Sophie slowly approaches the door. She almost reaches for the knob, but it's covered by tape. The tape stretches out in all directions. Masses of age-dulled tape connect the knob to the jamb, the wall beyond, and to the door itself. An index card sticks up out of the mass. It reads: *Don't Do It!*

Just below the poster is what was once a clear plastic bag. Now, it looks like something that was discarded on the street, kicked by innumerable feet, tossed by the wind, and then run over for days and days before being picked up. She touches it with shaking fingers, then tugs at it.

It finally tears, revealing folded papers covered by writing. After unfolding the papers, she can't hold her hands still enough to read the words. The paper is old, with yellowing edges and that slightly brittle feeling that only old paper has. She presses the papers against the poster on the door to keep them still. Tammy peers from the side, already reading. She gasps in distress.

Sophie begins reading.

Sophie,
My name is Coco, and I was here with your Grandma, Ruth. She asked

me to write this so you would know what happened. She couldn't decide what to say, and then she couldn't write anymore. She wanted me to tell you that she loves you as much as the world and that she's sorry.

Ruth found me in Year Five of the Loop. I didn't know anyone else was alive until she did. She was already very sick. She said she had liver cancer again. You probably know about the first time she had it. I stayed with her until the end, and she wasn't alone. I held her hand, and she thought I was you at the end. It made her happy to think that.

I wanted to bury her, but she was too heavy to carry and there's no place with enough deep dirt nearby. I wrapped her up as best I could on her bed. I don't know how long it will be until this ends, so you should not go in. I don't know what you'll see. You should call for help.

Ruth told me you know where she wants to be buried, and that when everything is over, you will be okay. I think things will probably be pretty crazy when you wake up. She's safe where she is until you get help.

Right now, you are here, and Tammy is here and you are both in loops. I don't know if you'll understand this, so I'll tell you what you're doing. I think if it were me in a loop, I wouldn't believe it either. So, this is the proof.

Every eighteen hours or so, you come into the house and part way up the stairs and then you say, "Grandma, you are the slowest person ever! You're going to make me late." Then you talk to someone. Then you call up that your mom is bringing coffee. Then you go downstairs and into the kitchen, and then you disappear.

I've seen you do this and heard it many times. Ruth told me she set a timer so she could see you happy. She said that it helped her survive the years alone. If your mom isn't here when you read this, then I'm sorry. Her loop got broken when the Looping started.

I'm sorry that you are reading this and hope you will be okay.
Love, Coco

Sophie stops and looks at the knob all covered in tape. Her grandmother is there? She's dead in that room? She just got here. How can this be?

"There are more pages," Tammy says, nodding at the small bundle of papers. "Read them. Maybe it will tell us what this looping thing is."

Sophie shifts pages, and sure enough, there's more. It's a different kind of paper and the handwriting is a little different, more mature somehow. It's in pencil instead of pen.

Sophie,

I have to leave Manhattan when the weather gets good enough. Food is getting harder to find, and the cold is worse every year. It's Year Eight of the Loop now, and soon, it will be Year Nine. I came back here hoping to eat the food Ruth never ate, but the cans are all exploding from the cold, just like everywhere else there's unlooped food.

I decided to leave another note because I understand more now. I want you to understand, and I'd like to ask a favor of you.

The three years since Ruth died have been awfully hard ones. Before I met her, I'd spent five years alone, but since I never expected to see another person, I carried on. Now, I know others are out there somewhere. I know I have to find them, and to do that, I have to leave Manhattan.

What got me through these past few years was Ruth. I didn't know her for long, but I loved her. She was the best person in the world for me to meet. I was twelve when the Looping began. I didn't truly realize it until after I met Ruth, but I was close to giving up. I met her and she saved me. I'm alive because of her. She was special, truly.

Now, I have to leave if I want to live. When I leave, I will also be leaving someone behind. When this ends, he'll wake up alone and he will be scared. It's my older brother, Corey. He's fourteen years old. I've put our address and all the phone numbers down. I don't remember my dad's new address in San Francisco, but I put down his phone number too.

I don't know what it will be like when this ends. I've thought about that endlessly over the years. At night, when it's too cold to sleep or I'm too hungry to let my mind rest, I think about the day when all this ends and all of you wake up. Most of the time, those are happy thoughts because it means you'll all come back and get your chance to live. Other times, I think about all those who won't be here when that happens. I think about the broken loops, the people and animals who disappeared when their loops were disturbed. I think about the chaos and the fear. Other times, I wonder if this can be fixed at all. How does someone repair an entire planet stuck in time? It's been so long, but no matter how big this problem is, I'll never give up hope that someone, somewhere, will figure out how to fix this.

And if my hopes come true and everyone wakes up, there is still my brother. If the broken loops don't come back to life, then he will be all alone. If your mom isn't here when you wake up, then you'll know he is alone. Can you help him? Help him get to my dad, or help him find out if my dad is even alive? Keep him safe? Our apartment is only a few blocks from you. Please?

Whatever happens, I hope you are all safe. I hope this all goes back to the beginning and you get your beautiful wedding dress and get married and live happily ever after. If that happens, then make sure Ruth goes to the doctor to check for her cancer coming back. If not, then I hope you can be happy knowing that Ruth loved you more than anything in the world and she wasn't alone.

Love, Coco

Sophie lowers the papers, glancing up at Tammy as she does. Tammy's hand is pressed to her mouth, tears streaming down her face. They both stand there looking at the door, knowing this isn't a trick. It isn't a joke. What lies beyond the layers of tape and peeling paint and the solid slab of wood has been there for years, possibly decades, if the condition of the house is any indicator. Gone for so long, yet only now becoming real.

Leaning against the door, Sophie presses the papers to her chest. Through her tears, she notices the air. The light. It shimmers. Just a hint. A suggestion of gold. She wipes away her tears, but it's still there. Swiping at the air, she rubs her fingertips together, but there's nothing.

"Do you see that?" she asks, her voice rough with tears. "Am I seeing things?"

Whatever this is, it must not be in her head, because Tammy nods and says, "Do you feel it too? It's warm. Or maybe it is. I feel it."

Closing her eyes, Sophie leans her head against the door that separates her from her grandmother. She tries to feel the light, because now she understands that anything is possible. There's an echo, as quiet and soft as a down feather falling to earth. Laughter and love and warmth and longing. Movement and stillness and hope.

The papers slip from her fingers as she looks down at her hands, her fingers breaking the light. It seems almost a gossamer veil, something not entirely substantial or insubstantial. Is this what remains of those decades? Will it pass, or is this a gift they will keep?

Her glance falls on the letter again, falls on the words *she wasn't alone*. Levering herself away from the door, Sophie draws in a hard breath, trying to pull in strength and resolve along with the air. She looks at Tammy and says, "My grandmother has been resting there for a long time. She would want me to help her friend. So that's what I'm going to do. I'm going to help her friend."

About This Book

A Letter from Ann

It wasn't until I finished the first draft of this book that I began to understand where it came from. All books come from some spot inside the author that has meaning, even if only in a very convoluted way. It took time for me to understand where this one came from.

Before I reveal that, I should say that until this book, I've had massive writer's block. As in, extremely extended, complete blockage. It crept up on me over a period of years. At first, I slowed down my writing because I realized it was much better when I had time to let things simmer. Slow cooker writing versus a fast broil.

Then, it slowed further because it's hard to be a post-apocalyptic science fiction author when our world begins to look dystopian. Finally, it ground to a screeching halt when the 2020 pandemic hit. I erased everything I wrote. I couldn't even complete stories and novellas that were more than halfway done and fully plotted. Part of that was my father. He caught Covid-19 early on, and it was a nightmare that never seemed to end.

So, no writing. Months and months. For those who've read my books before and connected with me via social media, you can probably guess how much that hurt. I live to tell stories.

Then, something strange happened.

I visited my parents and stole a hug from my dad. A little one that I wasn't supposed to get. But I couldn't help myself. It was the first one we'd shared in months. Afterwards, I drove to wait in a socially distanced line, voted, and headed home. When I went to bed that night, I had no idea how the election would play out. But I'd done my part. I voted.

Perhaps that's all my brain needed. A hug from dad and for some of the election anxiety to be over.

National Novel Writing Month had begun and I was seeing all those emails about it, bemoaning my lack of writing power. As I was getting ready for bed, I heard a tickle in my head. Like a distant voice, whispering. If you're a writer, you'll recognize this. It's the sound of a character being born.

Between going to bed and waking up, the whole story was lodged firmly in my head. The whole bleeping thing. The characters, their journey, their emotions, and motivations. All of it. I still didn't quite believe it was real, so I sat down to write.

In twenty-four days, I wrote over 110,000 words of the first draft. A completed draft. Holy macaroni! I've never done that. Portals took years of patient work. The Strikers trilogy took five years! What madness was this?

Of course, the subsequent drafts were much, much harder. It's taken two years to polish the novel. Lots to take out, batten down, and tighten up. I suppose that's only to be expected when one hammers the keys and lets it flow.

So, where did it come from? It was the virus. This book is my black box of a brain finally figuring out how it felt about Covid-19. More precisely, how my brain felt about the divisiveness the virus brought out in our world.

In the end, all factions had to work together in order to save the world in this book. And surprise, that's what we had to do too. This is a good thing, in my opinion. Despite our differences, we should continue to strive for the betterment of all humanity.

Now, I have a huge favor to ask of you. I used to be a reliable seller, but not anymore. I simply have no talent for the convoluted ad-buying system required to stand out from the crowd nowadays. It's a money in/fame out situation I'm not equipped for.

There is exactly one—and only one—other way for a non-famous author like me to have a book seen and gain traction. That's word of mouth, or as they call it now, social proofing. If you liked this book, please rate and review it on Amazon, Bookbub and/or Goodreads (or any retailer where you bought it). If you're on social media, please share a link, post your review, and tell someone that you liked it. Tell more than one person.

I know this is a big ask in today's world where the next ten thousand books are vying for your attention. Just know that I thank you for considering it and send you a big, virtual, and socially distanced hug for helping out.

Be well. Love. Gift someone a smile. I'll do the same.

Ann Christy

Acknowledgements

Though I've written many books, this is the first not entirely under my control. It was a terrifying experience, but also a great one. From the editors to the artists creating the covers and web art to the C-Suite at Campfire Technology, there have been many people who contributed something vital and good to the book you've just read.

First, I'd like to tip my hat to Jackson Dickert and Jason Louro, the CMO and CEO of Campfire Technology respectively. In case you don't know the story, the first draft of this book was written using their writing software and won their National Novel Writing Month contest in 2020. It was what Jackson and Jason saw in the story that started this journey toward publication under their new imprint two and a half years later.

Both of them contributed countless hours editing and providing creative insight to help make this book what it is today. I have much to thank them for and I hope they know it. Especially Jackson. I'm pretty sure he could mediate between an angry hippopotamus and an ornery alligator and they'd both walk away happy and feeling like they won. You're a genius, Jackson.

Thank you to the other folks at Campfire who worked on this book: Adam Bassett for his excellent worldbuilding insights and Cole

Field for bringing the Campfire Explore project to life with his art. If you haven't seen it yet, it's worth the trip. Go to www.campfirewriting.com/explore/NEEW and you can check out all kinds of behind the scenes and exclusive content for this book... Including an extra story or two from yours truly.

Working with Thérèse Plummer and Ari Fliakos, who so brilliantly narrated the audiobook, was a dream come true for me. Both are incredibly talented artists who worked hard to bring Coco and Forrest to life. I simply can't thank them enough for taking on the project, despite their packed schedules.

For his incredible cover art, I extend my thanks to Tom Edwards. Long time readers will likely have seen his creations on several of my other books. There's no question Tom is one of the most perceptive cover artists out there. I can't wait to work with him again.

For his wonderful editing, there's B. K. Bass. (See how nice and short that sentence was, B. K.?)

There are so many people to thank that not even a chapter's worth of words could cover them all.

There's one group that needs my final and most hearty mention... the readers. You've stuck with me for the years it took to publish this new book, and I certainly hope it turned out to be worth the wait. For readers who've been with me from the beginning, I hope you know how much your enthusiastic support contributes to keeping the stories flowing.

Thank you.

Ann Christy

Ann Christy is a retired Navy Commander with more than twenty-eight years of operational and scientific experience. A graduate of the University of South Carolina and the Naval Postgraduate School, she has a strong educational and professional background in oceanographic and meteorological physics, biochemical marine science, and coastal ecosystems.

Ann's hobbies include watercolor and oil painting (with varying degrees of success), fiber arts, thinking about science, and obsessively reading way too many books. Her favorite people tend to be animals or equally obsessive readers. She also sometimes writes books.

You can find Ann Christy on: Facebook @ann.christy.792, Twitter @AnnChristyZ, and at https://www.annchristy.com/.

Leave feedback, read exclusive bonus content, and support this project at www.campfirewriting.com/explore/neew